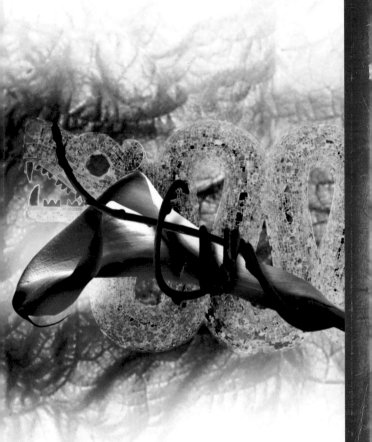

She is his dark possession...

Praise for Christine Feehan's Dark Carpathian novels . . .

"A HIGH PRIESTESS IN THE WORLD OF VAMPIRE FICTION."
—*Romantic Times*

DARK CELEBRATION

"[A] sex-and-magic-filled treat." —*Publishers Weekly*

DARK DEMON

"A terrific, action-packed romantic thriller."
—*The Best Reviews*

DARK SECRET

"The erotic heat . . . turns scorching." —*Booklist*

DARK GUARDIAN

"A skillful blend of supernatural thrills and romance that is sure to entice readers." —*Publishers Weekly*

DARK LEGEND

"Vampire romance at its best!" —*Romantic Times*

DARK FIRE

"If you are looking for something that is fun and different, pick up a copy of this book." —*All About Romance*

continued . . .

DARK
POSSESSION

A CARPATHIAN NOVEL

CHRISTINE FEEHAN

JOVE BOOKS, NEW YORK

THE BERKLEY PUBLISHING GROUP
Published by the Penguin Group
Penguin Group (USA) Inc.
375 Hudson Street, New York, New York 10014, USA
Penguin Group (Canada), 90 Eglinton Avenue East, Suite 700, Toronto, Ontario M4P 2Y3, Canada
(a division of Pearson Penguin Canada Inc.)
Penguin Books Ltd., 80 Strand, London WC2R 0RL, England
Penguin Books Ireland, 25 St. Stephen's Green, Dublin 2, Ireland (a division of Penguin Books Ltd.)
Penguin Group (Australia), 250 Camberwell Road, Camberwell, Victoria 3124, Australia
(a division of Pearson Australia Group Pty. Ltd.)
Penguin Books India Pvt. Ltd., 11 Community Centre, Panchsheel Park, New Delhi—110 017, India
Penguin Group (NZ), 67 Apollo Drive, Rosedale, North Shore 0632, New Zealand
(a division of Pearson New Zealand Ltd.)
Penguin Books (South Africa) (Pty.) Ltd., 24 Sturdee Avenue, Rosebank, Johannesburg 2196,
South Africa

Penguin Books Ltd., Registered Offices: 80 Strand, London WC2R 0RL, England

DARK POSSESSION

A Jove Book / published by arrangement with the author

PRINTING HISTORY
Berkley hardcover edition / September 2007
Jove mass-market edition / October 2008

For Jaunnie Ginn, with love

FOR MY READERS

Be sure to go to http://www.christinefeehan.com/members to sign up for my PRIVATE book announcement list and get a FREE exclusive Christine Feehan animated screensaver. Please feel free to e-mail me at Christine@christinefeehan.com. I would love to hear from you.

ACKNOWLEDGMENTS

As with all works, one has so many people to thank. Cheryl Wilson and Kathi Firzlaff, who spent an amazing amount of time with me helping with details. Brian Feehan, for the long nights you stayed up letting me talk the story line through with you. Domini, you were amazing, working with me at the end until we saw it through. Tina, for providing me with all the little things so I could get the job done. But most of all, my husband, the love of my life, for understanding and supporting me through everything.

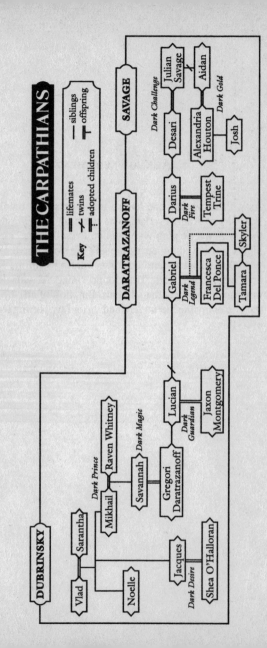

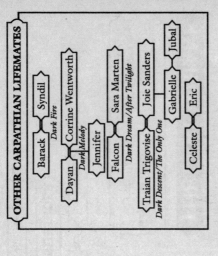

OTHER CARPATHIAN LIFEMATES

Barack ⋈ Syndil
Dark Fire

Dayan ⋈ Corrine Wentworth
Dark Melody

Jennifer

Falcon ⋈ Sara Marten
Dark Dream/After Twilight

Traian Trigovise ⋈ Joie Sanders
Dark Descent/The Only One

Gabrielle ⋈ Jubal

Celeste ⋈ Eric

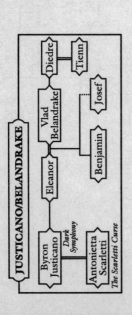

JUSTICANO/BELANDRAKE

Diedre ⋈ Tienn

Vlad Belandrake ⋈ Eleanor

Josef

Benjamin

Byron Justicano ⋈ Antonietta Scarletti
Dark Symphony
The Scarletti Curse

THE CARPATHIANS

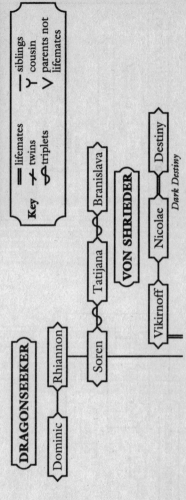

Key
= lifemates
⌣ twins
⌢⌢ triplets
— siblings
⅄ cousin
∨ parents not lifemates

DRAGONSEEKER

Dominic — Rhiannon

Soren ⌢⌢ Tatijana — Branislava

VON SHRIEDER

Vikirnoff — Nicolae — Destiny

Dark Destiny

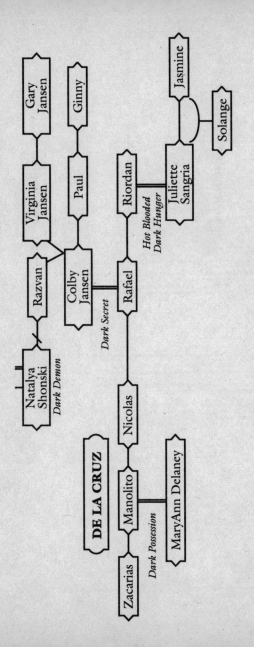

DARK
POSSESSION

1

Manolito De La Cruz woke beneath the dark earth with his heart pounding, bloodred tears streaking his face and grief overwhelming him. A woman's despairing cry echoed in his soul, tearing at him, reprimanding him, drawing him back from the edge of a great precipice. And he was starving.

Every cell in his body craved blood. The hunger raked at him with merciless claws until a red haze covered his sight and his pulse hammered with the need for immediate sustenance. Desperate, he scanned the area above his resting place for the presence of enemies and, finding none, burst through the rich layers of soil, into the air, his heart thundering in his ears, his mind screaming.

He landed in a crouch in the midst of dense shrubbery and thick vegetation, and took a slow, careful look around him. For a moment everything was wrong—monkeys shrieking, birds calling out a warning, the cough of a larger predator, even the brush of lizards through vegetation. He wasn't supposed to be here. The rain forest. Home.

He shook his head, trying to clear his fragmented mind. The last thing he remembered clearly was stepping in front of a pregnant Carpathian woman, shielding mother and unborn child from a killer. Shea Dubrinsky, lifemate to Jacques, brother to the prince of the Carpathian people. He had been in the Carpathian Mountains, not in South America, which he now called home.

He replayed the images in his head. Shea had gone into labor at a party. Ridiculous that. How could they keep the women and children safe in the midst of such madness? Manolito had sensed danger, the enemy moving within the crowd, stalking Shea. He'd been distracted, dazzled with color and sound and emotion pouring in from every direction. How could that be?

Ancient Carpathian hunters didn't feel emotion and saw in shades of gray, white and black—yet—he distinctly recalled that Shea's hair had been red. Bright, bright red.

Memories whirled away as pain exploded through him, doubling him over. Waves of weakness rocked him. He found himself on his hands and knees, his belly in hard knots and his insides heaving. Fire burned through his system like molten poison. Disease didn't plague the Carpathian race. He couldn't have become ill with a human disease. This was manufactured by an enemy.

Who did this to me? His white teeth snapped together in a show of aggression, his incisors and canines sharp and lethal as he glared fiercely around him. How had he gotten here? Kneeling in the fertile soil, he tried to sort through what he did know.

Another jolt of blinding pain lashed at his temples, blackening the edges of his vision. He covered his eyes to try to block out the shooting stars coming at him like missiles, but closing his eyes worsened the effect. "I am Manuel De La Cruz," he murmured aloud, trying to force his brain to work . . . to remember . . . pushing the words through teeth clenched tightly together in a grimace. "I have one older and three younger brothers. They call me Manolito to tease me because my shoulders are broader and I carry more muscle, so they reduce me to boy. They would not leave me if they knew I had need of them."

They would never have left me. Never. Not his brothers. They were loyal to one another—they had been through the long centuries together and would always remain so.

He pushed past the pain to try to uncover the truth. Why was he in the rain forest when he should have been in the Carpathian Mountains? Why had he been abandoned by his people? His brothers? He shook his head in denial, although it cost him dearly, as the pain increased, spikes seeming to stab through his skull.

He shivered as the shadows crept closer, ringing him, taking shapes. Leaves rustled and the bushes shifted, as if touched by unseen hands. Lizards darted out from under the rotting vegetation and raced away as if frightened.

Manolito pulled back and once again looked warily around him, this time scanning above and below ground, quartering the region thoroughly. There were shadows only, nothing flesh and blood to indicate an enemy close. He had to get ahold of himself and figure out what was happening before the trap was sprung—and he was certain there was a trap and he was close to being truly caught.

Throughout his time hunting the vampire, Manolito had been wounded and poisoned on many occasions, but still he'd survived because he'd always used his brain. He was cunning and shrewd and very intelligent. No vampire or mage would best him, sick or not. If he was hallucinating, he had to find a way out of the spell to protect himself.

Shadows moved in his mind, dark and evil. He looked around him at the growth of the jungle, and instead of seeing a welcoming home, he saw the same shadows moving—reaching—trying to grasp him with greedy claws. Things moved, banshees wailed, unfamiliar creatures gathered in the bushes and along the ground.

It made no sense, not for one of his kind. The night should have welcomed him—soothed him. Enfolded him in its rich blanket of peace. The night had always belonged to him—to his kind. Information should have flooded him with each breath he took into his body, but instead his mind played tricks, saw things that couldn't be there. He could hear a dark symphony of voices calling to him, the sounds swelling in volume until his head pounded with moans and pitiful cries. Bony fingers brushed at his skin, spider legs crawled over him so that he twisted left and right, flailing his arms, slapping at his chest and back, brushing vigorously in an effort to dislodge the invisible webs that seemed to stick to his skin.

He shuddered again and forced air through his lungs. He had to be hallucinating, caught in the trap of a master vampire. If that was the case, he couldn't call on his brothers for aid until he knew if he was bait to draw them into the web as well.

He gripped his head hard and forced his mind to calm. He *would* remember. He was an ancient Carpathian sent out by the former Prince Vlad to hunt the vampire. Vlad's son, Mikhail, had, centuries since, taken over guiding their people. Manolito felt one of the pieces snap together as a bit of his memory fell into place. He had been far from his home in South America, summoned by the prince to a reunion in the Carpathian Mountains, a celebration of life as Jacques's lifemate gave birth to a child. Yet he now appeared to be in the rain forest, a part familiar to him. Could he be dreaming? He had never dreamed before, not that he remembered. When a Carpathian male went to ground, he shut down his heart and lungs and slept as if dead. How could he dream?

Once again he risked a look at his surroundings. His stomach lurched as the brilliant colors dazzled him, hurting his head and making him sick. After centuries of seeing in black-and-white with shades of gray, now the surrounding jungle held violent color, hues of vivid greens, a riot of colored flowers spilling down tree trunks along with creeper vines. His head pounded and his eyes burned. Drops of blood leaked like tears, trailing down his face as he squinted to try to control the sensation of pitching and rolling as he viewed the rain forest.

Emotions poured in. He tasted fear, something he hadn't known since he'd been a boy. What was going on? Manolito fought to get on top of the strange tumbling of jumbled thoughts in his mind. He pushed hard to clear away the debris and focus on what he knew of his past. He had stepped in front of an elderly human woman possessed by a mage just as she thrust a poisoned weapon at Jacques and Shea's unborn child. He felt the shock of the entry into his flesh, the twist and rip of the serrated blade cutting through his organs and ripping open his belly. Fire burned through his insides, spreading rapidly as the poison worked its way through his system.

Blood ran in rivers and light faded quickly. He heard voices calling, chanting, felt his brothers reaching for him to try to hold him to earth. He remembered that very clearly, the sound of his brothers' voices imploring him—no—*commanding* him to stay with them. He'd found himself in a shadowy realm, banshees wailing, shadows flickering and reaching. Skeletons. Dark spiked teeth. Talons. Spiders and cockroaches. Snakes hissing. The skeletons drawing closer and closer until . . .

He closed his mind to his surroundings, to all shared pathways, so there was no chance anyone could be feeding his own fears. It had to be hallucination brought on by the poison coating the blade of the knife. No matter that he had stopped anything from entering his brain—something malicious was already present.

Fire ringed him, crackling flames reaching greedily toward the sky and stretching like obscene tongues toward him. Out of the conflagration, women emerged, women he'd used for feeding throughout the centuries, long dead to the world now. They began to crowd around him, arms reaching, mouths open wide as they bent toward him, showing their wares through tight, clinging dresses. They smiled and beckoned, eyes wide, blood running down the sides of their necks—tempting—tempting. Hunger burned. Raged. Grew into a monster.

As he watched, they called to him seductively, moaning and writhing as if in sexual ecstasy, their hands touching themselves suggestively.

"Take me, Manolito," one cried.

"I'm yours," another called and reached out to him.

Hunger forced him to his feet. He could already taste the rich, hot blood, was desperate to regain his equilibrium. He needed, and they would provide. He smiled at them, his slow, seductive smile that always foreshadowed the taking of prey. As he took a step forward, he stumbled, the knots in his stomach hardening into painful lumps. He caught himself with one hand on the ground before he fell. The ground shifted, and he could see the women's faces in the dirt and rotting leaves. The soil, black and lush, shifted until he was surrounded by the faces, the eyes staring accusingly.

"You killed me. *Killed me.*" The accusation was soft, but powerful, the mouths yawning wide as if in horror.

"You took my love, all that I had to offer, and you left me," another cried.

"You owe me your soul," a third demanded.

He drew back with a soft hiss of denial. "I never touched you, other than to feed." But he'd made them think he had. He and his brothers allowed the women to think they'd been seduced, but they had never betrayed their lifemates. *Never.* That had been one of their most sacred rules. He had never touched an innocent, not to feed. The women he had used for feeding had all been easy to read, their greed for his name and power apparent. He had cultivated them carefully, encouraged their fantasies, but he had never physically touched them other than to feed.

He shook his head as the wailing grew louder, the ghostly specters more insistent, eyes narrowing with purpose. He straightened his shoulders and faced the women squarely. "I live by blood and I took what you offered. I did not kill. I did not pretend to love you. I have nothing to be ashamed of. Go away and take your accusations with you. I did not betray my honor, my family, my people or my lifemate."

He had many sins to answer for, many dark deeds staining his soul, but not this. Not what these sensual women with their greedy mouths were accusing him of. He snarled at them, raised his head with pride and met their cold eyes straight on. His honor was intact. Many things could be said of him. They could judge him in a thousand other ways and find fault, but he had never touched an innocent. He had never allowed a woman to think he might fall in love with her. He had waited faithfully for his lifemate, even knowing the odds that he would ever find her were very small. There had been no other women, despite what the world thought. And there never would be. No matter what his other faults, he would not betray his woman. Not by word, not by deed, not even by thought.

Not even when he doubted she would ever be born.

"Get away from me. You came to me wanting power and money. There was no love on your side, no real interest other than to acquire the things you wanted. I left you with memories, false though they were, in exchange for life. You were not harmed, in fact you were under my protection. I owe you nothing, least of all my soul. Nor will I allow myself to be judged by creatures such as you."

The women screamed, the shadows lengthening, casting dark bands across their bodies, like ribbons of chains. Their arms stretched toward him, talons growing on their fingernails, smoke swirling around their writhing forms.

Manolito shook his head, adamant in his denial of wrongdoing. He was Carpathian and he needed blood to survive—it was that simple. He had followed the dictates of his prince and had protected other species. While it was true that he had killed, and that he often felt superior with his skills and intelligence, he had kept that place that was for his lifemate, the one spark of humanity, alive, just in case.

He would not be judged by these women with their sly smiles and ripe bodies, offered only to capture the wealthy male, not for love, but for greed—yet grief was pushing at his emotions. Cruel, overwhelming grief, coming at him and stealing into his soul, so that he felt weary and lost and wanting the sweet oblivion of the earth.

Around him, the wailing grew louder, but the shadows began to leach form and color from the faces. Several women pushed at their clothing and murmured invitations to him. Manolito scowled at them. "I have no need nor want of your charms."

Feel. Feel. Touch me and you will feel again. My skin is soft. I can bring you all the way to heaven. You have only to give me your body one time and I will give you the blood you crave.

Shadows moved all around him and the women came out of the vines and leaves, burst through the earth itself and reached for him, smiling seductively. He . . . *felt* revulsion and bared his teeth, shaking his head. "I would never betray her." He said it aloud. "I would rather die of slow starvation." He said it in a low snarl, a growl of warning rumbling in his throat. Meaning it.

"That death will take centuries." The voices weren't so seductive now, more desperate and whining, more frantic than accusing.

"So be it. I will not betray her."

"You have already betrayed her," one cried. "You stole a piece of her soul. You *stole* it and you cannot give it back."

He searched his broken memory. For a moment he smelled a wisp of fragrance, a scent of something clean and fresh in the midst of the decaying rot surrounding him. The taste of her was in his mouth. His heart beat strong and steady. Everything in him settled. She was real.

He took a breath, let it out, breathing away the shadows around him, yet more grief poured in. "If I have committed such a crime against her, then I will do whatever she wishes." Had he committed so great a sin that she had left him? Was that why the unfamiliar grief turned his heart to such a heavy stone?

Around him, the faces slowly dissolved as the forms blurred even more, until they were only wailing shadows and the sick feeling in the pit of his stomach eased, even as his hunger grew beyond craving.

He had a lifemate. He clung to that truth. Beautiful. Perfect. A woman born to be his mate. Born for him. *His.* Predatory instincts rose sharp and fast. A growl rumbled in his chest, and the ever-present hunger raked deeper into his gut, clawing and biting with relentless demand. He had been without color for hundreds of years, a long, emotionless time that stretched on and on until the demon had risen and he no longer had the strength or desire to fight against it. He had been so close. Kills had run together and feeding had become difficult. Each time he had sunk his teeth into living flesh, felt and heard the ebb and flow of life in veins, he had wondered if that would be the moment his soul would be lost.

Manolito shuddered as voices in his head once again grew louder, drowning out the sounds of the jungle. Little flashes of pain grew behind his eyes, burning and burning until he felt his eyes boiling. Was it the color? *She*, his lifemate, had restored color to him. Where was she? Had she deserted him? The questions crowded in fast and loud, mixing with the voices until he wanted to hit his head against the nearest tree trunk. The inside of his brain seemed on fire, as did every organ in his body.

Vampire blood? It burned like acid. He knew because he'd hunted and killed hundreds, or perhaps thousands. Some had been friends in his younger years, and he could hear them now, screaming in his head. Chained. Burned. Eaten by endless despair. His heart nearly burst in his chest, and he sank down into the fertile soil where he'd lain, trying to sort out what was real and what was hallucination. When he closed his eyes, he was in a pit, shadows surrounded him and red eyes stared hungrily.

Perhaps it was all an illusion. Everything. Where he was. The vivid colors. The shadows. Perhaps his wish for a lifemate was so strong he had created one in his mind. Or worse—a vampire had created one for him.

Manolito. You have risen early. You were to remain in the ground a few more weeks. Gregori said to make certain you did not rise too soon.

Manolito's eyes flew open and he looked warily around him. The voice held the same timbre as that of his youngest brother, Riordan, but it was distorted and slow, each word drawn out so that the voice, instead of resonating with familiarity, seemed demonic. Manolito shook his head and tried to rise. His body, usually graceful and powerful, felt awkward and foreign as he fell back to his knees, too weak to stand. His gut knotted and rolled. The burning spread through his system.

Riordan. I do not know what is happening to me. He used the path shared only by him and his youngest brother. He was careful to keep his energy from spilling from that path. If this was an elaborate trap, he would not draw Riordan into it. He loved his brother too much for that.

The thought made his heart go still.

Love.

He *felt* love for his brothers. Overwhelming. Real. So intense it took his breath away, as if the emotion had been gathering throughout the long centuries, building in strength behind a solid barrier where he couldn't access it. There was only one person in the world who could restore emotions to him. The one he'd waited centuries for.

His lifemate.

He pressed his hand tightly to his chest. There could be no doubt she was real. The ability to see color, to feel emotion: all the senses he'd lost in the first two hundred years of his life had been restored. Because of her.

So why couldn't he remember the most important woman of his life? Why couldn't he picture her? And why were they apart? *Where was she?*

You must go back to ground, Manolito. You cannot rise. You have journeyed long from the tree of souls. Your journey is not yet complete. You must give yourself more time.

Manolito withdrew immediately from his brother's touch. It was the right path. The voice would be the same if it wasn't playing in slow motion. But the words—the explanation was all wrong. It had to be. You couldn't go to the tree of souls unless you were dead. He wasn't dead. His heart was hammering loud— too loud. The pain in his body was real. He *had* been poisoned. He knew it was still burning through his system. And how could that be if he'd been healed properly? Gregori was the greatest healer the Carpathian people had ever known. He would not have allowed poison to remain in Manolito's body, no matter what the risk to himself.

Manolito pulled his shirt from his body and stared down at the scars on his chest. Carpathians rarely scarred. The wound was over his heart, a jagged, ugly scar that spoke volumes. A killing blow.

Could it be true? Had he died and been drawn back into the world of the living? He'd never heard of such a feat. Rumors abounded of course, but he hadn't known it was truly possible. And what of his lifemate? She would have journeyed with him. Panic edged his confusion. Grief pressed him hard.

Manolito.

Riordan's voice was demanding in his head, but was still distorted and slow. Manolito jerked his head up, his body shaking. The shadows moved again, sliding through the trees and shrubs. Every muscle in his body tensed and knotted. What now? This time he felt the danger as forms began to take shape in a ring around him. Dozens of them, hundreds, thousands even, so there was no possibility of escape. Red eyes blazed at him with hatred and malicious intent. They swayed as if their bodies were far too transparent and thin to resist the slight breeze rustling the leaves in the canopy above them. Vampires every one.

He recognized them. Some were relatively young by Carpathian standards, and some very old. Some were childhood friends and others teachers or mentors. He had killed every one of them without pity or remorse. He had done it fast, brutally and any way he could.

One pointed an accusing finger. Another hissed and spit with rage. Their eyes, sunken deep in the sockets, weren't eyes at all, but more like glowing pools of hatred wrapped in red blood.

"You are like us. You belong with us. Join our ranks," one called.

"Think you're better. Look at us. You killed again and again. Like a machine, with no thought for what you left behind."

"So sure of yourself. All the while you were killing your own brethren."

For a moment Manolito's heart pounded so hard in his chest he was afraid it might burst through his skin. Sorrow weighed him down. Guilt ate at him. He had killed. He hadn't felt when he did so, hunting each vampire one by one and fighting with superior intellect and ability. Hunting and killing were necessary. What his thoughts on the subject were didn't matter in the least. It had to be done.

He pulled himself up to his full height, forced his body to stand straight when his gut clenched and knotted. His body felt different, more leaden, clumsy even. As he shifted onto the balls of his feet, he felt the tremors start.

"You chose your fate, dead one. I was merely the instrument of justice."

The heads were thrown back on the long, thin stick necks,

and howls rent the air. Above them, birds lifted from the canopy, taking flight at the horrible cacophony of shrieks rising in volume. The sound jarred his body, making his insides turn to gel. A vampire trick, he was certain. He knew in his heart his life was over—there were too many to kill—but he would take as many with him as possible to rid the world of such dangerous and immoral creatures.

The mage must have found a way to resurrect the dead. He whispered the information in his head, needing Riordan to tell their oldest brother. Zacarias would send a warning to the prince that armies of the dead would be once again rising against them.

You are certain of this?

I have killed these in centuries long past, yet they surround me with their accusing eyes, beckoning to me as if I am one of them.

From a great distance away, Riordan gasped, and for the first time sounded like Manolito's beloved sibling. *You cannot choose to give your soul to them. We are so close, Manolito, so close. I have found my lifemate and Rafael has found his. It is only a matter of time for you. You must hold out. I am coming to you.*

Manolito snarled, throwing his head back to roar with rage. *Imposter. You are not my brother.*

Manolito! What are you saying? Of course I am your brother. You are ill. I am coming to you with all haste. If the vampires are playing tricks on you . . .

As you are? You have made a terrible mistake, evil one. I have a lifemate. I see your filthy abominations in color. They surround me with their vile bloodstained teeth and their blackened hearts, wizened and shriveled.

You have no lifemate, Riordan said in denial. *You have only dreamed of her.*

You cannot trap me with such deceit. Go to your puppet master and tell him I am not so easily caught. He broke off the connection immediately and slammed closed all pathways, private and common, to his mind.

Spinning around, he took in his enemy, grown into so many faces from his past he knew he was facing death. "Come then, dance with me as you have so many times," he ordered and beckoned with his fingers.

The first line of vampires closest to him howled, spittle running down their faces and holes for eyes glowing with hatred. "Join us, brother. You are one of us."

They swayed, feet carrying out the strange hypnotic pattern of the undead. He heard them calling to him, but the sound was more in his head than out of it. Whispers. Buzzing. Drawing a veil over his mind. He shook his head to clear it, but the sounds persisted.

The vampires drew closer, and now he could feel the flutter of tattered clothing, torn and gray with age, brushing against his skin. Once again, the sensation of bugs crawling over his skin alarmed him. He spun around, trying to keep the enemy in his sight, and all the while the voices grew louder, more distinctive.

"Join us. Feel. You are so hungry. Starving. We can feel your heart stuttering. You need fresh blood. Adrenaline-laced blood is the best. You can *feel*."

"Join us," they cried, the entreaty loud and swelling in volume until it was a tidal wave rolling over him.

"Fresh blood. You need to survive. Just a taste. One taste. And the fear. Let them see you. Let them feel fear and the high is like nothing you've ever felt."

The temptation made hunger grow until he couldn't think beyond the red haze in his mind.

"Look at yourself, brother, look at your face."

He found himself on the ground, on his hands and knees, as if they'd shoved him, but he never felt the push. He stared into the shimmering pond of water stretching before him. The skin on his face was pulled tightly over his bones. His mouth was wide in protest and not only his incisors but also his canines were long and sharp in anticipation.

He heard a heartbeat. Strong. Steady. Beckoning. Calling. His mouth watered. He was desperate—so hungry there was nothing to do but hunt. He had to find prey. Had to bite into a soft, warm neck so that the hot blood would burst into his mouth, fill every cell, wash through his organs and tissues and feed the tremendous strength and power of his kind. He could think of nothing else but the terrible swell of hunger, rising like a tide to consume him.

The heartbeat grew louder, and he slowly turned his head as a woman was pushed toward him. She looked frightened—and innocent. Her eyes were dark chocolate pools of terror. He could smell the adrenaline rushing through her bloodstream.

"Join us. Join us," they whispered, the sound swelling to a hypnotic chant.

He needed dark, rich blood to survive. He deserved to live. What was she after all? Weak. Frightened. Could she save the human race from the monsters preying on them? Humans didn't believe they existed. And if they knew of Manolito, they would . . .

"Kill you," hissed one.

"Torture you," hissed another. "Look what they've done to you. You're starving. Who has helped you? Your brothers? Humans? We have brought you hot blood to feed you—to keep you alive."

"Take her, brother, join us."

They shoved the woman forward. She cried out, stumbled and fell against Manolito. She felt warm and alive against his cold body. Her heart beat frantically, calling to him as nothing else could. The pulse in her neck jumped rapidly and he smelled her fear. He could hear her blood rushing through her veins, hot and sweet and alive, giving him life.

He couldn't speak to reassure her; his mouth was too filled with his lengthened teeth and the need to crush his lips against the warmth of her neck. He dragged her closer still, until her much smaller body was nearly swallowed by his. Her heart took up the rhythm of his. The air burst from her lungs in terrified gasps.

Around him, he was aware of the vampires drawing closer, the shuffling of their feet, their cavernous mouths gaping wide in anticipation, strings of saliva dripping down while their pitiless eyes stared with wild glee. The night fell silent, only the sound of the girl struggling for air and the thundering of her heart filling the air. His head bent closer, lured by the scent of blood.

He was starving. Without blood he would be unable to defend himself. He needed this. He deserved it. He had spent centuries defending humans—humans who despised what he was, humans who feared his kind . . .

Manolito closed his eyes and blocked out the sound of that sweet, tempting heartbeat. The whispers were in his head. *In his head.* He swung around, shoving the girl behind him. "I will not! She is an innocent and will not be used in this manner."

Because he was too far gone and might not stop. He would have to fight them all, but he might be able to save her yet.

From behind him, the woman wrapped her arms around his neck, pressed her lush, woman's body tightly against his, her hands sliding down his chest, his belly, lower still until she was stroking him, adding lust to hunger. "Not so innocent, Manolito. I'm yours, body and soul. I'm yours. You have only to taste me. I can make it all go away."

Manolito snarled, whirling around, shoving the woman from his body. "Go! Go with your friends and stay away from me."

She laughed and writhed, touching herself. "You need me."

"I need my lifemate. She will come to me and she will take care of my needs."

Her face changed, the laughter fading, and she yanked at her hair in frustration. "You cannot escape this place. You are one of us. You betrayed her and you deserve to stay here."

He didn't know—didn't remember. But all the temptation in the world would not make him change his mind. If he was to stay alive without food for centuries, enduring the torment of it, so be it, but he would not betray his lifemate. "You would have done better to tempt me to betray another," he said. "Only she can judge me unworthy. So it is written in our laws. Only my lifemate can condemn me."

He must have done something terrible. It was the second accusation of its kind, and the fact that she wasn't fighting at his side spoke volumes. He couldn't call her to him, because he remembered very little—certainly not a sin he had committed against her. He remembered her voice, soft and melodious, like an angel singing from the heavens—only she was saying she would have no part of a Carpathian male.

His heart jumped. Had she refused his claim? Had he bound her to him without her consent? It was accepted in his society, a protection for the male when a female was reluctant. That was not a betrayal. What could he have done? He would never have touched another woman. He would have protected her as he had Jacques's lifemate, with his life and beyond if possible.

He was in a place of judgment, and so far he didn't seem to be faring very well, and maybe that was because he wasn't remembering. He lifted his head and showed his teeth to hundreds, maybe thousands, of Carpathian males who had chosen to give up their souls, decimated their own species, ruining a society and a way of life for the rush of feeling rather than holding on to honor—rather than holding on to the memory of hope for a lifemate.

"I refuse your judgment. I will never belong with you. I may have stained my soul, perhaps beyond redemption, but I would never willingly give it up or trade my honor as you did. I may be all the things you have said, but I will face my lifemate, not you, and let her decide whether my sins can be forgiven."

The vampires hissed, bony fingers pointing accusingly, but they didn't attack him. It made no sense—with their superior numbers they could easily destroy him—yet their forms grew less solid and seemed to waver, so it was difficult to distinguish between the undead and the shadows within the darkness of the rain forest.

The back of his neck tingled and he spun around. The vampires receded deeper into the bushes, the big leafy plants seemingly swallowing them. His stomach burned and his body cried out for food, but he was more confused than ever. The vampires had him trapped. Danger surrounded him. He could feel it in the very stillness. All rustle of life ceased around him. There was no flutter of wings, no scurry of movement. He lifted his head and scented the air. It was still, absolutely still, and yet there was . . .

Instinct, more than actual sound, alerted him and Manolito spun around, still on his knees, hands going up just as the large jaguar sprang at him.

2

Clinical depression was an insidious monster that crept up and slid over and into a person before they had the chance to be aware and on guard. MaryAnn Delaney wiped at the seemingly endless tears running down her face as she went through the list of symptoms. Feelings of sadness. *Check*. Maybe even double check.

Sadness wasn't the word she would use to describe the terrible yawning emptiness she couldn't overcome, but it was in the book and she'd add it to the growing list of indicators. She was so freakin' sad she couldn't stop crying. And she could put a check on the no appetite because the mere thought of food made her sick. She hadn't been able to sleep since . . .

She closed her eyes and groaned. Manolito De La Cruz was a stranger. She'd barely spoken to the man, yet when she'd witnessed his death—his murder—she had gone quietly to pieces. She seemed to be grieving more than his family. She knew they were distraught, but they rarely showed emotion at all, and they certainly didn't speak of him. They'd brought his body back in the same private jet they used to return to their ranch in Brazil, but they hadn't taken him to their ranch.

Instead the plane had landed—with her on it—on a private tropical island somewhere in the middle of the Amazon River. And rather than give Manolito a proper burial, his brothers had taken his body to some undisclosed location in the rain forest. She couldn't even sneak out and visit his grave. How absurd and desperate was that? Visiting the grave of a stranger in the dead of night because she couldn't get over his death.

Was paranoia also creeping in, or was she right to worry that she had been brought to an island no one had mentioned when she was with her best friend, Destiny, in the Carpathian

Mountains? Juliette and Riordan had asked her to come to counsel Juliette's younger sister, a victim of sexual violence, and they often mentioned the ranch, but never a vacation home on a private island. The house was surrounded by thick forest. She doubted she could find her way back to the airstrip without a map and a machete-wielding guide.

She was a counselor, for heaven's sake, yet she couldn't find the discipline needed to overcome the growing desperation and suspicion, or the terrible, inexplicable anguish over Manolito's death. She needed help. As a counselor she knew that, but the sorrow was growing and putting dangerous and frightening thoughts in her mind. She didn't want to get out of bed. She didn't want to explore the opulent house or the lush rain forest. She didn't even want to get back on a plane and go home to her beloved city of Seattle. She wanted to find Manolito De La Cruz's grave and crawl into it with him.

What in the world was wrong with her? She was normally a person who believed in the glass half-full philosophy. No matter what the circumstances, she could always look around her and find something humorous or beautiful to enjoy, but since the night she had attended the Carpathian celebration with Destiny, she had been so depressed she could barely function.

She'd managed to hide it at first. Everyone was so busy getting ready to leave the Carpathian Mountains and fly home, they hadn't noticed she was quiet. Or if they had, they put it down to shyness. MaryAnn had agreed to come to Brazil in the hopes of helping Juliette's younger sister before she had realized the emotional trouble she was in. She should have said something, but she'd kept thinking the grief would subside. She'd traveled with the De La Cruz family in their private jet. And the coffin. They had slept on the plane, as was their way during the day, but she'd sat alone by the coffin and cried. She'd cried so much her throat was raw and her eyes burned. It made no sense, but she couldn't seem to stop.

The knock on her door startled her, made her heart jump and begin to pound. She had a job to do and the De La Cruz family would expect her to do it. The thought of trying to help someone else, when she couldn't bear the thought of getting out of bed, was terrifying.

"MaryAnn." Juliette's voice was puzzled and a little alarmed. "Open the door. Riordan's with me and we need to speak with you."

She didn't want to talk to anyone. Juliette probably had located her younger sister, who by all accounts had still been hiding out in the rain forest. Carpathians, vampires and jaguar people—sometimes she felt a little like Dorothy in *The Wizard of Oz*. "I'm still sleepy." She lied. She couldn't sleep if her life depended on it. All she could do was weep. And be scared. No matter how hard she tried to banish her fear and suspicion, the emotions wouldn't go away.

Juliette rattled the door handle. "I'm sorry to disturb your rest, MaryAnn, but this is important. We need to talk to you."

MaryAnn let out her breath. It was the second time Juliette had used the word "need." Something was definitely up. She had to pull herself together. Wash her face. Brush her teeth. Try to manage her hair. She sat up, once more swiping at the tears running down her face. Riordan and Juliette were both Carpathian and could read her mind should they choose, but she knew it was considered bad manners when she was under the protection of the Carpathian people, and she was grateful for that consideration.

"Just a minute, Juliette, I was sleeping."

They would know it was a lie. They might not read her mind, but they couldn't fail to feel the waves of distress pouring off of her and filling the house.

She stumbled to the mirror and stared at her face in horror. There was no way to quickly hide the evidence of tears. And there was certainly no rescuing her hair. It was long, long enough if pulled straight to reach her waist, but she hadn't thought to do it up in braids and the humidity had expanded her hair beyond all help. She looked ridiculous, her hair unmanageable and her eyes bright red.

"MaryAnn." Juliette rattled the door handle. "I'm sorry, but we're coming in. It's really an emergency."

MaryAnn took a deep breath and sank back onto the edge of the bed, averting her face as they came through the door. It didn't help that Juliette was beautiful, with her cat's eyes and her perfect hair, or that Riordan, like his brothers, was tall and broad-shouldered and sinfully handsome. She was so embarrassed, not only by the fact that her hair had grown into a mass the size of a beach ball, but that she couldn't control the terrible grief that was threatening her very life. She was a strong woman, and nothing made sense since she had witnessed Manolito's murder.

Juliette glided across the room toward the bed, her body compact and graceful, her gaze focused and alert, reminding MaryAnn of her jaguar ancestry. "MaryAnn, you're not well."

MaryAnn attempted a smile. "It's just that I've been away from home a long time. I'm more of a city girl and this is all new to me."

"When we were in the Carpathian Mountains, did you meet my brother Manolito?" Riordan watched MaryAnn with cool, assessing eyes.

MaryAnn felt the push of his questions in her mind. *He had given her a mental shove.* Her suspicions were well grounded. Something wasn't right. She felt the blood drain from her face. She had trusted these people, and now she was trapped and vulnerable. They had powers few humans could comprehend. Her mouth went dry and she pressed her lips together, one hand fluttering toward her breast where a spot throbbed and burned, as she remained stubbornly silent.

Juliette cast her lifemate a quelling look. "It's important, MaryAnn. Manolito is in trouble and we need information fast. Riordan loves his brother and he was using a shortcut that is expedient for our species, but not very respectful. I'm sorry for that."

MaryAnn blinked up at her, tears swimming again in spite of her resolve. "He's dead. I saw him die. And I felt it, the poison spreading through him, the last breath he took. I know he's dead. I heard people talking that even Gregori couldn't bring him back from the dead. And you brought his body back with us on the plane." Just saying it aloud was difficult. She couldn't add, *in a coffin.* Not with her heart feeling like a heavy stone in her chest.

"We're Carpathian, MaryAnn, and not so easily killed."

"I saw him die. I *felt* him die." She'd screamed. Deep inside, where no one could hear, she had screamed her protest, trying to hold him to earth. She didn't know why a stranger mattered so much, only that he had been so noble, so completely heroic to insert his body between danger and a pregnant woman. More, she had heard a rumor he had done the same with the prince of the Carpathians. Selfless in his protection, he had sacrificed himself for Mikhail Dubrinsky as well. And none of them seemed to care. They had rushed to the pregnant woman, leaving the fallen warrior down.

Juliette gave her lifemate another long, telling look. "You felt Manolito die?"

"Yes." Her hand moved up to her throat, and for a moment it was hard to breathe. "His last breath." It had been in her throat, in her lungs. "And then his heart stopped beating." Her own heart had stuttered in answer as though it couldn't beat without the rhythm of his. She moistened her lips with her tongue. "He died and everyone was more alarmed over the pregnant woman. She seemed so important, yet he *died*. I don't understand any of you. Or this place." She pushed back the wild mass of hair and rocked gently. "I need to go home. I know I said I'd work with your sister, but the heat is making me sick."

"I don't think it's the heat, MaryAnn," Juliette objected. "I think you're having a reaction to what happened to Manolito. You're depressed and grieving, yet you hardly knew him."

"That doesn't make sense."

Juliette sighed. "I know it doesn't seem to, but were you ever alone with him?"

MaryAnn shook her head. "I saw him a few times in the crowd." He'd been so good-looking, it had been impossible not to notice him. She considered herself to be a very sensible woman, but the man had stolen her breath away. She had even delivered the verbal smack-down to herself when she realized she was staring at him like a starstruck teenager. She knew Carpathians only had one partner. He might have used her for food, but beyond that, there was no hope for anything else.

In any case, she couldn't live with a man like Manolito De La Cruz. He was overbearing and arrogant, an ancient Carpathian male influenced in the worst possible Neanderthal ways by centuries of living in South America. She, on the other hand, was a very independent woman raised in an upper-middle-class family in the United States. And she'd seen way too many battered women to ever consider being with a man who had a domineering attitude toward women. But even knowing all that, even knowing Manolito De La Cruz was the last man in the world she could ever have a relationship with, she'd still looked.

"You were never alone with him? Not even for a short period of time?" Juliette questioned, this time looking her in the eye.

MaryAnn could see tiny red flames in the depths of those

turquoise eyes. Cat's eyes. A huntress inside the body of a beautiful woman. Behind Juliette stood her lifemate, and nothing at all could conceal the predator in him.

MaryAnn felt a hard "push," not from Juliette, but from Riordan, once again pressing to get past her natural barriers to find her memories. "Stop it!" she said, her voice sharp with sudden fury. "I want to go home." She didn't trust any of them.

She looked around at the opulent wealth and knew she was in a silken trap. She could barely function with the terror building. "I can't breathe." She pushed past Juliette and staggered toward the bathroom. She could see the killer in both of them, monsters lurking beneath the smooth, civilized facade. They had sworn to protect her, but they had brought her to this place of heat and oppression, away from all aid, and now they were stalking her. She needed help and everyone was too far away.

Juliette held up her hand, a frown settling over her face. *We're scaring her, Riordan. Stop pushing at her. Listen to her heart. She is very frightened, beyond what should be normal. Is it possible whatever is affecting Manolito is affecting her?*

Riordan was silent a moment. MaryAnn had always struck him as a strong, courageous woman. Although he didn't know her very well, she seemed to be acting out of character. *If she is his lifemate, then it might be so. But how could she be his lifemate? Why wouldn't he make his claim on her and put her under the protection of our family? It makes no sense, Juliette. He should not have awakened. Gregori locked him to earth, and when we brought him home, we took him to the richest soil in the rain forest and Zacarias ensured he would stay in the ground. I know of no others more powerful. How is it possible Manolito awakened before his time?*

Could the bond between lifemates override a binding command from the healer or from the head of our family?

Riordan rubbed his chin. The truth was he just didn't know. *Well she's scared to death and we have to do something.* Juliette took a deep, calming breath. "MaryAnn, I can see you're very distraught. I'm going to ask Riordan to step out of the room and we can talk about what's bothering you."

MaryAnn ignored her and ran the last few steps to the huge bathroom, slamming the door closed and locking it. She raced to the sink and turned on the water, hoping it would deter Juliette from following her. Splashing cold water on her face helped to clear her mind, although she was shaking, frightened at the thought of what she had to do. It wouldn't be easy to escape from the Carpathians. She had little defense against them, but Gregori, second in command and guardian of the prince, had been the one to put her under his protection, and he had given her a few safeguards. She just had to use them and keep from panicking until she could find her way back to the airstrip.

She had always had a sixth sense about danger, yet she hadn't seen this coming. Now the fear was growing inside of her, blossoming into full-blown terror. She couldn't trust these people. They weren't at all what they seemed. Everything was wrong. The huge estate, with its layers of beauty, was only designed to lure the unwary into the hands of the monsters. She should have seen through them all. *Gregori* should have seen through them all. Was it a huge conspiracy? Were they all involved?

No, she would never believe it of her best friend, Destiny, or Destiny's lifemate, Nicolae. They needed to be warned. Maybe they were already in trouble, or maybe it was just the De La Cruz family who had aligned themselves with the vampires. Spies in the Carpathian camp. All along there had been something different about them. She shouldn't have trusted them.

She stared at herself in the mirror, the red, swollen eyes, the signs of grief ravaging her face. The spot over her breast that never quite healed throbbed and burned. She had been certain it was a bite of some kind that she was allergic to. She'd had it ever since she'd been in the Carpathian Mountains, but now she feared it was far more. Perhaps Juliette or Riordan or Rafael De La Cruz had marked her in some way.

She had wanted to go home, desperate to be away from the violence of the Carpathian world, but Juliette had come to her with a story about her younger sister, one MaryAnn had been unable to brush aside, even though her grief and despair had been overwhelming. Was Jasmine even real? MaryAnn doubted it. They were supposed to be at a huge cattle ranch in Brazil, one where during the day many people surrounded them, but Colby and Rafael, Juliette's brother-in-law and his lifemate, along with Colby's brother and sister, had gotten off the plane at a private airport, and MaryAnn had continued on with Riordan and Juliette to an island.

She was trapped. MaryAnn drew in her breath and let it out slowly. She would not die in this place. She was a fighter, and she would somehow get word to Destiny and Nicolae that this branch of Carpathians was full of traitors. Fear skittered down her spine as she realized what she had to do. Escape into the rain forest, find her way back to the airstrip and somehow get the pilot to take her to an airport where she could catch a flight home. Hastily she looked around the huge room, trying to figure out what she could take with her.

Nothing. There was nothing. She would have to improvise. She went to the window and peered out. The grounds were fairly wild, the rain forest creeping toward the house like an insidious invader, vines and shrubs stretching toward the courtyard. It would be a short run. She caught the edge of the window and attempted to lift.

MaryAnn.

She shrieked, nearly jumping out of her skin, pressing her hand to her pounding heart as she whirled around. Vapor streamed under the door and through the small keyhole. Juliette and Riordan shimmered into human form, Riordan by the window, Juliette by the door.

"Where do you think you're going?" Riordan demanded, his black eyes snapping with fury. "You would be killed within five minutes of entering the forest. We are responsible for your safety."

His voice seemed slow to her ears, a growling rumble that reminded her of demons she'd seen in movies, as if the sound was being played far too slow. Fear beat at her, rage filled her and confusion reigned. The counselor in her stepped back to try to make sense of the jumble of emotions pouring in.

"MaryAnn," Juliette spoke gently. "I know you're puzzled by the things that you're feeling, but we think we have an explanation. We think that Manolito bound you to him in the way of our people. Riordan has reached out to him on their shared path and yet Manolito resists him, fearing him to be vampire, just as you are afraid of us. He claims he has a lifemate, and here you are, in despair, grieving for a man you say you've never met. Does that make sense to you? Something is happening here, and for both of your sakes we need to figure out what it is."

Riordan rubbed his temples as if they ached. There was worry in his eyes. "I fear for my brother's safety as well as his life. He seems confused, and one cannot be confused in the rain forest. We have powerful enemies. He is in terrible danger. He trusts no one but his lifemate. If you are that woman, you are the only one who can save him."

He stared at her with the unblinking eyes of a wild animal, shrewd and cunning and terrifying. MaryAnn shuddered and backed up until she was against the windowsill. A part of her thought they were crazy, deliberately trying to baffle her, but the counselor in her was always seeking information and adding it all up. She knew enough about lifemates from Destiny. She'd been around the Carpathian people for a while, and although she didn't understand the bond, she knew it was strong and unbreakable.

Juliette held out her hand. "Come back into the other room and let's try to sort this out. You don't remember at all being alone with Manolito?"

She would remember, wouldn't she? She'd dreamt of him coming to her. A daydream once—only a dream. He'd pulled her into his strong arms and his mouth had slid over her skin down to the swell of her breast. The spot throbbed and burned. Without thinking, she put her palm over the pulsing strawberry that wouldn't quite heal and held the warmth to her.

She shook her head. "It wasn't real. He was across the room at the Inn in the Carpathian Mountains, but I didn't ever really talk to him." He had looked at her. She'd expected his eyes to be flat and cold and empty like so many of the hunters', but he looked . . . dangerous, as if he might be hunting her. Instead of being frightened as she was now, she had been secretly thrilled, because, after all, it was a fantasy.

MaryAnn followed Juliette out of the room, aware of Riordan prowling behind her like a great jungle cat. He moved in silence, as his brother had moved. She needed air; the room seemed so hot and oppressive, much like the rain forest. That didn't make sense either. The house was well insulated and air-conditioned to comfortable coolness.

"I don't see how I could be his lifemate. I didn't even meet him. Wouldn't I know? Wouldn't he know?"

"He would know," Riordan said. "He would be drawn to his lifemate, and if you were the one, the moment you spoke, he would see in colors and his emotions would have been restored. He would not have been able to get very far from you." He frowned. "But he would have told us. You would have to be placed immediately under the protection of our family."

"She was already under the protection of Gregori as well as Nicolae and Destiny," Juliette reminded him. "He might not have thought it necessary."

He would have thought it imperative . . . unless . . . Riordan broke off his thought and studied MaryAnn's face. "You said it wasn't real. What did you mean by that?"

Color slid under her flawless skin. "I dreamt of him."

Juliette took a deep breath. "Oh, Riordan. What's happening? Something terrible is going on or he would be here."

Riordan immediately was at her side, gliding so fast he was a blur, his arm slipping around her waist as he pressed kisses to her temple. "MaryAnn is here. The three of us can figure this out and we'll find him."

For some reason, the fact that Riordan had included her, as if she could help find a solution, eased some of the tension in MaryAnn. She blinked several times, breathing deeply to try to see past the strange image of the vampire superimposed over the couple. The incisors receded a little, leaving them with normal white teeth.

"Is he really alive?" she asked, not daring to believe.

Riordan nodded. "We all tried to hold him to us, but he was dead, by our measures as well as human, his soul already leaving his body. No one believed we could bring him back, even with the healer and the rich soil and everyone working to keep him in this world, when suddenly he was back with us. If you are his lifemate, you could be the explanation. You may have kept a piece of his soul safe with you unknowingly."

MaryAnn opened her mouth to protest and then closed it abruptly. She knew the Carpathians weren't human. The same rules didn't apply to their species. She had seen things she would have thought impossible only a few short weeks ago. "But why wouldn't I know if I was his lifemate?"

"It is our men who are imprinted with the ritual binding words," Juliette explained. "As a precaution for the species to continue."

"You mean so the woman can't refuse him."

"It is the same thing," Riordan said. "And I doubt if he has bound you to him with the ritual words. It is more likely he has tied you together through a blood exchange."

Her heart leapt again, then settled down to a steady drumming. She had allowed Nicolae to take her blood in order to better protect Destiny, but she had never, *never*, contemplated exchanging blood. She shook her head. "I didn't. It wasn't real. I wouldn't have done that. I'm still struggling to understand and believe your world. I would never have voluntarily taken his blood."

Juliette and Riordan exchanged another long look. "You used the words 'it wasn't real.' What was this dream you spoke of?" Riordan asked.

MaryAnn pressed her hand tighter to her breast. She could still feel his mouth against her skin. She'd been outside and it had been snowing. Then later, when she'd gone back to the house and she'd been alone . . . Her skin felt cool and he had pushed aside her clothing. His lips had been warm and soft and so very sensuous. She hadn't thought to push him away, only cradle his head while he drank and then . . . and then . . .

MaryAnn gasped and covered her face with both hands, shaking her head. "It wasn't real. I wouldn't have done something like that. It was only a dream."

"Do you have his mark on you?" Juliette asked, her voice gentle.

"No. It's not that. It's not his mark. I wouldn't exchange blood with him. Or lead him to believe I'm something I'm not. I don't flirt. And I don't make promises I wouldn't keep." That's why she was there when she should be . . . somewhere else. Anywhere else.

"You didn't do anything wrong, you know. Let me see the mark."

MaryAnn swallowed hard, her hands reluctantly going to her blouse. She didn't want to show Juliette. The mark was private. Right now it pulsed with heat. She moistened her lips and summoned up all of her courage, pushing the material down to reveal the large strawberry, much like a love bite, but more intense and raw. Two telltale punctures were ringed with red.

Her stomach did a funny flip. "He bit me, didn't he? It wasn't a dream at all." And if he had, why did she feel more excited than betrayed?

"You are what kept my brother alive," Riordan said, his black eyes on the mark. "As his lifemate you are under the protection of my family, a sister to be loved and cherished. You did what no other could have done."

"Let's not jump to conclusions," MaryAnn protested. "I never even spoke to the man."

"That marks says you're his lifemate," Riordan reiterated.

She shook her head. "It could mean he took my blood and I was allergic to the anticoagulant. It could be a bug bite." She almost groaned at the desperate, all too absurd suggestion, but this couldn't be happening, not for real.

"Of course it's frightening," Juliette said. "It's unexpected to all of us, but at least you know why you've been so upset. Lifemates cannot be away from one another long without touching minds. Reach for him."

"I'm nobody's lifemate, Juliette," MaryAnn said. "I don't even like men all that much. The ones I see and hear about on a daily basis aren't very nice. I'm not lifemate material, and please don't take this the wrong way, but especially not to one of the De La Cruz brothers. They're far too difficult."

Riordan flashed a brief smile at her. "We make up for it in other ways."

MaryAnn couldn't find it in her to smile back. The entire idea was absurd, but she was beginning to believe it. "In order for us to be feeling the same emotions, wouldn't the bond have to be incredibly strong? Your brother never even really spoke to me. If I were his lifemate, wouldn't he at least introduce himself?"

"Not if he thought you would refuse his claim," Riordan said, ignoring Juliette's warning look. "He might hide his intentions."

MaryAnn frowned. "I would have refused. I have a life that's important to me in Seattle. This isn't my environment, nor would I want to be with a man as demanding as your brother obviously is. Of course I would have refused."

"Which explains why he would have said nothing. Manolito would never have accepted your refusal, but you are under the protection of the prince and his second. You also are best friends with Destiny. Not only would Mikhail and Gregori stand for you, but so would Destiny's lifemate, Nicolae, and his brother Vikirnoff as well as his lifemate, Natalya. Manolito would bide his time, stay close and wait until you were no longer surrounded by your protectors."

MaryAnn rubbed her pounding temples. "I feel sick and dizzy. Everything burns. Is that him? Or is it me?"

"I think he is the one feeling ill. He's still feeling the effects of the wound and the poison. He needs help fast. I touched his mind and he is very confused. He cannot tell where he is or what is real or not. He does not believe I am his brother because I did not know about his lifemate. That means he does not remember what he did or how he tied the two of you together without your consent. He's probably wondering what happened to you and why you haven't come to help him."

MaryAnn sank down onto the mattress and took another deep breath. She was a practical woman; at least she liked to think so. Everything was a big mess, but if it was all true, then Manolito De La Cruz was alive and in trouble. He needed her. Lifemates aside, she couldn't leave him alone and hurt in the rain forest any more than she could have Juliette's sister. "Tell me what to do."

"Reach out to him."

She didn't know what she had expected, but that wasn't it. Action. Soft words. A Jeep. "Reach out to him?" she repeated. "Are you crazy? I don't have any telepathic ability. None whatsoever. I'm not even psychic. You'll have to do the reaching and I'll try talking to him."

Juliette shook her head. "You can't be a lifemate without being psychic, MaryAnn. Gregori and Destiny both recognized your potential. With a blood exchange, Manolito would have established a private path for communication."

"Whoa. Back up. What do you mean my potential?" Suddenly she was furious. Shaking with it. Betrayal was bitter in her mouth. "Are you telling me they manipulated me into going with them to the Carpathian Mountains because they thought I was possibly a lifemate to one of the men? Destiny? Gregori?"

Juliette sent her lifemate a silent plea for aid. She felt like she was walking through a minefield and stumbling often.

He shrugged his broad shoulders matter-of-factly. *I doubt that Destiny had any idea, but Gregori has shared MaryAnn's blood. He would have known. We cannot afford to lose any more of our males. You know the situation is desperate. Of course Gregori would bring her to a gathering hoping she was someone's salvation.*

Juliette resisted the urge to take umbrage at his casual admission.

She will grow to love him if she is destined to be with him.

That is our way of life. You certainly resisted being with me. As I recall, you hid yourself deep within your jaguar and tried to escape your fate. You are happy and content with me, Juliette, as she will be with Manolito. Time takes care of many things.

It is still unfair that a man can dictate a woman's destiny.

It is equally unfair on the man. He has no choice either, Riordan reminded her. *And far more to lose.*

"I feel so betrayed," MaryAnn said. "I thought Destiny knew me, understood me. You don't do this to friends." Hurt colored her voice, but she couldn't help it. She had trusted Destiny, helped her to overcome her past so she could find a new life with her chosen lifemate. She had even left the excitement and sophistication of her beloved city of Seattle and headed to the remote, uncivilized forests of the Carpathian Mountains just to make certain Destiny would find happiness.

Juliette shook her head. "Destiny is new to the Carpathian society. I doubt she would have known, let alone allowed you to be placed in such a position. Gregori would have felt his protection would ensure you would not be bothered against your will. Most males believe a woman will fall in love with her lifemate. The pull between them is strong and the physical attraction is tremendous."

"Has there ever been a man or woman who didn't fall in love with their lifemate?" Because if Manolito was hers, she could see herself wanting to go to bed with him, but living with him was an altogether different matter.

"Like any species, we have some born not quite right. No one knows why or how it happens, but yes, there have been aberrations," Riordan admitted. "Manolito is dedicated to his lifemate. He would never dishonor her with another woman. We have waited far longer than you could ever comprehend for our women, and, although you may think us overbearing and arrogant, we cherish and hold our women above all else."

The sincerity in his voice made her feel a little better. And Juliette was no pushover. It was just that MaryAnn found all that testosterone a little annoying. The De La Cruz brothers would demand full surrender in all things. She couldn't see them compromising all that much. Even the very tone of their voices put her on edge. She couldn't imagine herself with one of them as a husband. They might be easy on the eyes, but she'd probably develop ulcers trying to be with one.

"That's admirable, Riordan, it really is." She could be sincere as well. "But I'm not certain you're right about me being meant for your brother. If he did put this mark on me," she struggled not to blush, remembering the heat of his mouth and her body's reaction to it, "then he did it without my consent. I don't know why in your society you would think that was okay, but in mine, it's wrong."

"You're no longer living in your society," he said without a trace of remorse. "Our rules are rules of survival. We only have one chance of survival after centuries of living as honorably as possible. That chance lies in finding our lifemates. Without our women, our species cannot exist and our men must either commit suicide or become vampire. There is no other choice for us."

MaryAnn sighed. Without grief and despair eating at her, she should have been able to think much more clearly, but now confusion reigned above all else. Were her own emotions to blame, or was it Manolito? And if it was Manolito, how could he survive in the rain forest without knowing what was happening to him?

"How do I reach out to him? I've never even tried anything like that before."

Riordan and Juliette exchanged a long, puzzled look. They'd never had to explain what seemed to come naturally to them.

"Picture him in your mind. Use details, down to the smallest thing you remember about him, including scent and emotion," Riordan advised.

Great. She remembered feeling he was the most sensuous man she'd ever conjured up in her life. Heat swept through her body. Had his mouth really traveled down her throat to the swell of her breast? Had his teeth sunk into her skin to draw her life's blood out of her into him? The thought should have been repulsive to her. Any sane woman would have found it repulsive. She closed her eyes and thought of him.

His shoulders were broad, his arms powerful. His waist and hips were slender, his chest muscular. Muscles rippled beneath his skin like a great predatory cat's when he moved. And he moved in absolute silence. His face . . . MaryAnn took a breath. His features were exquisite. He was the most handsome man she'd ever seen. Dark, mysterious eyes, shiny black hair accenting the strong angles and planes of his face, a straight masculine nose and high cheekbones that any model would envy, his jaw strong, with just a dusting of a shadow over it. But it was his mouth she hadn't been able to stop staring at. Sensual, with a hint of danger. Just enough to drive a woman wild.

She reached toward him and to her astonishment felt her mind expand, as if it had only been waiting, as if the path was already familiar. She felt him, just for a moment, touching her, reaching for her, but then . . . Her eyes widened in terror and her hands shot out defensively. A huge, fierce cat leapt between them with murderous intent. The teeth exploded out of the muzzle, driving for Manolito's throat. She screamed and thrust her body in front of his, feeling the hot breath fan her face. *Jaguar.*

3

Manolito spun around, still on his knees, his hands going up instinctively to catch the large, heavy cat as it sprang for his head. The force and power of the jaguar was tremendous, driving him down and onto his back. Was this real, or was this an illusion like the shadowy vampires must have been?

His fingers sank into thick fur. Claws raked his belly, tearing through skin and muscle. Hot, fetid breath exploded in his face, and wicked teeth scraped along his arm as he used sheer strength to keep the beast from getting to his throat and skull. For one moment, as he lay beneath the cat, keeping its massive head from his, he felt someone—*her*—his lifemate—move in his brain.

Her cry of terror echoed through his mind, replacing hunger and confusion with a focus he might not otherwise have found. He saw her reaching for the cat, trying to aid him. Not wanting to risk her life, he broke the telepathic connection between them and dissolved. His body turned to vapor, streaming up and around the cat to reshape into that of a male jaguar with a broad, heavy head and a larger, stockier body the color of the darker shadows. Droplets of blood fell like mist, spattering the leaves and roots as he took the form of a rare black jaguar. He snarled a challenge and leapt. The two cats crashed heavily together, rolling across roots and boughs, the sounds of battle disturbing the night.

Many cats used strangulation to kill, but the jaguar, with its exceptionally powerful jaw, would bite directly through the skull between the temporal bones, killing prey instantly. As the Amazon had been their home for so many years, the De La Cruz brothers had come into regular contact with the cats.

Jaguars were extraordinarily strong, with compact, muscular bodies and broad heads. Stealthy and nearly invisible, they lived a solitary life in a shadowy world of dusk and dawn. With their incredible night vision, retractable lethal claws, piercing canines and well-muscled bodies built for ambush and stealth, they commanded the rain forest, yet they were leery of fighting one another. The heavy moisture was a perfect breeding ground for infection.

Manolito's first thought was to kill in self-preservation. He was weak from hunger and already dripping precious blood. The wisest and safest course of action would be to end the battle quickly. Respect for the rain forest's strongest predator made him hold back. He and his brothers had always lived in harmony with the creatures of the forest. He would not take this animal's life if there was another choice.

He growled a warning, clearly telling the male to back off. Testing the air, he could find no female leaving scent that might give the cat added incentive to fight.

The jaguar circled Manolito's powerful furred body, showing teeth and rumbling with challenge. Hoping to subdue the animal, Manolito leapt. The jaguar rushed to meet him, slashing with stiletto-like claws even as Manolito reached for the mind of the beast. The jungle erupted into an explosion of sound as the two cats came together.

Birds screamed and took to the air, high in the canopy above. Monkeys shrieked warnings and threw twigs and leaves down on the two jaguars as they rolled in the vegetation. Boughs broke beneath the heavy bodies, scattering debris into a thick cloud around them. Manolito pushed past the red rage in the cat's mind and tried to find the spirit of the animal as he kept its lethal fangs from sinking into him.

Jaguars possessed extremely flexible spines that allowed them to turn and twist, move their legs in lateral sideswipes, even change direction in midair. And the ropes of muscles all over their bodies gave them tremendous strength. Manolito took another vicious rake on his side as he tried to focus on calming the cat.

He pushed harder, breaking through the wall of rage and found—*man*. This was no jaguar. This was one of the rare and solitary jaguar-men who still made their homes in the rain forest. The Carpathians and the jaguar people had always lived in harmony, avoiding one another, yet this one had deliberately attacked.

Manolito dissolved and took his human form, this time from the comparative safety of a distance away. Cats could cover amazing distances in a single leap, and the jaguar people had cunning and strength beyond normal. He stood, breathing hard, watching for any signs of aggression as the cat faced him, sides heaving, a snarl on its face.

"I know you are a man. You will die here if you continue. You cannot use my respect for the jaguar to defeat me. Why have you broken our unspoken treaty?" He deliberately pitched his voice soft, calming, a mesmerizing tone of notes to aid in soothing the cat's temper.

The jaguar bared teeth, but held his ground, the eyes never leaving Manolito's face, as if he was just waiting for one moment of weakness that would give him an advantage. And Manolito was weak. He held the pain of his wounds at bay and ignored the raging hunger nearly consuming him. The scent of blood was heavy in the air. Both jaguars had been torn, and droplets showered bright spots of crimson over the leaves. Deliberately the jaguar licked at the blood drops, to remind Manolito that he had scored.

Manolito exploded into action, ice-cold fury washing over him at the insulting taunt. He leapt on the animal's back, knees digging tightly into the banded muscle, legs nearly crushing the animal as he locked his ankles under the belly. One arm snaked around the thick neck in a half nelson to drag the head up. He sank his teeth deep into the jugular and drank. The animal tensed with resistance, but the man inside the cat form forced stillness, realizing Manolito could—and would—rip out his throat.

The hot blood pumped into his starving body, soaking into tissue and cells, and rejuvenating muscles. For a moment he was flooded with euphoria, the adrenaline-laced blood too rich and addictive when he'd been so long without and so very close to turning.

So good. Do not stop. Feel the rush. Do not stop. There is nothing like it in the world. Join us, brother. Be with us. Take it all. Every drop.

Manolito heard several voices whispering the temptation. The buzzing in his head grew louder until it was almost painful. *It is forbidden to take a life.*

A cat only. Nothing to one such as you. He attacked you.

Why should you give him his life when he would have killed you?

The enticement was strong. Hot, rich blood. And he was starving. The cat had attacked him first. It would still kill him, given the chance, even now, when he had spared its life.

Although he felt the difference in his body, he felt sick again, as if his stomach was cramping, which didn't make sense. Insects buzzed in his ears, loud and obnoxious, but when he wished them away, the noise didn't abate. Around him the ground rolled, as if an earthquake had taken place deep beneath the soil. His gut rolled with it.

You need strength. The cat wounded you. You need blood to heal, and it is so good. Drink, brother. Drink it all. The persuasive whispers continued.

Beneath him, the cat began to shake. The man prowling within the animal shouted something unintelligible, something human.

Human. He could not kill while feeding.

Not human. A cat. Tear its throat out. Rejoice in the power. Feel it, brother, feel the absolute power of a life ebbing away beneath your hands. Be what you were always meant to be— what you are.

What was he? A killer? Yes. There was no doubt he had killed so many times he could no longer remember all the faces. Where was he? He looked around, and for a moment the rain forest was gone and he was surrounded by shadowy forms, the stretched and knotted fingers of the dead pointing accusingly. Branches clacked together like brittle white bones, sending a shiver down his spine.

He killed—yes. But not like this. It was wrong. Self-defense was one thing. And there was justice and honor in dispatching a fallen brother when he had given his soul over to evil, but murder while feeding was against everything he believed. *No.* Whatever, *whoever*, was trying to get him to kill was no friend.

It took discipline to take only what he needed to survive, only what he needed to push past the beast's barriers and lay open the mind of the man hidden inside. He swept his tongue across the punctures to seal them and dissolved into vapor, only to reappear a distance away, taking a careful look into the shadows around him. Were those faces in the shadows, peering through the leaves and coming up out of the ground? Were vampires lurking? He shifted onto the balls of his feet, ready for anything. The jaguar roared, drawing his attention back to the danger closest to him.

Manolito forced a careless smile. "You have the taste of my blood in your mouth. And I have the taste of yours. You have information I seek. You tried to kill me and I owe you no quarter."

The cat remained motionless, not a muscle moving, eyes focused intently on Manolito.

The jaguar people were as elusive and secretive as the great cats, and like their animal part—or because of it—they preferred the dense rain forest near streams and riverbanks. They were rarely encountered and, most likely, were stealthy enough and too familiar with the rain forest to ever be seen unless they wished it. The men, like the animal, were heavily built and enormously strong. They had tremendous night vision and excellent hearing. They were good tree climbers and strong swimmers. Little was known of their society, although Manolito knew they had bad tempers when aroused.

Before he probed deep into the brain of the jaguar, the hunter took another slow, careful look around him, scanning as he did so. The voices hadn't completely abated, whispering in his ear, urging him to kill. The shadows his sight couldn't quite penetrate seemed to hold a thousand secrets. Something slithered across the ground, just under the surface, displacing dirt as it moved. His mouth went dry.

The jaguar shifted, crouching a little lower, muscles bunching, drawing Manolito's instant attention. Centuries of hunting in dangerous situations kept his face expressionless, his eyes flat and cold and his mouth a little cruel. "Dare to attack, cat-man, and I will have no mercy for you." And he wouldn't. Not with the vampires closing in around him. He would have no time for mercy, not if he wanted to live.

The blood Manolito had taken from the jaguar-man enabled him to follow the brain pattern, push past the last of the shields to extract information. Hatred, deep and violent, toward Carpathians. The need to find and destroy them. A sense of betrayal and righteous anger. Puzzled, Manolito probed deeper. The two species had never been great friends, but neither had they been enemies. They held different values, but had always managed to respect each other's society.

There was a touch there in the memories. A dark stain. Something off. He examined it carefully. The spot was very dark in the center, but rings formed around it, lighter in color, stretching out to encompass the entire brain of the jaguar-man. The closer Manolito got to the spreading discoloration, the more agitated and disturbed the jaguar became.

The moment Manolito merged, as soft a touch as he used, he felt evil shift, become aware of him. Around him the shadows swelled and took form. Within the jaguar's brain the blemish stirred as if disturbed. He backed off, not wanting to rouse the ire of the cat any further. The animal was shaking, fur wet and dark as its sides heaved. The man was beginning to lose the battle for control of the beast.

"You have been touched by the vampire," Manolito said, his voice low and carrying the ring of truth. "I can try to aid you to rid yourself of the poisonous influence, but it will fight to keep ahold of you." And it would leave him vulnerable to attack, perhaps even from the jaguar. It was a risk, not even a good one, but Manolito felt compelled to help. The jaguar species, both man and beast, was losing the battle for existence just as the Carpathian species was. And Manolito very much feared that the De La Cruz brothers had unwittingly played a large part in the destruction of the jaguar people.

The man stayed quiet within the jaguar. Tied to him by blood, Manolito could feel his alarm. He was no young man, cocky and full of bravado; he was old enough to know the danger of the vampire, and he had been questioning what was happening among his kind for some time. The cat crouched low and nodded the broad head, the gaze shifting from Manolito to their surroundings, as mindful of the danger as the Carpathian.

In the canopy above them, the leaves rustled ominously. Clouds moved across the dark skies, bringing the promise of more rain. Already the air was heavy with moisture and the rivers and streams were swollen beyond the banks. Water poured over rocks and out of banks and made waterfalls where there had been none before. Most of the water was white and bubbling, but on the edges of the rocks, the water was stained with tannin and appeared a dull reddish brown.

Manolito took a deep breath and pulled his gaze away from the blood-colored water, and let his air out, breathing away everything but the task at hand. He had to let go of his physical body, making himself incredibly vulnerable to a potential enemy already occupied by the vampire. It was much more difficult than he expected, now that he could feel emotion and it mattered that he stayed alive.

The dark spot in the jaguar-man's brain recoiled, minute wormlike creatures writhing as his spirit entered the other man, bathing the brain in white-hot energy. Manolito heard the jaguar roar and the man hiss out a warning. Manolito hesitated, afraid of injuring the warrior.

Do it. I do not want that thing inside of me.

Manolito attacked the stain, breaching the outer rings and burning them clean with healing light. The tiny parasites tried to dig deeper into the brain in an effort to escape. As they scattered, Manolito could see to the core of the jaguar-man. The parasites tried to keep the light out of the jaguar-man's memories and hide what the vampire had done, but, unexpectedly, the jaguar-man joined his strength with Manolito's, using his well-developed telepathic abilities and their newly established blood tie.

He opened his memories to Manolito and flooded him with as much information as possible. His name was Luiz. For many years he'd worked to restore the dwindling strength of his species. Too many of their women had left, seeking companionship and love with human males rather than the careless abandonment of their own males. He'd influenced the others to follow the way of the Carpathians and mate for life, to provide a home and a family, a reason for women to stay with them. At first, many had gone along with his ideas and had begun to give up their solitary way of life, but recently, they had become divided in their thinking, as a slow, subtle change occurred.

Packs of men had begun committing terrible crimes against women. A "new order" of jaguars had begun searching for women of their kind and raping them in an effort to have pureblood children. Luiz hadn't known of the horrors, other than unconfirmed rumors, for the first few years, but now more and more men had joined the bands of marauding rebels. He feared not only for the women, but for their entire species. What woman would want to be with men who did such terrible things? He had heard that some of the women now were rescuing those in captivity. Their world had turned upside down, and Luiz had never once considered a vampire might be at work. Now it all made sense.

Vampire. The vilest creature on the face of the earth. Since when had they tried to kill off an entire species? Manolito knew.

He and his brothers had once known the Malinov brothers. Sadness crept in. The five Malinov brothers had been best friends with his family. Now it seemed as if they may have all turned vampire. The idea of losing all of them was distressing now that he was capable of emotion. With the Malinov brothers, they had spent many hours discussing how they could take over ruling the Carpathian people. The possibilities of destroying an entire species, allies of the prince, had been a hot topic of conversation. In the intellectual debate, they had devised many ways, and one had been to influence self-destructive behavior, to capitalize on a species' weakness. *Just as the jaguar society had done.*

When their prince had sent them out into the world, away from their native land to protect humans, the subject had once again come up. In the end, the De La Cruz brothers had sworn to serve their prince and people. Once their word was given, no De La Cruz would ever go back, given a choice. The Malinov brothers had done the same.

Manolito was careful to keep that information to himself. Just the talk of betraying the prince had been bad enough and he was ashamed. He had never felt shame before and it was an uncomfortable emotion.

You were right all those years ago. The voices whispered once again in his mind. *You and your brothers should have followed your own path completely. You allowed a weaker man to reign, to lead our people down a path of destruction. Had Zacarias ruled, the Carpathian people would be thriving, not driven into the ground, hated and feared and hunted by the very people they protect.*

Manolito let out his breath in a long hiss of challenge. *Show yourselves. Do not hide in the shadows. Come out where I can see you.* He couldn't maintain the energy to stay long within the jaguar-man's body. He had to rid the man of the taint of the vampire and get back to his own unprotected body.

There is no need to feel shame. It was a brilliant plan.

Manolito took another breath and blocked everything out but the task at hand. The voices from the shadow world would have to wait. The jaguar-man was straining to hold the beast, keep it from leaping on Manolito and tearing apart his unprotected body.

The hot white light, pure energy, spilled over the center of the dark stain with terrible purpose. Manolito focused his entire attention to the task, risking everything to do so, not only because it was the right thing to do, but because he wanted to make up, in some small way, for his part in the plot devised so many years earlier. What had only been an intellectual debate had at one time exploded into angry possibility, but Manolito thought they had discarded all notion of betrayal and sabotage. Obviously one or more of the Malinov brothers had decided at some point to implement the plan. Manolito had witnessed firsthand the attempts to assassinate the prince, and then to kill the women and children of the Carpathians. Now, it seemed, the enemy had also put into motion a plan to wipe out the jaguar people.

Manolito utilized every bit of energy to fight the small threads of wriggling parasites, burning them out of their hiding places, following them as they raced through the jaguar-man's brain in an attempt to evade the attack. It was exhausting and time-consuming work.

When he was done and returned to his own body, Manolito staggered and nearly went down. His earlier need for blood had barely been satisfied, and using such energy had drained him. Only iron discipline kept him on his feet.

Beside him, the jaguar contorted. Fur rippled and muscles stretched and lengthened. The shifting of the jaguar people was different from that of the Carpathians. Skin and bands of muscle appeared; long, dark hair with streaks of gold running through it covered a noble head. A man crouched on the ground where the cat had been.

Luiz straightened slowly until he was standing upright in front of Manolito. Like all jaguar-men, he was comfortable with his nudity, his body roped with muscles, his hair shaggy. "I apologize for attempting to take your life." He spoke with great dignity, his eyes meeting Manolito's without flinching, even as he gestured toward the blood dripping steadily down the hunter's body.

Manolito bowed slightly in acknowledgment, while keeping every sense alert for another attack. "No man is responsible for what he does under the influence of the vampire."

"I owe you a great debt for aiding me in getting rid of him."

Manolito knew better than to deny it. The jaguar-man was stiff with pride, the face edged with guilt and worry. "It must have been difficult living with such a thing when you have worked so hard to save your people from the very thing that infected you."

"I know the difference between right and wrong. Most of our remaining men do as well, but the vampire is like a disease. We can't stop what we don't see. If I go back and try to tell the others, I have no proof. I don't have the ability, as you do, to find the taint of vampire and expel it."

"If you do not, there is no hope for your species," Manolito pointed out. "Your women flee, as they should. The vampire is destroying you from the inside out."

Luiz nodded in agreement. "I knew something was wrong, but the hatred toward your kind festered. The vampire must have planted the seeds among us. Carpathian males stealing our women. I don't remember ever encountering a vampire, or one who said such a thing, but I have known for some time that I was not thinking correctly."

"He underestimated your strength. He must have chosen you because you're a leader."

"At one time I was. Not so much anymore. The men are scattered, running in packs now, looking for women of our blood." Luiz frowned, rubbed at his temples as he tried to recall what they'd been told. "I believe the vampire wants a specific woman, one of pure blood who can shift every bit as quickly as a man, fight as hard, as tirelessly. He was insistent if we find her, that she be brought to the Morrison Research Institute in order for his researchers to duplicate her DNA." He sighed. "At the time he made it all seem sensible, but now it makes none at all."

The leaves rustled and both men spun toward the sound. The jaguar-man slipped toward Manolito, his every movement fluid and stealthy, as quiet as any cat as he went back to back. *There are eyes in the forest. And ears. My people are no longer trustworthy now that the vampire has gotten to them.*

Manolito searched his memories for information that was eluding him. He couldn't show vulnerability, or point out that he was seeing on two different levels and didn't know which was real and which was imaginary. Nor did he even know if the shadow world was an illusion. Could he be walking in two worlds at the same time?

You removed the taint of the vampire from me. Is it possible to do the same with my brethren?

Manolito could feel the jaguar-man stretching his mind, reaching with all of his senses to find danger. He sniffed the air, listened, his eyes moving restlessly, unceasingly.

"Whatever is out there is far from us," Luiz said, "although others have entered the rain forest."

Manolito's heart jumped. His lifemate. He was certain of it. She was coming to him. She had to be. No lifemate could stay separated from the other for long and survive. They were two halves of the same whole and needed each other for completion.

Come to me . . . It was a command. A plea. Yet he didn't know her name. He couldn't fully picture her. He closed his eyes to hold his memories to him. Skin. He remembered her incredible skin, softer than anything he'd ever touched, like silk burning under his lips. The taste of her, wild and spicy like the woman herself. His pulse quickened and his breath came in a rush, body tightening unexpectedly. He'd forgotten what it was like to desire. To lust. To think of a woman and want to sink his body forever into hers, making them one. Or maybe he'd never really known the feeling. Maybe he'd scanned so many other males it was merely an illusion until this moment in time. Now his body recognized the woman he needed, and it was demanding to be sated in every way.

"Carpathian. You are swaying with weariness. This thing you have done for me, driving the vampire from my body, it was difficult on you." Luiz made it a statement.

"Yes." But it was more difficult to look into the leaves of the shrubs and ferns, the boughs lying broken on the ground, and see the shadowy faces of evil staring at him. In the numerous waterfalls and streams, eyes stared as if from a watery grave. Everything appeared to be translucent, a gray, dank veil drawn over the brilliant colors of the rain forest.

The jaguar-man relaxed, the tension easing out of him, but Manolito was more alert than ever. In the distance, others had entered the forest, that was true, but whatever faced him in the shadow world was still there, still waiting and watching. The jaguar-man couldn't see or sense the other world, but Manolito knew he was still in danger. Or maybe the shadow world really was illusion and he was losing his mind.

Because his legs refused to hold him any longer, Manolito slowly crouched down, careful to appear to stay in control. He took another slow look around him, a small frown on his face. Why was he seeing everything through a veil, as if he were only half in his world and half in another? He plunged his hand into the soil he had slept in, hoping that it would anchor him and keep him from the shadows.

Just as he'd expected, the soil was terra preta, fertile black soil found among the poorer reddish clay or white sand in the rain forest. Unlike the other soils of the rain forest, the terra preta maintained fertility. Finding the precious soil had been a deciding factor in his family's decision to purchase the island.

The De La Cruz brothers had realized the soil was their key to survival and hope. Far away from their homeland, without their native soil, they searched the rain forest and most of Brazil in the earlier centuries for something rich and rejuvenating that would aid them not only in healing wounds and sleeping, but also in giving them strength needed to maintain their honor so far from their prince and people and without lifemates to sustain them. He took handfuls of the precious dirt and packed the wounds on his belly and sides to keep from losing any more blood.

Even with the soil in his hands, the large, lacy fronds darkened in color, turned from vibrant green to a drab gray. His breath caught in his throat as a thought occurred. If his lifemate was dead, would he cease to see in color?

The rain forest was capable of overwhelming newcomers with its sheer intensity of vivid, brilliant color and raw beauty. Manolito was at home in a place many saw as threatening and oppressive. Now, with his lifemate having restored his emotions and his ability to see in color, he should be blinded by the vivid colors, but as his surroundings fluctuated between color and shadow, could that mean she was dead? Was that why she wasn't with him? For a moment time seemed to stop. His heart thundered in his ears, a frantic cry for his other half.

No. He let out his breath. She was alive. He felt her. Touched her mind-to-mind. It had been brief, but her mind had pushed against his. Close to him, the jaguar-man stirred, bringing Manolito's attention snapping back to him. Feeling vulnerable, not knowing what was real and what was illusion, he forced his body to his feet once again, facing the man.

"Let me aid you," Luiz offered, frowning as he observed the

sheen on Manolito's skin. He kept his voice low and friendly,
seeing the sudden flare of heat in the Carpathian hunter's eyes.
"Are your wounds so terrible?"

Manolito shook his head. He could not afford to go drifting
between worlds. Not when he didn't know friend from enemy.
That only put him in more danger than ever, yet he couldn't
seem to stop it. One moment the forest would be vivid with
brilliant colors and the familiar, comforting night sounds, and
the next, it would be a dull version, the colors muted and hazy,
the shadows alive with something not alive, yet not dead. He
made an effort to force his mind back to the situation, to extract
as much information as possible when he had the opportunity.

"Do you know who this woman is that the vampire is sending your men to acquire?"

At once the jaguar-man's expression changed to one of wariness. "I am not certain. There are few purebloods left even
among our males. There are even fewer women, and only one or
two of noble blood."

"My youngest brother has found his lifemate. She is jaguar.
And from an aristocratic lineage. Are you referring to her?"
Manolito wanted to get it out in the open. If this was some
elaborate plan to recapture Juliette, Riordan's lifemate, the jaguar-
men would have a war on their hands. The De La Cruz brothers
would protect Juliette with their lives, and every other Carpathian would do the same.

"No one would ever be that stupid, Carpathian."

"Manolito."

Luiz inclined his head in acknowledgment of the courtesy.

Carpathians often didn't reveal their names to enemies.
Manolito hadn't given his birth name, because he was being
careful, but Luiz didn't need to know that.

"This other woman is in danger. Perhaps my people can
help."

Luiz took a deep breath, hesitated and then nodded. "I would
ask your help to aid my brethren. If I bring one to you, would
you consider removing the stain of the vampire?"

There was a silence filled only by the night insects. Manolito
knew what was being asked of him—a tremendous favor—yet
also a huge matter of trust.

"I would have to take blood to do such a thing," he admitted.
"This is a master vampire, one not so easily defeated. I could

try healing without the bond, but if it is as difficult as it was with you, I am not certain it can be done." He had recognized the vampire's touch. One of the Malinov brothers for certain. He'd grown up with them, run wild with them, laughed with and fought beside them. They had been friends.

"Perhaps if we do this quietly, we won't alert the vampire to what you are doing to aid us."

"If you wish me to help your people, I need you to tell me who the woman is so that we can put her under our protection. You and I both know your men are too far gone to turn her over to the Morrison Laboratory. They will brutalize her, force her submission and eventually break her. And if by some miracle they didn't, and they gave her to the vampire, she would be dead anyway."

"I will protect her."

"The vampire got to you once already and you didn't know. He walks among you unseen. Give me her name."

"She will not surrender easily to you."

"I do not ask for her surrender, only her safety." Manolito took another look around him. The shadows were stretching, moving closer and closer. He could see the faces in between the leaves. Skin stretched tight over bones. Black holes for eyes. Jagged, brown-stained teeth. Manolito shifted his weight slightly to the balls of his feet, readying himself for the inevitable attack. He blinked and the images faded.

"She has long rescued the women of our race and she's fought our warriors. She detests the men. She won't come in to be sheltered. That isn't her way."

"You speak of Juliette's cousin, Solange."

Luiz nodded. "There is no other like her that we know of. She is nearly as strong as any of our warriors and as good a fighter. She comes from a long, pure line that can be traced back hundreds of years. We look upon her as the future of our species. She will have nothing to do with us. I've tried to convince the others to talk with her, to try to form a friendship and get her counsel on what needs to be done to bring our women back among us. The women listen to her, but I have no more voice. Not unless we can destroy the vampire's influence among us."

Manolito knew that Solange and Juliette's younger sister, Jasmine, refused to come to the De La Cruz ranch to visit Juliette, but they had agreed to stay in the De La Cruz home on

their privately owned island retreat. The island was wild and
the house was protected on three sides by the rain forest. He
had wondered why Luiz was on their property, not that the jaguar people didn't consider the entire rain forest their domain.
They had amazing swimming skills, and the swollen rivers
were never much of a deterrent.

"You came here looking for her."

Luiz shifted his gaze for just a moment. "Yes. We thought it
a possibility that she might come here. We knew she wouldn't
go to your ranch."

"And you knew the younger woman was with her. The one
Juliette and Solange took back from your men."

"Not my men. I can't control them. I had hoped to find her
before the others."

"And what would you have done with her?" Manolito demanded, his black eyes glittering dangerously.

Luiz shook his head. "I don't know. I thought I came to talk,
but then I scented you, and I became very confused." He rubbed
his forehead. "I began to think you were here to take our women
and I wanted you dead."

"You came to the island in control, but then something happened. You had to have encountered him here," Manolito said
in alarm. That meant the master vampire was close, somewhere
on the island, and no one knew. Solange, Jasmine, Juliette and
even his brother Riordan weren't safe. "Who did you meet?"

"Not a vampire. An old friend. He had taken shelter here
and was leaving because he realized the house was occupied by
the De La Cruz family."

Manolito kept his expression blank, but his heart jumped
and pounded. Fear was an incredible emotion, and now that he
felt it, he knew it was for those he loved rather than for himself.
"Your old friend is long gone, Luiz. Avoid him at all costs. You
met a master vampire, and only because he has a plan and
needed you did you escape unscathed."

"You think my friend is dead?"

"If not dead, then certainly tainted."

"Thank you, Manolito, for your aid," Luiz said, and for the
first time he looked defeated. His body crouched, a quick graceful move, fur rippling as his muzzle lengthened to accommodate a mouthful of teeth. In absolute silence he slid into the
underbrush and disappeared.

Just to be safe, Manolito dissolved into mist and joined the low, gray vapor drifting around the tree trunks only a few feet off the ground. It was far better to err on the side of caution with the jaguar-man.

He took form again atop a boulder facing a roaring white waterfall that poured over the rocks and fell into the swollen river. He needed his lifemate. Needed to touch her. Hold her. Taste her. His hunger had returned, bringing confusion with it. He needed to warn his family of the danger lurking on the island, but most of all, he needed his lifemate to anchor him.

Where are you? The echo of his cry was in his mind, the sound lost and lonely.

4

MaryAnn placed one foot carefully out of the all-terrain vehicle and watched her beloved Kors boot sink deep into the muck. She gasped in horror. The boots had been a treasured find. Dark brown, antiqued stressed leather with a tapered toe, they were stylish with their high, thick heels, but comfortable, and very rain-foresty. More than that, they matched her Forzieri jacket in the same elegant color and leather, cut short, trendy and butter soft. She had even carefully rainproofed both for any and all occasions such as a trek in the forest. She'd come totally prepared, yet she wasn't out of the vehicle and already she was ankle deep in mud. She *loved* those boots.

As she pulled her shoe out, a squishing sound accompanied the unpleasant odor of too-sweet flowers mixed with rotting vegetation. She shifted back onto the seat to examine the damage, wrinkling her nose in distaste. What in the world was she doing in this place? She needed to be in a coffee shop with the music of the street singing to her and the bustle of people everywhere, not in this strangely silent world of . . . of . . . *nature*.

"Hurry, MaryAnn. We have to walk from here," Juliette said.

MaryAnn gingerly dragged her backpack to her and peered out the open door at the strangely quiet interior of the forest. "It's pretty muddy, Juliette," she said, grasping for any reason to stay in the relative safety of the Jeep. The forest terrified her in ways she could never explain to anyone. Her fears were deep-rooted and she'd never been able to overcome them. She couldn't just make herself walk calmly into that oppressive darkness like a sacrificial lamb. "Maybe you could just call him and tell him we're here. You can do that sort of thing, right?"

"He would not answer," Riordan reminded. "He believes we mean him harm."

"I did mention I've never been camping, right?" MaryAnn said, scanning the ground for the driest spot.

"Three times," Riordan said, his mouth set in grim lines.

He was suddenly in front of her; he caught her around the waist and deposited her a short distance from the vehicle. There was impatience in the bite of his fingers. She didn't sink into the ground, but insects raced all around her. She bit her lip and heroically refrained from saying anything as she took a cautious look around. Whipping the can of bug spray out, she doused the insects in a businesslike manner, "accidentally" managing to spray a little on Riordan's stiff neck.

"Whoops. Sorry." She put the can neatly into one of the loops at her belt, ignoring his glare. Fulfilling the childish urge had given her a little burst of satisfaction. She knew she was stalling, but she'd work up to this her way, not be rushed by anyone.

The rain forest wasn't anything like what she'd expected. It was dark and a little frightening. The air felt heavy with moisture, yet was still with expectancy, as if a thousand eyes watched her. The drone of insects and the unceasing cry of birds were the only things she could hear.

MaryAnn swallowed hard and stayed perfectly still, afraid of moving in any direction. For some reason she thought the forest would be noisy, with the shrieks of a million monkeys, not just the calls of birds and the rustle of insects. Her heart began to pound. Somewhere in the distance a jaguar roared. A chill went down her spine and MaryAnn cleared her throat.

"I may have forgotten to tell you about my weird little thing with cats. House cats. I don't know any other kind, but cats scare me. They have that focused stare and dig their claws into people." She was babbling and couldn't stop herself. It was pathetic and a little embarrassing, but she hadn't signed on for this. "So don't, you know, turn into a big cat or anything. And if one happens to be stalking us, it's probably best not to tell me. I'd much rather remain completely ignorant."

"We'll keep you safe," Juliette assured her.

"I thought you knew you were coming to the rain forest," Riordan said, trying not to sound annoyed. Was this really his brother's lifemate? She wasn't in the least bit suited to their lifestyle. Manolito would eat her alive.

"*Cattle ranch*," MaryAnn corrected. "You said cattle ranch on the *outskirts* of the rain forest." And that had been bad enough, when she was thinking *luxury five-star hotel close by*. "You didn't say a word about an island and being in the *middle* of the rain forest. I thought you would be bringing Juliette's sister to me there. I made it very clear I'm a city girl. Give me a mugger and an alley any day of the week."

For reassurance, she touched the two small canisters of pepper spray tucked safely beside the bug spray in the belt loops beneath her jacket. She'd come prepared for jaguar-men, not jaguars. And she could read Riordan's expression; he didn't bother to hide it. His opinion of her was hitting an all-time low, but she just didn't care. He wasn't the reason she was forcing herself to go into a place she knew was extremely dangerous to her. She had nothing to prove to anyone; she never had.

Riordan beckoned with his fingers, and MaryAnn forced one foot in front of the other, reluctantly following his lead. Juliette was behind her, looking small and compact and alert. She moved with grace and ease through the surprisingly spacious forest floor. The forest was damp and so relentlessly dark, yet she could see colors she shouldn't have been able to see. MaryAnn was a little shocked at the vast variety of shades. As she walked, she was surprised by the absence of animals. She'd always thought creatures were everywhere in the forest, waiting to pounce on the unwary visitor, but as they walked single file, there was only an occasional flutter of wings overhead.

She had also expected the forest floor to be an impenetrable jungle, but it was open and easy to walk through. Trees rose all around her, giant, smooth trunks rising without branches, nearly to the canopy. Roots flared out of the bases like snakes, writhing across the ground. Some trees appeared as if they were held up by a myriad of stilts. Climbing plants hung everywhere. Lianas tangled like ropes, knotting the trees together and forming a hidden highway up in the canopy. Vines crept up the trunks, weaving their way through orchids and over shrubs, ferns and the moss sprouting from the branches. She walked over dead leaves, seedlings, fallen boughs and twisted roots reaching in all directions like tentacles across the forest floor.

MaryAnn was so scared. Terrified in fact. She hadn't been this frightened since a man had broken into her home and nearly killed her. If her best friend, Destiny, had been there, she would have admitted it aloud, talked it over and maybe even laughed at herself. But she didn't know these people. She was entirely out of her element, and it was only her intense need to help others that drove her forward.

She'd dressed in her most comforting clothes, trying to give herself courage. Her Forzieri embroidered jacket, short and stylish in brown distressed leather, matched her boots and gave her added confidence. The embroidery on the back was too cute for words, and the linen ruffles gave the jacket an elegant renaissance look. Pairing the jacket with her Seven jeans, with their wide waistband settling below her belly button and so comfortable she barely knew they were there, and her all-time-favorite, wear-anywhere-and-look-like-a-million-bucks Vera Cristina V-neck tee with intricate beadwork in turquoise, gold and clear beads, she couldn't have looked better. Well. If you didn't count her hair. She reached up to pat it. Out of desperation, she'd managed to braid it into one very thick braid. She hadn't bothered with more than stud earrings because she figured anything else might be a hindrance. As her heel sank into the vegetation, she realized she was hopelessly out of her depth and totally inappropriately dressed. She blinked back tears and kept walking.

If Manolito was alive, where was he? Why couldn't she reach for him after she had that horrible moment when the knowledge had hit her that a jaguar was attacking him? She had tried to stop it, throwing up her hands to catch it, to put herself in its path, screaming a warning, but no one had understood, and how could she explain without sounding crazy that for one moment she had been there—in the forest—standing between Manolito and certain death.

Riordan and Juliette looked grim, but hadn't provided answers to her fearful questions. They had practically thrown her in the truck, Riordan almost rude. He had been intimidating, much like his brothers, but never really rude, not until now.

As if reading her thoughts, Juliette moved up beside her. "I'm sorry. This must be difficult for you."

"It's not my thing," MaryAnn admitted, wanting to turn around and run for the safety of the truck. She kept walking after Riordan. "But I can handle it." Because that's what she did when someone needed help. And she wasn't about to leave Manolito De La Cruz alone in the rain forest with jaguars attacking him. She could barely breathe with her desire to see him alive and well.

Her chest hurt, her heart felt like a stone, and her eyes burned constantly with the need to weep for his death. She needed to see him. Hear him. Touch him. It made no sense, but right then it didn't matter. She *had* to be with him or she wasn't going to survive. Although she tried hard to keep her face averted from Juliette, she was aware of the woman casting anxious glances at her.

"He is alive," Juliette said quietly.

"You don't know that," MaryAnn choked out. "The jaguar—" She stopped to try to regain control before speaking. "It was attacking him. I felt the claws tearing through his flesh." She pressed her hand to her stomach as if she were wounded.

"Riordan would know." Juliette cast a swift, worried glance at her lifemate as she kept pace with MaryAnn. She didn't know why, but she was beginning to have misgivings about whether or not Manolito was alive. It was crazy, because the De La Cruz brothers would know if he was dead, and through them, she would know. "My people are jaguar. If one of them attacked Manolito, I fear what Riordan and his brothers might do in retaliation. The jaguar has always left the Carpathians strictly alone. Out here, one chooses one's battles. A single scratch can result in a life-threatening infection."

Riordan, are you certain Manolito is alive? I am feeling grief and a terrible sense of oppression and dread. Juliette needed her lifemate to reassure her; she was no longer able to discern the truth.

Riordan took a breath. He, too, was feeling grief and an unreasonable fear for his brother's life. He reached out to his eldest brother, Zacarias, the one person they could always rely on. *Do you feel Manolito? Can you tell if he still lives?*

There was a moment while Zacarias touched Manolito. *He is alive, but shielding himself. Do you have need of me?*

Zacarias was at the ranch house with the rest of the family, and Riordan wanted him to stay there. Zacarias would not allow Juliette's younger sister and cousin freedom. He would insist on bringing them back to the ranch to protect them, and neither would come willingly. That wouldn't stop Zacarias. He ruled with a snap of his bared teeth and his enormous power, expecting—and getting—everyone's instant obedience.

It is best if no one is here when we contact Jasmine and Solange. Jasmine needs MaryAnn's help, and neither she nor her cousin will come forward voluntarily if you and Nicolas are here.

Do not cater to stupidity, Riordan. I realize you must make your lifemate happy, but not at the expense of endangering women, especially potential lifemates. Just like that, Zacarias was gone, giving his opinion and expecting that Riordan would follow his advice. It wasn't that easy if you had a lifemate. Solange would fight him to the death for her freedom, and if he put so much as a scratch on her, Juliette wouldn't forgive him.

Riordan sighed and once more tried to reach out to Manolito. The man was hiding. He had risen, and he was most likely close to the fertile bed of terra preta. As badly as he was wounded, he would need the rich black soil to survive.

MaryAnn was very aware of Riordan's scrutiny. She didn't turn around to look at Juliette, but she knew they were talking telepathically about her. She didn't quite trust them; after all, what did she really know about them?

Juliette prodded Riordan. *Why am I feeling so upset?*

I believe it is the woman broadcasting. She may be a much more powerful psychic than we were led to believe. I, too, am feeling her emotions. Is it possible she is jaguar?

Juliette inhaled MaryAnn's scent and watched the movements of her body closely. MaryAnn was nearly running in her fashionable, high-heeled boots, the soles barely skimming the forest floor. She looked utterly out of place but . . . *There is no sound, Riordan. She makes no sound when she moves. No leaves crackling, no branches snapping. She should be awkward—she feels awkward—but she moves like one born and bred here. But she is not jaguar.*

Riordan sucked in his breath, slowing the pace just a bit so that MaryAnn wouldn't notice. Was the woman part of a trap? What did they know about her after all? Manolito had never claimed her openly, as any lifemate would. He had never told his brothers to watch over her, as a true lifemate would do. Riordan probed gently, keeping the touch light and casual.

MaryAnn brushed her head with her hand as she continued walking, and Riordan felt the psychic slap as if she'd actually struck him. He jerked back to himself and threw a quick glance at his lifemate, truly shocked.

What are we dealing with, Juliette?

MaryAnn had been protected by no less than three powerful Carpathian hunters. If she was vampire, surely they would have detected it. Deliberately, just to be safe, he turned the wrong way, moving away from where he knew his brother had been buried.

MaryAnn took three steps and immediately everything in her shifted and reached back in the other direction. The feeling was so strong she stopped. "That's the wrong way. He's not there. He's . . ." She gestured, her heart pounding.

What was Riordan doing, leading them the wrong way? Didn't they want to find him? Why were they keeping him away? The seeds of suspicion were growing, and she couldn't suppress them. She turned away from the direction Riordan was leading, suddenly confused. She couldn't figure out why she thought she knew where Manolito was. She tried repeatedly to reach for him, to brush her mind against his, but she couldn't do it, couldn't find him. The more she tried, the more she knew she wasn't in the least psychic. She had no talents, and no ability to be anyone's lifemate. Still, she was afraid the man was in trouble, and she had to get to him.

Confused, she took another step away from the Carpathians and stumbled over the stabilizing buttress roots from one of the taller emergents, an enormously tall tree bursting through the canopy to tower over the other trees. The roots were twisted into an elaborate, artful shape, roaming along the surface of the ground, tips probing for nutrients. A small tree frog, bright green in color, leapt from a particularly thick root to land on MaryAnn's shoulder.

She stifled a scream and froze. "Get it off. Get it off me, right now," she ordered, her hand closing around the small canister of pepper spray.

Where are you? I need you. Please be alive. Because she wasn't a woman made for tree frogs and beetles, but she wasn't leaving the rain forest until she found the man or his body. She could handle the dark of an alley in the city any day of the week, but she detested walking in the mud and rotting leaves, with the oppressive darkness and the silence closing in around her. She felt eyes watching every step she took.

Juliette whispered softly, although it was her mind she reached out with, to ask the frog to get off MaryAnn. Juliette had an affinity for animals, and even reptiles and amphibians sometimes responded, but in this case, the frog moved closer to MaryAnn's neck, clinging with its sticky feet.

Get off me! MaryAnn screamed it in her head, not able to wait for the frog to obey Juliette's command. *Right now!* "Get off!" she yelled aloud.

Evidently the creature had had enough of humans, and it leapt to the nearest tree trunk, landing near two other small frogs. Overhead, in the canopy, a small monkey threw leaves at the trio of amphibians.

MaryAnn closed her eyes, took a deep breath and began walking again, this time, in spite of the high heels on her boots, picking up the pace until she was practically running. She pushed past Riordan, who looked shocked. When he would have started after her, Juliette caught his arm and gestured to the trees around them. Small frogs dotted the trunks and branches, leaping from one tree to the next, following MaryAnn's progress. Overhead, in the canopy, monkeys used the highway of tangled vines to converge and follow the woman as she made her way through the forest.

Do you think the vampire is here? Juliette asked.

Riordan did another, much more careful and thorough scan of the surrounding forest. *If so, he is a master at hiding his presence. I know they are getting much more clever about such things, so we will need to be fully alert to all danger to her. She is drawn to Manolito, and perhaps can find him even faster than we can, as he is shielding his presence from me.*

Juliette frowned as they began to follow MaryAnn. *Your blood bond should keep you informed of his whereabouts.*

Riordan sent her a small smile. *We are ancients, Juliette, and we have studied many things over the centuries. Manolito can hide his presence even from our best hunters, and there is no detecting Zacarias when he does not want it known that he is near.*

MaryAnn realized tears were running down her face. The sense of dread and fear was overwhelming. *Where are you? Find me.* She continued to try calling to Manolito mentally, although clearly she didn't have the psychic gifts they all thought she did.

As she moved deeper into the interior of the forest, she noticed that the greens weren't quite so vivid. Leaves and shrubs appeared to have a veil of fog over them, changing the vibrant color to a dull gray. Shadows grew where there had been none. First she had seen bright colors in the dark, and now she was seeing shadows when she shouldn't be able to. Terror moved through her, but she couldn't stop going. Whispers plagued her mind as she began to jog. She didn't jog. She wasn't a jogger, or a runner of any kind, but she found herself hurrying through the forest in an effort to get to Manolito.

Something pushed her onward when all around the forest grew darker and the rustling above her head more pronounced. Once, she risked a look up, but there were small furry things swinging over her head, and it made her feel dizzy and slightly sick. She stumbled and nearly fell, putting out her hand to break her fall. Her long, beautifully manicured nails dug into the wet moss. One nail broke. A dozen green frogs leapt onto her arm and clung with their sticky webbed feet.

She froze. The frogs stared at her with huge, black, green-lidded eyes. They were shiny, with spots on their underbellies and matching green toenails, as if they wore polish. Tongues darted out, tasting the leather of her jacket. MaryAnn shuddered and looked back at Juliette.

"Why are they doing that?"

Juliette didn't have an answer for her. She'd never seen the frogs congregate together in such numbers before, and she'd spent most of her life in the rain forest.

"I don't know," she admitted. "It's unusual behavior." *Riordan, they ignore even the strongest of pushes.* There was alarm in both her voice and her mind.

Riordan set Juliette behind him, regarding the frogs with suspicion. "When creatures do not act as they should, it is best to destroy them."

MaryAnn's breath caught in her throat. She shook her head. "No, I didn't mean for you to kill them. Maybe they're just curious about my jacket." She made a scooting gesture with her free hand. "Move along, little froggies." *Hurry before the big bad Carpathian fries you all. I mean it, you've got to move.* Silently she urged them to cooperate, while mentally rolling her eyes. For heaven's sake, how much damage could a tiny little innocent tree frog do, after all? She didn't want to see Riordan do anything like rain down fire on the poor helpless things. "Shoo, shoo. Go back to your little froggy homes."

The frogs took to the trees, the movement sending a strange wave of green over the tangle of roots, as dozens of frogs skittered away toward the safety of the higher branches. MaryAnn sent Riordan a small little sniff. "What were you going to do, make them into shish kebab? Poor little things. They're probably as scared as I am."

Did you feel that, Juliette? That surge of power? She made the frogs leave. And she's sneering at me. Sneering. He was going to have to revise his thinking about his brother's lifemate. "Those frogs are poisonous. Natives used them for years to tip their arrows," he couldn't resist adding.

MaryAnn straightened slowly, automatically looking at her broken nail. Her nails grew abnormally fast, they always had, but now her nail polish was going to be a mess. And it was hurting like hell. It always did when she broke off a nail. Her finger would throb and burn and tingle as the nail regenerated.

She flicked a scowl at Riordan. "Don't try to scare me with frogs. I don't like them, but I'm not that big of a city girl." She was, but he didn't need to know that.

"They really are toxic," Juliette confirmed. "Riordan is telling the truth. It isn't normal to see so many frogs in one area, and they certainly shouldn't be following us."

MaryAnn glanced at the frogs surrounding them. "Are they following?" The idea made her nervous. She didn't want them killed, but she wanted them gone. Out of sight. Of course then they might be hidden in the foliage, staring with their giant eyes just like everything else in the rain forest seemed to be doing.

"Yes, and so are the monkeys," Riordan said, folding his arms across his chest and indicating the canopy with a nod of his chin.

MaryAnn was afraid to look. Frogs were one thing—and she chose to leave out the poisonous part—but monkeys were furry little beasts with near-human hands and big teeth. She knew that because once, just once, she'd gone to the zoo and the monkeys had all been insane, screaming and jumping around, baring *huge* teeth at her through what appeared to be smiles. It had been a horrible day, not as bad as this one, but she'd vowed never to go to a zoo again.

MaryAnn squared her shoulders and elevated her chin a

notch. "Do you have an explanation for why these creatures aren't behaving normally?"

"I thought I did," Riordan admitted. "I believed a vampire might be using their eyes and ears to gather information, but now I am not so certain."

Her heart jumped when she heard the word "vampire." She'd been expecting it ever since she'd entered the dark oppression of the rain forest, but she still wasn't prepared. She longed for the normalcy of gangs hanging out on the corner. She could quell the street toughs with one look, but a herd of frogs or monkeys commanded by vampires . . . Was it herd? She didn't even know. She didn't belong in the animal kingdom. She desperately wanted to go home.

As soon as the thought was completed, grief welled up, swamping her. More than sorrow, she felt need, a compulsion to keep moving, to hurry. She turned away from Riordan and Juliette, toward the direction the pull was strongest. She couldn't leave this terrible place until she found Manolito.

She turned her head from side to side, not seeing anything, only thinking of him, the lines of pain and fatigue etched deep into the handsome features. His broad shoulders and thick chest. He was tall, much taller than she was, and she wasn't exactly short. Where was he?

She could hear the high-pitched sound of bats calling to one another, and somewhere in the raging river one porpoise beckoned to another. The world seemed to narrow, or maybe her senses expanded, making her hearing far more acute, so that her brain processed every individual noise. The rustles in the leaves were insects, the flutter of wings were birds settling for the night, the monkeys overhead disturbed leaves as they kept pace. She heard the sound of voices, two men, about six miles away, and she recognized Manolito's sensual tone. His voice shimmered in her mind, sent goose bumps skittering over her skin and her stomach clenching in anticipation of seeing him.

MaryAnn walked fast, urgency driving her. He was in trouble. She knew it. She felt him now, close, where before she couldn't reach him. She didn't try connecting mind-to-mind; she wasn't psychic, but it didn't matter. She heard his whispered command floating in the air. *Come to me.* She knew he was injured. Confused. He needed her. Scents burst through her brain, the three-day-old trail of a tapir rooting for vegetation. A mar-

gay hidden deep in the canopy a mile to her left. So many creatures, even . . . *jaguar.* Her breath hitched and she drew her
knees higher, pumping her arms, picking up speed.

She cut through a series of slopes running along a swollen
stream, uncaring when the lower shrubbery tore at her hair.
Water poured from every conceivable outlet, creating waterfalls everywhere. The sound was loud in the stillness of the
forest. With little moon and the thick canopy overhead, the interior was dark and eerie. Low-lying fog wove a trail of ghoulish gray vapor in and out of the trees, covering the buttress of
tangled roots so when she got close to them, the thick knots and
snakelike limbs appeared to be dark fortresses hiding secrets.
The huge trunks rose up out of the fog, seemingly disembodied
from the roots holding them to ground.

Juliette's nails dug into Riordan's arm as they paced behind
MaryAnn. *Look at her. She runs so smoothly. She's not jaguar,
but I don't know what she is. I've never seen anything like her.
Have you?*

Riordan struggled with his memories, trying to remember if
he'd ever seen such a transformation. It was difficult to see
MaryAnn as more than the beautiful fashion plate she always
appeared to him to be. She was intelligent and courageous for a
human, he had always given her that, but her courage wasn't
the kind needed to be the lifemate of a Carpathian hunter like
Manolito. Riordan's brother was dominating and hard, with no
soft edges to make him more palatable for a woman like Mary-
Ann. Yet there was a steel core in her. And there was far more
to the package than met the eye. She wielded power and energy
without conscious deliberation, yet the moment she thought
about it, she became inept and afraid.

*The biggest question is whether or not she is a danger to
Manolito.*

*I think she is very confused about all of this, Riordan. I feel
sorry for her. The blood tie to Manolito is strong. If it was only
the one exchange, why is the connection so strong in her that
she knows more than you where your brother is? Because,
make no mistake, she knows exactly where he is and she's
heading straight to him. He's a good six miles away, but she's
making fast time even though she's never been in a rain forest
in her life.*

MaryAnn felt a buzzing in her head, as if insects were fluttering in her skull. The Carpathians were talking to each other again. She detested that. Were they using her to get to Manolito? If Riordan really wanted to find his brother, why didn't he approach him directly, call to him, draw him out? Why hadn't they simply buried the body at their ranch, where Manolito would have risen among family members who would have helped him? Why hadn't they mentioned a second home? And why were Juliette's sister and cousin too afraid to even go to the De La Cruz home? Something was very wrong.

It all should have frightened her—and it might have—but Manolito's voice once again slid into her head.

Where are you? He sounded so lost and lonely. Her heart twisted in answer, aching for him.

She wasn't a runner, but she picked up the pace, smoothly, easily, leaping over fallen tree trunks as if she'd been born with the reflexes, something inside her urging her to hurry. As she ran, her mind became still, quiet and certain, assessing everything around her with uncommon speed.

Her vision was odd, as if her other senses being so enhanced had robbed her of normal vision. The vibrant greens and reds of leaves and flowers blended and dulled until it was hard to distinguish color, yet even with the dull gray, she caught the movement of insects and lizards, the flash of the tree frogs and monkeys as they scurried overhead. Her night vision had always been excellent, but now it seemed more so; without the colors to dazzle and blind, she could identify a wider spectrum of things as she raced by.

It was exhilarating to have all of her senses so sharp. Her hearing was definitely much more acute. She could hear air rushing out of Juliette's lungs. The ebb and flow of blood in veins. Deep inside of her something wild unfurled and stretched.

MaryAnn caught her breath, frightened. She stumbled and nearly fell, stopping so abruptly Riordan and Juliette nearly ran her over. She backed away from them, her palm covering the mark over her breast where it throbbed and burned.

"What did he do to me?" she whispered. "I'm changing into something else."

Juliette caught at Riordan's wrist and squeezed tightly to prevent him from saying the wrong thing. He might not see how fragile and lost MaryAnn looked, but she did. There was a different, very real fear in her eyes now, wary, like a cornered animal. They didn't know how MaryAnn would react, but more importantly, *she* didn't know, and that had Juliette spooked.

"We don't know exactly what Manolito did do to you, other than he probably took one blood exchange." Juliette drew in a deep breath, trying to be honest. "Maybe two. You're not Carpathian, so he didn't convert you."

"But Nicolae took my blood to better protect Destiny."

And she wasn't afraid of him. Riordan picked that out of her mind. *Not like she is now. Why wasn't she afraid to have Nicolae take her blood when it would be the natural thing to be?*

MaryAnn put a hand to her head, brushing as if to sweep away insects, taking another step backward, away from them. Fear grew with every breath she took. Something was terribly wrong; she knew it, could feel it deep inside her. Closing her fist, she dug her nails deep into her palm to test herself. She was beginning to doubt what was real and what might be illusion.

She knows we are talking privately, Riordan cautioned, *and it upsets her.*

And have you asked yourself how she knows? She shouldn't. She doesn't even think she's psychic.

She's more than psychic, Juliette, Riordan said. *She wields power without effort.*

Or the knowledge that she's doing it. "This is crazy, Mary-Ann," Juliette added aloud. "Neither Riordan nor I know what to make of it."

"I want to go home." Even as she said it, MaryAnn knew she couldn't, not until she found Manolito De La Cruz and assured herself he was alive and well and not in some kind of terrible trouble. Damn her nature, the one that always needed to help and comfort others. She lifted her shaking hand. Her nail had already grown, much, much faster than even the accelerated rate normal for her. "What do you think he did to me? You must have a guess. And is it reversible? Because I'm human and my family is human and I *like* being human. This is what comes from having a skinny bloodsucking white girl as my best friend." And she was *so* going to have a few things to say to Destiny when she saw her again—*if* she ever saw her again.

Juliette cast Riordan another anxious glance. "I'm so sorry, MaryAnn. If I knew what was happening, I'd tell you. The thing is this—humans have lived for centuries side-by-side with other species. In all those years, you and I both know, eventually the species are going to mix. Maybe several centuries ago, there was something we don't know about. I have jaguar blood. So do a lot of the women who are psychic."

MaryAnn shook her head. "Not me." It felt wrong. She knew her mother and father and her grandparents and great-grandparents. There weren't any spots in her family and no one sucked blood.

Could she be mage? Juliette ventured.

Mages hold power, that's for certain, and most are good people, but she would be weaving spells. She does not appear to be doing that. She gathers energy as we do and uses it, but she is unaware. That is why she is such a good counselor. She unwittingly urges them to feel better. She wants them happy, so they are. She senses the right thing for each person to hear and she says it.

MaryAnn's heart went into overdrive. They were clearly talking to each other again. She turned on her too-high heel and ran headlong into the underbrush, thinking she might outrun them, forgetting they could take to the air if they wanted. And they wanted.

She felt the rush of displaced air all around her, and Riordan dropped down out of the sky, cutting her off.

MaryAnn screamed and backpedaled, her heels catching on one of the many roots snaking across the ground. She went down hard, landing on her bottom, looking up at him as he stood over her.

"That way is dangerous," Riordan explained, extending his hand to her.

She kicked at him, furious with him, but mostly angry with herself for being in such a vulnerable position. How many times had she counseled women about going off with strangers —people they met through the Internet, or through friends, but didn't really know themselves. She curled her fingers around the small canister of pepper spray. Did it work on Carpathians? Or vampires? No one had mentioned them in her pepper-spray class.

"MaryAnn," Riordan cautioned, frowning at her. "Don't be silly. Let me help you up. You're sitting on the ground. Did you know that there are a million and a half ants per half acre in the rain forest?"

MaryAnn suppressed a yelp of fear and scrambled to her

feet without help, backing away again, brushing at her clothing, feeling the swarm of insects on her legs and arms. *I hate this!* She screamed it so loud in her head she felt the echo through her clenched teeth. Her eyes burned with tears again.

The air around them charged with electricity so that the hair on her arm prickled.

"Take cover," Riordan yelled and leapt back.

Thunder rolled. The ground shook. Monkeys howled. Birds screeched and rose from the trees. Lightning sizzled and snapped, slamming to earth in a near-blinding display of energy. Fog poured in all around her. MaryAnn felt strong arms slide around her, and one hand pressed her face into a large, muscular chest. Her feet left the ground, and she was flying through the treetops so fast it made her dizzy.

Riordan swore and caught Juliette's arm when she would have pursued. "That was Manolito and he gave us a clear warning to back off. We have no choice but to do so. She's his lifemate and we have no business interfering."

"But . . ." Juliette trailed off helplessly. "We can't just leave her."

"We have no choice, not unless we want to provoke him into a battle. He will take care of her," Riordan assured. "We cannot do any more here."

5

MaryAnn circled Manolito's neck with her arms and buried her face in his shoulder. The wind whipped viciously at her face and neck, tugged maliciously at her hair and managed to slip under the leather jacket to wrap icy fingers around her skin. If she thought the rain forest was bad, flying in the canopy was a thousand times worse. She felt dizzy and sick, and her stomach did rolling flips. She'd face the million ants and the tree frogs before she'd do this again.

As a child you must have wanted to fly.

She was certain he was reading her mind easily, and she could feel his superior male amusement, reminding her why she didn't care all that much for men. And since she wasn't in the least bit psychic or telepathic, she answered out loud, pressing her lips against his throat. "*Never.* Not once. I like my feet firmly on the ground." But his skin smelled so good. It was hard to not sniff and drag him into her lungs.

Manolito settled them down in a relatively protected area, which she was grateful for because it instantly began to rain. Not a soft drizzle, or even a steady one, but a hard, pounding downpour, as if the heavens simply opened up and dumped an ocean on them.

MaryAnn stepped away from him the moment she had her legs working. Her stomach was still rolling and pitching, and she swore her nose twitched wanting another good sniff, but she refrained and sent him a long scowl. The problem was, he was looking at her. Not just looking. Staring. Her heart did a slow roll and her stomach did the butterfly thing, but with a lot more wing. And her womb clenched and her nipples . . .

She jerked her jacket tight around her and summoned a

glare to go with the scowl. Who looked like that? Honestly. Men didn't really stand there looking gorgeous and hot in the rain forest. Not just hot. Smoking hot. He was the sexiest thing she'd ever laid eyes on, and he was looking at her like he might devour her in one utterly delicious bite. His eyes smoldered with a dark sensuality, making her forget all about leeches and ants, and making her wholly aware she was a woman. She hadn't felt that way in so long—if ever—that she was flustered.

"So," Manolito said, his black eyes burning with such pure sin she nearly melted on the spot. "You came at last."

Oh, God. Her stomach did another roll right along with her heart, and she tasted sex in her mouth. He dripped with it. "I came to rescue you." She blurted the words out before she could think. She couldn't actually think with him staring and her brain short-circuiting, so really, as stupid as the remark might have been, it wasn't half-bad under the circumstances.

He smiled, a slow, sensual smile that sizzled and dazzled and tightened the spirals in her already curly hair. Maybe he was the Carpathian secret weapon against women, because it was working on her. The man was a menace. Truly. She had to get ahold of herself. She snapped her fingers. "Consider yourself saved and let's get out of here." Because wanting to jump him was most likely the effect of the rain forest, all sultry and sweaty. She'd read a lot of Tarzan books in her youth. She was just programmed for sex in the jungle, and the sooner she got out of there, the faster she'd return to normal.

He crooked his finger at her. "Come here."

Her mouth went dry. "I'm perfectly fine right here, thank you." With her favorite boots sinking into the muck. She couldn't move if she'd wanted to. Her heart pounded and fear crept in, not of him, of herself. For herself.

His gaze slid over her, and there was dark possession glittering in the black depths. Not love. Possession. Ownership. Raw sensuality. Her body responded, but her brain screamed a warning. She wasn't dealing with a human male who lived under the rules of her society. She was alone with a Carpathian who believed he had every right to her. Who knew he could control her mind and persuade her to do his bidding. This man would demand total submission and surrender from his partner. And she was a no-submission, no-surrender kind of woman. How the hell had she gotten herself into such trouble?

"I said come here to me." His tone didn't rise, or even harden; rather he pitched the command lower so that his voice felt like the velvet rasp of a tongue sliding over her skin. His black eyes compelled her obedience.

She stepped closer before she could stop herself, and strong arms whipped around her, crushing her body against his. She fit like a glove. He was hard and muscular, and she was all soft curves and aware of every one of them. He whispered something in his own language, something soft and utterly sensual. *Te avio päläfertiilam.* He repeated the words as his tongue swirled against the pulse beating so frantically in her neck. "You are my lifemate."

It couldn't be true because she knew one had to be psychic, but right then, in that precise moment, she wanted it to be true. She wanted the feeling of belonging to this man. She had never had such a physical reaction to another being in her life. *Entolam kuulua, avio päläfertiilam.* His lips whispered over her pulse, teeth nipping gently as his tongue stroked another caress. She thought her body might go up in flames. "I claim you as my lifemate."

She lifted her head, opened her mouth to protest, but his mouth fastened on hers, taking her breath, exchanging it with his. Her legs turned to rubber, and to anchor herself she wound one leg around his thighs while her tongue tangled with his in a long, slow dance of pure erotic pleasure. The feeling burst through her so that her blood pounded and her heart thundered in her ears. She almost missed the soft words brushing along the walls of her mind and embedding there.

Ted kuuluak, kacad, kojed. Elidamet andam. Pesamet andam. Uskolfertiilamet andam. Sivamet andam. Sielamet andam. Ainamet andam. Sivamet kuuluak kaik etta a ted. "I belong to you. I offer my life for you. I give you my protection. I give you my allegiance. I give you my heart. I give you my soul. I give you my body. I take into my keeping the same that is yours."

The kiss deepened, and she was falling, burning, wrapping herself inside Manolito De La Cruz. She felt her heart and soul reaching for his. Merging. Her breasts ached and grew heavy. She felt the damp eagerness in her deepest feminine core, and her mind blurred even more with the hot passion rising.

Some small, sane part tried to save her, some little untouched portion of her brain raising a red flag, but his mouth was unlike anything she'd ever experienced and she wanted more, his taste addicting. His hand slipped inside her jacket, pushed up the edge of her shirt and closed over her breast so that she gasped and drew his head down to her, wanting him. *Wanting.* No, *needing.*

His lips wandered down her throat as one hand settled into her hair, bunching the thick braid in his fist, anchoring her to him while he explored the satiny soft skin. He found the swell of her breast, the mark he had placed there branding her his.

Ainaak olenszal sivambin. "Your life will be cherished by me for all time." The words vibrated through her, so that she pressed closer, pushing against his thigh, easing the terrible aching emptiness, wanting to fill it with him.

She cried out when his mouth settled over her breast, drawing her sensitive nipple into his mouth right through the sheer lace of her gold peekaboo bra. He suckled strongly, his tongue flicking, teeth scraping. All the while she heard his voice murmuring in her head.

Te elidet ainaak pide minan. "Your life will be placed above my own for all time."

His tongue danced and laved. He lifted his head, his gaze holding a mesmerizing dark possession. "And your pleasure." Once more he captured her mouth, stealing her breath, taking her will, lighting a fire in her veins.

His mouth burned a trail of flames from her throat to her breast, his teeth teasing and nipping with tiny little bites, each one sending a rush of hot, welcoming liquid sizzling through her feminine channel. She was weak with wanting him. She nearly whimpered when his mouth found her other breast, pulling strongly, until she could no longer think clearly. She arched into him, wrapping her leg more firmly around him, aligning their bodies so she could press tightly into him.

Te avio päläfertiilam. Ainaak sivamet jutta oleny. Ainaak terad vigyazak. "You are my lifemate. You are bound to me for all eternity. You are always in my care."

He lifted his head and once more found the spot where he had marked her. His teeth sank deep. Fire burned, pain flashed through her like a storm, then pleasure so sweet, so erotic, she moved with restless abandon against him, cradling his head, holding him to her while his long, inky hair spilled over her arms and she buried her face in the silky strands. She felt herself slipping further and further from the woman she knew into another realm entirely.

He murmured something else in his language, his voice so sensual, she pushed aside the small warning going off in her head and kept her face buried in the silk of his hair because nothing in her life had ever felt so right. She belonged. She'd found what she'd always been looking for. Content with her life, she had always assumed she would grow old and die with the comfort she'd achieved, but now this was a gift. Passion. Excitement. Belonging. It was all hers.

There was nothing shy about MaryAnn. She had chosen to abstain from sex simply because she would not share her body with a man she didn't trust, didn't love, a man she wasn't going to spend the rest of her life with, but at that moment, she knew Manolito De La Cruz was her other half. She would share everything with him, was eager to do so.

His tongue swept across her breast, making her shiver with need. His voice whispered again, and the strangest thing happened. She found herself standing off to the side observing as she ran her hands beneath his shirt and pushed it up his chest, revealing the defined muscles flowing beneath his skin and the shredded rips in his belly where the jaguar had raked him. Her hand slid up over the terrible claw marks, her palm covering them, infusing them with warmth. She saw herself press kisses up his belly and chest to a point just above his heart.

Her tongue found the pulse she was looking for, that steady, strong beat. Her body clenched in anticipation, throbbing and weeping with need. Her hand slid over the spot, and she stared at her fingernail, the one she'd broken earlier. It lengthened into a sharp talon. To her shock, she opened his skin and pressed her mouth willingly to his chest. He groaned and threw back his head, ecstasy mixing with passion. His hand came up to hold her to him, urging her to take more. And she did. There appeared to be no revulsion, no hesitation. Her body writhed against his, a sensuous slide of curves, an invitation for much, much more.

And he took her up on it, his hands rough, intimate, possessive. He yanked at her clothes, wanting bare skin against his. When she rubbed her body along the thick, hard bulge straining his jeans, he shuddered and murmured his approval; he cupped her bottom and half lifted her to align their bodies so that he was pressed against her most intimate spot.

As if she knew exactly what to do, how much she could take of the hot, addicting exchange, she swept her tongue across the wound and lifted her head to look into his mesmerizing eyes. She looked different, her eyes dark and sultry, her lips curved and voluptuous, so sexy she couldn't believe it was her, so ready to do anything and everything Manolito would ask of her. She wanted to please him, pleasure him, and have him do the same for her.

He smiled down at her and her heart went crazy, reacting every bit as strongly as her body.

Päläfertiil. "Wife." He kissed the tip of her nose, the corner of her mouth, hovered there, a breath away, looking into her eyes. *Tell me your name that your koje, your husband, will be better able to address you.*

MaryAnn gasped as the words sunk in. He couldn't have done worse if he'd thrown a bucket of ice water over her. Mary-Ann blinked and shook her head, trying to clear her thoughts. What in the world was she doing wrapped around a man who didn't even know her name, but professed to be her husband? And what in the world had gotten into her that she let someone mesmerize her to the point of doing things totally against everything she believed in? Manolito made her weak. He'd taken complete control of her, and she'd just gone along with it as if he could rule her life with sex.

Fury burst through her, a fury she'd felt only one other time before, when a man had burst into her home and threatened to kill her. He dragged her out of her bed, punching her viciously before she could defend herself, throwing her to the floor and kicking her. He had leaned down and stabbed her with a knife, and when the blade had gone into her flesh, something wild and ugly and out of control had lifted its head and raged. She'd felt her muscles bunch and knot, and strength had poured into her. At that moment Destiny had arrived, and she'd killed the man, saving MaryAnn's life and maybe her soul, because whatever had been inside of her frightened her more than her attacker.

MaryAnn was a woman who absolutely abhorred violence and could never condone it, yet now she had an indescribable desire to slap that handsome face as hard as she could. Instead she leapt away, at the same time screaming in her mind. She put every bit of fear and loathing at herself and her own actions into her cry because no one could hear her, and no one would know the terror she lived with trying to contain that slumbering beast dwelling deep within her.

Get away from me. For one terrible moment she didn't know if she was yelling at Manolito—or at whatever lived inside of her.

Manolito staggered, fell back into the broad trunk of a tree and stood shocked and staring. No one had ever delivered him a psychic slap before, but that was what his lifemate had done to him. Not just any slap, but one hard enough to knock him off his feet. No one had dared treat him in such a manner, not in all the centuries of his existence.

Dark anger crawled through his belly. She had no right to deny him—or defy him. He had a right to the solace of her body whenever he wanted it. She was his. Her body was his. Blood pounded and surged through his veins. His cock was filled to bursting. He'd waited a thousand years—more even—faithful to this one woman and she was denying him.

"I could make you crawl to me and beg forgiveness for that," he snapped, his black eyes smoldering with dark, telling smoke. He could feel the pull of her, so powerful he couldn't stop the frenzy his body had gone into. Hard and hot and crawling with such a need—the feeling was far worse than any hunger for sustenance. He drank in the sight of her, shocked at her beauty. Her skin was so soft-looking he ached to run his fingers over it, to slide his body over hers, into hers. She had full, luscious curves and a mouth he couldn't stop staring at, sinful and wicked and so tempting his body hardened into one long, painful ache. He imagined her fingers on him, her mouth, her body surrounding his, tight and hot and killing him with pleasure.

He needed to bury his face in her wealth of blue black curls, inhale her scent and keep it for all time in his lungs. He needed the warmth of her arms and the sound of her laughter. But his body needing sating first. He couldn't look at her and not want to be inside her, not want to ravage her, bring her to fulfillment, to have her cry out his name. He wanted her on her knees in front of him, wanted her to admit she belonged to him and no one else, admit that she wanted—even needed—to give him the ultimate pleasure of her body.

MaryAnn wasn't certain exactly what had happened. He'd

fallen back, but she'd only yelled at him, the arrogant ass. In any case, crawling didn't figure into her plans. And begging forgiveness wasn't exactly her style. He looked furious, and dangerous, and altogether far too handsome for his own good. A spoiled, arrogant man whom everyone had obviously catered to all of his life. Women must have done whatever he said, when he commanded it. And he must have done a lot of commanding.

She bit down hard on her lip to keep from telling him to go to hell, because . . . MaryAnn spread her hands out. "Look, I'm as much to blame as you are. I had choices here." She wasn't going to blame just him. She was a grown woman and believed in responsibility, although nothing that had happened to her since entering the rain forest had been normal. "I bought into the entire lifemate thing because you're . . . well . . . you're gorgeous. What woman wouldn't want you?" And she'd reached the point she'd been darned sure she was never going to experience soul-searing, hot-as-hell, unforgettable sex. Manolito looked like a man who could—and would—deliver it. So yeah, she was guilty, but he could forget all about her crawling to him for forgiveness.

Manolito studied his lifemate's face, gently probing her brain at the same time for some clue as to what their relationship had been like. Stormy obviously. And her name was MaryAnn. MaryAnn Delaney. He was hazy about details, such as when and where they'd been first together, but he knew the addicting taste of her. He felt a driving need to dominate, to hear her breathless pleas and see ecstasy cloud her eyes.

He had reconfirmed the sealing of their souls in the age-old ritual because his mind had insisted he do so. But she was a woman who needed a firm hand. Stripping her naked, yanking her across his knees and delivering it to her unbelievably beautiful bottom was something he'd take pleasure in doing. And then he'd lay her out and taste her, eat her, lap up every drop of that feminine cream, memorize every luscious curve, learn what drove her mad until she did beg him for forgiveness. And then he would bring her over and over to the brink of fulfillment, until she knew just who her lifemate really was.

He took a step toward her and something crossed her face, fear maybe. He didn't want her afraid of him, not really, although a little healthy fear might win him some cooperation. Confusion for certain. He stopped when she backed away from him and looked around as if she might run.

"I could never harm my lifemate, you should know that. At most I would find a pleasurable punishment, one I could be certain you would ultimately enjoy."

MaryAnn frowned at him. "Whatever you're talking about you can forget. I'm too old to be punished. Look, we've made a mistake. Both of us. I came out here with the intention of counseling Juliette's sister, and Riordan told me you were in trouble. I've never actually been introduced to you before. We've never met. I saw you in the Carpathian Mountains, at the Christmas party, right before you were attacked, and a few times in the distance, but we were never introduced. I have no psychic ability. I'm a normal human being who counsels women in need."

Manolito shook his head. Could this be the truth? "Impossible. You are no stranger to me. You are the other half of me. My soul recognizes yours. We are sealed as one. You belong to me and me to you." He pushed an impatient hand through his long, silky hair, then reached back to tie it with a leather thong he drew from his pocket.

Maniacal laughter slid into his head, so that he whipped around, scanning in every direction, his body language changing to protective. He leapt the distance separating them and placed her behind him.

"What is it?"

"You did not hear anything?" He knew what was out there. The vampires emerging slowly out of the shadows to stare with pitiless eyes and gaping maws for mouths, to point bony fingers in accusation at him.

MaryAnn listened but only heard the annoying call of cicadas and other insects. Who knew they'd be so loud. She shook her head, feeling her heart break for him. "Tell me, Manolito. You look so sad. You should never be sad." She willed him to be happy. To go back to being furious and smoldering instead of lost and lonely.

He turned then, catching her upper arms and dragging her close, staring down into her guileless face and meeting her eyes for one long, endless minute. He raised one hand to her face. The pad of his thumb slid along her high cheekbone, regret etching deep lines around his eyes and mouth. "I just found you, MaryAnn, but if you do not hear the voices, it means I am not quite sane. I do not remember things. I have no idea whom I can trust. I thought you . . ." He trailed off, groaned softly and covered his face with his hands. "It is true then. I am losing my mind."

"I'm human, Manolito, not Carpathian. I don't see and hear the things you are able to see."

Manolito wished that were true, but the ground was rippling beneath their feet and she didn't see the face in the leaves or the disturbed soil forming a mocking mouth. He stood very still for a time before lifting his head, while the rain poured steadily down.

"You must leave me. Go back to where you feel most safe. Stay away from me. I do not know why I believe you belong to me, but I fear for my sanity—and for your safety. Go now, quickly, before I lose my resolve."

Because he couldn't bear the thought of her being out of his sight. Until that moment he hadn't realized how much he needed her. His needs no longer mattered. She had to be safe—even from him—especially from him.

There it was—her freedom. She looked around her. The rain forest was dark and somber but for the water. It was everywhere, forming both small and large waterfalls, finding new paths and converging into wide, rushing streams. The water poured down, relentless and steady, adding to the falls pouring out of the rocks and dirt. She was so out of her element here, so completely without a clue what to do.

Manolito appeared just the opposite, even if it was true that he was losing his mind. He was at ease in the world, confident and powerful, his eyes once more searching the area around them, trying to assess the danger to them—no—that was wrong—he was trying to assess the danger to her.

She took a deep breath and slipped her hand into his. "We can figure this out together. Are you hearing voices now?"

"Yes, mocking laughter. And I see vampires in the ground, in the trees, in the shrubbery. They are surrounding us."

MaryAnn closed her eyes briefly. Just great. And she'd been worried about jaguars. Vampires were much worse. Reaching with her free hand, she settled her fingers around the canister of pepper spray. "Okay. Show me what you see. You can do that, right? Open your mind to mine."

He felt her moving inside his mind, already merging and stretching to meet him. She seemed unaware of it, but the integration was initiated by her. Her mind slid easily and seamlessly into his. Her fingers tightened around his. A tremor went through her body.

You see them.

MaryAnn stared around her at the hideous faces. No wonder he didn't know reality from illusion. The vampires were all too real there in his mind. At least she thought they were there in his mind. "Do you trust me?" she asked.

"With my soul," he answered promptly. He believed she was his lifemate and there could be no betrayal, no lies between them. And if he was wrong, so be it. He would die protecting her.

"Let go of my mind and I'll get us out of here." She tried to step in front of him, gripping the canister of pepper spray hard, prepared to do battle with whatever came their way, so she could get him to safety.

He caught her chin and forced her to look at him. "I am not the one holding the merger. You are. I cannot release you; only you can do that."

She moved closer to him as if for protection. "I can't be the one holding the merge. I'm not psychic."

"It is going to be all right, *ainaak enyem*. Forever mine," he translated. "I will not allow harm to come to you while we dwell in *lamti ból jüti, kinta, ja szelem*."

"I don't speak your language." And whatever he'd said couldn't have been very good. It sounded demonic. She braced herself for the translation.

"The literal meaning is the meadow of nights, mists and ghosts. We seem to be partially in our world and in some measure in the netherworld. I am not certain how that occurred or why, but we have to find our way out."

"I was afraid it might be something like that." She *so* didn't belong in this world. She didn't even watch horror films. "All right, tell me what to do, because that really ugly vampire to our left is moving closer."

The world was gray. A dull, veiled gray with shrouds of fog hanging like moss, draping along sticks of blackened tree branches. And there were insects everywhere. Big ones, flying around her face and every available inch of exposed skin. She whipped out the bug spray and doused them with a burst from the canister. The mixture came out of the nozzle a weird grayish green vapor, drifting slowly and thickening as it went. The sound was a slow hiss, animal-like, overly loud in the sudden quiet of the world.

"They don't make any noise," she whispered to Manolito. "The bugs. It's so quiet here."

Immediately ghoulish heads turned, and demonic, glowing eyes bored into her. Shock registered. The vampires looked at one another, then back at her. A murmur of glee rose, and one of the vampires pushed closer, his hideous mouth gaping open to expose pegs of stained teeth filed to a razor-sharp point.

"Delighted to have you join us," the vampire hissed, his foul breath hot on her skin. "It is long since I dined."

Steam rose around them, enveloping them in a thick fog. Manolito dragged her into his arms, wrapping them around her head to keep her from seeing the monsters as they moved closer, the pitiless eyes staring hungrily at her neck.

"Now would be a good time for flying," MaryAnn urged.

"I cannot in this world. I am bound to the laws of the land of mist."

The ground shifted and more faces stared at them. The vampire jerked closer, each movement labored. MaryAnn tensed as a long, bony finger pointed at her and the creature crooked his fingers, beckoning her. He blew foul-smelling air as cold as ice toward her. Before it could touch her face, Manolito whipped around, so that he took the shot in his back, rather than allow the vampire to strike her in the face with his poisonous breath. Even so, MaryAnn felt the ice shards pierce through Manolito's body, straight into hers.

"The hell with this," MaryAnn snapped. "You flew before. Get your butt in gear and get us out of here." She willed him into the air. Commanded it. She even wrapped her arms around his neck, buried her face against his chest and crushed her body up against his.

Manolito might have to follow the dictates of the meadow of nights, but MaryAnn evidently did not. He was locked into the shadow world, a half dweller, but she was mortal, walking in a place she did not belong, drawn in and held by their shared soul. She had only to desire to leave without him and she would be free, but she refused to consider it. He was beginning to know her mind now, and to realize his lifemate had a spine of steel. He found himself in the air with her, moving fast away from the faces staring up at them, the wail and gnashing of thousands of teeth.

He found a small shelter of boulders and dropped down to place her on the ground, hoping they would be safe, but as he knew nothing of the unnatural realm they partially dwelt in, he feared nowhere was safe. MaryAnn clung to him, her body trembling as her feet touched the rock. She slid down his body as if boneless and sat, her knees drawn up and her body rocking.

"You can leave this world, MaryAnn," he said gently. "I know you can."

"How?"

She looked up at him and his heart clenched painfully in his chest. She looked close to tears. His fingertips pushed back strands of her curly hair, lingering against the warm satin of her skin. "You have only to make a conscious decision to leave me here. Condemn me for whatever wrong I have done you."

She looked genuinely puzzled. "What wrong did you do to me?" She waved her hand. "Other than looking gorgeous and driving me a little crazy, you haven't done anything to hurt me. I'm responsible for my own hormones going into overdrive, not you. You can't help the way you look."

He sat beside her, his thigh touching hers, and reached for her hand, bringing it to his chest, over his heart. "At least you like the way I look. That is a start."

She shot him a small, mischievous grin. "Every woman likes the way you look. You don't have a problem in that department."

"So it is my personality you object to."

It was hard to think of just what she objected to when his thumb slid over the back of her hand in a mesmerizing caress and his thigh delivered enough heat to warm up half the world. His white teeth were dazzling and his smile so sensual her body hit overdrive before she even knew her engine had been started. It didn't seem to take much around him. It should have embarrassed her, but in the midst of the strange world she found herself in, potent chemistry was the least of her worries.

"You're still living in the dark ages, my man," she said, patting his knee, trying to feel auntlike and wise. Instead her heart was tripping, her stomach fluttering, and all she could think about was pressing her mouth to his to see if rockets went off again. Because she sure didn't want to think about being alone when the sun came up, and he was going to point that out any minute.

He brought her hand to his mouth and nibbled on her fingers, his teeth sending little electrical currents zapping through her bloodstream with each nip. "The dark ages? I thought I had adapted to this century quite well."

She laughed; she couldn't help it when he sounded so shocked. "I suppose for someone as ancient as you, you have adapted." And maybe it was the truth. He was born into a species and time when males protected and dominated women. He lived in a country where the same rules of society still often held. Of course he would feel he had a right to her if he believed she was his lifemate.

Husband. She tasted the word, aware of the very breath moving through his lungs. He was too gorgeous for her, too wild and far, far too dominating, but she could dream and she could fantasize. She couldn't imagine *really* belonging to the man, not like Destiny belonged to Nicolae. But if he kept looking at her with those black, black eyes filled with such raw hunger, she might just forget all of her misgivings and try for one glorious night with him.

"I just know what is right for my woman, how to protect her as well as please her, and she should have faith enough in me to trust that I will see to all her needs as well as every pleasure she—or I—could imagine."

His teeth nipped at the sensitive pads of her fingers. It shouldn't have been erotic, but it was. He made everything sound that way, even his ridiculous suggestion of punishment. It was the velvet rasp of his voice, the way he could make it slide over her skin like a caress. If someone else talked the way he did, she would have laughed, if not aloud, at least to herself, but with Manolito, she was tempted to try some of his more outrageous fantasies.

"I'm reading your mind," he said softly, "and we need to be concentrating on how to get you out of here."

"Well, they are just fantasies." She was *not* going to blush. Being stripped naked and tormented until she begged was frankly as sexy as could be, although the reality might not be the same as the imagination.

"I can promise you that you will enjoy every moment with

me," he assured her, and bit lightly on her finger before sucking it into the warmth of his mouth.

His tongue teased and danced until she wanted to scream surrender. And he was just kissing her finger. She fanned her face. Maybe she was up for the reality of it after all. "Would you consider terms? Like not ordering me around? I might concede to working on being adventurous."

"To be adventurous, you have to be willing to surrender yourself into my care," he countered.

There it was again, that slow, sexy smile that burned through her skin and found hidden wild desires she shouldn't be contemplating with a man who was bent on her utter and complete surrender. "Tempting. But no. I'm not a woman who could ever turn over my life to a complete stranger."

His chin nuzzled the back of her hand. Her breasts ached, as if his shadowed jaw had brushed her soft skin there. "But surrendering in the bedroom is not the same as surrendering out of it."

"Is that an option with you?"

"There is no option. There is only what is. You are my lifemate. We will find a way because that is the way of lifemates." The smile faded from his face. He kissed her knuckles and brought her hand once more over his heart. "You cannot stay here with me, MaryAnn; it is much too dangerous. I cannot tell what is real or illusion, and with our bodies in one world and our spirits in another, we are vulnerable in both places."

"I don't know how to leave, and I wouldn't if I could. Not without you. How about I forgive you for anything you may have done to me." She looked around at the dull gray of the world. It appeared to be the rain forest, but without the vibrant color and sounds. Water ran out of the rocks and down the slope, but instead of clear or white, it ran in dark streaks.

"I do not think it is that simple. First I have to figure out what I did to bring me to this place of ghosts and shadows."

6

Ghosts and shadows. She *so* didn't like the sound of that. MaryAnn rubbed her chin on the top of her knees. There was always an answer; she just had to use her brain.

Manolito leaned in close—close enough to envelop her in his pure male scent, to warm her body and make her feel feminine and protected. She sent him a faint irritated glare. She was trying to think and didn't need her brain shorting out. His smile sent every electrical pulse sizzling and snapping throughout her body.

"Tell me what wrong I have done you. I would not hurt you for the world. I know I was never unfaithful. Tell me, *päläfertiil*, and I will do whatever it takes to make this wrong up to you, not to get out of here myself, but because I would never want to wrong my lifemate in any way."

There was enough hurt in his voice, and concern, to turn her heart over. "Manolito, I honestly don't know what's going on, but you haven't had a chance to wrong me. I barely know you. I am not Carpathian. I live in Seattle and counsel battered women. That's how I met Destiny. We became friends, and through her, I ended up traveling to the Carpathian Mountains."

He frowned. "That cannot be so. You say you are human, yet you can do things only a Carpathian can do. You have much power, MaryAnn. I feel it surging within you even when you talk to me. You are reaching out to soothe me, to make me feel better."

She shook her head. "I'm human. My family is human. Everything about me is. I really, honestly just met you today. I saw you." *And thought you were so beautiful it hurt.* She closed her eyes and leaned her head against his shoulder. "You scared the hell out of me. Everything about you is frightening, some of it, most of it, in a good way."

His kiss was the merest whisper of his lips over her cheekbone, but she felt it lodge right in her heart. "Why would I be frightening to you? You are the other half of my soul." He looked puzzled.

She had a mad desire to rub away the frown lines between his brows, but she resisted, curling her fingers together. "You wouldn't understand." Because she wasn't all that attracted to men, not like this. Not so that she wanted to do anything and everything he asked. Not so she couldn't breathe or think with wanting him. She liked her calm, controlled life. She wasn't in the least adventurous, in bed or out. Definitely not in. He was exotic and mysterious and oh, so dangerous. She was—well—just plain MaryAnn with her feet firmly on the ground. She didn't indulge in wild fantasies. Or obsessions, and Manolito could certainly be characterized as an obsession.

Manolito swept his arm around her. "You have only to talk to me about your fears, *ainaak sivamet jutta*, and I will find a way to reassure you. I will get you out of here. We need to do so quickly, as the sun will be rising. When our bodies are in the realm of the living and our souls are in the meadow of mists, it is difficult to protect ourselves out in the open in the rain forest."

"Then take us to your home. If we're there, we won't have to worry so much about something big attacking our bodies."

"We must go to ground. The richest soil is the terra preta. Better to stay where the soil has a chance to rejuvenate us."

Her heart slammed hard in her chest. "I'm not Carpathian. I don't go to ground. I'd die if the earth covered me. My heart doesn't stop like yours does. Please, believe me when I tell you, I'm not Carpathian."

Manolito rubbed the bridge of his nose and regarded her through long lashes. "I know you feel our connection. I can read your thoughts much of the time, not because I'm invading your privacy, but because you're projecting them to me." He sent her a small half smile. "You try to comfort me. I can feel your energy wrapping me up in warm arms and stroking me, reassuring me all will be well."

He was so close, all she had to do was lean in and kiss his sinfully sensual mouth. He was temptation sitting there, in the midst of danger and mystery. Wicked, shocking temptation.

And she couldn't resist. MaryAnn pressed into him, crossing the scant inches that separated them until her lips brushed his. Just once. A slow savoring. Because if she was going to die, or stay in hell, she might as well get a taste of heaven while she was at it.

His arms slid around her, and the earth dropped away along with her stomach. His mouth simply took her over. She hadn't known anyone could kiss like that. She tasted addiction and need. She tasted hunger and the biting edge of raw, carnal sex. For one terrible moment, either terrible or sheer ecstasy, she thought she might have an orgasm just from his kiss.

"I can't breathe." She didn't care if he knew how much she wanted him. Everything ached. Everywhere ached. There wasn't a single cell in her body that wasn't aware of him; aware of wanting—no—*needing* him. In that moment she knew no one else would ever satisfy her. She would crave this man's taste, his touch, his face and body, even his wicked smile. She would dream of him and lie awake at night needing him. It was a terrifying realization that her life was no longer her own and that with him, she had very little control.

"Easy, *sivamet*, you are in good hands."

His voice was mesmerizing, every bit as sexy as his mouth. Strangely, he wasn't taking advantage; rather, he gathered her closer and held her protectively as if he knew her uninhibited and all-encompassing reaction to him scared her.

"I'm out of my depth with you," MaryAnn admitted. She tried to breathe, tried not to hyperventilate, but she couldn't get her lungs to work. If it was possible, she thought she might actually be experiencing a panic attack over a kiss. Cool, unflappable MaryAnn was losing control over a man, and there wasn't even a sister close by to talk to. She was *so* out of her world here.

"No, you are not," he said, the gentleness in his voice whispering over her skin. He kissed her again, breathing air into her lungs. "We are both in an unfamiliar situation."

She wanted to laugh at the understatement, but she was too close to tears. Not because of the danger, but because this man who needed to be with some glamorous movie star or model was looking as if he had eyes only for her. She didn't dare talk about it anymore.

Lifting her chin, she brushed his sensual mouth one last time and took a deep breath. "Let's try for the house. I should be safe there. Riordan and Juliette have to go to ground like you, but Juliette told me that her sister and cousin use the house during the day when no one is there. With three of us there, we should be safe. Vampires can't walk around during the day, can they?"

"No, but they often have puppets who do their dirty work for them. The jaguar-men have been tainted by their evil."

"How do you know?" MaryAnn took a cautious look around, aware that all the while Manolito had been kissing her, holding and comforting her, driving her wild, he had been scanning for enemies. She wasn't going to be able to resist his lovemaking if he ever got serious about it, but she really, really wanted the opportunity to try.

"I met one of them, Luiz, not too far from here. He attacked me. When I reached for his mind to calm him, I knew the vampire had been influencing him. He actually was not a bad man at all. In other circumstances, perhaps we could have been friends."

"I felt his attack on you. I tried to stop it," she admitted. "How bad did he get you?" She frowned. "He wanted to kill you."

"It was brave of you to try to intervene, although you must never place yourself in harm's way. Trust me to take care of us." He had felt her, for that one moment, standing between the leaping cat and him, and he had slammed his mind closed to prevent any injury to her, but he had felt proud of her and, most importantly, part of her. "A few scratches is all he managed."

He lifted his shirt to show his very muscular stomach. Mary-Ann licked her lips. "I didn't think men were really built like you," she blurted out and then covered her face with one hand. He was holding the other one or she would have used that one, too.

She was so shallow. That was it. *Shallow.* Because she was fixating on his six-pack, his ripped muscles, and how could she not notice the impressive bulge in the front of his jeans? He wasn't even trying to hide it. She should be thinking wounds and *oh no* and *are you all right?* But no, she was thinking about stripping him naked and having her way with him. She hadn't always been shallow, so maybe it was the strange shadow land they seemed to be in. But while she was at it, she might as well go all the way. She glanced down at her once beautiful boots.

Maybe she needed some thigh-highs and a good long whip to be in control of herself—or of him.

"I'm reading your mind again." There was male amusement in his voice.

"Well good. Try to make some sense of it, because I'm not doing so well myself. Are you all right?" There. That was certainly appropriate. A little slow in coming, but she got it out there.

The rain forest surrounded them, the water still pouring out of rocks and flowing into rivers. Everything appeared the same, yet different. Fouler. Much more frightening and strangely still. Before, when she'd first entered the forest, she had noticed it was quieter than she had thought it would be, but as she walked, she began to hear the cicadas and other insects, the cries of the birds, and wind and rain in the canopy. After a time, the forest seemed loud and filled with occupants, so that she didn't feel quite so alone. Now it seemed less vivid, drabber and dark, not so alive, and ominously quiet.

Snakes slithered along the forest floor and coiled over twisted branches. Worms, leeches and ticks made the vegetation writhe and move as if alive. The beetles were large, with thick, hard shells, and the mosquitoes were ever present, searching endlessly for blood. The flowers gave off a rotten fragrance, and the scent of death seemed to cling to everything. But sometimes, when she blinked rapidly, or she thought about Manolito and how gorgeous he was, the rain forest was all vibrant color again. It made no sense, but it gave her hope that if she just took a little time, she could unlock the secret to getting them both out of the shadows.

"Take me back to the house. Can you find your way?"

"I do not want to lead danger back to the others."

"If a vampire is hanging around the neighborhood, my guess is he knows all about the others. We're safer in numbers, especially if you aren't going to be with us." The idea of him leaving her alone caused instant panic. Her throat swelled until air could barely get through to her lungs, but she refused to give in to fear. He was Carpathian and she was human . . .

MaryAnn went rigid. "Wait a minute. Wait a minute." She held up both hands, palms out as if she could block the information flowing into her. "Did you take my blood?"

"Of course."

There was that puzzlement again, as if she was maybe not quite as bright as he'd expected. "And you think I'm the other half to your soul. Destiny told me that in your society the man can marry the woman without her consent and bind them together. Is that true? Did you do that to us?"

"Of course."

MaryAnn scrubbed a hand over her face. There was a sinking feeling in the pit of her stomach. "How many times does it take to convert a person to Carpathian?"

"It takes three blood exchanges if they are not already Carpathian."

She bit down hard on the end of her thumb, memory flooding her. She looked down at her fingernail—the one she had broken earlier in the forest. It had grown to the length of the others and then some. All of her fingernails had grown. Sometimes that was a problem. She had to cut them often, but not daily. Maybe it was the Carpathian blood accelerating the growth. "How many times have you exchanged blood with me?"

Her palm slid over the mark on her breast. It still throbbed and burned as if his mouth was on it. Why could she imagine that all of a sudden? Why was she so certain his mouth had been there? Why could she *feel* his mouth, burning like a brand, against her skin when his lips should never have been there? Not skin to skin. He had kissed her, slid his mouth over her; she still had a warm, wet spot on the nearly nonexistent lace of her bra. As sexy as it had been, it wasn't his mouth on her skin, so why was the memory suddenly so strong?

"I would imagine many times."

She inhaled sharply. "You don't really know, do you? Manolito, if you don't know, and I don't know, we could be in real trouble. I am not Carpathian. I was born in Seattle. I went to school there and then to Berkeley, in California. If it's true that you've exchanged blood with me, I know I haven't gone through the conversion. I would know if I had to sleep in the ground. I'm still just me."

"That cannot be so. I remember taking your blood, binding us together. You are a part of me. I cannot be mistaken."

She opened her mind and memories to him. "I'm telling the truth when I say I haven't met you before. It's the truth that I saw you at a party in the Carpathian Mountains, but we were never formally introduced. I am physically attracted, but I don't know you at all." Okay, wildly physically attracted, but this was serious and she could overlook it—she hoped. Everything was falling into place. The things Riordan and Juliette had told her were beginning to make sense. Her heart thudded hard.

He was silent, assessing her memories of him, dwelling a little too long over the one he found of a man coming into her house and attacking her. He felt the lengthening of his sharp teeth and the demon within roaring for release. Very carefully, he hid his reaction. She was coping with enough, and if he had somehow brought her into his life without her knowledge—or his—raging like he wanted to because she hadn't been safe would only make things worse.

"If what you say is true, MaryAnn, then how is it we are lifemates? Speaking the ritual words cannot connect two people who are not one. I could say them to every woman I met, but it would do me no good."

"Maybe you made a mistake," she ventured. "Maybe we aren't really connected."

"I see in color. I feel emotions. I can think of no other woman but you. I want no other woman. I recognize your soul. We are lifemates." His voice was firm, brooking no argument.

MaryAnn couldn't find an argument. While it was true that she didn't know everything about Carpathian life, she knew enough that the possibility was strong. Judging by her reaction to him alone, she had to admit it was probable. "All right. Say we are lifemates, Manolito. You say you wronged me in some way and that is why you're stuck here. Why do you think that?"

His thumb slid up the back of her hand, stroking tiny caresses over the silky smooth skin. He bent his head to nibble the pad of her thumb while he thought about it, the gesture automatic, sexy, burning through her with ease. "I felt like I was being judged for something I had done to you. I should know if I wronged you."

"I should know, too," she conceded, trying not to react to the feeling of his teeth scraping erotically over her thumb. How could such a small thing be felt in the pit of her stomach? Or make her womb clench? Or her breasts feel swollen and achy? There was no way she could ever let this man touch her in a bedroom. She'd never get over it.

"I'm reading your mind again."

"You do that a lot." She wasn't going to apologize. "Stop being so sexy. I'm trying to think here. One of us has to get us out of here." She sent him a smoldering look from under her lashes, but he only grinned at her, his smile sending need skittering over her body as easily as his caresses had. She was in trouble. Big trouble. Huffing out her breath, she pulled her gaze away from his, determined to find a way to free them.

"Could that be the wrong, Manolito, because tying us together without my consent and taking my blood without my knowledge shouldn't be okay by anyone's standards. Maybe you need to feel remorse in order for us to get out of here."

"I can say I feel sorry for claiming my lifemate, but it would not be true."

She sighed. "You aren't exactly getting into the spirit of the thing here. If we want out of this shadow world and you somehow wronged me, shouldn't we be figuring out what you did?"

"The wrong cannot be binding us together. That is a natural act for a Carpathian male. I would be wrong not to bind our souls. I would turn vampire and you would eventually die of heartache."

She snorted. "Of heartache? I don't even know you." But she'd grieved for him. Cried for him. Had been clinically depressed and now she was feeling hot and bothered and exhilarated in spite of the fact that she was surrounded by ghouls and insects and spiders the size of dinner plates. She tried again to make him understand. "What if I was married? You didn't even wait to find out. I could have been." Because a *lot* of men thought she was fine.

His fingers tightened around her and tiny flames leapt in his eyes. "There is only one man for you."

"Well maybe you were late in coming. The point is, I could have been married. I had a life before you came along and I liked that life. No one has the right to turn someone else's life upside down without that person's consent." She forced herself to look into his eyes. "I don't love you."

His eyes went very black, liquid heat, turning her inside out and stealing reason along with her ability to breathe. "That may be, *ainaak enyem*, but it cannot change what is. You are my lifemate, the other half of my soul, as I am yours. We are meant to be together. I must find a way to make you fall in love with me." He leaned close, so that she felt the warmth of his breath on her skin, so that when he whispered to her, she felt the brush of his lips, soft and firm and tempting, over hers. "Rest assured, *päläfertiil*, that I will focus my complete attention in that direction."

Her heart went crazy, pounding and slamming so hard she thought she might have a heart attack. "You're lethal. And you know it, too, don't you? Were there other women? Maybe that's your big wrong." And the thought set her teeth on edge, even though it was silly. He hadn't known her, he still didn't, but reason didn't seem to enter into her emotions. That strange wild thing hiding deep within her began to awaken and stretch, raking with sharpened claws at the inside of her belly.

Horrified, MaryAnn jumped up, yanking her hand away from his. She was buying into this entirely. The nonexistent shadow world. The lifemate of a man she didn't know. A species that dealt with vampires and mages. Nothing made sense in this world, and she didn't want to be there. She wanted Seattle, where the rain came down to clear the air and the world was right.

MaryAnn felt Manolito's restraining fingers circling her wrist, but when she looked down at his hand, it was gray. She blinked. All around her, the rain forest was vivid and bright, the colors so brilliant they nearly hurt her eyes. The sound hit her then, the continual drone of insects, the rustle in the leaves and the shifting of animals moving through the underbrush as well as the canopy overhead. She swallowed hard and looked around her. The water was pure and clean and rushing with enough force to sound like thunder.

She reached for Manolito, clutched him to her, afraid she would lose him. His form seemed solid enough, but there was something not right about his response, as if part of him was otherwise occupied. "I think I just did something."

"You are fully back where you belong," Manolito said, relief in his voice. "We need to get you to safety before the sun comes up. You may not be Carpathian, MaryAnn, but with at least two blood exchanges, you will suffer the effects of the sun."

"Tell me what's happening." She hadn't liked that other world, but being alone in this one was terrifying. "I don't want to be separated from you."

The anxiety in her voice turned his heart over. "I would never leave you, especially not when danger surrounds us. I can fully protect you even with my spirit locked in this world."

"What if I can't protect you?" she asked, her dark eyes filled with trepidation.

Manolito pulled her close to him to try to comfort her. Even as he did, the ground beneath him heaved and a huge plant burst through the soil close to his feet. Tentacles slithered across the ground, searching even as the middle of the bulb opened and a yawning mouth gaped wide, revealing thick tubes topped with poisonous stigma, sticky knobs waving toward him, trying to touch his skin.

"Watch the ground, MaryAnn," he warned, whipping his arms around her and leaping back. He landed ten feet from the seeking plant, scanning quickly to pick up signs of an enemy. His senses didn't work as well in the shadow world, but he feared whatever happened to him here could very well mirror what happened in the other world.

"What is it?" She raked the ground with sharp eyes, her vision clearing entirely so that she almost felt as if she was seeing in an entirely different way. She could see Manolito, but whatever attacked him in that world she couldn't focus on. She saw it as blurring shadows, something nightmares were made of, insubstantial and eerie. His arms were fading, as if he was being pulled more and more into the other world.

"Don't let go of me!" She tried to grab his shirt, but she felt him letting go of her mind. She hadn't even known he'd been in it, but once he was no longer there, his form became nearly transparent.

"I cannot allow you in danger here. We do not know what can happen in this realm. You are safer where you are while I deal with this."

"What is 'this'?" She yelled it, called him, implored him, but he was gone, other than that wavering shadow flicking in and out among the shrubbery, until even that was gone and she was alone.

Fearful, mouth dry, heart pounding, MaryAnn looked around her. No matter how hard she wished it away, the rain forest surrounded her. She swallowed hard and backed up a few more steps, her heels sinking into muddy water. Leaves and aquatic vegetation hid the shallow channel she'd accidentally stepped into. Water and mud were everywhere.

The rain poured down, making its way through the canopy to pepper the forest floor. Leaves rustled and something moved in the water. She wrapped her fingers tightly around the canister of pepper spray and tugged it from her belt loop.

"Great time to disappear," she whispered aloud, spinning in a circle, trying to see around her.

The branch overhead shook, and she tilted her head to look upward. She could see a snake looking down at her through the leaves. She swore her blood froze in her veins. For a moment she couldn't move, staring up at the thing, mesmerized. A hard tug at her ankle yanked her back to reality. Teeth bit through her boot and into her skin. She gasped, instinctively trying to pull her foot out of the water, but a snake with a very broad head held her while its long, thick body coiled around her legs, preventing movement.

She screamed. It was pure terror, a reflexive action she couldn't have stopped if she'd wanted to. In her wildest imagination, she had never been attacked by a hundred-pound anaconda. She tried frantically to get to the head, hoping if she sprayed the pepper spray she'd have a chance, but the body seemed endless, without a head or tail. Already she could feel it crushing her bones. Panic wasn't far away, and deep inside, the wildness that she kept locked up so tight began once again to unfurl.

"Hold still! Don't fight." The command was sharp, the voice unfamiliar.

MaryAnn clutched the pepper spray and forced her body to quit fighting. A hand with a wicked-looking knife came into view. Pain speared through her, as teeth sawed for a better purchase on her ankle. Anacondas didn't chew, but they held their prey while their muscular bodies crushed, and this one wasn't giving up so easily.

She saw the hand slash in and out of sight. The snake slumped to the ground and MaryAnn scrambled out of the water, knocking her heel sideways so that it wobbled under her as she ran away from the snake. She caught a tree trunk, hugging hard, breathing deep to try to calm the panic.

"What are you doing here? Are you lost?"

She turned around to find a man calmly pulling a pair of jeans from a small pack around his neck. He was totally naked. His body was strong, muscular, with scars here and there. She bit down hard on her lip, the urge to either laugh or cry very strong.

"You could say that." As men went, he was built. He had a strong face, and even though he'd tugged up his jeans, she could see he was well endowed. "Do you just walk around the rain forest naked?"

"Sometimes," he admitted, his serious eyes studying her and the can of pepper spray she had in her fist. "I suggest you stay out of the rivers and channels. Anacondas and jaguars and other predators patrol through here."

"Thanks for the tip. I hadn't noticed or anything. Those snakes aren't poisonous, are they? Because it bit me."

"No, the danger is infection. Let me take a look."

MaryAnn inhaled sharply, everything in her rebelling at the idea of the man touching her. Shaking her head, she stepped back. "Thanks, but no. I've got some antibiotic cream I can use."

He studied her face for a long time, as wary as she was. "This island is private property. Who brought you here?"

"I'm staying with the De La Cruz family. Manolito is around somewhere." She didn't want him to think she was alone.

His eyebrow shot up. "It doesn't make sense that he left you, even for a minute."

The worry in his voice gave her a small sense of assurance. "Do you know Manolito?"

"I met him earlier this evening. Dawn is approaching, and many animals hunt along the riverways at dawn. Let me take you back to the house, and Manolito will follow when he is able."

MaryAnn searched the shadows for Manolito. She couldn't touch his mind or feel him at all, let alone see him. *Where are you? I don't want to leave you.* She reached out but found only a black void.

If her rescuer ran around naked in the rain forest and he'd met Manolito earlier, there was a good chance he was a jaguar-man. Juliette's younger sister had been captured and brutally attacked by the men of the jaguar species. MaryAnn took a firmer grip on the canister of pepper spray. She'd never find her way out of the rain forest, and she was terrified of being left alone, but she couldn't leave Manolito, especially since she knew something was happening to him, and she was afraid to trust this man.

"I'm Luiz," he said simply, obviously reading her unease.

"Manolito did me a great service today. I am simply returning the favor."

"I don't want him to come back and find me gone. He'd worry." She didn't want the only person there—human or not—to leave her alone. She couldn't look at the body of the snake. She hadn't wished it harm, but she didn't want to die here either. Getting consumed by an anaconda was on her list of least favorite ways to go.

"Carpathian males worry about very little," Luiz said. "Come with me. You cannot stay alone. If you wish, you can carry the knife."

MaryAnn sighed. Carrying the knife meant getting close enough for him to hand it to her. It also meant that she might really stab him with it if he made a wrong move, and she was definitely opposed to that idea. "You keep it." She had the pepper spray and that she wasn't afraid to use.

He smiled at her. "You are a very brave woman."

She managed a short laugh. "I'm shaking in my very favorite pair of boots. I don't think brave is the word I'd use. Stupid. I'd be safe at home in Seattle if I just hadn't been the save-the-world kind of idiot I tend to be."

He started down an almost nonexistent path. She could see it had been used by an animal. Taking a deep breath, she followed, sending up a silent prayer that Manolito would find her soon. Maybe if she got to Riordan and Juliette, they would be able to find Manolito again and help him.

Luiz glanced back at her. "Can you walk with the heel of your shoe broken? I can cut them off for you."

That was sacrilege. He'd saved her from the snake, but he deserved pepper spray for even contemplating cutting the heels off her favorite pair of boots. It wasn't too late to salvage them. "No, thank you." She stayed polite, because he had to be a little crazy to think of such a dark deed.

They walked in silence for a few minutes, MaryAnn trying to keep her mind from straying to Manolito. It was difficult. Part of her wanted to rush back to where she had left him and wait until he returned. Part of her was angry with him for deserting her, and another part—the biggest—was terrified for him.

"Why are the tree frogs following us?" Luiz asked.

"Tree frogs?" MaryAnn bit her lip and glanced around,

peeking through her eyelashes, hoping the jaguar-man was wrong. "I have no idea." She took a quick look at the trees. Sure enough, frogs leapt from roots to branches, from trunk to trunk.

"They seem to be following you."

"Do they?" She tried to sound innocent even as she hissed at the frogs, gesturing with her arms to go back. "You must be mistaken. More likely they're migrating in the same direction we're going." Did frogs migrate? Maybe that was geese. Rain forest creatures were complicated. She glared at the brightly colored amphibians. They continued to hop happily alongside of her.

"You're gathering quite a crowd." He sounded amused as he politely held the shrubbery back so she could walk freely along the path. He continually raised his face to sniff the air in every direction.

"Maybe they're attracted to my perfume." *What part of "go away" don't you understand? You're making me look bad.* She tried a mind-to-mind telepathy, hoping some of Juliette's and Riordan's psychic abilities really had rubbed off on her, but the frogs ignored her complaint.

"Can you walk faster?" Luiz asked.

He didn't look nervous. In fact he appeared quite steady, but she had the feeling he was looking for trouble, scanning the canopy overhead and watching their back trail. The monkeys began to scream and throw leaves and twigs. Luiz held up his hand and signaled for her to remain quiet.

Mosquitoes buzzed by her face, and she calmly pulled out the bug spray and liberally doused the air around her.

Luiz whirled around, his nose twitching. "Don't do that."

"The mosquitoes are biting me everywhere."

"That foul stench hinders my ability to catch scents. I need to know what we're likely to be facing."

Okay. That sounded ominous, and quite frankly, she was tired of being scared. There was only so much scared you could do without a friend to egg you on. She sighed and put the bug spray back, resorting to slapping at the insects with one hand and retaining possession of the pepper spray with the other.

She was *so* out of here the moment she could get to a phone. Well, after she made certain Manolito was all right. She was beginning to feel sick with worry, and that just made her madder at him. The mark at the curve of her breast throbbed and burned and ached for him. Tears blurred her vision, and she stumbled on a twisting, snakelike root, nearly falling, throwing out both arms to catch herself before she face-planted in the muck—and it saved her life.

The large jaguar missed and hit the ground just inches from her head. Snarling, it whipped around, raking at her face with claws, but Luiz was there first, already half changing, his face broadening, muzzle lengthening to accommodate teeth. The two cats crashed together, raking and clawing. The rain forest erupted into a frenzy of noise.

Pushed beyond all endurance, MaryAnn jumped up, took two long strides to the marauding cat and let loose with a stream of pepper spray directly into the fully formed jaguar's eyes and nostrils. She gave it several short bursts, fury shaking her hand, but her aim was perfect.

"Enough already. I've had it—absolutely *had* it with this jungle crap. I may be an urban woman, damn it, but I can deal with anything this horrible place throws at me. Get out of here now!" she yelled at the top of her lungs, sending another stream right at the jaguar's face for good measure. The command blasted through her brain and out into the air even as she shot several short streams.

The jaguar raced away as if she'd bitten it. Luiz fell onto his butt, jeans half-shredded. "What the hell was that?"

"Pepper spray," she said and sat down beside him, bursting into tears.

7

Manolito avoided the seeking tentacles as he studied the fi-brous bulb. His body was in the rain forest with MaryAnn. He was intelligent; he could reason it out. If he was trapped in the spirit world, as he was certain now he was, then only a spirit could reside in this place. He had no body here, so the attack was merely a distraction. It must have to do with MaryAnn. Not only had her spirit entered, but her warmth and vitality with her. The vampires had sensed hot blood and the light in her soul. He had to lead the attack away from her, just in case she inadvertently stepped back into the shadow world where he was trapped.

He moved slowly away from her. The shadowy figures who called to him to join them, who threw accusations at him and wanted to sit in judgment of him, didn't seem to be able to look past the veil into the world of the living. Perhaps if he could get far enough away that they couldn't sense her, she might be safe. He could lay a false trail and get back to her and escort her to safety before dawn. He shouldn't have been able to feel sensation, but the farther from MaryAnn he traveled, the more he felt cold.

"Join us. Share her. She has already condemned you to a half life." The voice shimmered in the air, soft and persuasive, becoming louder as he moved farther away from MaryAnn. "You have always belonged with us, not with sheep, following the speaker of lies."

Maxim Malinov, dead from the battle in the Carpathian Mountains, slain by the prince himself, stepped out of the shad-ows and approached Manolito. "Why would you give your life for the prince when he cares nothing for you or yours? He knows you are in the meadow of mists, yet is he watching after your lifemate? Is he protecting your body while you wander in this world? He is selfish and thinks only of himself, not of his people."

Manolito drew in his breath. It had been long since he'd seen his boyhood friend. He looked young and strong, handsome as always, with intelligence shining in his eyes. As young men growing up, they had enjoyed debates and discussions throughout the nights, talking about the issues they felt best for their people. Following Mikhail, the current reigning prince, hadn't been anyone's idea of what was best.

"We were wrong, Maxim. Mikhail has led our people from the brink of extinction. The Carpathians are beginning to grow powerful again, but more importantly, we have become a society filled with hope instead of despair."

Another plant erupted from beneath the surface, the long vines reaching like arms toward him. He leapt into the nearest tree, more out of reflex than need. He might feel the piercing cold as ice shards began to rain down, but the stinging wounds as the icicles stabbed through him were no more real than the plant. He gave himself a moment to force his mind to accept it was all illusion. The plant slid back beneath the soil, but the stabbing ice continued to fall.

When he leapt back down, Maxim shook his head. "In the old days you would not have settled for looking at so small a piece of the real picture. We hide from the people who should serve us. We hide in fear, when it is they who should tremble before us."

"And why should they tremble, Maxim?"

"They are nothing but cattle."

"That is why you do not lead and I would not follow if you did. They are people with hopes and dreams. Good, hardworking people who fight every day to do the best they can for their families. They are no different than we are."

Maxim gave a snort of derision. "You have become brainwashed. You have taken a human for a lifemate and she has already corrupted your ability to see sense. We are noble, the better race, the one deserving of this earth. We could rule, Manolito. Our plan is in place. Eventually we will take over and humans will bow before us." His smile was wholly evil, the red flames in his eyes leaping with maniacal fervor.

Manolito shook his head. "I do not want them bowing before

us. Like all species, many of them have mixed from ancient ancestors. Most likely, Carpathians, mages, jaguar-men and even the werewolf have integrated into the human society."

The red flames leapt and the vampire hissed out his disbelief. "The jaguar-men have tainted their bloodline, it is true. They threw away their heritage and their greatness because they refused to take care of their women and children. They deserve to be wiped from the earth. *You* were the one who said it. You and Zacarias."

Manolito held himself still as another large piece of ice stabbed through his shoulder. The sensation was fiery, sickening, but it disappeared when he refused to give it credence. "I was young and stupid, Maxim. And I was wrong. We all were."

"No, we were right."

"The jaguar-men made mistakes, and those mistakes cost them, but they are not Carpathian and their needs were different from ours. You chose not to wait for your lifemate, Maxim. In doing so, you have given up every chance of having a wife and children and helping to create a lasting society. You saw the power of the prince's bloodline. He is the vessel for all of our people."

"His power is false, a sham. Look at the scar on your throat, Manolito. How many times are you willing to die for him? You have taken the knife twice for him and once for his brother's lifemate. You are here, in this world of shadows, to be judged for your 'dark' deeds. What dark deeds? You lived with honor and you served your people, yet you are here." The voice became hauntingly beautiful, filled with truth and mesmerizing zeal. "All the ancient races are myths now, forgotten by the world. The jaguar race, once powerful, is found only in books. They clothe themselves with shame. They brutalize their women. Would you have that happen to our species?"

"If you really believe what you're saying, Maxim, then you would have chosen another path. Why turn vampire? Why make kills for power? Why not gather your army and march against Mikhail right out in the open?"

"That was not the plan."

"Becoming the undead was never part of the plan either. Our families lived with honor, Maxim. We hunted the vampire, not embraced him."

Maxim ignored him. "My brothers and I studied how to take over. If we approach the prince directly, we would be defeated. You know the majority of Carpathians believe in the old ways. They are cattle."

Manolito curled his lip. "Humans and jaguar are cattle to you. Now Carpathians. You certainly have risen high in your own opinion, Maxim. You have contradicted yourself repeatedly."

Maxim folded his arms. "You seek to anger me, Manolito, but you cannot. You were once a great Carpathian, from a powerful family, but you have given your loyalty to the wrong person. You should have joined us. You still can join us. You are already lost to the next world."

For the first time Manolito's pulse jumped in response to the vampire's twisted logic. Vampires were deceivers, but they often wove truth in. What had he done to his lifemate? Why couldn't he remember his crime? MaryAnn didn't seem to be angry with him. In fact she had protected him, or at least tried to.

The thought of his lifemate warmed him, driving out the ice shards that had pierced his body and frozen his blood. He blinked and looked down at his hands. They had been almost transparent, but now were gathering a deeper shade as if his body was regaining substance and form.

"I see there is danger here after all," he said. "Maxim, you were always clever, but you have never believed in lifemates or the concept of them. You were wrong then, and more so now. I am not lost as long as I have my lifemate."

"And what do you think your lifemate is doing now, while you dwell in the shadow world? Do you think she lives without a man's touch? She craves the jaguar-man and she will lie with him."

Manolito felt the knots twist in his belly. He hadn't known jealousy was such a dark and ugly thing until he had found his lifemate. "She will not betray me. She holds the other half of my soul. You cannot pull me wholly into this world, because she will always anchor me in the other one."

This time Maxim did snarl, his eyes glowing fiercely, his teeth sharp spikes as he hissed his annoyance. "She does indeed hold the other half of your soul. We have only to acquire it and you belong to us. You are a traitor, Manolito, to our family, to our cause. The plan was your idea, yours and Zacarias's, but at the first test you failed us."

"We all agreed it was silly, boyish talk, taking over and ruling the world. Your brothers, my brothers, we said many foolish things that have taken shape and grown into a path of destruction for too many species. There are lifemates waiting for us among the humans, Maxim. Think beyond your hatred and know that humans are the salvation of our people."

"Mixed blood," Maxim sneered. "That's your salvation?"

Manolito sighed his regret. He remembered Maxim as a friend—more than a friend—a beloved brother, and now lost beyond saving. "I have my emotions, Maxim, honor and a future. You have death and disgrace and nothing to sustain you in the afterlife. Any mistakes I have made I will answer for willingly, but I will not help you bring down our prince. Aside from my own honor, I would never dishonor my lifemate by making us traitors to our people."

"We will kill her. Your precious lifemate. Not only will we see her dead, but it will be brutal. She'll suffer a long time before we give her death. *That* is the wrong you have done your lifemate. You have already betrayed her by trading her life for that of your prince."

Fear nearly blindsided him. Terror of what a monster could do to MaryAnn. She was light and compassion, and she would never understand what something as evil and hideous as Maxim could do to her. His breath left his lungs in a long rush of apprehension, of panic. He had never known panic before, but it nearly consumed him with the thought of MaryAnn in the hands of his enemies.

Had he fallen into a trap after all? Had Maxim led him away from MaryAnn so one of his brothers could kill her? She was alone in the rain forest. How much time had passed? Was time the same in the realm of shadows? Was it possible for someone to pierce the veil and help plot murder, or was Maxim deliberately goading him into fear? Fear led to mistakes. And mistakes led to death. He simply would not accept the death of his lifemate.

Manolito kept his features expressionless, his gaze filled with contempt. "You do your worst, Maxim, but you will not prevail. Evil will not drive good from this earth, not while one hunter still lives." He dissolved into mist and streamed through the tortured, twisted trees.

Once out of Maxim's sight, he blasted through the air, racing back to the place where he'd left MaryAnn. He could feel blood pounding in his temples and thundering in his ears as he shifted shape almost before he hit the ground. She was gone. Time stopped. His heart stuttered. The beast within roared and clawed for release. Teeth lengthened and sharpened in his mouth and razor-sharp talons tipped his nails.

She betrays you with the cat-man. Voices filled his head. Anger and jealousy pushed aside reason.

Manolito lifted his head and scented the air. His woman had been there and she hadn't been alone. He knew that scent. He had taken the jaguar's blood.

She lies beneath him, moaning and writhing and calling his name. His name. Not yours. He has stolen her from you and she thinks only of his touch.

A snarl shaped his mouth in cruel lines and his eyes glittered with menace. He studied the tracks, saw the dead snake and the pattern of footprints. Luiz had approached her in jaguar form, but had shifted to his human form. That meant he had stood without clothes in front of MaryAnn. Fury nearly blinded him. He should have killed the treacherous devil while he had the chance. Jaguar-men were notorious for their escapades with women.

Luiz had crooked his little finger and she had followed, like a mesmerized puppet. Both male and female jaguars were very sexual beings. MaryAnn claimed she wasn't jaguar, but if even a small amount of their blood ran in her veins, would Luiz's presence set her off? She might go into her cycle, and then she would need a man to attend her.

She has gone off with him, needing him to give her a child. He will spill his seed in her. Fill her. Take her over and over until he is certain she is with child.

He let loose a roar of anger at the thought. The idea of another man touching her soft skin set the beast raging. No one touched his woman and lived. No one lured her away from him. Luiz was either after MaryAnn for personal reasons, or he had been sent by the vampire to kill her. Either way, the jaguar-man was dead.

Kill him. Kill her.

Manolito shook his head. Even if MaryAnn had betrayed him with another, he could never harm her.

He moved fast, rushing through the rain forest, avoiding hitting the trees by scant inches. If Luiz dared to lay a hand on her, harm one hair on her head, he would tear the man limb from limb. He spotted them, MaryAnn on the ground, tears running down her face, Luiz standing over her. She looked disheveled and angry and afraid, so much so that he ached inside, his heart contracting when he saw her distress. He put on a rush of speed, his body a blur, bursting out of the shrubbery just as Luiz turned.

Manolito hit the jaguar-man hard, driving him backward, then picked him up, slamming him so hard to the ground it drove an indentation in the soft soil. Somewhere in the distance, he heard MaryAnn scream. He pounded Luiz's face, giving him no time to shift into the form of a cat. His arm reared back, and he drove his fist toward the chest wall to penetrate and rip out the black heart of a monster.

"Stop." MaryAnn screamed the command. Then again, with a silent shocking fury that sent Manolito flying backward through the air. *I said stop!*

He found himself sprawled on the ground, ears ringing, from the force of the psychic command. She'd thrown him back, away from the jaguar-man, who lay motionless in the muck. The telepathic punch was harder than any physical one he'd ever received. He blinked up at her, anger at her mixing with awe.

"Are you crazy?" MaryAnn demanded, standing over him, hands on her hips, face furious, eyes glittering dangerously at him.

He wanted her. That was all he could think in that split second. He wanted all that passion and fury under him, fighting him, submitting to him. She was amazing, with her lush curves and incredible face. She usually looked so calm on the outside, presented such an elegant picture, but underneath she was all fury and claws, as wild as their surroundings.

He got up slowly, his eyes steady on her, unblinking and focused. Saying nothing, he stalked toward her across the uneven ground. She had the good sense to back up a couple of steps, wariness and defiance mixing with the fury. He walked right up to her, forcing her to look up at him through her long lashes. One hand fisted in the thick mane of hair, tilting her head further, while the other caught her around the hips and drove her forward into him, crushing her breasts against his broad chest.

She opened her mouth to protest and he took possession. The kiss was rough, the edge of his fear and anger still riding him hard. His tongue drove deep, sliding into her mouth and taking her over, using her own passionate nature against her. She had done what no man had ever done, knocked him on his butt with a thought. *A thought.*

Need burned deep and hot in him. Lust rose sharp, consuming him with the desire to dominate her, to bring her so much pleasure she would never think to leave him, never think to deny him anything. He bit gently at her lower lip, caught it between his teeth and tugged, licked at her pulse and kissed his way down her neck and over to her throat. She breathed in, a harsh sound of need that sent his body into a hard, knotted ache. The rush of hot blood filled him, and he closed his eyes to better absorb the feel and texture of her. Soft and pliable, moving against him like so much silk. Filling every empty place in his heart and soul. He kissed her again, the miracle called woman.

Heat and his scent surrounded her. His erection pressed hot and thick against her stomach. His lips were firm and warm, his kiss rough and arousing. She'd always pictured sex with the man of her dreams as being gentle and slow, but heated passion flared hot and bright inside of her, arousal building into something frightening. Her heart hammered loud and hard, storming against his chest. Her muscles contracted and clenched. Her body turned to liquid, fiery heat.

She ached for him. The need so strong she slid her hand under his shirt to touch his bare skin, to feel his heart beat. Her heart picked up the rhythm of his. Blood pounded and tiny flames licked over her skin.

He pulled away, black eyes glittering down at her. "Do not interfere again."

She blinked up at him, shocked at how easily he controlled her. "Damn you for that." She wiped at her mouth, trying to remove the desperate aching need, the brand he'd put on her, but the taste and feel of him remained. She stepped back, slapped at his hand when she stumbled and he steadied her. "You owe that man an apology. A huge apology. He saved my life twice and sure doesn't deserve to get beat to a bloody pulp because he was escorting me back to the house."

It amazed her that she could talk. Her body burned from the inside out. She stole a look at him. His eyes were heavy-lidded, dark with hunger and arousal. He looked every inch the predator. Dangerous and hungry—starved for the taste and feel of her.

"Do I?" His gaze flicked to where Luiz was beginning to sit up. "He knew you belonged to me."

"I *don't* belong to anyone but me. And he saved my life. You weren't here to play hero." She was appalled at the accusation in her voice.

His gaze softened. "You were afraid without me."

She was afraid for him, and that made it worse. She swallowed hard and spread her hands out. "Look. I'm used to a semblance of control in my life. I don't know what I'm doing here. I don't know what's happening. I'm feeling things I've never felt before."

She was dependent when she'd never been. She needed time to think, to just be quiet, yet she couldn't bear the idea of being away from him. And that was more frightening than anything else, because she wasn't a woman to give up her independence.

Manolito stopped the words burning to be said. She did belong to him—as he belonged to her. But the confusion and weariness on her face turned his heart to mush. She stood there, looking soft and kissable and thinking she was tough, and all he wanted to do was hold and comfort her.

Instead, he stalked across the ground and reached down to yank Luiz to his feet. The man swayed unsteadily and managed a half grin.

"You pack a punch."

"You are lucky I did not kill you."

Luiz nodded. "Yeah, I got that." He looked past Manolito to MaryAnn. "Are you all right?"

A soft warning rumbled in Manolito's throat. "It is not necessary for you to inquire after her state of being when I am here."

"I think it is," Luiz said.

"That's because he has *manners*," MaryAnn snapped. "Thank you so much for your help, Luiz. Especially for saving my life." She turned and walked away. The cave man could keep up or not, but she was close enough to the house that she recognized the Jeep trail. She could just follow that.

Manolito shrugged when Luiz's eyebrow shot up. "She's very good at reprimanding me." For a moment, amusement flickered in his eyes.

"I have a feeling she'll need to be," Luiz said, rubbing his jaw. "She's amazing."

Manolito's face darkened, the brief flash of humor fading

away. "You do not need to find her amazing. And keep your clothes on, jaguar."

Luiz's grin widened. "Women can't help but be impressed."

"I doubt it feels good to have one's heart ripped out of one's chest, but if you like I can arrange for you to find out."

Luiz laughed at him. "She may just rip your heart out, Carpathian. Take care."

Manolito looked down at the blurred shadow of his hand. He was still in both worlds, but he was seeing much more clearly and his form was more substantial than it had ever been. Luiz hadn't noticed, and jaguar people were not only observant, but they could read things in the forest few others could. And they'd spot another of their kind instantly . . .

He caught up with MaryAnn. "He did not call you jaguar, and if you had even a small trace of blood, he would know."

Her dark eyes went stormy. So she still hadn't forgiven him. Deep inside, lust uncurled claws and raked him sharply.

"I'm not jaguar. I told you that."

He dropped behind her to take a good look at her bottom encased so snugly in denim. His heart nearly stopped. The woman was built like a woman should be, all curves and temptation.

"Stop it," she hissed and sent him another smoldering look over her shoulder. "I'm so mad at you right now, nothing you do is charming." Because she knew it wasn't about his lack of manners or his arrogant, ridiculous behavior, it was about *her* behavior. Whether she liked it or not, she was different inside. Whether she liked it or not—whether she even admitted it or not—she was burning and aching for this man, *only* this man, to touch her, to be inside of her. His obnoxious dominating ways should have repelled her, but instead she found him fascinating, mesmerizing even. And that shouldn't have been acceptable.

"I cannot help it if I find you attractive," Manolito protested. "Looking at you puts ideas in my head. I am more than happy to share them with you."

"Well don't. Sex isn't the same thing as love, Manolito, and couples, husband and wife and lifemates, are supposed to be in love. That's how it works."

"You will learn to love me," he said, confidence stamped on his too-handsome face. "It will come with time."

"Don't count on it," she muttered, stomping up the walkway

on her wobbly heel. Yeah. Because it was all about him. She was supposed to learn to love him. That's how things worked in his world, but not so much in hers. When she had raw, passionate sex with this man, she wanted *him* to love *her*.

She was halfway to the door when she really looked at the towering palace he and his brothers called a vacation home. A retreat. Yeah. Who retreated to a place the size of an apartment building? She stopped abruptly at the door. It was a freaking palace. She sighed and rubbed her temples. Man, she needed to be home, back in the real world.

Manolito reached past her to open the solid double doors and gesture for her to go in. "Please enter my home."

MaryAnn drew a deep breath and took a step back, shaking her head. *Nobody*, but nobody, lived this way. She stood in the middle of the huge double doorway, staring at the gleaming marble entryway. She had forgotten what the house was like, or maybe she hadn't noticed when she'd first arrived because she'd been too grief stricken. Set in the middle of nowhere, it was like a palace of days gone by.

"I'm *so* not setting a foot on that floor," she said, backing away from the door. And she had great shoes, too, shoes meant for walking on a floor like that. *Great* shoes—well, she used to. Her beautiful boots were ruined and muddy, the left heel loose and wobbly. She wasn't going to take a chance on scratching the gleaming marble floor that stretched for miles. Her entire house in Seattle could fit into the entryway.

Behind her, Manolito pressed a hand into the small of her back and gave her a little push forward. "Get inside."

Okay, the shoving thing was not working for her any more than his penchant for issuing orders. Besides underscoring the fact that he was the biggest jerk on the planet, every time his fingers brushed her body, every nerve in her system simply went haywire. Her body refused to listen to her brain screeching macho jerk alert.

Even though she couldn't stop the shiver of excitement and the slow burn that spread through her veins like a drug each time he touched her, he wasn't getting away with ordering her around the way he obviously thought he could.

"I know you didn't just shove me," she snapped, tossing her long, thick braid as she glared at him over her shoulder.

It was a mistake to look at him. His gaze burned over

her—into her. No one had eyes like that or such a sinfully sensual mouth—or a house like this. She wasn't into opulence and decadence. She wasn't impressed by it or comfortable with it. And she certainly wasn't into hot, arrogant men who gave orders as naturally as other people breathed.

"It was a gentle aid to assist you into my home, as you seemed to be having trouble entering."

His voice slid under her skin and filled up every empty place inside of her. The deep-timbred rasp was wrapped in velvet and seemed to stroke over her skin. She set her teeth against the dark lure of pure sex.

"I'm not going in there. You must have another house. A little one. Anything else." Because he was planning on leaving her—*again*. He got her all hot and bothered, ordered her around, acted like a jerk, brought her to this—this—*palace*—and he was going to dump her. She could read it on his face. So screw him. She wasn't going in. Being alone in the middle of the rain forest on an island, palace or no palace, was not happening again.

She pushed back against Manolito's hand. Maybe if she found Luiz again, he could help her find the airstrip and she could sweet-talk the pilot into flying her back to civilization. Provided there was a pilot. And a plane. She didn't even know that, but Luiz might.

A flicker of fury bloomed in Manolito's black eyes, and he caught her up and tossed her over his shoulder, striding into the cool of the house, right past the entryway and double sweeping staircases and into an enormous room of marble and glass.

Shock stunned her into silence, and then pure anger blasted through her veins. MaryAnn, who never resorted to violence, who didn't believe in violence, who actually counseled against violence, wanted to beat the man into a bloody spot on the floor.

It was utterly humiliating to be carried over his shoulder, her arms and legs dangling like spaghetti. She pounded on his broad back only to be further infuriated when he didn't even flinch. "Put me down, right now," she hissed, clutching the back of his shirt. "I mean it, Manolito. If someone saw me like this, I'd be so upset." The thought was completely mortifying.

"No one is in the house," he assured her, not liking the distress in her voice. Anger was one thing, but not distress. "Riordan and

Juliette must be with her sister and cousin in the rain forest. And since you asked so politely." Manolito set her on her feet and stepped back, a smooth, fluid glide, just in case she took a swipe at him.

MaryAnn straightened her jacket and blouse with great dignity. "Was that display of machismo really necessary?" Sarcasm dripped. If she couldn't smack him like he deserved, she could take him down with words. She was very good at crossing verbal swords.

Manolito stared down at her furious face. She was so achingly beautiful with her perfect coffee-and-cream skin, so soft he found himself brushing his fingers over her whenever he could get the chance. *His.* He tasted the word. Let it sink into his mind. She belonged to him. Had been made for him. She was his alone, and he would have her for all time.

She'd given him back colors and emotions after hundreds of years without. And she had no clue what she was to him. She stood there in front of him, a small spitfire of a woman with her shiny midnight black curls and chocolate doe eyes, innocent and vulnerable. Need crawled through his body with savage, raking claws, merciless and dangerous, but something else was creeping into his heart. Something soft and gentle when he had long forgotten tender things.

"It seemed an expedient way to get out of the early morning sun."

"Your mama sure didn't teach you a thing about manners, did she?" She tried to maintain her anger, but it was nearly impossible when he was looking at her in that strange way—as if she was—*everything.* And fear was beginning to swamp her, the need to cry, because she could feel the resolution in his mind to leave, to go to ground. She couldn't go with him, and that meant she'd be left alone.

He took a step toward her, obviously reading her dismay.

MaryAnn held up a hand to stop him, because if he touched her, she didn't know how she'd react. She'd never, *never* even contemplated turning her body over to a man and allowing him to do anything he wanted, but Manolito could so easily make her want to do just that. He could make her want things she'd never dreamt of, and that scared her almost as much as the idea of being left there alone.

"Look at my boots," she said, to keep from crying, and sank

down onto the chair to pull them off. "I loved these boots. They've always been my favorite."

He knelt down in front of her, gently pushing her hands away to remove the boots himself. She looked down at the top of his head, his hair silky midnight black and falling in disarray around his face and shoulders. She couldn't stop herself from touching it as his fingers slid down her calf and sent shivers of awareness up her leg.

He was only helping her remove her boots, yet somehow that small gesture seemed sexual. She tried to pull her foot away, but he circled her ankle with strong fingers and held her still. "Don't, MaryAnn. I have no choice but to go to ground. I do not want to leave you alone. It is the last thing that I want. If you continue to be so upset, you will leave me no other option than to convert you now and take you with me."

He raised his head, his dark gaze meeting hers. Her heart jumped as his tongue touched his lips and his gaze dropped to her mouth.

"Don't even think about it." Because *she* was thinking about it, and that just plain scared her to death.

"Go take a shower. I will look after these boots for you," he instructed. "The hot water will relax you and help you to sleep."

MaryAnn swallowed a protest and left him kneeling there on the floor, her boots in his hand. She didn't look back, wouldn't allow herself to look back, even though she was certain he would be gone when she came out.

She turned the water on as hot as she could stand it, letting it pour over her sore, tired muscles while she cried. It was silly, really, but she couldn't help herself after everything that had happened. A relief valve, but still her heart felt heavy. The shampoo took the poof out of her hair, and the conditioner smoothed it once again. She emerged feeling tired and lost and wanting Manolito more than she ever had, but she was determined not to cry anymore.

She wrapped a towel around her and went into the bedroom to find something to sleep in. Manolito sat in the chair by the window holding up her boots. They were clean and shiny and looked new. For a moment, she could only stare in shock, clutching the towel to her as joy burst through her. Fresh tears burned, happy tears this time, but she swallowed them and managed to nod casually toward the boots.

"You fixed them."

"Of course. You love them." He set the boots down and held up a pair of high-heel sparkling red shoes that went with a little slip of a dress that clung like a second skin to her every curve. "I love these."

"You have good taste."

"Put them on for me."

Her eyebrow shot up. "Now? I'm in a towel and my hair is soaking wet." She had the mass of curls wrapped up turban-style, and she was suddenly self-conscious. "They look great with a dress I have, but I'm not so certain what effect they'll have in a towel."

"Right now." His voice was low, compelling, that hypnotic, sexy rasp that tightened her nipples and made her ache with need.

She put her hand on his shoulder and slipped one heel on her foot, all the while watching his face. *He* looked mesmerized. Hungry. She slid the other red heel onto her foot and stepped away from him with confidence. The heels made her legs look great. How could they not? Towel or not, she had a good figure, and he was definitely appreciating it. He made her feel like the sexiest woman alive.

He stood up, an easy casual ripple of muscles, his walk cat-like as he advanced on her, nearly stopping her heart. His hand cupped her face, thumb sliding over her cheekbone. "You are so beautiful. I have no idea what I did to deserve you, but you take my breath away."

He bent his head and kissed her. It was a gentle, lingering kiss, his breath warm and his mouth coaxing. He trailed kisses down the side of her face to her neck, nuzzling her, nipping with his teeth and teasing with his tongue. Her blood thundered in her ears as his hot, seductive mouth roamed down her throat to the curve of her breast. Liquid heat pulsed between her thighs.

Manolito tugged on the towel, and it dropped away from her body, leaving every inch of her bare to his hungry gaze. He stepped back to take in the sight of her, the expanse of satin skin and full, lush curves, achingly soft and inviting. His thumb brushed her sensitive nipple and she gasped in response. He drew a line from her chin to her navel. "I swear, MaryAnn, I have never seen a sight more beautiful in all my centuries of living." Lust roughened his voice, but honesty turned it to velvet. He stepped back, his hand sliding down her arm until his fingers tangled with hers. He tugged so that she would take a step toward him.

8

Manolito slid his hand over the curve of her hip, the pads of his fingers lingering lightly on her skin. MaryAnn's stomach muscles tightened. Small flames of arousal flickered over her thighs, spread up to her belly and teased her breasts. His eyes had grown hot and possessive, his mouth sensual, the edge of hunger sharper. She could barely catch her breath, her body craving his. Everywhere his gaze touched her, she felt it like a brand.

Was she seducing him? Or was he seducing her? She couldn't tell and didn't care. All that mattered was that he couldn't take his eyes from her. His body was hard and tight, the bulge in the front of his jeans impressive. Heat rolled off him in waves. And his touch was sheer magic, the pads of his fingers teasing at some wild creature inside of her, one that demanded to be free—one that physically responded to everything about him.

"I waited several lifetimes for you," he confided, his gaze hot as he bent his head to her neck. His tongue teased her earlobe, swirled over her pulse. "I thought of you. What I would do with you. How many ways I would give you pleasure."

Manolito inhaled the ripe scent of her. All woman. His woman. He ached for her, his erection so hard, so thick, he knew he would never find peace until he buried himself deep inside of her. It mattered little to him that dawn was approaching and he had been unable for some time to even tolerate the early morning sunlight. He would risk everything to stay with her, to be inside of her, to claim her for his own. Her breath quickened, drawing attention to the rise and fall of her full, firm breasts. *His.* He was going to take every second he had with her and live it to the fullest.

He forced himself to let his hand slide from her arm. Walking to the bed beside the fireplace he dropped onto the thick mattress. "I want to look at you."

She stood for a moment, her hand on her hip, her hair streaming down her back, her beauty robbing him of breath. She took a single step in the sexy red heels, and desire hit him with a brutal blow, a fist of need that might have driven him to his knees had he been standing. He drew in his breath and let the intensity of lust take him. His body felt hot, too tight, bursting with the need to drive into her. Images ran through his head of her spread out before him like a feast.

With each step she took, the hunger increased, until his blood pounded in his body and every cell raged for her. The sheer pleasure of wanting her shook him to the very foundations of his existence. He had never wanted anything the way he wanted her. He had never needed anything, but suddenly her body was everything. The shape and texture. Her skin, gleaming with invitation. Every soft inch of it waiting to be explored, to be touched. Every secret hollow and shadow. His. All for him. When nothing in his long centuries of existence had ever been for him, the sight of her was almost too much to be believed. Looking wasn't good enough. He would have to touch her—possess her—or none of this would be real.

For the first time in her life, MaryAnn felt absolutely, totally sensual, without inhibition, moving around the room in her high heels, knowing every step she took brought Manolito De La Cruz closer to the edge of his control. It was exhilarating to see him draw in a harsh breath, to see his eyes go smoky and dark, to see the dark need in him etched deep into his face. He was so handsome she couldn't breathe for looking at him. And he wanted her. Oh, yeah, he wanted her. Lust was carved deep. Hunger lit his dark eyes, the intensity feeding her own needs.

Her body was alive with sensation, her breath coming in gasps. She was aware of the aching tingle in her breasts, the way her nipples were tight and hard. The damp heat gathering at the junction between her legs. All because he looked at her with that fierce possessive need. She wanted to rub her body along his, stroke him, please him, do whatever it took to satisfy those leaping flames of hunger in the depths of his eyes.

He crooked his finger at her. "Come here." He patted the bed beside him.

She licked her lips. If he touched her, when she wanted him

this much, what would happen? She threw back her mane of rich, dark hair and sauntered over, watching with satisfaction the way heat flared in his eyes as his gaze drifted over her body.

"You really are beautiful, MaryAnn."

His voice was that blend of rasping velvet, but this time, a small rumbling growl was added. The note seemed to play over her skin, stroking like fingers. Her womb clenched, triggering tiny like quakes. His foot hooked the inside of her leg, ran up and down her calf and then tugged gently until she stood with her legs spread for him.

He shifted, leaning forward to circle her bare ankle with his fingers. Very slowly he ran his palm up her leg. When she would have moved, his grip tightened in warning. "Don't."

She tried to stay very still, but his touch sent electric currents slicing through her bloodstream and she couldn't stop shaking. His palm traced the shape of her leg, moved up to her knee, caressing, stroking, sending tiny flames licking along her calf and up her thigh as he moved higher, his fingers pressing into her body, imprinting the shape and texture of her into his mind.

"I'm not certain I can stand for much longer." Was that her voice, a thick sensuality coating every note? Why was this so sexy, to stand completely naked while he was fully dressed? To have every inch of her explored by his wandering hands while she stood still. "I'm not a toy, Manolito." But it felt like it. His toy. His woman. His body to touch and tease and worship with his large, warm hands. And why did that turn her on? Why did she like being on display for him, seeing his body's reaction to her and feeling more empowered with every passing moment?

"Of course you are. Your body is a beautiful playground and I want to know every inch of it. I want to know exactly what makes you respond and what gives you the most pleasure." He rubbed his thumb over her slick, wet entrance and watched her eyes glaze over. "I want to know what makes you scream, what makes you beg." His hands made circles along her inner thighs, moved up and over the flare of her hips and then down to caress her buttocks. "I want to eat you alive, listen to you moan and whimper for more. And that's exactly what I intend to do, MaryAnn, feast on the taste of you."

He bent forward, and his tongue swiped a long, slow tease along her cleft, wrenching a whimper from her.

"Much, much more."

"More? Surely there isn't more?" She was certain she couldn't stand wanting him any more than she already did.

His hands shaped her bottom, fingers sliding skillfully down the center, feather-light, caressing, stroking small streaks of fire through her body.

"There is always more, MaryAnn, and all of it will bring you more pleasure than you ever imagined."

Right at that moment she could imagine a lot. She drew in her breath, shocked at the things she wanted from him, shocked that all that mattered to her was that he touch and taste her. The wildness in her was growing, and all her normal inhibitions seemed to be disappearing rapidly.

Manolito had to resist throwing her to the ground and taking her the way his body demanded, hard and fast, pounding into her over and over until he felt sated. His cock throbbed and burned, stretched beyond limits, but he was not rushing this. She was so beautiful, with her lush body and her soft doe eyes glittering with a mixture of fear and excitement. She was a woman who liked at least the illusion of control. He wanted to drive her past her comfort zone and take her to a place of pure sensation.

He drew her down, into his arms, onto his lap, so that her body fit tight against his. The soft linen of his trousers rubbed against her skin as he locked her to him, tilting her chin up so her eyes met his. He inhaled her, drawing her feminine scent deep into his lungs, heard her heart thundering in his ears, felt the soft skin, the lush silken texture of it, and had to resist the urge to thrust her beneath him. The need to blanket her, dominate, sink his teeth into her was growing stronger with each passing moment.

She relaxed into him, her body trusting him. She felt small and soft, little shivers running up and down, so that she burrowed closer to him. Her eyes looked dark and filled with the mystery of woman.

He took her mouth, gentle at first, savoring the spicy tang of her as his tongue tangled with hers. She sighed, her body going pliant, moving against his in invitation.

"Such a temptation," he whispered as he shifted her in his arms, laying her across his lap, her body stretched out, breasts thrust upward, thighs open and moisture glistening along her cleft. "You're so wet for me, *sivamet*, so ready."

His teeth tugged at her lower lip, teased and nipped, loving the curve of it, memorizing the shape. "I love your mouth." He loved everything about her. And that was the problem. The more he tried to find a way to hold her to him, to make certain she would never want to leave him, the more he wanted her. He would never get enough of her body. And her body would never be enough for him. He wanted her eyes to shine with more than lust and need.

Manolito kissed her again, a slow taking of her senses, wanting her heart and soul, knowing he could only have a small part of her. It made him more determined than ever to bind her to him sexually. She was unaware of her allure, of the fact that she was as sexy as hell; she thought it was all him. His kisses were long and drugging, shaking her deliberately, not giving her a chance to think, only to feel. Her moans were soft, and he swallowed each one, taking them into his body to hold forever.

He loved watching her arousal heighten, knowing it was for him. Knowing that he had put that dazed look of utter need in her eyes. She turned her face to his, nuzzling under his chin, her tongue sliding in a heated rasp over his skin before she whispered his name.

"Manolito."

The soft breathless entreaty hardened his body even more. He nibbled his way down her chin to her throat. Her skin was warm honey. He couldn't resist a small bite, teeth scraping gently over her pulse, his tongue soothing the small sting with a gentle swirl. She reacted with another breathy moan, tilting her head to give him better access to her throat. Her hair fell like a waterfall around him, and he wanted the feel of it against his skin. Her breasts rose and fell as her breathing grew ragged.

"You like that, don't you," he whispered, his teeth nipping her skin again, his voice mesmerizing. He noted the elevated pulse, the scent of her calling to him, ripe and ready. Heat emanated from her. "Oh, yeah, baby, you definitely like that."

His brow furrowed in concentration and his clothes dissolved in swirls of mist, leaving his body naked, so that he held her skin-to-skin. The cascade of her hair fell over him in a sensual slide, so that his erection, so thick and hard and aching was pressed tight against her soft body. MaryAnn stood between him and the monster he could become—the undead. She alone had the power to save him, and the miracle was, she was offering up her body to him. There was nothing more powerful or more erotic.

His mouth moved over her hungrily, her coffee-cream skin like hot silk. He could hear and feel her blood calling to him, surging in her veins with the ebb and flow of life. Her heart followed the rhythm of his, beat for beat, beneath the full mounds of her breasts. His lips traced a path along the rising swell and down into the valley, his tongue flicking over her pulse points, his teeth teasing as he moved his attention to the tight peaks of her nipples.

Her body arched as he blew warm air over the tightening buds. She tried to move, to bring up her arms, but he stopped, lifting his head, watching the arousal burning in her eyes. "Stay still, *sivamet*. Very still. I want you to feel every stroke of my tongue, every touch of my fingers."

"I can't," she gasped. Her body was too edgy, too restless, the need growing fast and ferocious. She wasn't certain she could take any more. She had never been like this, in a fever of need, craving his touch, his mouth, the small nips that seemed to tug at her womb so the fire inside built higher and higher. So high she felt on the edge of desperation, when she wasn't a desperate woman. She needed him inside her more than she needed to breathe, but instead of giving her more, he kept up his slow, sensual assault until she thought she might die with need.

"Yes, you can. You will. Whatever I give you, you'll take and more," he said. "Let me make you scream, MaryAnn. Let me make you so mindless with pleasure you do not know any other name but mine." He allowed his voice to be a seduction, caressing her skin the way his fingers did. He bent his head to her breast, his lips brushing her nipple as he spoke. "Give yourself to me completely."

His hand cupped the firm ripeness of her breast and took the tip into the hot cavern of his mouth. His teeth tugged; he suckled, licked, nipped, assaulting her senses, back and forth between tiny bites of sensual pain and exquisite ecstasy. Need was on him, shaking his control as she writhed against his groin. He flattened his tongue to flick her nipple as his hand slid down to the gathering heat at the junction of her legs.

She cried out, a soft little tormented plea, twisting in his arms even as she tried to obey his command to stay still. Nerves in her thighs jumped and she opened her legs further, squirming against the thick erection. Fire raced through his body and his cock jerked. Another growl escaped his throat as his fingers glided to the vee of dark curls just above her moist cleft. He sent another heated, feather-light breath across her darkening nipple so that she arched into him again, thrusting toward his mouth in an agony of need.

Manolito gave her several slow, lingering licks, flicking his tongue, suddenly tugging gently with his teeth, deliberately sending flickering flames dancing through her body. He alternated between hard and gentle, slow and fast, a bite of sensual pain and a torturous swirl of his soothing tongue. All the while, his fingers teased just above that glistening cauldron of heat. Muscles rippled in her stomach, and her hips arched in desperation, striving for release he wouldn't give her.

Her breath came in a little sob. "You have to do something."

Satisfaction lit his dark eyes with tiny amber pinpoints of light. He lifted his head to look down at her, his gaze hot and possessive as it drifted over what was his. Deliberately he shifted her again, laying her on the bed, his tongue and teeth gliding over her body, tasting sex, tasting lust, tasting fulfillment of his every fantasy. It was the display of a dominant male, one that slightly shocked him, but he needed to imprint his scent on her, needed her—and everyone else—to know whom she belonged to.

She trembled, her breasts heaving, her legs splayed wide as he traveled down her body, claiming every inch as his own. Her head tossed back and forth as he teased the ultrasensitive flesh of her breasts, traced each rib, moved over her quivering tummy, stopping to tease her intriguing belly button.

She murmured something hot and erotic, and his body jerked in answer. He was completely focused on her now, absorbing the feel of her, the sheer beauty of her, the silky glide over her skin. The scent of his mate enfolded him, called him and commanded, and his body throbbed and ached with the need to answer. Lust and love rose up together, one not separated from the other, this woman, this female, courageous enough to follow him into the land of mists and shadows, brave enough to walk into a rain forest when everything in her told her to run. *His.*

His rich hair slid over her flat belly and curved hips as he dipped lower still. He was at the very center of her heat, and she lay beneath him, fingernails raking the sheet, her body arched, her throat exposed as she flung her head back and lifted her hips. Her gaze met his, aroused, desperate. His smile was pure sin as he caught her thighs and spread her wider for him. His gaze grew hotter, much wickeder and all too sensual. He bent his head and drank.

The moment his tongue speared deep, she screamed and dug her nails into the mattress, trying to hold on as the world around her exploded. Her body seemed to fragment. The edges of her vision blurred as fire raced down her spine and the muscles in her tight channel pulsed. Her throat shut down so it seemed impossible to catch her breath as waves of pleasure rocked her.

He lapped at her, speared her, and scraped with his teeth, feasting like a man possessed. His hands held her down with a strength she hadn't imagined he possessed, holding her helpless and open to his erotic assault. He licked and sucked, his tongue stabbing deep, drawing the hot cream from her center while she tossed and whimpered beneath him.

"I can't stand it," she gasped, digging her fingers into the mattress, trying desperately to find something to hold on to. "You have to stop." Because there was no control left to her.

His tongue was pressing against her clit, and her body was in meltdown. Pleasure burst through her with the force of an exploding volcano, spreading like white-hot lava, until her muscles clamped down viciously and her stomach tightened and spears of fire raced up her spine and around to her breasts. She bucked hard against his mouth, unable to stop herself when the mind-numbing pleasure had her spiraling completely out of control.

Before she could catch her breath, he was flipping her over, dragging her to her knees when her body shook with wave after wave of pleasure. He rose over the top of her, catching her hips and pulling her bottom back toward him, one hand pressing on her back to hold her in place. He pushed the broad head of his erection against her tight entrance.

"Is this what you need, *sivamet*?" he whispered hoarsely.

She realized she was chanting something, a keening plea. Lightning flashed through her body, streaks of it, as his body began to invade hers. He was thick, so hard, like a steel spear pushing through her soft folds, stretching and burning. "You're too big," she gasped, afraid for the first time that she couldn't accommodate his body, not like this, not when he gripped her hips and pulled her bottom back toward him as he drove relentlessly, mercilessly through her tight channel. Yet even when she protested, she was arching her hips, wanting more, needing more, nearly crying with the pleasure spreading through her. Even the too-tight invasion, the burning that accompanied him taking her, couldn't stop the waves of ecstasy, or maybe it added to it.

In the dominant position, Manolito held her completely under his control, taking his time as he thrust into that hot channel, soft as velvet, surrounding him with living walls of silk. "You're so tight, MaryAnn." His voice was rough, the growling rumbling in his throat. He bent over her further, deepening his invasion, filling and stretching her impossibly. "Don't move, *meu amor*, don't do that."

But she couldn't help the way her muscles locked down around him, gripping and kneading, the action shooting darts of fire through her body. She felt him push deeper and deeper. His hips pulled back and then he thrust forward, driving through her soft folds, the friction hot and wild, sending vibrations through her entire body, so even her breasts felt the fiery flames and her body pulsed, saturating him with welcoming fluid.

His fingers bit hard into her hips, holding her still, his whisper a guttural sound, as he plunged into her again and again, wringing shocked cries from her with every stroke. She felt the edge of pain as he swelled, locking himself inside of her and beginning a hard, thrusting rhythm that went on and on, sending shafts of lightning streaking to every part of her body, but never easing the torturous ache.

He pushed her beyond any boundary she'd ever had, driving the need higher and higher, until she was sobbing, pleading for release. She tried to move, tried to crawl out from under him, terrified of losing herself, terrified it would be too much to handle, but he suddenly snarled, the sound animalistic, and leaned forward, his long body stretching over hers, locking her down, one arm under her hips as his teeth sank deep into her shoulder.

Unexpected pain washed through her, blending with dazzling white-hot streaks of pleasure as he rode her, his breath coming in harsh gasps, his strength enormous, as he drove into her over and over. She heard her own gasping cries, the sound of flesh hitting flesh, felt his balls, slapping against her body in a rough caress as he continued the furious pounding deep in her tight channel. A firestorm started, building hotter and more out of control, and she writhed against him, needing more, yet terrified he would give it to her.

His arm locked tighter, dragging her hips up so her bottom slammed tightly against him and he buried himself so deep he lodged against her womb. She felt him swell, felt her muscles tightening, until she was afraid she would shatter into a million pieces.

Manolito heard her harsh breath, the sobbing pleas, and knew she was there, riding the edge. *That's it,* sivamet, *come for me. Burn for me.*

Multiple orgasms tore through her body, sweeping through every part of her in a tidal wave, each stronger than the last. The sensations ripped through her in powerful spasms. Her body arched, her hips reaching back for more, his hoarse cries echoing hers.

His release was brutal, the fire tearing up his spine and coiling in his belly, while her channel squeezed and gripped and milked jets of hot semen from his body. He felt the explosion in his toes, up his legs and gut, right through his chest to the top of his head. It should have sated him, but his body refused to be completely satisfied.

He held her to him, her smaller body soft and open and vulnerable to him. His erection remained thick and aching, the pulsing pleasure continuing as the tight walls around him rippled with aftershocks, locking him to her. He couldn't move, breathing hard, trying to still the wild pounding of his heart, trying to keep from allowing his incisors to lengthen. Surprisingly, his canines had done so, and he had buried his teeth in her shoulder, holding her still.

The urge to take her blood, to bring her fully into his world, was on him, but he fought it back, afraid he might trap her with him in the meadow of ghosts and shadows. Still, he craved the taste of her, so he held her beneath him, on her knees, his body covering hers while he let the urge pass. He ran his tongue over his canines, savoring the wild taste of her, one hand stroking her breasts, enjoying the rush of hot liquid bathing his aching cock every time he flicked her sensitive nipples.

"I could keep you here forever," he whispered, running his tongue along her spinal column.

MaryAnn bit her lip and tried to still the wild pounding of her heart. Never in her life had she imagined she could give her body so completely over to another person. When he touched her, when he was close to her, she had no inhibitions whatsoever. Fear maybe, but not of what he might do, only that she could lose herself in the absolute madness of physical pleasure.

There was no going back. She couldn't even blame Manolito. She had done as much seducing as he had, and it was purely physical. She closed her eyes and tried not to feel the pounding in her blood. This was addicting. *He* was addicting, and she would crave his touch for the rest of her life. No one would ever make her feel the things he could. And nothing would ever seem right with anyone else. But it wasn't love.

"How do you know, *sivamet*, how do you know what love is with me?"

"You're in my mind."

"You merged with me." He kissed the smooth line of her back. "Easy, *csitri*, I am going to ease you down onto the mattress." She was trembling so much he was afraid she would fall over once he allowed his body to leave hers.

The moment he moved, her muscles clamped down on him, sending fresh sensations through both of them. He kept his arm tightly around her waist as he let his body slide reluctantly from hers. Very gently he let her collapse onto the bed before rolling over, taking her with him so that her body was pillowed by his.

"I do not think I can move." The truth was, he didn't want to move.

"I know I can't," MaryAnn whispered, unable to so much as lift her head. Her body still quivered with small aftershocks. It was impossible to get enough air, her lungs burning and her body on fire. She lay beside him, listening to their combined heartbeats. "What did you mean when you said I didn't know what love is with you?"

"How could I not love the woman who braves everything she fears to save me from the unknown? How could I not love you when you stand between me and the darkness? How could I not love you when you give me more pleasure than I ever dreamed possible?" He didn't say she brought him peace. That the moment he was in her company everything inside of him simply settled, calmed, became right. "It is you who do not love me yet, but you will learn to."

He wrapped his arms around her shivering body and held her closer still, his chin nuzzling into her neck, warm breath against her ear. There was no censure in his voice, only a matter-of-fact statement.

Her body throbbed and burned and craved his all over again, and that was just downright frightening. He had such confidence in himself, was so certain he could make her fall in love with him. Even if she didn't, she knew it would be nearly impossible not to want to be with him, not when he could make her burn from the inside out.

"Don't you think that was just a little bit scary?"

"You are safe with me." He buried his face in the wealth of her hair. "I want to stay here with you and sleep the sleep of humans." He had never once, in all of his existence, thought he would want that simple pleasure, but now he wanted nothing more than to curl his body around hers and fall asleep with her in his arms.

"Why the sleep of humans?" she asked, snuggling against him. "That seems an odd thing for you to say."

"I want to dream of you. Drift off to sleep dreaming of you, and wake up to you by my side."

She rubbed up against him like a cat. "Well don't fall asleep. You have to go to ground, Manolito. Even I know that."

He looked around the room. Light was already creeping in through the windows. It should have been burning his eyes, but instead he wanted to stretch and arch his body, bathe in the early morning glow. "Maybe I will stay here. We can cover the windows."

Her heart jumped. "It isn't safe. No way. You have to leave."

He propped his head on his hand and stared down at her, his eyes once again totally black. "You do not want me to stay, do you?" he said with sudden insight. "You want me to leave you."

She swallowed the urge to deny his accusation. It would be a lie. "I can't think straight around you."

"No?" The edgy aggression in his voice softened to a throaty purr of male satisfaction. His hand cupped her breast, his thumb sliding over her nipple so that she shivered beneath his touch.

"No. Do you think I always act so—so *submissive*?" She nearly spat the word. "I don't do bondage and submission."

"Maybe I know more about what you like than you do," he

said. "I am in your mind and look for the things that please you."

She closed her eyes briefly, wondering if it was true. She had liked the things he had done. *Like* was a tame word for how she felt. She couldn't blame him for her own actions. She had wanted him fast and hard, almost brutal in his possession of her. She had wanted—still wanted—to belong wholly to him. To do whatever it was he asked of her. And that scared her on a whole different level. It was a major personality shift and needed consideration.

Manolito studied her face. She was puzzled by her behavior, and in turn, he asked himself why he had needed to be so dominant with her. He was a dominant man, so much so that he had no need to prove himself to anyone else, yet something in him had needed to mark her, to leave his scent, evidence of their mating. He brushed the hair from her shoulder and touched the small wound there. Carpathian males left pinpricks, maybe a strawberry, and he had left such a mark on her breast the first time he had ever taken her blood. The wound on her shoulder was something altogether different. Puzzled, he focused his gaze on it. It had been made with his canines.

MaryAnn turned her head to look at the mark as well, a small frown on her face. Why in the world had she found it sexy when he had held her like that? "I think you must have put some sort of spell on me."

"I believe it was the other way around."

"Did you?" she asked suspiciously. "Because Destiny can do that sort of thing. Get inside minds and influence them."

"Merge with me again and I will see what kind of influence I have. This time, I think I will have you kneeling at my feet, taking my cock into your hot, very sexy mouth." His hand stroked her throat, the pads of his fingers caressing. His body hardened all over again at the thought, pressing tightly against her, jerking at the erotic fantasy. "I might not live through it, but I am more than willing to sacrifice for the experiment."

She should have been alarmed, but the thought of exploring his body, of driving him over the edge, of him commanding her to give him that kind of pleasure and her robbing him of control, sent a coil of excitement spiraling through her body. His tongue was flicking at her shoulder, teeth nipping, and already her body responded with those light quakes that spread up her belly to her breasts.

"Maybe I'm the one influencing you," she said. "You're always telling me I'm the one merging with you."

"Of course you influence me. I am reading your every fantasy and sharing mine with you." His hands cupped her breasts and teased her nipples before sliding down the curve of her body to her buttocks. He began a slow, rhythmic massage. "When I come for you, tomorrow night, wear something feminine."

She gasped, outraged. "I *always* wear feminine clothing. I have the *best* taste in clothes. I can't believe you insulted me like that."

Male amusement gleamed in his eyes. "I apologize, *meu amor*, if you took that the wrong way. You are always beautifully dressed. I am old-fashioned and would prefer a dress or skirt." His hand slid up to her belly, fingers splayed wide. He rubbed in gentle circles, sliding lower, even as his voice turned husky. "Aside from showing off your beautiful body to its utmost advantage, I would be able to touch you like this so easily."

His fingers slid lower still, found warm, welcoming moisture waiting. "I want your body available to my touch. I look at you and want to slide my palm over your skin. There is nothing like it in this world."

His fingers slid over her cleft, making her gasp. Her thighs clenched. Her womb spasmed, and just like that she was his. Every thought of resistance was gone. His fingers stroked and teased and began an intimate exploration all over again. His rough whispers in her ear only heightened her senses and nerve endings and increased her need of him.

Morning rays of sunshine crept in through the window, and light illuminated the stark arousal etched into his face. He rolled onto his back and simply lifted her so that she straddled him. She gasped as she looked down at his erection. It seemed impossible that she could take him inside of her, but her body burned and pulsed and wept for him. He positioned her thighs on either side of his hips, pushing the broad head of his cock into her. His smile was genuine, white teeth flashing at her, black eyes gleaming with something close to joy as she settled over him.

He drove right through her tight folds until he was seated

deep inside her where he belonged. He brought her hands to his shoulders so she could brace herself as he began to move, to fill her, this time slow and easy so she could feel every stroke when she was already so sensitized.

She began to move to the rhythm herself as his hands guided her to ride him in a slow, sensual slide. He stretched her slowly, steel encased in velvet, moving through the tight, clenching muscles until the friction robbed her of breath—of sanity. It was different from the wild possession of before, but no less pleasurable. And there was something decadent in sitting on him while his gaze followed the sway of her breasts and his eyes focused on her with such hot lust and appreciation.

MaryAnn was exhausted by the time Manolito left her, but the sun was high. She did recognize that it was dangerous for him to be out at such a time. Her own body was so worn, she couldn't do more than return his kiss and wave a weak hand as he pulled the covers over her and left her alone. She barely registered his whispered command to sleep, already closing her eyes.

9

MaryAnn woke to the feel of tears on her face and the soft sound of feminine voices on the other side of her door. She groaned and turned over, her body sore in places she hadn't known she had.

"It was just sex," she said aloud. "He doesn't love you. Love matters, and he doesn't love you."

He might not love her, but he owned her body. She would have done anything he asked, and she hadn't known that was possible. There were whisker burns between her thighs and on her chin. She throbbed and pulsed with need the moment she thought of him. Her breasts ached and felt heavy. There wasn't an inch of her body he hadn't claimed or that she hadn't given him freely.

Her loss of control was terrifying. How could she crave his body to the point of letting him push her beyond every boundary, real or imagined, she thought she had? The only safe thing to do was leave, and it was far too late for that. She was practical, a woman who reasoned things out, and there was no reasoning this.

She sat up and wiped more tears away. She hadn't cried this much since she was a child. A shower only added to the sensations whispering over her skin. Memories of his fingers tracing every shadow and hollow, every curve and dimple. His mouth driving her mad with cravings. "This isn't normal," she said to her reflection in the mirror. "It isn't normal to want him like this and be afraid he'll come to me and more afraid he won't."

Could she leave? Was it possible to go back to her life in Seattle? Manolito was still trapped between worlds; could she leave him knowing he might never make it back if she didn't help him?

MaryAnn dressed with care, using clothes as armor, as she often did when she needed confidence and to feel in control. Manolito had told her to wear a dress, so she put on slacks and a silky top. She stood trembling, staring at herself, wanting to wear a dress because it would please him. Because he'd look at her with that look of dark hunger she'd never be able to resist. For a moment her hands went to the small shell buttons on her blouse, but she forced her hands down. She wouldn't give in—not to herself and not to him. If she couldn't leave him, she could at least stand up to him.

Lifting her chin, she walked out into the common room. A young woman sat curled up on a window seat, her long hair cascading down her back like a waterfall. She looked up with a hesitant smile that was not at all real, her emerald eyes watching carefully.

"You must be Jasmine. I'm MaryAnn Delaney. Did Juliette tell you I was coming?" She approached the girl slowly, her movements gentle and nonthreatening. This was why she had come in the first place, this young woman with the too-old eyes and the sorrow already etched into her face.

Jasmine smiled and held out her hand. "It's such a pleasure to meet you at last. Juliette speaks so highly of you."

"You reek of Carpathian male," another voice said, the tone filled with disdain.

MaryAnn turned to face Solange. It could be no one else. She was beautiful in a wild, untamed way. She had cat's eyes, amber, focused and wary. She prowled instead of walked, her quick restless movements graceful and agile. MaryAnn could see the anger in her, deep and held in tight. She had seen too many horrors to ever go back to innocence.

Solange wore loose-fitting drawstring pants and a belt around her hips. Where MaryAnn relied on pepper spray, Solange wore knives and guns with familiar ease. She had weapons MaryAnn had never seen before, many small and sharp and very efficient-looking. Her hair was shaggy but suited the shape of her face. Where Jasmine was ethereally beautiful, thin and shapely, with gentle curves and flowing hair, Solange was earthy, with full curves, temper in her eyes and passion stamped on her mouth.

"Do I? I took a shower." MaryAnn smiled at the woman, wanting to soothe her, to help her relax.

Solange halted in mid stride, her nose wrinkling. "I'm sorry. That was rude. I have a very acute sense of smell. I shouldn't have said that. We've been roaming in jaguar form and it makes me ultrasensitive."

"No, it's all right. You're entitled to say what you think." MaryAnn sent her a quick, appreciative smile. "Even if you are saying I smell."

"On, no," Jasmine said, rising to her feet. "Solange didn't mean that at all." She sent her cousin a warning look and reached out to take MaryAnn's hand. "Are you hungry? We were about to make dinner. We just got up a few minutes ago. I'm sorry if we woke you."

"You were crying in your sleep," Solange said. "I have exceptional hearing, too. Are you all right?"

MaryAnn kept her smile serene. Jasmine's fingers had tightened around hers, and the young woman was trembling. "I'm a city girl. The rain forest is a little scary to me. I'd guess neither of you feel that way about it. Although I did use my canister of pepper spray on a jaguar last night when it attacked me."

Solange whirled around, her dark eyebrows drawing down in a frown. "You were attacked by a jaguar? Are you certain?"

MaryAnn nodded. "I was very close to it."

"Did it have a collar on its neck, or a pack of any kind that you could see?" Solange pursued. She was already hurrying from window to window, peering out.

"Now that you say that, maybe he did." MaryAnn kept Jasmine's hand in hers. The girl shuddered, but kept walking through the wide hall to the large, open kitchen. "I can't remember. It all happened so fast."

Solange scented the air again, lifting her face and sniffing. "Were you near a jaguar male? A man aside from the Carpathian?"

Jasmine gasped and covered her mouth, her eyes going wide with fear. "Are they here? On the island?"

"It's going to be all right," Solange assured her. "I can protect you, and Juliette wrapped the house in safeguards. As long as we stay inside, we should be fine. I'm just going to check the upstairs, make certain the balconies and windows are all closed and locked. The windows have bars, Jazz."

Jasmine rushed to her, grasping her arm. "Don't leave me alone again. I don't want to be alone."

Her young face looked haunted, and for just one moment, MaryAnn saw anguish in Solange's amber eyes. She put her arms around her cousin and held her close. "MaryAnn is here, honey. I'm just going upstairs. She'll sit with you and I'll be right back. Why don't you get MaryAnn some food? She's hungry, remember?"

Jasmine swallowed and nodded. "Yes, I'm sorry. Of course I'll get you food. Do you drink tea?" She watched Solange leave the room. "She'll be right back, don't worry," she added.

"Of course she will," MaryAnn said soothingly and wrapped a comforting arm around the younger girl. Jasmine had gone pale beneath the gold of her skin. "Tea would be lovely, thanks."

Jasmine's hands shook so much the teacups rattled, but she poured both of them a cup of tea, added milk and sank down across from MaryAnn at the table, facing the door, watching for her cousin.

"It must be difficult to let Solange out of your sight," MaryAnn said gently. She concentrated on putting the young woman at ease, soothing and comforting, wanting her to realize she had someone she could talk to.

I'm here now. It's going to be okay. I'll make everything okay. You're strong and we can handle this. Jasmine was barely out of her teens, and yet already her world was one of violence and fear. MaryAnn wanted to pull her into her arms and rock her like a baby, somehow set the world right again for her.

Jasmine nodded. "I try not to be a burden to her, but I can't sleep most of the time and she has to sit with me."

"I'm sure she doesn't mind, Jasmine. It's obvious she loves you."

Solange might be as tough as nails, but she was loyal and loving to her family. She would fight to the death for this child, and she would use her last breath to comfort her. MaryAnn could read that much in both of them, but Jasmine was more than just afraid after her terrifying experience. She was holding something else, some dark secret that she hadn't shared with Juliette or Solange. MaryAnn mentally stroked the girl as she would a child, warmth and caring in her mind. She longed to make it right for Jasmine, longed to remove the sorrow from her eyes and take fear and trepidation away for good.

Jasmine took a deep breath. "I'm so glad you came. Thank

you. Juliette said you're from the city and this is all difficult for you."

MaryAnn shrugged, willing the girl to quit making small talk and come out with whatever she was on the verge of saying. It was frightening to her, and she wanted to tell MaryAnn without Solange in the room. "I wanted to come so you'd have someone to talk to. Sometimes it's easier when it isn't family." *It's okay, honey. I'm here now. I won't betray you. I've come a long way to help you. Trust me now. Trust me with the burden you're carrying, and the two of us will sort it out.*

"And you've talked to other girls, girls like me, right?" Jasmine asked, lowering her voice, glancing at the doorway to ensure Solange was still upstairs.

"What happened to you was particularly brutal," MaryAnn said. "You have to give yourself time." *Come on, baby. Share it. It's eating you up inside. Whatever it is, we can handle it. I know what I'm doing. You can rely on me.* She wished she could find a way to convey to Jasmine that she would help, that she would never betray her confidence.

"I don't have time," Jasmine whispered. She ducked her head and set the cup down. "It makes it easier that you know what happened. I haven't told anyone yet, but I'm going to have to soon."

MaryAnn held her breath, her heart beating hard. She wanted to cry for the girl, little more than a teenager, her life already shattered. She laid her hand over Jasmine's, connecting them, willing the girl to be calm, to be comforted. "You're pregnant."

Jasmine covered her face with her hands. "There's a plant we can use after, you know, to make certain, and Solange gave it to me, but I couldn't . . ." She trailed off and looked at Mary-Ann through her fingers. "I already knew. The moment it happened. I just knew and I couldn't do it."

"You didn't do anything wrong, Jasmine. Those men took away your choice and you stood up and made your own decision. Are you afraid you did something wrong?"

"It's complicated. We live a complicated life and I've made it so much worse. They'll never stop now. Those men. They'll come after us no matter where we are." She looked at the doorway again. "Solange . . ." She broke off. "It's been so hard for her."

"Are you sorry about your decision?"

"I don't know how I feel and I can't bear for Solange to be upset with me. She's done so much already and it will be one more person for her to take care of."

"You would keep the baby?"

Jasmine's eyes flashed with something close to fire, and for the first time, MaryAnn saw the resemblance between Jasmine and her cousin. "I would never give my baby to them. *Never*. If Solange wants me to leave, I will, but I won't turn a child over to them even if it is a boy."

"No, of course you wouldn't. What those men did was criminal, Jasmine." MaryAnn took a sip of her tea and regarded the younger girl. She chose her words carefully. "Manolito told me he met one of the jaguar-men, the same one who saved my life yesterday from the jaguar who attacked me. He said that a vampire had tainted him, turning the men to commit crimes against their women. If that is so, in a sense, they are victims as well."

"What are you saying to her?" Solange demanded.

MaryAnn turned as the woman entered the room. She moved in absolute silence, her body perfectly balanced, her bare feet making no sound on the cool marble floors. She crossed to Jasmine's side and put an arm around her, glaring at MaryAnn.

Jasmine stiffened, alarm spreading on her face. She sent MaryAnn a quick, nervous shake of her head, not wanting her secret revealed.

MaryAnn suspected Solange already knew. She was pureblood jaguar, with all the senses of the animal. It wouldn't be possible for Jasmine to hide such a thing from her, but MaryAnn wouldn't betray a confidence no matter what she thought.

"Just that if a vampire is influencing the men to hunt their women, it is a terrible tragedy for everyone." She kept her voice mild and matter-of-fact. "If what Manolito found is the truth, the vampire is deliberately killing an entire species."

Solange bit her lip and poured herself tea. "Maybe the vampire has the right idea. If our men are capable of the things they're doing, the species shouldn't survive."

"Solange," Jasmine protested.

MaryAnn caught the hurt look in her eyes and wished she could comfort her. *She doesn't mean it the way it came out. She's seen too much, been through too much and has been traumatized, too. She would accept the baby.* She couldn't assure Jasmine, even though she thought it was the truth. Solange would never turn her back on Jasmine or a child. It wasn't in the woman.

Solange shrugged. "You know how I think, Jazz. I've never made a secret of my contempt for men."

"You've never wanted a family?" MaryAnn asked.

"Sure. Sometimes. When I'm alone in the middle of the night, or when I go into heat." She dropped a hand on Jasmine's shoulder. "There's no other way to put it. We suffer from mating urges a little more than most women, I think, but I'm not willing to live the kind of life a woman has to in order to have a family."

"What kind of life is that?" MaryAnn asked, spooning a little honey into the tea. For some reason, she was having a difficult time drinking it. The food on the table turned her stomach. She hadn't eaten in a long time and should have been starving, but even the fruit didn't appeal to her.

"Giving up freedom. Being under a man's thumb."

"Is that what you think most marriages are like? Is that what Juliette's marriage is? Is she forced to do everything Riordan's way?"

Solange opened her mouth, took a breath and closed it. Sighing, she sank down into a chair. "To be fair, maybe not. It looks like it on the surface, but the way he looks at her, the things he does for her, no, I think she has just as much say as he does. She *wants* to make him happy." There was curiosity in her voice. "I can't imagine wanting to do anything for a man."

"Surprisingly, Solange, I felt the same way for a very long time. In my line of work, I see the worst in men—much, I suppose, as you do. But we're seeing a very small section. There are a lot of good men out there who have women they love, and they treat women with love and respect."

MaryAnn willed her to understand and see what she was saying, because Solange was bitter and bitterness eventually ruined lives. *You're too good a woman to live your life that way, honey.* She wished she could take away all those terrible memories, all the tragedy that had befallen the two of them. Solange had been rescuing female captives from the jaguar-men for some time. She'd seen too much death and brutality. There were no policemen on the corners to call. It was a life-and-death struggle in the rain forest, and Solange had managed not only to survive, but to save many other women as well.

"Maybe you're right," Solange agreed. "I keep thinking

eventually Jasmine and I have to leave this place. It's my home and I love it, but if we keep up this fight, we'll eventually be killed. They already know us and our reputation."

It was logical, but more than that, the fight with the jaguar-men colored every aspect of their life. "It isn't the best place for Jasmine," MaryAnn agreed.

Solange nodded. "I know. We've known for some time that we have to find another home, haven't we, Jazz?" She ruffled her cousin's hair.

There was too much sorrow in Solange, as if a great weight sat on her shoulders. She was younger than MaryAnn, and that was shocking. She looked older, her face serious and womanly rather than innocent, but she had to be only a few years older than Jasmine.

"We've talked about it," Jasmine admitted, "but where would we go? Neither of us could live in a city, so close to other people."

"Juliette said that Riordan had a house built on their ranch property for us," Solange said, her voice ultracasual. "We might try it."

Jasmine stiffened and shook her head mutely.

MaryAnn was too adept at reading people. Solange did not want to go to the ranch. She had such a distrust of men, and the De La Cruz main home was a working ranch with men every-where. But it would place both women under the protection and eye of the De La Cruz brothers, all of whom took their roles very seriously. Solange was worried about Jasmine. If she knew about the pregnancy, as MaryAnn suspected, she would want to take Jasmine to the comparative safety of the ranch house.

"Have you met Rafael and Colby?" MaryAnn asked. "Col-by's younger brother Paul and her sister Ginny are living at the ranch. They seem to really love it there. Ginny is particularly wild about horses."

Solange sent her a grateful smile. "Ginny is still young, right? I've heard Juliette talk about her. Eleven or twelve maybe."

"It's not going to work, Solange," Jasmine said. "I'm not go-ing to go to the ranch without you."

"Did I say without me? I would go, too, if you did," Solange said. "And you're not eating enough to keep a bird alive. Eat."

Jasmine scowled as she took a banana. "You'd go to the ranch,

Solange, but you wouldn't stay there and you know it. You'd leave me with Juliette and come back to the rain forest and try to work here by yourself."

Solange sat back in her chair and regarded Jasmine with a sober face. "I said I'd go with you and I will. I'll try to stay. That's all I can promise. I'll try to stay. I thought we'd be safe here, but if the jaguar-men know of this house and that most of the time the De La Cruz brothers aren't using it, they'll come for us. Maybe we should go back with Juliette and Riordan when they go."

MaryAnn caught the underlying anxiety. Solange didn't believe for a moment that she would be able to stay at the ranch, but for Jasmine, she would try.

"What do you fear at the ranch the most?" She leaned her chin into her palm and studied Solange's face. Jasmine would never stay if her cousin didn't.

Solange was silent for so long MaryAnn was afraid she wouldn't answer. "I am not good with people. Men especially. I get claustrophobia in confined spaces. I haven't had anyone telling me what to do since I was about twelve, and I can't imagine living in a place with rules—someone else's rules. I've made my own for too long and I can't fit in anywhere." She looked at Jasmine. "I don't want that for you, Jazz. You deserve a life."

"So do you," MaryAnn said quietly—firmly.

"I'm not such a nice person," Solange said, her amber eyes going flat and hard. "I've done things and I can't take them back."

Jasmine put her hand over Solange's. "You saved lives."

"And I took them."

There was no regret in her voice, and none on her face, but MaryAnn could feel the sadness coming off her in waves. She was a warrior, and there was nowhere in the world left for a woman like Solange.

"Don't feel sorry for me," Solange said. "I made my choices."

"And I've always made mine," Jasmine asserted. "I stay with you. Here or at the ranch, or wherever. We're family and we stick close. Juliette feels the same way. She can't join us during the days, but she's with us when she can be."

Good for you. MaryAnn flashed Jasmine an approving

smile. The girl had spunk after all. She wasn't going to give up on Solange.

Jasmine flashed her a small, conspiratorial smile, and Mary-Ann realized she was glad she'd come. *Both* women needed her. She was a born counselor, she helped people find their way and she was good at it, proud of her ability. Solange seemed more lost than Jasmine because she'd given up on life. On people. On everything.

Solange suddenly lifted her head, coming to her feet, her body still. Jasmine pressed a hand to her mouth to stifle a cry of alarm.

"It's okay, baby," Solange assured.

"They're here," Jasmine whispered. "Outside the house, and it's another couple of hours until sunset."

"Take MaryAnn into the safe room," Solange instructed. "Wait for me there."

"MaryAnn will be just fine helping you out," MaryAnn said. "I'm not hiding from these men. If they dared come here to harm you—"

"They'll rape and kill. That's what they do," Solange said, her voice hard. "We live by the law of the forest here, kill or be killed, and you have to be prepared to do just that. Go with Jasmine."

Jasmine pushed back her chair and reached under the table for the gun taped there. MaryAnn's eyes widened. They'd obviously been prepared for an attack.

"I'll take the upstairs," Jasmine said. "You defend down here, Solange. MaryAnn, they won't be able to breach the safe room. If we get into trouble, we'll fight our way back to that, so leave it unlocked as long as possible."

"I'll stay with you," MaryAnn said. "I know how to shoot a gun."

"Riordan and Juliette set safeguards on the house," Solange said, not bothering to waste time arguing with them. "Jasmine, see to the windows. Stay back out of sight. If they see and recognize you, it might make them do something crazy to get in, but if they breach the window, shoot to kill. Do you understand me? Don't you hesitate."

"I won't," Jasmine assured.

"I'll be with her," MaryAnn added. Jasmine looked so

young and frightened. Her pregnancy made her even more vulnerable.

Solange caught Jasmine to her, stared into her eyes. "Be safe, little cousin."

"You too." Jasmine brushed a kiss along Solange's cheek and then turned and hurried up the stairs.

MaryAnn followed her, but paused to watch Solange move through the huge kitchen toward the hall. The woman looked like a jungle cat, sleek and powerful and deadly. It was impossible not to admire her—or believe in her.

"She'll get us through this," Jasmine assured her.

"I have no doubt she will." Still. It was always better to have a backup plan. They had to hold out until Manolito, Riordan and Juliette managed to wake and get to them. She glanced at her watch. A little under two hours. The safeguards should hold that long.

"Uh oh," Jasmine said, peeking out the window and ducking back against the wall. "They've got someone out there and he looks like he knows what he's doing."

MaryAnn risked a quick look. The man was no jaguar; his build was all wrong. He was short and slender, his close-cropped hair blond. He stood facing the house, hands in the air, weaving a graceful pattern. She had only seen something like that once before and it chilled her to the bone. "Mage." She whispered the word.

"He's taking down the safeguards, isn't he?" Jasmine said.

"It looks like it."

Solange swore. Once again she'd crept up behind them. "I counted four of the jaguar-men. I recognize one of them. He's a tough fighter, Jazz. He knows our scent. The one you identified as a mage I've never seen before. He must have been brought here specifically to unravel the Carpathian guards."

"And that means they're here for a reason," Jasmine said, choking on fear, voice shaking. "They came here deliberately for us, didn't they, Solange? For me."

"Calm down, baby," Solange said. "You know they hunt any women with jaguar blood, particularly those who can shift. Both of us are of the age to have children; we carry purer bloodlines and we can shift."

Jasmine shook her head. "Not me. I can't."

"You don't want to. That isn't the same thing. Give me the gun, Jasmine." Solange held out her hand.

Jasmine shook her head again, this time much harder. "No. I need it."

"I mean it. Give it to me."

MaryAnn winced at the steel in Solange's voice. "Jasmine, there's no need to panic. It will take time for the mage to unravel the safeguards. After Juliette and Riordan put the locks in place, Manolito came with me in the early morning hours and he added to the safeguards. Give Solange the gun and let's get ourselves something cool to drink and we'll wait downstairs near the safe room. If we block off or rig some kind of alarm on the stairs, we won't have to guard them. We can concentrate on defending the downstairs, a smaller area. It will be easier and we can leave a clear path to the safe room. No matter what, we'll be fine until the Carpathians get here."

She kept her voice soothing, her features serene, dissolving the tension that had been building in the room.

Solange smiled at her. "That's right. Let them play their little games out in the hot sun. We're inside where we have plenty of food and water and shelter from the rain. It's started pouring again. The poor mage is looking like a wet dog."

Jasmine's smile was thin, but she managed one as she put the weapon in her cousin's hand. "What is a mage exactly? And why is he here?"

Both women looked at MaryAnn. She bit her lip and shrugged. "I'm not really certain. I can only tell you what I picked up here and there when I was in the Carpathian Mountains. Juliette or Riordan can explain better than I can. My understanding is mages were the most like humans, but with psychic powers and the ability to weave energy. They were close to Carpathians and shared a great deal of knowledge. Something happened and there was a war between the Carpathian people and the mages."

"This was all years ago," Solange acknowledged. "I heard a bit about it from some of the storytellers when I was a child, but I thought they were long gone from this world."

"Apparently not," MaryAnn said.

"And they're all against the Carpathian species?" Jasmine asked. "Does that mean the jaguar species is as well?"

"It's been my observation, Jasmine," MaryAnn said, "that no entire race of beings is all good or all bad. Most don't hate simply because others do. I met a jaguar-man who saved my life and was very troubled with what was happening to his people. I'm certain there are mages who don't approve of what is being done here. Many probably don't even know. Vampires are wholly evil, and once they infiltrate and influence anyone, they disrupt the entire balance of nature."

"So the vampires used the violent tendencies of our males to corrupt them and end our species," Solange said, a tinge of sarcasm in her voice.

"Not all males are bad, Solange, and reiterating over and over that they are, influencing Jasmine so that she fears a normal life, is no better."

"You haven't seen what these men do."

"Be honest, isn't it a small percentage? One small group? I believe the other jaguar-men have been trying to stop them. If that's the case, you are condemning some of the same men who have been working to stop this."

"I've never met any of these mythical men," Solange said, then glanced back at Jasmine. "But there may be some."

"Many men sacrifice themselves for the common good. I saw Manolito step in front of a pregnant woman and take a poisoned knife for her. He died, n-nearly died." Emotions rushed up and overwhelmed her before MaryAnn could stop them. She was unprepared for the grief and sorrow sweeping through her, shutting down reason and logic.

She turned away, blinking back tears, staring out the window at the mage. His hands followed a pattern and he looked triumphant, as if he knew exactly which safeguard had been used and how to unravel it.

If only he would grow tired standing in the pouring rain. Tired and wet, his arms feeling like lead. So tired he couldn't see straight or think to remember the ancient words and flowing movements.

MaryAnn watched the mage through the window, imagining his fatigue, hoping he was exhausted standing there, the rain pounding down on his unprotected head. *He felt weak and weary and he desperately needed to get out of there.* If they were really lucky, he was a little afraid of the jaguar-men and visualized them attacking him, tearing into his body with terrible teeth, crunching his skull with a single bite . . .

The mage staggered back, lifting one hand to his head and

staring back at her through the window. He pointed at her, saying something she couldn't hear, but it was clearly an accusation.

"There in the trees," Solange said. "You drew them out."

MaryAnn peered into the heavy canopy where the forest met the wide expanse of yard. One half-formed jaguar moved in the branches. He was a big man, well built, with shaggy hair and cruelty etched in his face.

Jasmine shrank back into Solange's arm. "That's the one they call Sergio. He's terrible. They all listen to him."

Solange nodded. "I remember him. He's a strong fighter. He could have killed me, but he knew I was a shifter and didn't want to take chances." She flashed Jasmine a small, humorless smile. "It gives us a little advantage."

"Why did you say I drew them out?" MaryAnn asked, her hand going to her throat in a defensive gesture. The mage was staring at her now and once again moving his hands in a flowing pattern. She had the feeling he wasn't unraveling the safeguards so much as trying to do something to her.

Solange pulled her back away from the window. "He knows you stopped him. We should go downstairs."

"I didn't stop him. I was only hoping he would get a little tired."

"Well, your hoping delayed him, but not for long. I want you and Jasmine in the safe room." She led the way down the stairs. "You just set yourself up as a target. Sergio will know you aren't jaguar and that you're dangerous."

"I'm not dangerous."

"If you can break the concentration of a mage, you're dangerous. He'll want to kill you. Stay behind Jasmine."

That was the last thing MaryAnn intended to do. Jasmine looked determined, but so frightened, MaryAnn wanted to gather her up and rock her. "I've got a couple of weapons as well," she said, and held up the pepper spray. "They won't be expecting it."

"I won't let them take me this time," Jasmine said. "Not again, Solange."

"They'll have to kill me to get to you, baby," Solange assured. Her voice was quiet and steady. "Believe me, I'm not going to let that happen. If we're very lucky, MaryAnn bought us enough time for the sun to go down and Juliette to get here to help."

MaryAnn noticed Solange didn't name either of the two male Carpathians, as if she couldn't—or wouldn't—count on them for support. Solange was far more damaged than Jasmine appeared to be. MaryAnn smiled at Jasmine. "Don't worry. Manolito will rush to help us, and so will Riordan, although you know him better than I do and probably are well aware that he would never let anything happen to you if he could help it."

Jasmine looked down at her hands. "I haven't taken the time to get to know him. I've had a difficult time adjusting after the attack."

"We stay to ourselves," Solange said. She met MaryAnn's steady gaze and understood the reproof, accepting it with a slow nod and a deep breath. "That probably hasn't been the best way to deal with things though. I think we need to go to the ranch and try to make a new and very different life for ourselves."

"Do you really think that, Solange?" Jasmine asked. She pressed a hand to her stomach, fear in her eyes.

MaryAnn knew the look was fear of Solange's disappointment in her decision to have a baby, a jaguar child with nearly pure blood. Solange had seen too many horrifying events to ever be able to look at the jaguar-men without prejudice, and Jasmine knew it. Still, she'd been strong enough to make her own decision, and that was a good sign.

"Of course I do. We can't live in the forest forever, and the jaguar-men know who we are now and are hunting us. I think it's more than time that we got out."

Solange caught Jasmine's arm and gave her a little push. "Get moving now. They're going to break through any second. MaryAnn, go." She glided to the window with purposeful strides, her knife in one hand, a gun in the other.

She turned, swearing, "They're coming. Be ready!"

The front doors burst open and a large frame entered, half-jaguar, half-man, rushing across the cool marble straight toward them. It launched its body into the air, straight at Solange, snarling muzzle filled with wicked-looking teeth, hands curved into razor-sharp claws.

10

Jasmine screamed, and clapped her hand over her mouth to muffle the sound. She stumbled backward, reaching behind her to find the door of the safe room.

Solange rushed the jaguar with no hesitation, gun out, firing shots as she ran at him. A second jaguar, the one Jasmine had identified as Sergio, hit Solange from behind, where he'd stalked her, unseen and unheard. He brought her down, slamming her to the floor and slapping the gun from her hand. The sound was loud as furniture and lamps crashed on the marble.

They rolled, Solange partially shifting to bring jaguar strength into play, swiping at Sergio with a sharpened claw as he used his size to pin her beneath him. The attack had obviously been orchestrated, their adversaries having studied Solange's abilities. The first jaguar staggered, his sides heaving as blood dripped steadily from the two bullet wounds. He went straight for Solange to aid Sergio in restraining her.

MaryAnn blasted him with the pepper spray, using short bursts, hitting him in the eyes, mouth and nose repeatedly. Jasmine followed her into the fray, slamming a lamp against his head and driving him backward.

The first jaguar-man fell hard, landing between MaryAnn and Solange. He pawed at his face, howling, rolling back and forth and leaving blood smears on the marble.

Solange punched Sergio's throat, hitting hard, using her body weight as well as her cat's strength. She raked up his muzzle and tore at his belly. His cat's weight crushed down on her, and his teeth sank into her throat. She went still beneath him, sides heaving, amber eyes defiant, her body rigid and tense.

Jasmine leapt across the room after the gun where it had skittered across the floor. Before Jasmine could scoop it up, the mage was there before her, kicking the gun out of reach and shoving her against the wall so hard it knocked the wind out of her.

Jasmine's leap had taken her over the huge males just as another male burst into the room, fully changed, fierce, eyes glittering. He swerved around Jasmine and knocked Sergio off Solange. The two males reared up, slamming together so hard they rocked the walls.

The wounded jaguar roared with rage, swiping at MaryAnn's leg, and she gasped with pain. A claw raked her calf, tearing through her slacks and ripping skin and muscle nearly to the bone. MaryAnn's leg went out from under her and she fell, hitting the marble hard, digging her heels in to push backward in a crablike crawl to try to stay out of reach of those raking claws. Like sharpened spikes, the claws found her ankle and with a victorious roar, the jaguar pulled her to him, his teeth going for her skull. MaryAnn punched the cat's throat, the canister in the fist adding a more solid contact, but the animal continued to drive forward. He erupted into a killing frenzy, whipping claws from side to side as he blindly sought prey. His face was wet with tears, his nose and muzzle streaming, but he was dangerous, whipping around the room hunting for his attacker.

Solange landed on his back, all cat now, wild and furious, teeth clamping down on the broad head, her bite enormously strong. The jaguar forgot all about MaryAnn, rolling in an effort to dislodge Solange. Mercilessly she raked at the cat's belly while she clamped down with her teeth on the muzzle.

MaryAnn dragged her leg out of the fray. Four jaguars rolled on the floor, fighting to kill one another. Jasmine's scream pulled her out of her haze of fear and pain. The mage had Jasmine by her long hair and was dragging her backward out of the house.

Fury swept through MaryAnn, fury and something dark and wild and dangerous. She felt it so close, deep inside her, ripping at her to get out. Her bones ached. Her mouth and teeth hurt. Her hands curled into fists, but her fingernails had lengthened and cut into her palm.

"Stop!" *Stop right now!* MaryAnn jerked to her feet. *Enough already.*

To her astonishment, all four jaguars ceased moving, heads hanging, sides heaving, tongues lolling out of their mouths. Only the mage kept moving, although he was sweating and shaking, his gaze on MaryAnn as he dragged Jasmine out of the house and kicked the door closed.

The sound of the door slamming triggered the jaguars back into action. At once, Solange drove deep again, tearing at the other jaguar's throat. The two males slammed into one another, all teeth and claws. MaryAnn pulled herself to her feet, skirted around the fighting cats and, shoving the agony of her leg into a mental compartment, stumbled after Jasmine and the mage.

Deep beneath the ground, Manolito woke to a burst of pain and fear. His heart began a strong, steady gallop, his pulse thundering in his ear. He knew, in the way of all Carpathian people, that the sun hadn't set but was slowly beginning to sink from the sky. He couldn't wait. MaryAnn was in desperate trouble. He burst from the rich, dark soil, one arm across his eyes as he shifted into vapor and at the same time called on the clouds to block the sun. The dense canopy helped, but still he was caught for a microsecond in the rays. Flames should have raced over his skin, turning it into a melting inferno. He should have been a mass of blisters, and smoke normally would have mingled with the vapor as he shifted—but only his eyes burned.

He put aside the pain and streaked through the canopy toward the house. *MaryAnn. Connect with me now.* In spite of the fact that he had taken her blood and he knew exactly where she was, she had strong barriers in her mind. Right now they were in place, a steel wall he couldn't penetrate. If he could access her eyes, he could aid her from a distance.

He had left her with a command to sleep, but there had been something, a small block in her mind that he couldn't identify, and maybe that had kept his compulsion from working as it should have. He had to find a way around that shield in her mind in order to access her brain. She didn't seem to be closing him out purposely, but he couldn't get in. *MaryAnn. I can help you. Let me aid you.*

They were connected, yet they weren't. Her mind should have been open to him at will, yet he couldn't penetrate that dense spot no matter how he tried. It made no sense, the on again, off again connection. He was an ancient, entirely capable of placing powerful beings under his control, yet not his own lifemate.

He could feel her fear for Jasmine. Her sense of determination. There was pain, but she was ignoring it, pushing it to one side as her mind worked frantically on a plan to get Jasmine away from the mage. He felt all of those things and more. He felt Jasmine's emotions through MaryAnn, as if her connection with the other woman was as strong as a blood connection between Carpathians. Terror, regret, absolute determination to escape or die—Jasmine would not submit. MaryAnn was keenly aware of Jasmine's resolve and redoubled her efforts to find a way to save the younger girl.

Because Manolito was touching MaryAnn's mind, he felt the gathering of energy, a sudden surge within her brain. The air around him grew unstable. Wind shrieked, buffeting him and sending leaves and twigs spinning like missiles through the air. Lightning veined the clouds. Electricity sizzled and crackled. Below him, a branch snapped off a tree and plunged through the canopy, hurtling toward the ground. Power, uncontrolled, unstable and very dangerous, pulsed through the region.

MaryAnn narrowed her eyes as the mage spun to face her, pulling Jasmine in front of him, his fingers digging deep into Jasmine's throat.

"Stop or I'll kill her."

She halted her forward progress, her stomach churning, anger welling into a hard, determined knot. She had come to the rain forest to help this girl and she would not fail. Jasmine had endured enough and it would stop *this minute*. MaryAnn longed for the abilities of a Carpathian, a way to let the wild wind take her high into the air and set her at the top of the tallest tree. Fury burned through her like a brand, and the mark over her breast pulsed in time to her heartbeat. She pressed her hand over the spot. *Manolito. I cannot stop it.*

Did she mean the mage? Or the feral thing unfurling inside of her? She didn't know. Her hands and feet hurt, bones cracking and jaw popping. Her injured leg felt on fire. Prickles swarmed up and over her body, thousands of tiny pinpricks itching and stinging. The forest around her wavered, lost the brilliant colors, but her sense of smell increased acutely. She could smell fear pouring off the mage. He kept Jasmine firmly

in front of him as if her slender body could protect him from
MaryAnn.

Jasmine struggled wildly. The mage's fingers bit hard into
her throat, choking her. "Stop it, Solange," he hissed. "You will
cooperate." He spoke in a singsong voice, weaving a holding
spell to keep her from fighting him.

MaryAnn felt his words like a buzzing pressure in her head.
"Knock it off," she snapped. *Stop it now!* She was so furious she
shoved her palms outward toward him, instinctively wanting to
push the intense force right back at him. If he was attacking
them with his mind, there was little she could do about it. She
didn't know about mages and their abilities, but it made her angry that he choked Jasmine with so little care for her life.

The mage stumbled back, dragging Jasmine with him, coughing repeatedly as if something had lodged in his throat. Maybe
they would get lucky and his stupid spell would backfire and
leave a lump in his windpipe, making it difficult to breathe.

The mage grasped his throat in horror as if he could read
her mind. And why would he think she could do anything to
him? She had her canister of pepper spray, but it was nearly
empty. She doubted if the second one held much more. But if
he didn't take his other hand off Jasmine's throat, she knew she
would tear him limb from limb. *There would be nothing left of
his body for the vultures.* She glanced overhead and they were
there, floating in lazy circles, just waiting.

The mage's gaze followed hers; he spotted the gathering
birds and paled visibly.

"They know you're a dead man." She was shaking, not with
fear, but with something else, adrenaline pouring into her body,
the itching everywhere, her scalp tingling, her toenails hitting
the ends of her shoes so that they felt far too tight.

Her vision blurred until she was seeing him through a haze
of yellow. She fixed her gaze on him, wanting him to realize
she was willing to fight to the death for Jasmine. "Let her go
now."

She felt it then, the gathering storm inside of her, fighting for
release. The wind shrieked and lightning flashed. Thunder rolled
and the trees shuddered under the gathering force. The air felt
heavy with crackling energy. Tiny sparks snapped and crackled,
orange and yellow flames sizzling in the air all around them.

"Her eyes," the mage choked out. "Look at her eyes."

Jasmine slammed her elbow into the mage's stomach, calling on her cat, a rarity for her, but the animal answered her, lending enormous strength. The air rushed out of her attacker's lungs. She leapt away, running toward MaryAnn, tears streaming down her face and blurring her vision. MaryAnn caught her wrist and thrust her behind her, steeling herself to meet an attack.

The mage retreated two steps and lifted his hands. Before he could weave a spell, a thick branch toppled from above them and dropped like a stone, driving the man into the soft soil. Jasmine screamed and buried her face against MaryAnn's shoulder. MaryAnn wrapped her arms around the girl and held her tightly.

"We can't leave Solange to fight the jaguar alone," she whispered. "I have to go back and help her."

Jasmine nodded her agreement, straightening up and stepping away from MaryAnn. She glanced at the huge tree limb that had fallen. The leaves hid most of the fallen man from her sight. "Do you think he's really dead?"

"I don't much care right now," MaryAnn said, shocked that it was true. She caught Jasmine's hand and began to run back toward the house, trying to think how she could keep Jasmine safe with the two jaguar-men waiting inside. She was fairly certain the cat who had attacked Sergio had been Luiz, but if she was wrong, Solange was fighting alone for her life.

They ran through the trees back along the path leading to the house. As they sprinted, leaping over the fallen boughs and tangled roots, monkeys began to scream in warning. Jasmine skidded to a halt and whipped her head from one side to another, searching the canopy above them. Hundreds of monkeys threw leaves and twigs and jumped in agitation, baring teeth toward a group of trees close to the house.

"There's another one," Jasmine whispered.

"Of course there is, because it would just be too easy to have three of them after us." MaryAnn took a deep breath. "It's stalking us, isn't it?"

"Yes," Jasmine said. "There in the tree, I can see part of the fur. They want me alive, so maybe if we split up they'll come after me."

"You can forget that," MaryAnn said. "We got lucky with the

mage, we might get lucky again, but whatever we do, we're *not* splitting up."

Jasmine's eyes widened. "Is that what you call luck? I thought your aim was excellent."

"I didn't do that. The lightning both hit it and sheered it off, or the wind took it down. Either way, it helped us and that's all that matters."

The air suddenly charged with electricity, their hair crackling. Clouds boiled dark, edged with flashing light. MaryAnn caught Jasmine and threw her to the ground, covering her body as best she could with her own. The sound of lightning striking the tree was loud, the trunk splitting, the jaguar howling. The roar ended abruptly with the smell of burnt flesh and fur.

Jasmine shivered continually. MaryAnn held her tighter. "That's Manolito," she whispered, trying to assure the girl.

"I knew it had to be a Carpathian," Jasmine admitted. "I thought it might be Riordan and Juliette."

"It's a good thing. We have help. Solange is in trouble, Jasmine, and we have to get her out of there. He'll help us."

Jasmine swallowed visibly and sat up slowly, blinking as the tall Carpathian male came striding toward them. The cloud cover helped and the last of the sun was sinking, allowing him to move with more freedom. He looked like a warrior of old moving fast through the smoke and ruin of a battlefield. His face was chiseled and set. His hair was long and flowing behind him. Muscles rippled beneath warm gold skin, and his ice-cold eyes were bleak and dark, holding too many secrets.

The gaze swept right past Jasmine to find MaryAnn. Warmth pushed the chilling ice aside, and his eyes went hot as MaryAnn rolled over and sat, blinking up at him. He didn't miss a stride, moving fast, leaning down to scoop her up, even as he caught Jasmine's arm and pulled her off the ground as well. His fingers on Jasmine's skin were impersonal, and he never even looked at her, other than a quick cursory glance to make certain she was all right. His gaze registered the finger marks at her throat, but then jumped to do a thorough inspection of MaryAnn.

The pads of his fingers brushed over her skin, absorbing the feel and texture of her. He could breathe again, knowing she was alive. A storm of fury gathered in his eyes as he took in the gaping wounds on her leg.

"MaryAnn." He said her name. Breathed it. A mere thread of sound, but he made it poetry, as if she was his entire world.

She tried not to react. He was just so intense it was difficult not to respond to his complete focus. She swallowed the searing pain in her leg and attempted a smile. "Thanks for getting here so fast. Solange is inside fighting off a couple more of them. I think Luiz is here as well, trying to help."

He bent to examine the rakes on her legs.

MaryAnn caught his arm and tugged. "You have to go help her."

"I cannot leave you like this."

"I'm coming with you, so it's all right." MaryAnn wasn't going to argue, not when he set his jaw in that stubborn line. She pushed past him and began an awkward jog toward the house, certain he would follow her.

Manolito scooped her up and ran, cradling her to his chest as he covered the distance with blurring speed. He set her aside at the last moment, shifting to vapor and sliding beneath the door, leaving MaryAnn on the other side.

Blood and fur were everywhere, furniture turned over, glass smashed, chairs reduced to splintered sticks. A female jaguar lay on her side, her coat dark with blood and saliva. Her sides heaved as she tried to drag in air, and with every movement, blood gushed into the air. She valiantly tried to go to the aid of the male fighting two others. He was in a corner, shredded with claw marks and covered in puncture wounds, but he was too fast to knock off his feet, and one of the other males was nearly blind from his weeping, burning eyes.

As Manolito entered, Sergio lunged forward and grasped Luiz by the throat, closing strong jaws and ripping. The other male leapt for Luiz's back, but before he could land, the hunter seized him around the neck, surprising the shifter as he was jerked away. Manolito wrenched hard, his features set in harsh, merciless lines, his eyes without emotion. There was an audible crack and the jaguar-man sagged to the floor, tongue out of his mouth, breath ceasing instantaneously.

Manolito raised his head and looked at Sergio, death swirling in the dark depths of his gaze. Sergio dropped Luiz and leapt, crashing through the door and racing to the safety of the rain forest.

Jasmine barely managed to get out of his way as he sprang past. She stood in the doorway, one arm around MaryAnn's waist to help support her as they entered. She gave a little cry when she saw Solange and raced to her side, dropping down on one knee to clamp her hand hard over the gushing blood. "Do something. She's going to die."

Manolito took two steps toward the door to follow Sergio, but Jasmine's cry stopped him. He turned back. The scent of blood was everywhere, triggering not only the inevitable hunger, but aggression as well.

"MaryAnn, sit down before you fall down. I will aid you in a moment. Let me look at the wounds and see what I can do."

"Where's Juliette?" Jasmine asked. "I thought she would come."

"I do not know, but they will come," Manolito said. He knelt beside the jaguar and ran his hands over the shuddering cat.

Solange bared her teeth and turned her head. The effort cost her remaining strength, and blood geysered from the wound in her throat.

"Can you do anything?" Jasmine asked anxiously.

"I would have to seal her wounds and give her my blood. She resists even my touch, let alone the offer of my blood." Manolito shook his head. "I am sorry, little sister, there is nothing I can do for her."

"Solange!" Jasmine stretched out on the floor beside the cat. "Please. Don't leave me alone. Let him help you."

Manolito sighed. "She feels she has nothing to live for, that her day in the rain forest is over. She cannot adjust to life elsewhere, and she wants no part of Carpathian blood."

The room grew cold and the walls pulsed as power flowed in. MaryAnn sank to the floor beside Luiz, trying to stem the flow of blood with her hands. It was everywhere, and the jaguar lay as if already dead.

Manolito. Hear me now.

She heard the voice distinctly. It was hard-edged, as if teeth were bared and snapping together. It was a clear command with no room for argument. *Heal her and give her blood. Riordan's lifemate is distressed. There can be no other choice.*

There was the impression of danger, of a force and intelligence she had not encountered, nor did she wish to. She found herself holding her breath, watching Manolito. He seemed unfazed by the strength of power and merely shrugged his shoulders casually.

"Zacarias has given an order and it will be done." He struck hard and swift, his mind plunging into Solange's before she could form a strong enough shield to stop him.

Who is he? MaryAnn thought the question more than she sent it to Manolito, but to her surprise, she actually connected with him.

Now you speak to me in the way of lifemates. There is no need to stroke his fur. He is dying. There was a definite reprimand in his voice.

MaryAnn heard the death rattle herself in the cat's throat. "Well he isn't going to die. You're going to save him."

There was absolute conviction in her voice. And trust. When he spared her a quick glance, her eyes were shining with an emotion that made his heart melt. He couldn't recall anyone ever looking at him that way, not once in all the long centuries of his existence. He wanted to make her proud of him. He wanted to hold on to that look for eternity.

"Keep him alive, then," he said. "Will him to live. You seem to be able to get people to do almost anything."

MaryAnn flicked a small, determined smile his way. Her leg was hurting so bad she thought fainting might be a good idea, but when she looked at the carnage around her, she decided her wounds were very small in comparison. Manolito had to heal Solange and then Luiz and then her leg. He had just risen, and the one thing she knew about Carpathians was they woke hungry, and when they used energy to heal, they needed blood. "I'm good. You do what you have to do."

Manolito turned his attention to Solange. She fought him, in her mind, trying to throw him out, but she was far too weak. He held her to earth, refusing to allow her spirit to slip away as he shed his physical body and slipped into hers. He was an ancient and powerful, but if she hadn't been so severely injured, he might have had to resort to a more dangerous and violent method of keeping her mind imprisoned within his. She had a will of iron and she fought hard to keep him away from her.

At first he thought it was her distrust of men, but as he merged his mind firmly within hers, he saw the fear was of Juliette and Jasmine realizing she was a killer—beyond saving, beyond hoping. There was no other way of life left for her. She didn't know if she could stop. Somewhere, she'd crossed a line and there was no going back.

And then he felt it, a soft warmth flowing gently into Solange's mind. He recognized MaryAnn's touch instantly, so light as almost not to be there, but steady and calming, a feeling of tranquillity and hope, bathing Solange in her warmth and absolute belief that life was good and filled with beauty and adventure and love.

He almost forgot himself, where he was, what he was doing, in awe of this woman who was his lifemate. She smoothly, seamlessly, blended with Solange, so that there was no way of knowing she had entered. He wouldn't have known if he hadn't exchanged blood with her, her touch was that light, but she filled Solange's mind with hope and belief. Under MaryAnn's influence, Solange grew cooperative, relaxing in the soothing cocoon of warmth. It was difficult to leave the comforting waves and seek out the torn and bleeding organs to repair them.

Manolito reluctantly allowed his spirit to travel through the body of the cat. Sergio had not wanted to kill her, but she had fought hard, and when the second jaguar had attacked her, it hadn't been so careful. The artery was nearly shredded, the jaguar body filled with blood. He knew what it meant, knew what had to be done to save her life. He let go of everything he was and became only healing energy, repairing every wound as quickly as possible, relying on MaryAnn to keep Solange cooperative.

MaryAnn held the male jaguar head in her lap, stroking the velvet fur, murmuring softly to keep him with her. He was struggling for breath, his lungs filling with blood. She kept talking to Solange as well, afraid if she quit, the woman would try to rip out Manolito's throat. It was a frightening situation, two people on the brink of death and only Manolito there to save them. Jasmine held towels to Solange's wounds and whispered to her, tears streaming down her face, fearful she was losing her.

Stay with us, Solange. MaryAnn prayed silently, trying to reach the other woman, to let her know that no matter how dark things seemed at the moment, it could all be better. It *would* be better. MaryAnn would make it her mission in life to help Solange and Jasmine after all the sacrifices they'd made rescuing women and helping them to a safe place.

Luiz was dying. She could see his life slipping away, see the spark fading from his eyes, and all she could do was watch helplessly. She willed him to live, the same way she willed Solange to have hope and see a future, but she couldn't do what Manolito was doing, healing from the inside out. How did you let go of everything you were and become an instrument of healing? She had seen Manolito sacrifice his life for a woman and unborn child. She had heard that he had gotten a scar around his throat, when Carpathians rarely scarred, from saving his prince. And now he had managed to let go of who he was in order to save a life.

Few could know what that really entailed, but she was with him, connected to him, and she realized just what had to be given up to become spirit. The body was vulnerable to all attacks, yes, but much more than that, Manolito had shed his personality, all ego, all hopes and dreams, his own needs, *everything*, and he had done so willingly.

She had been inside his mind when he had so quickly shed his opinions and ideas, his very personality, and become selfless in his effort to save Solange. She couldn't help but admire him. Manolito was a strong personality with set beliefs about women, yet with all that, he had immediately cast himself aside. What kind of true character did he have hidden under all that arrogance? And were his seemingly dominating ways with women maybe really about protection? His species certainly treasured their women and children. All of them. It didn't seem to matter that Shea was Jacques's lifemate, Manolito had stepped in front of her and taken the death strike meant for her without a qualm.

Live, Luiz. Hang on until he can help. He'll save your life. She was positive. She was in his head and she could see his absolute resolve to keep Solange alive. Manolito was so focused, so completely wrapped up in healing that he thought of nothing else. She saw goodness in him, something she might have missed if she hadn't been connected by his blood exchange, and for the first time she allowed herself to think about that exchange as something good. She might have dismissed the Carpathian as impossible if she didn't know about his other, much softer side.

She stroked back Luiz's hair, the gesture idle as she watched Manolito's face. Time seemed to stop. Everything around her faded until there was only Manolito. His eyes, dark and shadowed, with absurdly long lashes. They should have been feminine, but his face was too masculine, the strong jaw and straight nose. She felt his breath move in and out of her body. She felt his heart beat, strong and steady. Her heart. His. Luiz's. Solange's. They were all tied together by one man. One incredible man.

Manolito pulled out of Solange's body, swaying with weariness, his gaze seeking his lifemate. She had kept them all connected, sharing strength, keeping up a steady flow of absolute conviction of life. Of love. Of wholeness. Solànge was still alive because MaryAnn had given her a reason to cling to life. Luiz still lived because she held him tight to earth, refusing to even consider allowing him to go.

She thought it was all Manolito. He didn't know whether to laugh or simply grab MaryAnn and get out before she could find out he was a fraud. He needed to give Solange blood, and it would take strength to force her. He was already ravenous. And the bright colors around him were fading into much duller spectrums, as if he couldn't keep his mind from wandering back to the land of shadows.

MaryAnn's gaze collided with his, and for a moment he couldn't move or breathe. She could never stop looking at him like that. The trust and belief, the absolute faith shining in her eyes, was a gift he would never forget. The shadows receded. "I need to give Solange blood. See if you can get her to accept what I offer. It will heal her faster and make her stronger. I will not exchange with her, merely give her enough to survive."

He sounded so tired. The lines in his face were etched deep. She wanted to put her arms around him and hold him, comfort him, give him whatever he needed to help him continue. She read the determination in him.

"Hurry, Manolito. I know you're tired, but Luiz can't last much longer."

His gaze flicked to the hand stroking Luiz's furred head. For a moment a flicker of black jealousy raked at his gut. He tasted ashes in his mouth, and once again the shadows drew close. Faintly, he heard voices calling to him. *Join us. Join us.* Shaken, he touched MaryAnn's mind and instantly found those fingers were really stroking his head; it was Manolito who consumed her thoughts. He sent her a quick smile before slashing his wrist and forcing the female jaguar to swallow his offering.

Jasmine made a small sound of distress and turned her head away.

"It is okay, little sister. She will not become anything else. Once she has enough of my blood mixing with hers, she will survive and be strong again," he reassured her, his voice gentle.

"I know. I do, really. I just feel a little sick. Thank you for doing this. It can't be easy. She may not show you appreciation, but what you've done matters," Jasmine said.

"I do not need her appreciation. She is under the protection of our family, as are you, little *sisar*, and we would never let her die if we could save her."

Manolito was matter-of-fact, uncaring of the cost to himself. He worried more about the cost to MaryAnn. She would have to provide for him, and the innocent faith he read in her eyes might fade for all time. He couldn't let himself think about that, or falter in his duty just to make his own life easier.

Solange was a family member, and as such was guarded with all care whether she wanted it or not. After this fiasco, Zacarias would issue a decree to the women and they would be forced to obey. He would want them close, where all the De La Cruz brothers and their people could help protect them.

He closed the wound on his wrist himself and turned his attention to Luiz. It took a little more effort to shed his body, as his hunger had built to an alarming need. He could scarce keep his teeth under control, and the scent of blood was a constant torment. The jaguar-man's body was ripped to pieces, powerful jaws having cut through tissue and bone. Blood was filling the lungs, the man slowly dying. Even if he repaired the damage and gave Luiz blood, there would be no saving him.

Manolito came back to his own body and shook his head with regret. He respected Luiz. "I am sorry, *päläfertiil*, I cannot save him. It is a great loss to the jaguar people."

"Of course you can save him. I talked to Gabrielle at great length when I was in the Carpathian Mountains. Do you remember her? She was working for the prince to try to come up with a solution for so many stillbirths. She was human. When her injuries were so severe, one of the men saved her life by converting her. You would have converted Solange had you needed to. I could read that in your mind."

"That was different." He was so weak, his body swaying. He blinked rapidly to stay focused, but his vision blurred. The moment it did, colors dimmed.

"How is it different? If Luiz is jaguar, he must be psychic. Isn't the jaguar species the origin for a lot of the psychic abilities?"

"You do not understand."

"What I understand is if Luiz was a woman with psychic ability, you would move heaven and earth to save her life. He's a man, so he isn't as valuable to you."

The jaguar nuzzled MaryAnn's hand. *It is all right. I am tired.*

"No," Jasmine said suddenly. "Save him. He saved Solange. If he hadn't come when he did, Solange would be dead, or those terrible men would have her. Please. If you are my brother as you say, I'm asking for this favor."

Manolito closed his eyes briefly. "You do not know the heart of this man."

"But you do," MaryAnn said. "You drove the vampire from his mind. You saw his memories, saw what he was like. Is he worth saving?"

11

"You do not know what you are asking for him, MaryAnn. Longevity is not always a good thing. The life of a Carpathian male is extremely difficult. You may be asking for something he wouldn't want."

"Then ask him. Don't let him die simply because he's a man."

Manolito sighed. She had a point, but then, she couldn't know what it was like for a Carpathian male to know just how low the odds were of finding a lifemate. She hadn't lived centuries alone.

"I'll need to feed, MaryAnn. Are both of you willing to contribute? Because I cannot do this without blood." He was desperate to feed. The world around him was fading fast. *He* was fading. When he looked down at his hands, they were gray and growing transparent.

MaryAnn looked at Manolito's glittering eyes, saw the tiny red flames and felt her heart jump. She always forgot he wasn't human, even when she was asking him to do things that weren't at all human. She took a deep breath and nodded.

Manolito switched his attention to Jasmine. The girl sat on the floor, petting the spotted fur more to comfort herself than to keep Solange calm. "I think I can do it," she agreed, without looking at him. "Tell me what to do."

"Give me your hand."

Jasmine slowly extended her arm. Manolito's fingers settled around her like a vise. The whispers began in his head. Soft. Insidious. Temptation eating at him.

She gasped and tried to jerk away. "Wait. Wait. I forgot to tell you. I'm pregnant. Will this hurt my baby?"

Manolito dropped her hand as if she'd burned him. His gaze

went obsidian black, his mouth set in a firm line. "You have no business offering blood, or fighting jaguars. No, I will not take your blood. You must take great care to guard the child."

Before Jasmine could reply, Luiz gave a gasping wheeze and the jaguar shifted, bones crackling, body contorting as death reached for him.

MaryAnn gave a soft, alarmed cry and knelt, leaning over the broad chest to listen for a heartbeat. She immediately started CPR. "Do something, Manolito. You can't just let him die."

She had no idea what she was asking. The other world was so close. He was starved. Weary. Shadows moved everywhere in the room. MaryAnn looked at him with her wide, dark eyes, so trusting. She had so much faith in him. More than he had in himself with the whispers pushing at the back of his mind and his own body fading. He blinked and forced himself to focus.

Hear me, jaguar-man. I can make you Carpathian. You will never be jaguar, yet you will live and be able to shift. Know that this gift is a dark one. If you do not find the other half of your soul, you will eventually lose emotion and color and live only on memories. You will need blood to survive. You will have to live under the rule of our prince and pledge your allegiance and protection, your very life, to him and to our people. I will hold your life in my hands. I will be able to touch your mind at will and find you no matter where you are. If you betray us, I will kill you without remorse as quickly as possible. You have the choice of going to another place and seeking peace or remaining in this world and continuing your fight.

This was no small matter. He would forever be responsible for anything Luiz chose to do. It was an obligation few males wanted. They knew the risks, and knew what it was like to hunt and kill former friends. He allowed Luiz into his memories, into that long, seemingly endless corridor of darkness. There could be no way to describe to the jaguar-man what it would be like; he could only show him the fading emotions, the centuries of hunting and waiting, relying only on honor and then memories of honor. He was as honest as he was able.

I have not yet finished my fight to save my people.

Luiz was far away, but he clung to life. Strangely, the further Luiz's spirit retreated, the more clear the misty world around Manolito became. Voices grew louder. The room became still. Shadows with stretched skin and gaping mouths, with sharpened pegs for teeth, slithered across the walls and floor. Hunger burned and raked, clawing at every cell and organ in his body. He felt thin and stretched beyond endurance.

Manolito made an effort to concentrate only on Luiz. *They will no longer be your people. Your blood will be Carpathian. Jaguar will avoid you. Be very certain you understand what you are getting into before you choose.*

I cannot allow the vampire to continue to prey upon my people whether my blood is Carpathian or human or jaguar. We are all the same, struggling to find a life and live it well. I choose life.

It will be painful. Very painful.

And MaryAnn would be witness. How could it not scare her to death? Everything in him ached to stop, to take his lifemate and leave, but there was no doing so, not after merging so deeply with Luiz, knowing what kind of man he was and the hard fight he'd waged to save his people, to honor his women. Manolito could not abandon him to *lamti ból jüti, kinta, ja szelem*, the meadow of night, mists and ghosts, nor could he wait much longer or the man would be half-dweller, as Manolito was certain he was.

I choose life.

Manolito put a restraining hand on MaryAnn's shoulder to stop her from continuing CPR. He simply took over with his mind, keeping Luiz's heart beating and the air moving through his lungs. "I cannot do this without blood."

MaryAnn could see that Manolito had grown weak and pale, his skin nearly gray. He was swaying with weariness. It was a frightening thing to stretch out her arm and offer her wrist, but she trusted him; even with the red flames flickering in the depth of his dark eyes, she trusted him with her life.

Ignoring her wrist, he wrapped his arm around her and pulled her close. "I could never harm you, *sivamet*."

The way the last word rolled off his tongue was sensual and alluring. More than that, she caught the meaning in his mind. *My love.* Was she his love? Did he already feel more than physical need for her? Having been in his mind, she realized that the sharing of memories and the inability to hide from each other made the relationship so much more intimate than she could ever have imagined. If he was courting her, he was doing a good job, simply by being himself.

She went into his arms willingly and nuzzled his throat. He tilted her chin so that her gaze met his, was captured by his, mesmerized and lost in the dark depths of his eyes. Lost in the seduction of stark need and raw hunger. He never tried to disguise or lessen the way he felt about her. Her breath caught in her throat. Her heart did a curious melting as her stomach flipped and her womb clenched.

This man could be hers—was hers. She hadn't claimed him back. She didn't even know if she could live with what and who he was, but she admired and respected him. She could feel the hunger beating at him. The weariness. He was torn between two worlds, and to stay in hers drained him. His sense of honor toward Solange, and to her, had only added to his burden.

"Take what you need." Her lips whispered over his.

Temptation. Oh, lord, the temptation she was inadvertently offering him. His tongue was a velvet rasp over her pulse. She was warm, living silk in his arms. No one had softer skin. His emotions had long been frozen in a place deep inside him, buried so deep he thought it impossible to taste or feel or know the pleasure a woman's shape could bring to a man's body. Her touch, the sound of her voice, her very breath had awakened him. She had given him life again. He wanted her with him for all time. He wanted to ensure she was always by his side.

Temptation. He now knew what it felt and tasted like. He knew temptation was a woman and that he would have to use every ounce of control to keep from whisking her away to a place where they could be alone.

His teeth sank deep, and the taste and essence of her flowed from her to him, completing him body and soul. A sultry, smoky flavor and so MaryAnn. His arms tightened, and he closed his eyes to better savor her. At the same time, he allowed one hand to wander down the curves of her body to her leg. She was curled up in his arms, her legs in his lap, and he could easily find the tears in her flesh.

No one, woman or man, should have been able to push aside the pain and function, not only sitting, as she was doing now, but running as she had earlier in the rain forest. The pain should have dulled her thinking and affected her ability to manipulate energy. The pain was there in her mind. She felt it. But she pushed it into a center of her brain he was unfamiliar with.

He'd never seen the pattern before. He was ancient. He had used mage, jaguar and human for sustenance at one time or another, and as the species mixed, the patterns became less distinct over the ages. He ran his hands over her thigh, an intimate exploration. She shivered in his arms, her body moving restlessly against his.

She is yours.

Yes. She was his. Made for him. Shaped for him. The other half of him.

She was made for you.

Of course she had been, her body curved just so, soft and pliant, hot silk moving in his arms so that he would know what it would be to bury his body deep within her, drive them both over the edge into ecstasy.

It is your right.

He had every right to her body. He owned her, body and soul, just as she did him. He could take pleasure when and where he wanted. His hand slid along her thigh, moved toward heat—his heat—she belonged to him. He knew exactly the things that would please her, would bring her to a fevered frenzy of sexual need.

Why bring the jaguar-man across? He will only turn vampire and you will have to hunt and kill him as you have so many others.

It was madness to consider bringing another male into their world when there were so few lifemates. He might try to steal MaryAnn.

He was alone with her. Naked. Showing her his body in order to lure her away from you. He wants her. He'll do anything to take her from you.

The jaguar-men had all proven to be deceivers. They did lure women and hold them captive, treat them brutally.

He touched her. He touched your woman. He saw your mark, smelled your scent all over her, yet he touched. You saw him standing over her. He was stark naked. What do you think he was trying to force her to do?

She defended him. Said he'd saved her life.

She wants him. Make her yours. Take her now. Take what belongs to you. Bring her to your side for all eternity.

He couldn't stop. He needed this. He was starving. *Starving.*

The hunger drove him mad. Nothing could sate him but his lifemate. The rich, hot blood burst through his system with the rush of the most powerful drug.

He needed her body submitting to his, all heat and fire, sating the desire that had him so hard and hot and beyond caring of anything but sinking deep into her. He wanted to hear his name called out in a storm of need. He wanted to see her eyes glaze over with passion; he wanted to hear her beg for him to join them. He had waited an eternity through darkness and hell, and now she was there, in his arms, her body ripe and ready for his, her blood mingling with his.

Take her. It is your right. She cannot deny you. Anything you want she must provide. Yours. Take her now before the jaguar claims her. You cannot stop now when you are so close. Take enough to convert her and she cannot leave you. Taste her. The whispers grew. Voices joined in.

For one moment, his arms tightened possessively and his body urged hers backward so that he bent her beneath him. For what? Would he take her right there with Luiz dying beside them? With Jasmine and Solange there as witnesses to his madness?

Yes. Yes. You take her now before it is too late and you lose her.

Fear rose in him. Fear that he couldn't control the addiction to her taste, that he wouldn't—couldn't—stop. He was losing his mind, and he was going to harm the one person he had sworn to care for. He shouldn't be listening, but the voices were insidious, creeping into his mind and preying on his worst fears and his worst traits.

His worst traits. The need to dominate. The need for her to see only him and no one else. The terrible need to force his will on her, so that she not only wanted to but *needed* to do everything he wished. He wanted her on his terms and knew he could control her through a sexual relationship. He knew her desires and fantasies, and he knew how to exact every erotic response. Not for pleasure—hers or his—but for control.

He would not only dishonor himself and everything he stood for if he took her blood and her body, if he brought her wholly into his world, but he would ruin any chance he had of gaining MaryAnn's affection. That was not what lifemates were all about. He was her lifemate and would be in every sense of the word.

The voices became louder, more persuasive. The shadows around him lengthened and grew. He caught at MaryAnn's arms, prepared to wrench her away from him, but she moved in his mind, a soothing warmth, a feeling of well-being.

That is not so, Manolito. I hear them and they speak falsely. Of course you feel I am yours. If I am your lifemate, I am the other half of your soul. MaryAnn was grateful that Destiny had taken the time to try to explain the bond between Carpathian lifemates. *Naturally you would want me wholly in your world. They are preying on your instincts, but you are stronger than they are. We are stronger than they are.*

You can hear them? He was desperate for her to know that he walked in two worlds. It seemed so implausible. And yet he was surrounded by the shadows, the voices and the cold chill he couldn't shake, when a Carpathian could control body temperature.

Of course I hear them. She wouldn't let them take him. Whatever was happening was real, not imagined. She was an urban bush woman, and she could handle whatever the trash wanted to throw at her or her man.

Her stomach did another odd little flutter. She was already thinking of him as her man. Whatever. She wasn't going to desert him until he was safely in the land of the living, without vampires and ghouls hanging around.

Manolito tried to still his pounding heart and the surge of hot blood racing through his body straight to his groin. The good thing was, with her body heat, her soft skin and total acceptance, she had dimmed the voices enough for him to dull the demon rising to claim her, and for him to reason once again.

She had been aware of his thoughts, yet she hadn't fought him, hadn't pulled away. She had waited for him to sort it all out, believing in him through the entire exchange. Her faith terrified him. What if he let her down? What if the man she believed him to be didn't exist? She humbled him with her confidence in him.

He swept his tongue across the pinpricks, careful this time not to leave his mark. Once was enough, and he made certain it was still there to remind her, in his absence, of the connection of their souls. He held her for a moment, his heart pounding. Had the voices been more than a temptation to do her wrong? Had those in the shadow world sensed she was connected to him and had Maxim tried to draw her into the world of mists, where he could kill her?

"Let me heal your leg." He couldn't bear to see those marks on her, and she had been suffering long enough while he helped others. His fingers slid over the tears on her calf, the ripped flesh and the exposed muscle gaping from the wound.

"But Luiz . . ."

"I am keeping him alive. Allow me to do this."

MaryAnn pressed her lips together to keep from protesting, sending one quick glance toward Jasmine and Solange, hoping they weren't witnessing her reaction to Manolito's attention. Because quite frankly, it was sexual. In the midst of blood and chaos, her body was doing things and thinking things it shouldn't. Solange lay without moving, eyes closed, holding Jasmine's total concentration.

"Go ahead then, but hurry." Her voice came out choked. She could hardly think, let alone speak, with his fingers trailing up and down her thigh.

He bent his head toward her calf, his fingers circling her ankle to hold her still. Her breath caught in her throat, as she watched his silky hair cascading like a waterfall around his shoulders. She could see his profile, his long lashes and the outline of his lips. He was just too gorgeous to be real. She lifted a hand to her out-of-control hair. Even braided, it was trying to grow into a wild mass. The action drew her attention to the bloodstains on her silk blouse.

She looked with dismay down at her really chic black dress pants. One trouser leg was ripped and torn, the really cute cuff shredded into strings. Beneath it, her leg had deep rake marks, so deep the muscle poured from the slashes. Pain exploded through her, robbed her of breath, and for a moment she thought she might get sick.

"Manolito." She gasped his name, shocked at the pain burning through her. Tears swam in her eyes. "It hurts."

"I know, *sivamet*, I can take that away as well." He found it interesting that the moment her mind had become aware of the wound, she had felt the entire load of stabbing pain. It was no longer compartmentalized in her brain, shut off from her conscious self.

Manolito shouldered the pain and began the task of healing the wounds from the inside out. When the lacerations were sealed and free of all infection, he came back to his body and bent to inspect her leg. She closed her eyes when she felt his tongue rasp over the wound like the stroke of warm velvet.

She knew he had a healing agent in his saliva, and that there should have been an "ick" factor for her, but there wasn't. Instead, a million butterfly wings brushed at her stomach and her muscles clenched. Heat pulsed between her legs. He was doing something with the pads of his fingers, up higher, on the inside of her thigh, something that threatened her sanity, but before she could lose her mind, he lifted his head, eyes heavy-lidded and smoky with desire.

"We need to focus on Luiz." His husky voice was thick with emotion.

She nodded, unable to speak. "Tell me what to do to help you."

Carpathian men did not share their women, and Manolito was definitely the jealous type, but his heart went out to Luiz when he sensed his apprehension as Manolito bent to his throat.

Try to hold him to you, MaryAnn, to make his transition easier. I fear his cat is strong and will not relinquish him easily. It wasn't easy to make himself ask her, but he was already firmly merging with the jaguar-man, and the taste of fear was bitter for a man who had fought so many battles and worked so hard for his people. Manolito didn't want Luiz moving from one life to the other in a state of anxiety. He allowed himself to merge completely to calm the man, but the cat sensed what was about to happen and raged.

You will still exist. How could you not? You have been a part of Luiz for so many years. You two are the same. This will allow you both life. He has chosen to save you so that you can save your people. MaryAnn stroked the man's hair, her fingers lingering, caressing.

She touches another man.

The same man who was with her earlier.

The voices were hideous demons, designed to undermine his confidence in her. He chose to look at her hand, to feel her intent—to trust her instead of the voices. Her fingers were mesmerizing, and Manolito felt the touch in his own hair—on his own scalp. The three of them were fused tightly together through MaryAnn, but he was certain she had no knowledge of what she did.

He was beginning to figure out how she did it. Her abilities were unlike any he'd encountered. She gathered energy and used it as automatically as breathing. She reached out to those around her, anyone suffering or in need of comfort and "read" them without even knowing she did so. After she gathered and processed the information about the person and their trouble, she used the energy to give them whatever was needed in the way of hope or comfort.

She gave Luiz her compassion, soothing and calming him, but she gave Manolito something altogether different. Partnership. She wasn't following him as he felt a woman should do; she was standing beside him, working with as much energy to protect and save him from the shadow world he dwelt in as he used to protect her. It was simply a different energy and a different approach.

He drew the life, blood and spirit from Luiz and took them into his keeping. Slashing his wrist, he gave the command to drink, and Luiz, submerged so deeply, didn't fight. The jaguar gave one roar of protest and then allowed MaryAnn to calm it.

MaryAnn bit her lip and continued stroking Luiz's hair, trying to figure out how best to help the situation. She didn't know what to expect, but she didn't want Jasmine to be around if anything bad happened. "Can you help Solange to the bedroom?" she asked, uncertain if the jaguar was unconscious or simply not moving.

The door burst open and Riordan strode in, Juliette a step behind. She was obviously frantic, pushing against him to get to her sister and cousin. There were burn marks down Riordan's arm and left cheek. A slash of blood along his thigh. Juliette appeared unharmed, but shaken. A small cry escaped when she saw the amount of blood spattered on the floor and walls, but Riordan's body blocked hers from any possible danger while he took in the scene.

"Does Solange need further assistance?" he asked Jasmine as he stepped aside to allow his lifemate to rush to her cousin's side.

"We need to put her in a room and allow her to shift back to human form," Jasmine said. "She's quiet now, but in pain."

"I'm so sorry." Juliette was close to tears. "We tried to get here, but our enemies are near. They must have guessed our resting place, and when we tried to rise, they attacked us."

Manolito flicked a quick, hard glance at his brother, to ensure the man had no wounds that needed immediate attention. Riordan shook his head to assure him.

"Jasmine and I can take Solange to her room," Juliette said, "while you help Manolito."

"What are you doing?" Riordan demanded, although he already knew. He just didn't want it to be true. "Have you lost your mind? We cannot bring a jaguar male over."

"Why?" MaryAnn challenged. "You have no problem converting women. Wasn't Juliette human with a little jaguar blood thrown in?"

Riordan's gaze flicked to her face and then down to her shredded leg.

"Riordan?" Jasmine called his attention back to her.

At once his expression softened. "What is it, little sister?"

"I asked Manolito to save the jaguar. If he hadn't come to Solange's aid, she would have been captured or dead."

"A mage traveled with them." Manolito supplied the information, his features set in grim lines as he stopped Luiz from feeding. "He unraveled the safeguards to allow the jaguar into the house and then he came in behind them and grabbed Jasmine."

Juliette spun around, her face paling. "Oh, no, it was a trap after all. We feared so when we spotted a jaguar watching the battle. Jasmine. Are you all right?"

Jasmine nodded. "But he wasn't after me. He thought I was Solange. He actually called me by her name. I didn't react or deny it, but he was definitely after her."

Manolito sat back away from Luiz and wiped the back of his hand across his forehead, leaving behind a smear of blood. "Luiz had been tainted by a vampire. The Malinov brothers are using the plan to gain control. They are destroying the jaguar race from within, just as we discussed when we were young. They are looking for royal blood, but I don't know why. I thought Juliette or Jasmine at first, but Luiz told me Solange is the target. A vampire has placed a compulsion within the men of the jaguar race to capture and turn her over to him." He sent his brother a quick mental recap of all that had transpired.

Juliette shook her head. "Solange is pureblood and of the royal line."

"Solange cannot stay on the island," Riordan said. "We have to take her to the ranch as soon as she is able to travel."

"She won't go," Juliette said.

"She spoke of going," Jasmine countered. "I think we can persuade her."

"Take her up to her room," Riordan ordered. "I'm going to get rid of the mess in here and clean up. This time we'll use only the safeguards never woven by mage."

"Burn the jaguar I killed. He was tainted by the vampire and would most likely be used again," Manolito advised. "I do not want him to be used by our enemies."

"What plan?" MaryAnn asked, watching Manolito's face closely.

He remained expressionless, but flicked a glance at his brother.

It was Riordan who answered. "We were very young and thought of ourselves as intellectuals. We thought we could make the world a better place."

"We thought we were superior to everyone around us," Manolito corrected. "We all had quick brains and fast reflexes. Few hunters were better. When we sat in the council circle, it was always Zacarias who came up with the strategies for battles. It was always one of us who managed to think up the ideas for keeping our people from heading toward disaster."

"What happened?" MaryAnn prompted.

Manolito sighed and dragged both hands through his hair. "Now I realize everyone's thoughts flowed together, flooding us with information. Our gifts allowed our brains to work fast to develop the answers we needed. That was what we contributed to the council meetings, just as everyone else had something of value to contribute. But back then, we thought we knew the direction our people should go, and it wasn't the same as Vlad Dubrinsky decreed. He was prince then and our women were so few."

Riordan shook his head. "Back then there was little hope of finding a lifemate. Few children survived and none of them female. We all could see that the extinction of our species was at hand. It was a matter of time. Many resented being regulated to the murmurings of old men and ancient peoples. We were becoming myth along with the others—the mage, the werewolf and the jaguar. There were many species of shifters, but most had died out, and the same was happening everywhere we looked."

"We wanted to save our people, so we would sit around with

our friends and come up with plans to take over. We had to lead the *Karpatii* people out of the dying shadows and back into the world. Anyone who would follow the Dubrinskys and fight on their side had to go. So we played with ideas on how it could be done."

"They were stimulating intellectual debates," Riordan added. "We didn't mean anything by them." He spread his hands out in front of him and looked at them, as if he might see the blood of his own people on them.

"Regardless of what we thought back then," Manolito said, "the Malinov brothers are implementing that exact plan."

"Who are the Malinov brothers?" MaryAnn prompted.

Luiz stirred, eyes snapping open, a gasp of air escaping. His body writhed, muscles locking and contorting.

MaryAnn leaned over the convulsing body with a small sound of distress escaping. "It isn't working, Manolito."

Manolito caught MaryAnn and set her away from the jaguar-man. "This is going to be rough, *ainaak enyem*. He would not want you to witness his conversion."

She lifted her chin, looking from one brother to the other. "You don't want me to witness the conversion because you don't want me to know what happens," she guessed.

"That as well," Manolito conceded. "But his body will have to rid itself of toxins as the cat fights for supremacy."

"Juliette's conversion was extremely difficult," Riordan added.

MaryAnn kept her gaze locked with Manolito's. "I honestly believe I can help him with the transition."

Riordan shook his head. "No one can help. If we could, we would bear most of the pain, but we cannot, not even for our *avio päläfertiil*, the other half of our souls."

MaryAnn reached her hand out to Manolito. He immediately took it, lacing his fingers through hers. "I can help him, Manolito. I comfort people. It's what I do."

"I am sorry, beloved," he said as gently as he could. "It is too big of a risk. You are unaware of your gifts and you merge with people without even knowing it. I cannot take the chance that you might be locked with him and his body give out before the struggle is complete. I will not risk it."

"It isn't your risk."

Something dark and dangerous flickered in the depths of his

eyes. A muscle jerked along his jaw, but his features remained absolutely expressionless. "I said no."

MaryAnn scowled at him. "Manolito, you can't tell me what I can or can't do."

He moved faster than she expected, his body a blur as he wrapped her up in strong arms, so strong there was no chance to fight. Before she could think to even object, he was striding with her through the house. In all her life, MaryAnn had never had anyone restrain her physically. Furious, she kicked at him, but his strength was enormous and his will made of iron. There was no stopping him.

"I am sorry, *ainaak sivamet jutta.*"

Forever to my heart connected. She read that in his mind as he glided through the house to her room and deposited her on the bed. His lips brushed a caress into her hair and he left her, closing the door firmly behind him.

Manolito stood there for a moment, murmuring a binding spell to keep the door locked should she manage to remove the hinges. She was entirely capable of such a thing, if any woman was. She was going to be spitting mad at him, but for both Luiz's and MaryAnn's sakes, he preferred she not witness what was about to happen. A shoe thunked against the door, and then a second one. Yeah. She was angry all right.

"Manolito, hurry," Riordan called. "This is going to be bad."

MaryAnn heard Riordan's urgent yell to his brother, and she caught up the pillow and held it to her stomach, feeling sick. She had been the one to push Manolito into saving Luiz, but now she'd deserted all of them. Luiz was alone, facing a terrible ordeal. She didn't know what it was, but sensed it was traumatic both for him and the two Carpathian males.

Had they ever converted a male before? If it had never been done, maybe there was a reason why. A good reason. She'd been rash to push them into it. She buried her hot face in the pillow, feeling tears burn. Luiz was going to suffer, and somehow she knew Manolito would suffer right along with him. She wanted to hold onto her fury at his high-handedness in locking her in her room, forbidding her, as if she was a small child, from witnessing the change, but because a part of her was still there, with Luiz, with Manolito, and she felt their agony, she couldn't sustain her anger.

She went into the bathroom and ran hot water in the tub, needing to relax her cramped, hard muscles. Her stomach was in knots. She caught impressions of convulsions, of Luiz's body contorting, wrenched into the air and dropped down hard. She could get glimpses only and realized Manolito was blocking her from merging with him. It had taken a bit to get the trick of their connection, and most of the time when she tried, she simply wasn't that good at it. But now it seemed impossible.

She took a deep breath and let it out. She would not desert Luiz at this stage, not when he needed her most. Manolito was trying to shield and protect her, but whether he knew it or not, he needed her, too. She concentrated on him. The feel and texture of him. The layers in his mind. The intimacy of the path between them—such an unexpected gift. As much as she thought him arrogant, she knew him better now, the gentleness he hid from the rest of the world. She saw his compassion as he held Luiz, felt the way he had reached to calm him.

She felt the cat rake and claw, fighting for survival, and then the sensation was gone. She let her breath out slowly and continued to picture Manolito holding the jaguar-man. She caught a small wave of compassion from both Riordan and Manolito and then the cat again, the alarm building to panic, snapping and biting as it defended itself against the onslaught of Carpathian blood.

She went to her knees, stomach heaving. She knelt, hands and knees on the bathroom floor, gasping for breath as pain rippled through her. She caught Manolito's startled awareness that she was with him, and he once again put her firmly away from him.

There was an agony in being alone, knowing Luiz was suffering and Manolito needed her with him. She felt the need, but couldn't do anything to help either of them. Manolito had been uncompromising, not realizing, or maybe he did, that he was asking her to go against her nature. Once more she pushed away fear and concentrated on Manolito, because in that moment she had connected with him, she felt his struggle with the shadow world. She might not be able to reach Luiz, but she could Manolito. The connection between them was incredibly strong.

And then she was solidly in his mind, in Luiz's mind, and saw for herself the true horrors of conversion. The agony wrenching at the jaguar-man as death called, as the cat fought. Manolito took way too much on himself, shouldering as much of the pain as nature would allow. Both men were stoic, each fully aware of the other, Luiz trying to bear it all with great dignity. Manolito strove to be compassionate and comforting while allowing the jaguar-man his self-respect. In that moment, with tears running down her face and her body writhing in the shared pain of the two men, she knew she could love Manolito wholly, with everything in her.

The attraction may have been started with some ancient ritual. She may have been obsessed physically with him, but in the end, she saw his true character. He was open to her as he tirelessly worked to help Luiz come fully into his world, and her heart responded in the only way MaryAnn knew—completely.

12

The conversion was the most frightening thing she could imagine, a dark, painful death and rebirth. She knew she was facing it and that Manolito, watching what Luiz had gone through, was not as certain as he had been that he wanted to risk her. Strangely, for the first time she did consider risking everything, because what she had learned here today was that Manolito De La Cruz was far more than a gorgeous man with a too-arrogant attitude, and she was already more than halfway in love with him.

She French-braided her hair in the tub, her hands adept at the familiar task, giving her comfort when she wanted to weep a little for what Manolito, not Luiz, had gone through. His brothers thought him insane. He even believed he might be, but he had handled the jaguar-man with great care and respect and had suffered greatly for it. He had known she was there, helping Luiz and soothing him as best she could, and he would have done anything to spare her that, but it only made her feel closer to him.

She pulled on lacy thong underwear in midnight blue, the ones with the tiny gold chain on either hip that made her feel sexy and courageous in the worst of circumstances. Her skirt was calf length and fell in ripples of material, a fall of royal blue that looked dynamite with her butter-soft matching blue knee-high boots with the cuffed tops. They molded to her feet like slippers and whispered when she walked. The skirt showed off her nicely rounded butt to the best advantage, and she was going to need every advantage she could get with Manolito when she discussed with him the dos and don'ts of their relationship. Because she'd made up her mind they were going to give it a try.

Her demi push-up bra matched the thong, dark and exotic, giving her curves a nice allure and enhancing the fit of her short, royal blue sleeveless blouse with the little pearl buttons up the front. Accessories were everything, and she had plenty. As she pushed bangles onto her wrist, she conjured up his image.

The way he smiled. His thick, jet black hair, even more shiny and luxurious than she had realized the previous evening. His eyes. Oh, lord, he had those hot, demanding eyes and that wickedly sensual mouth, and what the hell was she dressing to seduce him for? She was trying to get a handle on her emotions, and she was definitely dressed to get him to sit up and take notice. She was playing with fire, and she knew enough about life to know that if she did that, she couldn't cry when she got burned.

The tension in the house was gone, and she let her breath out slowly and sank down onto the bed to wait for him. She could hear the clock ticking. Endlessly and loudly ticking. He was coming. Soon. Immediately. She waited, but as the minutes passed, the smiled faded from her face. Her teeth clicked together as she—dare she use the word—*gnashed* them. He wouldn't leave her locked in her room like an unruly teen. He had better come. Now. Before she lost her sweet *forgiving* nature for all time.

She stalked across the room and gave the door a thump with her fist. "Come on, jungle man. Enough is enough. Get me out of here."

Silence met her demand. She was going to kill him with her bare hands. Her nonviolent beliefs were wasted in the rain forest and definitely obsolete with jungle man. "I take back every good thing I ever thought about you," she yelled at the door, and smacked it with her open palm for good measure. Right where his face should be. "You need someone to slap you upside that hard head."

And a good hard slap wouldn't be enough. She might have to think up other, much more savage punishments, although she didn't have that kind of imagination. Whips and chains. But that conjured up black leather boots with stiletto heels, fishnet stockings and a leather bustier. And that was *so* not happening, because he didn't deserve it to happen. What he needed was the smackdown of a lifetime. Those horrible shows on television with men fighting in cages and one of them pummeling the other, that would be the way to go, not leather and boots.

The door swung open, and Manolito's broad shoulders filled the frame. He stood there blinking down at her, rubbing his jaw ruefully, a quizzical look on his face. "I believe it best if you only think nice thoughts about me."

She opened her mouth to slay him with words, then snapped it shut abruptly. He looked exhausted. Totally exhausted, weary from his fight to save two lives, heal her and keep the two worlds he existed in separate. She felt the weariness like a great weight on his shoulders—on hers. She knew what he'd been through, and she knew why he had tried to spare her.

MaryAnn put her hands on her hips and regarded him from head to toe. "You managed to exhaust yourself. Did your brother give you more blood?" She felt courageous asking the question, forcing herself to face who and what he was without flinching away from his needs.

A faint smile softened the hard edge of his mouth and pushed the deep shadows from his eyes. "I did exhaust myself. You look beautiful, MaryAnn. One look at you and everything else fades away." He held out his hand. "Come with me."

She wanted to be alone with him so badly she actually took a step back instead. "Where?"

"I have a surprise for you." He kept his arm extended toward her, gaze steady on hers.

Letting her breath out, she put her hand in his. At once his fingers closed over hers and he drew her close to the warmth of his body. She could feel the heat and the pull of their connection wash over and into her.

"Luiz?"

"He is in the ground, well guarded. This time we used safeguards no mage should be able to penetrate. It is long since we have had dealings with that species, and over the centuries we have grown careless. The recent battle with them should have taught us we must always factor them in when guarding our homes and sleeping chambers. Such a mistake will not happen again."

"Thank you for what you did for him."

He leaned down to brush his lips against hers, a soft, lingering touch, nonaggressive, as if he simply was savoring her.

"You are welcome. We will see how Luiz feels about it all when he rises."

Manolito would have to control Luiz's natural instincts to feed. Luiz already had years of jaguar instincts and he would awaken ravenous. If he gave in to the need to kill his prey, Manolito would have to dispatch him fast and efficiently, but he didn't want to think about that now. He wanted to fill his mind with nothing but his lifemate, MaryAnn. He didn't want to think anymore about the shadow world, or the real world, or the mess he had gotten himself into just to see a look of gratitude on a woman's face.

"He can't feel pain, can he?"

Manolito tucked her hand beneath his chin, his thumb sliding over her skin in a slow caress. "No. He is safe. He will stay for two or three nights before he rises, and I will be there to help him as much as possible when the time comes."

"And Solange?"

"Juliette and Riordan are with her." He rubbed her knuckles back and forth against his jaw. "The house is clean and protected. Everything is quiet. I want to take you away from here and have you to myself for a little while."

Her heart gave a funny little jump. More than anything she wanted to be with him. She had dressed with care and made certain she looked her best so that she would have the courage to face him and whatever was between them, but now that he stood in front of her, looking better than any man had a right to look, she wasn't certain being alone with him was the smartest idea. He was just too sexy and appealing. She didn't want to relate to him just physically, and her newfound feelings made her feel more vulnerable than ever.

"I find my lifemate absolutely fascinating and would very much like to get to know you," he added. There was no push to see it his way. There was no order, or demand. His simple statement held the ring of truth and cut through every defense she had.

"You're certain I shouldn't check in on Jasmine and Solange? I came here to try to help them, not that I've done much good."

"You helped saved their lives," he said, drawing her gently beneath his shoulder. "Solange is resting and Juliette is with her sister." He took a breath, drew her scent deep into his lungs.

"I need you." His voice roughened with hunger. His black eyes smoldered with smoky lust.

She nodded, her heart pounding hard. Her pulse seemed to hammer right through her entire body, bunching muscles and tightening her nipples, making her ache. Her mouth went dry, and she touched her tongue to her lips, gasping as his watchful gaze followed the action.

"I'm not certain it's safe."

"No harm will come to you," he promised. The pad of his thumb traced the path her tongue had taken, outlining her lips with a brush of heat. "Not as long as I am with you."

"You." She could barely breathe, let alone get the word out. "You're not safe. I have this crazy reaction to you." It was best to be honest and let him know. "The thing is, I set rules for myself a long time ago."

"Rules?" His eyebrow arched in question, but his gaze was still on her mouth.

"For me. For men. I don't just sleep with anyone." This *so* wasn't coming out right because she honestly couldn't think with him looking at her like that.

"I am grateful for your rules."

There was a faint quirk to his mouth that only added to his allure. How could she explain she felt her self-respect and years of restraint were about to go flying out the window? If she was alone with him, she'd be doing her best to seduce him, or just plain beg for him to slam her up against the nearest wall and have his way with her.

She had never wanted a relationship with a man that was comfortable. She had wanted all-consuming passion or nothing at all. She'd settled for nothing at all. She had fantasized about a relationship with a man who could inspire hot erotic licks of electricity running up and down her spine, where she met him in a grocery store wearing absolutely nothing beneath a coat, or danced with him in a sensual haze at a party, his hands moving on her skin, knowing, *needing*, that they wouldn't make it home before they succumbed to their desire for each other. Now here it was, every fantasy she had ever dreamt of.

MaryAnn was fairly certain Manolito De La Cruz was the hottest man alive. He dripped sensuality. From every look and mannerism to the set of his shoulders, the thickness of his chest, the way his hips narrowed and the all-too-impressive bulge in the front of his jeans. His eyes were heavy-lidded and smoky with lust for her. While that stark hunger made her heart pound and her body go into serious meltdown, the truth was, in every single fantasy, the man had been wild about her, deeply in love. One without the other wasn't acceptable to her.

"If I go off alone with you again now, Manolito, I'm not certain I could live with myself afterward."

"I will do nothing you cannot live with."

From the sound of his voice, he hoped to do things she couldn't live without, and that was *exactly* what she feared. Because she so wanted those things. She wanted him to teach her all the things she dreamt about, she wanted to belong to him, to have him love her, show her that the things in her mind could be real, not just imagined.

"You are not letting me into your mind."

Was there hurt in his voice? The last thing she wanted to do was hurt him. "I don't know how to let you in or out of my mind. I honestly have no idea why you all think I'm psychic. Jasmine thought I saved her from the mage. The wind was horrendous; a branch broke off and fell on him. I didn't do that. How could I have?"

In a way she was very grateful he couldn't get into her mind. He would never get in if she had anything to do with it. All she needed was for him to read her fantasies and she would be in more trouble than she could imagine—and she had far too vivid an imagination when it came to sex.

Manolito's dark eyes drifted possessively over her face. "Come with me, MaryAnn. Let me show you my world."

She shouldn't go. She was asking for trouble if she went. She sighed. Of course she was going with him. She was going because she'd lost her mind, because she could still taste him in her mouth and feel his hands on her body and she ached inside and out for him. "I'm bringing the pepper spray."

His faint smile sent tiny, flickering flames of arousal licking over her breasts and down her belly, dancing along her inner thighs until she felt searing heat scorch her most feminine core. She let her breath out, feeling as if she'd just leapt off a cliff.

"I would expect nothing less than pepper spray," he answered, his voice tinged with amusement.

That small note of humor, one she suspected was rare in

him, just added to his allure. She lifted her gaze to his and was lost in the absolute focus and intensity she saw there—for her. Nothing—no one—existed for him but her in that moment.

With exquisite gentleness, he wrapped his arms around her and drew her slowly up against his body. His skin was hot and hard and smelled masculine. His midnight hair brushed across her face as he lifted her, sliding her body up his so that she felt the thickness and length of his erection pressed deep into her softer body. "Put your arms around my neck and your legs around my waist. If you still fear flying, press your face into my neck so you cannot see. Trust me to take care of you, Mary-Ann."

There was a terribly intimate note in the velvet rasp of his voice, husky and promising and altogether shocking, as if sin lived and breathed in him and reached to wrap her in nothing but passion. The double meaning sent a shiver of desire spiraling through her body. MaryAnn was all about control, and this man was all about taking it away. Her pulse followed the rhythm of his. Her heart hammered out the same beat. Temptation to taste the forbidden was so strong she let her hands bunch for a moment in his silky hair, absorbing the texture, feeling shaken inside.

She closed her eyes when her feet left the floor. He took her breath so easily, shaking her up until she forgot about being MaryAnn the counselor and became, wholly and completely, MaryAnn the woman. The hollow of his neck was warm and inviting, and she nuzzled his shirt aside so her face could rest against his skin. Her lips moved against him, tasting him, because she could. Because when she did, a shudder of pleasure shook his strong body.

The night was surprisingly warm. As he whisked her through the forest, she could hear all sound cease, as animals, birds and insects became aware of their presence. A shiver went down her spine as she realized they were sensing a predator. It was impossible not to feel alive with him. He created energy, both sensual and exciting, most of all dangerous, and wrapped her in his voracious sexual appetite for her, his need for her elevating her own needs and desires.

For all of that, his looks and his sensuality, it wasn't her virtue in the most jeopardy, because he was a good man and her heart responded with the same passion as her body. The biggest risk was letting him into her heart. He gave of himself so quickly to others, without thought of consequences to himself, and no other trait in a man could appeal to her quite so much. He was starkly honest about everything, and that appealed to her as well. He showed her vulnerability when he told her about seeing and hearing things from another world. He let her inside of him without reservation.

And just like that you open your mind to me.

She felt warm, as if he'd enfolded her in a velvet wrap. "Did I?"

If she did, she hadn't thought about the danger of opening her mind. Only her heart. She kept her face buried in the hollow of his neck, feeling safe as they moved through the sky.

Look now, MaryAnn.

"I'm afraid of heights."

She was afraid of loving what he showed her. Afraid of loving this man and changing her life—one she'd worked so hard for—forever. She just really enjoyed her little niche. She knew she helped others; she was good at it, and she liked her independence. And there was that very frightening thing inside of her, something that terrified her, one she kept locked away, but it was drawn to this man. In the city, surrounded by people and the hustle and bustle of life, it stayed quiet and under her control. Here, with this man, she could feel it stretching and reaching inside of her, anxious for freedom. And she didn't dare let it free.

His lips brushed the top of her head. *You will not be afraid, I promise you. You will see my world the way I see it.*

She closed her eyes briefly and pressed tighter into him. That was *exactly* what she feared. She didn't want to see beauty in the rain forest. She wanted to see the insects. Lots of nasty, biting insects. And leeches. They had leeches, she just knew it. When she looked, she'd dwell on that. It was the only way she could think of to stay safe. Armed with a picture of big, fat, blood-sucking bugs, she cautiously raised her head and looked around her.

They were in the canopy of a huge tree, vines tangling rapidly beneath them to form a solid deck. The vines continued to twist and climb, adding a solid railing so she could walk around in the treetops and feel as if she were on rooftops in her hometown. He slowly let her out of his arms, watching her turn her face to the sky.

MaryAnn caught her breath as she looked around her. Mist

looked like diamonds falling across a midnight sky. Stars scattered and sparkled, tiny crystals glittering everywhere she looked. Up so high, she felt she might touch the moon. It wasn't close to being full, but it was a magical sight. She crossed to the railing, holding firmly with both hands, and looked beneath her. She saw treetops, leaves shining silver instead of green, branches forming highways for animals; the flutter of wings, the moonbeams catching the colors of feathers as the birds settled in for the night. Tendrils of fog wound in and out of the tree trunks, adding to the mystery and beauty.

She turned back to him, resting against the railing as she drank in the sight of him. He belonged to the night. A lord or a prince. The strong bones gave his face a noble, masculine appearance, and that molded mouth held a hint of both sensuality as well as cruelty. Danger and passion. She pressed her hand to her stomach to quell the butterfly wings.

"It is beautiful, Manolito. Thank you for bringing me here."

There was no smell of blood or death. No horror in the eyes of young women. There was only the night and Manolito.

She smiled at him. "I feel the mist, yet it isn't cold and my clothes aren't wet."

"I am Carpathian. I can control such things." He waved his hand, and the leaves began to tangle with flowers, forming a solid bed, thick and soft and inviting.

Her heart jumped in anticipation.

"Why do you wear your hair in such a tight braid? It's so beautiful, all the curls and waves and the color of it shining in the moonlight. Let it down." His hand went to the fastener holding her hair in some semblance of control.

She caught his hands to stop him. "I have natural curl, Manolito. In this weather my hair would be huge and kinky, and with no stylist around, I'd be in serious trouble."

"It's wild and beautiful." His fingers were busy stripping the band from her hair.

"You don't understand. It's wild all right. I could use tons of products to hold it in place, but the mist would wash them right down my face and into my eyes and that would sting and streak and be a huge mess. So leave it." She tried to sound tough, but it was impossible with the feel of his fingers tugging her hair out of the braid. She only succeeded in sounding breathless.

"I like the skirt. Thank you for remembering for me."

She had put it on for him. She was giving too much of herself away, but she wouldn't be less honest than he was being. The skirt and blouse were not only ultrafeminine, but made her feel sexy and desirable as well. She wanted to feel that way for him. She wanted him to see her that way.

"It's one of my favorites." Was that her voice? She sounded more seductive than he did, and she didn't want that. She wanted to know him. She wanted a chance at—*everything*.

Her hair was out of the braid now, flowing around her face and shoulders. He reached under it to cup the back of her neck, his thumb sliding over her skin, as if savoring the feel of it. There was an unexpected tenderness in his touch. She could feel heat all the way down to her toes. It was suddenly difficult to breathe.

"Does your leg hurt?"

The memory of his mouth on her leg, the feel of his tongue rasping over her skin, sent another wave of arousal washing through her body. She shook her head, afraid to speak, when his thumb smoothed over her ear and teased a shiver down her spine.

"Come lie down with me, look at the stars while we talk."

She wasn't certain she could speak when it came right down to it, not without babbling or, worse, pleading for his touch.

She sank rather gingerly onto the bed of leaves and flowers, trying to hold the image of leeches in her mind, but the flowers gave off a wonderful fragrance and the bed was as soft as the best mattress she'd ever lain on. Because she was afraid, she stayed in a sitting position.

Manolito caught her calf in his hands, drew down the zipper to her boot and pulled it off. "You may as well be comfortable, MaryAnn."

There was a command in the firm touch of his fingers, but gentleness in his voice. She made no objection, just let him remove the boots and set them aside so she could draw her knees up. He sent her a faint, mocking smile and stretched out, fingers laced behind his head.

"I thought I'd be afraid up here," she admitted, to break the silence. To find a safe subject.

"You are afraid."

"This is an unusual situation." She snuck a peek at him over her shoulder. He lay like an offering, casual and lazy and very deceptive when she could feel heat radiating off his body, when she could see the ripple of muscle and the bulge he didn't bother to hide. His features were stamped with raw desire, his eyes devouring her.

He brought one arm down to his side, the fingers curling against her thigh, rubbing back and forth through the thin royal blue silk. "I am your lifemate, MaryAnn, your husband. There is no need to fear the things I want from you. Like your hair and your skin and whatever dwells within you, what is between us is as natural as breathing."

"I don't know you well enough to give you that kind of trust. A woman like me needs to trust a man completely to give herself to him like you're asking."

"I do not ask." There was a faint smile in his voice.

For a moment she thought he was saying he didn't want her, but then she realized he meant he would demand what he wanted from her. She rubbed her chin on the top of her knees, contemplating instructing him in human law.

The fingers along her thigh bunched in her skirt, continuing to slide up and down in mesmerizing strokes. "I am not human, *sivamet*, and more than anything else, I wish to bring pleasure to my woman. What is wrong with that?" He sounded genuinely puzzled.

"Maybe I don't want that."

His laughter was low and sexy, playing over her body with the same mesmerizing stroke as his fingers. "But you do. It is what you fear most, but it is also what you want most. As I know you are safe in my keeping, there is no reason to deny you what you want—or need."

"I'm afraid that may take some time." His touch was light, but the heated silk against her skin made her muscles bunch in reaction.

"I do not think so, MaryAnn. When you lie beneath me, when my body is in yours, you trust me more than when we are apart."

Color swept up her neck and into her face before she could control it. She couldn't deny it. She would have done anything he asked of her. She *had* and more. But it was too much, too soon. She moistened her dry lips with her tongue. "I'm not ready yet."

"Fair enough."

His answer was so unexpected she turned to look at him. It was a mistake. His black eyes glittered with possession, with raw lust.

He patted the mattress of flowers. "Lie down beside me. We'll talk."

There was no hint of compulsion in his voice, at least she didn't think so, but she still found herself lying down beside him. Thigh to thigh. Hip to hip. She stared up at the sky and watched the mist sparkling above them and searched for a topic that would lead to a real discussion, one that might reveal more of who and what he was.

"Do you like living here?"

"I have grown to call this land home. I love everything about it. The rain forest, the cattle ranch, the people, even the horses. I was not the best of riders when we first began ranching." He laughed softly at the memory. "I have not thought of that time in years. We knew nothing at all, but wanted to appear human. Fortunately, we had the Chavez family to aid us. We had the money and they had the knowledge. We have worked closely ever since."

"I would have liked to see your first ride on a horse."

"I did not spend a lot of time in the saddle. I wished to be macho like the Chavez brothers so I didn't use my mind to control the horse."

She relaxed a little, laughter bubbling up. "I wish I'd been there."

The pads of his fingers traced the shape of her thigh. "I am very glad you weren't. Unless you had controlled the animal for me."

"That would have been interesting, and very tempting, although I have no idea why you think I have psychic ability."

"Because you do."

"If I do, how can I not be aware of it, yet everyone else is? What exactly do I do psychically?"

His fingers once again began that steady caressing through the silk of her skirt. "You are actually quite powerful. You gather energy and use it when you need it. I think you have been doing so all of your life, probably since you were a child, so it is normal to you. Completely natural. Like your hair." His hand slid up to the intriguing curls. He tugged gently, just enough to bite at her scalp.

She felt the pull through her body, a flash of heat she couldn't deny or control. "I don't do that." She didn't think she did. "How would I even use something I don't know about? How would it work?"

His hand slid from her hair down her arm to her wrist. He circled it lightly as if his fingers were a living bracelet. "If I knew that, *päläfertiil*, I would never be concerned about you knocking me on my rear."

"I didn't."

"You did." He brought her hand to his mouth to scrape his teeth over her palm. "It was a good jolt, too. I was proud of you—once I got over the fact that my woman had slapped me down." His tongue swirled over the exact center of her palm, easing the tiny sting of his nipping teeth.

"You're very oral, aren't you," she said, tugging at her hand. He didn't let go, and the sensation of his mouth, hot and moist, closing tightly over her finger sent flames dancing across her skin straight to the junction between her legs.

"Very," he admitted, his voice dropping low, his black gaze burning through the thin material of her blouse to her full breasts as they rose and fell with the fast tempo of her breathing.

She licked her lips again and stifled a groan when his gaze jumped to her mouth. "Stay on track here, Manolito. I really want to figure out how I could be psychic." Because she was fast losing her ability to think with her brain.

"Of course you're psychic. You can read people, and you know exactly what to say to them to help them find their way."

She laughed. "I was hoping for a real revelation, not fantasy. I went to school a very long time to become a counselor. Whether or not I'm any good has nothing to do with being psychic. I'm trained and I have a lot of experience."

"You are able to get inside their heads. You think it is instinct, and maybe that is another word for your talent. You act a lot on intuition." He turned her hand over and bit gently at her knuckles. "We could use a little instinct right now."

"I don't think psychic ability is much good if you don't know how you're using it," she protested. If she really did have some talent, it would be kind of cool, but not if she couldn't wield it properly. "I can connect with you because of the blood thing, but can't really do much else."

"You do plenty well with your power. You throw people out

of your mind at will. Very few people can do that, MaryAnn. It is a very intriguing ability." His hand dropped to his side between them once again, fingers bunching in her skirt.

"Where does it come from?"

"Many sources. I think all societies had a few who possessed some ability to manipulate energy. Some species were stronger than others, but once they began to mix, over the years, you find both amazing talent and none at all."

It made sense. She felt the caressing pads of his fingers as he bunched her skirt higher to expose the long expanse of skin along the leg closest to him. He remained lying beside her, staring up at the stars, but his hand slid under the silky material to move along her thigh and hip, shaping her curves.

Everything in her went still. Every muscle clenched in response to that light touch. "What are you doing?"

"Memorizing you. You have such soft skin. It is hard not to touch you."

He wasn't trying that hard, not that she could see. She moistened her lips again and tried to concentrate on conversation. "Did you know the jaguar people when there were still quite a few of them?"

"The shifters, especially the jaguar and werewolves, were always secretive societies. They kept to themselves. We all had a 'live and let live' philosophy, so we didn't mix unless someone committed crimes in our territories. *Karpatii*, mage and humans were close. The others stayed away from us and from each other. The other shifters disappeared so fast they are barely a memory. It was obvious that if the society did not take care of its women and children, that it was impossible for that species to continue, but the jaguar refused to acknowledge or learn from the mistakes other species had made. They wanted to keep their animal instincts and live free."

She was silent a long moment, watching the shimmering mist and the wheeling and dancing of bats as they hunted insects in the night sky. There was a kind of beauty and peace in the strange ballet they performed. Lying there, she could understand why some people preferred the rain forest to the city, especially if they were with a Carpathian who could keep insects and rain from ever touching them.

"Has it been difficult living through so many changes?" He

must have seen so much. Learned so much. Suffered so much.

"Longevity is both a curse and a blessing. You see people you care about coming and going while you endlessly remain. War is the same. Poverty. Ambition and greed. But there are such wonders, MaryAnn, wonders worth all the rest." He turned his head, his dark gaze liquid black in the moonlight. That was what she was to him. Wonder. A miracle. She had no idea. He caught glimpses of her thoughts when she opened her mind to him. She didn't understand how a man like him would ever look at her, let alone want to spend eternity with her. She had no idea of her own appeal. The light in her shone like a beacon.

Everything about her appealed to him. She was courageous, yet didn't see herself that way. She had more compassion in her than any other person he had ever encountered. Often, at great risk to herself, she went to the aid of others. There was an innocence about her, yet her eyes were old. She'd seen life at its worst, but refused to give up hope.

"What are you looking for?" She tilted her chin a little at him.

"Acceptance." He didn't think to hide himself from her. One never did, not from one's lifemate. He needed that from her. That she could see him, all of him. He wanted to stand before her with all his flaws and know that she could still accept who he was. It had never mattered before. Now acceptance was everything.

He rubbed the pad of his fingers along her glowing skin. Nothing had ever felt so soft and inviting. It seemed a miracle—another wonder in life—to be able to touch her like he was. To lie beside her with the stars above them and talk quietly together.

"Tell me your worst trait."

His teeth flashed white in the moonlight. "I think we should start with something good."

"If we go with the worst, then we get it out of the way fast. We know what it is and whether we can handle it. I'm stubborn. Not just a little bit, either. I'm really stubborn. I don't like being pushed around."

"I am always right."

Her soft laughter teased at his groin like caressing fingers. He had forgotten, or maybe he had just never experienced, perfect enjoyment like being with a woman who could arouse him the way she did. He could listen to that laugh for all time and never get tired of it.

"So you think."

"So I know."

"And you expect everyone to do what you say because you're right."

"Of course."

She wrapped his hair around her finger. "Since we're telling secrets, does it bother you to be called Manolito instead of Manuel? I know that 'little man' is often used for boys instead of men in some countries."

"It is a term of affection to my brothers. I do not care, and have never cared, what others think, only that those I love accept me. Does it bother you?"

"Manolito in other countries is a more commonly used name, with nothing else attached to it. I grew up thinking it was a great name with a beautiful sound to it. It's nice to know your brothers tease you with affection."

Shadows moved in the depths of his eyes. "Nicolas and Zacarias have not found their lifemates. They only have the memory of emotion, and it is more difficult to maintain with every passing night."

"I'm sorry, Manolito." She could feel his worry.

"They will endure because they must." His hand brushed down her face. "Tell me what's wrong, MaryAnn. I can see how upset you are."

She hesitated, pressed her lips together, then sighed. "Whatever is inside of me scares the hell out of me."

Overhead, the branches swayed with more than birds. She could see small, furry bodies gathering for the night in the trees. Most congregated to one side of the tree, just across from her, while a few of the monkeys settled in branches on Manolito's side.

"You cannot be anything but who you are, *ainaak enyem*. Never be afraid of what is inside of you. I'm not."

Her eyes met his. "You should be."

13

Manolito felt the sudden tension in her. He touched her chin with gentle fingers. "Why would I ever fear what is inside of you? I can see your light shining so bright, there is never a need to fear any part of you."

She ducked her head so that the mass of curly hair fell around her face. "Maybe you don't see me as well as you think you do."

"Then tell me."

"I don't know what to tell you. How to tell you. I can't see it. I only feel it, and it scares me to death."

He was silent a moment, trying to find a way to help her confide in him. She wanted to. It wasn't that she intentionally was hiding anything, but she was struggling to come to terms with something she knew or suspected and she wasn't quite ready.

"Tell me about your childhood," Manolito said, his dark gaze holding hers, his voice gentle.

She looked uncomfortable, shifting slightly away from him. "I had a normal childhood. You'd think it was boring, but I enjoyed it. My parents are great. Mom's a doctor, and Dad owns a little bakery shop. I grew up working there and earned most of my money for college. No brothers or sisters, so it was a little lonely, but I had a lot of friends in school."

His gaze drifted over her face, noting her eyes, the pulse beating so frantically in her throat. "There were things that happened. Unexplained things. Tell me about those."

Her heart began to thunder in her ears. She felt her breath catch in her lungs. She didn't want to think of those moments, and yes, there had been plenty, incidents there was no explanation for. MaryAnn pulled away so her body didn't touch his, just in case he could read her. She felt a shift inside of her, something moving and nudging at her almost in inquiry. *Do you need me? What is it?*

She gasped, bit down hard on her lip and tried to thrust the truth back into that deep abyss where she never had to face it. Out here in the rain forest, where everything was wild and it was kill or be killed and she faced enemies unknown in her safe world, she could no longer contain that other being unfolding inside of her.

Manolito remained still, not moving a muscle, sensing her sudden withdrawal, not only from him, but from something that had been close enough for her to see. She had slammed that impenetrable barrier between them again to keep him from seeing it. The moment she withdrew her mind from his, he was aware of that other world he still dwelled in.

The colors around him dimmed significantly and the noise of the rain forest disappeared until silence surrounded him. Strangely, his sense of smell was even more acute, as was his hearing. He not only could detect the position of animals and birds around them, but he also knew *exact* locations. He didn't need to reach with his mind to find those surrounding him; his nose and ears gave him the information. The longer he dwelled in the shadow land, the more heightened all his senses became—well, almost all of them. His vision seemed different, familiar in the way of when he shifted to animal form, but still, he caught movement instantly. He just didn't like the graying in the color, as it reminded him too much of the centuries of darkness.

He curled his fingers around hers and held tight. He had been vaguely aware of the land of mists creeping into his mind and vision since he had sent Luiz to ground, but it had been distant, as if he had made his way closer to the world where MaryAnn lived. Now, without her mind merging with his, everywhere he looked the gray was consuming color.

Manolito squeezed her hand in reassurance, although he wasn't altogether certain who was reassuring who. "You are safe here with me. Whatever it is you fear, share it with me. Burdens are much less when shared."

He was aware of every detail about her in that moment, and she was very much afraid. He heard her heart, saw the frantic beat of her pulse. She had insisted on standing by him, refusing to leave him alone in the meadow of mists, even when she was unsure of him. He wanted her to know he would do no less.

She shook her head even as she began to speak, obviously not wanting to remember the incident, or speak of it aloud, yet almost compelled to share, needing at least someone to know she wasn't crazy. "There was one time when I was in high school that I went out for track. My parents really wanted me to play sports, but I had no interest. I'm a girlie girl, always have been, but my dad thought if I got involved in sports I'd be less inclined to follow the latest fashion trends."

He stayed silent, watching the shadows chase across her face, waiting for her to make up her mind to tell him the entire story, not the watered-down version.

"I showed up for practice and took off running. At first all I could think about was how I was going to fall on my face, or trip and humiliate myself. But then I forgot myself and how uncomfortable it was running and I felt . . . *free*." She let her breath out, obviously remembering the feeling. "I wasn't aware of what I was doing at all, but I outdistanced everyone and ran without thought. I didn't feel pain at all, only a type of euphoria."

He brought her hand to his mouth and kissed her fingertips. "Don't stop, *sivamet*. What else did you feel? Obviously this made an impression on you."

"At first it was wonderful, but then I began to notice things." She pulled her hand away, as if she couldn't bare her soul while touching him. "My bones began to hurt, my joints cracked and popped. Even my knuckles ached." She rubbed them, clearly remembering the feeling. "My jaw throbbed, and I had the sensation of stretching thinner and thinner. I could hear tendons and ligaments snapping. I ran so fast, everything around me was a blur. My vision changed, my hearing and sense of smell were so acute, I could tell where every single runner was behind me. *Exactly* where they were, without looking. I could hear their breathing, the air rushing in and out of their lungs. I could smell their sweat, and hear their hearts beating."

How could she explain to him what had happened that day? How she felt something changing and growing and reaching to get out of her, to be acknowledged and recognized. *It* wanted out. She moistened her lips and clung tighter to his hand.

"I was different in that moment, completely different, yet the same. I could leap over obstacles without even slowing down.

Every sense was alive in me. My body was—singing, as if it had come alive for the first time. I can't even explain how it felt, every sense so open and gathering information. And then things began to pour into my mind, visions I couldn't stop or make sense of."

He brought her hand to his chest in an effort to comfort her. She didn't seem to realize she was becoming agitated and that her state of mind was affecting the monkeys in the surrounding trees. Wings displaced air overhead as birds stood on branches and beat them, squawking and chirping anxiously. He slid the pad of his thumb over the back of her hand and felt hard knots under her skin as her tension mounted. "What did you see?" Whatever it was had terrified her.

"A man calling to a woman, telling her to take the baby and run. The baby was—*me*. I was lying in a crib, and she wrapped me in a blanket, kissed the man and clung to him. I could hear voices and saw dancing lights outside the windows. The man kissed me, too, and then her one last time and jerked open a trapdoor in the floor. I felt dread and fear. I didn't want to leave him and neither did she. I think we all knew it was the last time we'd see each other."

She licked her dry lips. "The infant was surrounded by forest while I was running the track, hearing my heart, my footfalls, smelling the others, and I remember stars bursting around me. But they weren't really around me at the school; the lights were flashing around the woman and me, the infant in the forest. I could hear something whistle as it went past us, and then the woman flinched, stumbling. The next thing, I was running on the track, yet at the same time the woman was running through the trees with me—the baby."

"Was the woman your mother?"

"No!" MaryAnn nearly shouted more denial, but caught herself, breathing hard, trying to push down the shock of what that would imply. "No, I don't know who she was, but she wasn't my mother."

He reached out and tugged until she lay against him, her head pillowed on his shoulder. "Do not be upset, *sivamet*." His voice was soft, that mesmerizing sweep of velvet whispering over her skin. "Be calm. It is a beautiful night and we are simply talking, getting to know one another. I am very interested in this dual run you had. Do you think it really happened? How old do you think you were when this flight through the forest took place? And where were you? The United States? Europe? What language was spoken?"

MaryAnn sucked in her breath and lay very still, absorbing his warmth and strength. She could feel it flowing over and into her, as if Manolito was sharing himself and who and what he was with her. He didn't probe her mind, but he sent her complete understanding and acceptance. He was accepting something in her that she couldn't seem to accept in herself.

"Not English. I don't know. I was afraid. Very afraid." And every single time she entered a forest, that fear nearly choked her. "They wanted to kill us. I knew that, even as an infant. Whoever was torching the house wanted all of us dead, even me."

She was barely able to breathe, her chest tight, her heart pounding. "The woman ran and ran, but I knew something was wrong with her. Her rhythm was off and her breath came in great gasps. We both knew the exact moment the man who had stayed behind in the house was killed. I heard her silent scream, and it echoed mine. Sorrow consumed her and then me, almost as if we shared the same emotions. I knew she was desperate to get through the forest to a neighbor's house. The place was usually empty, but they were there, on vacation."

A shudder went through her and Manolito gathered her closer. Her skin was ice cold, and he turned, fitting his body around hers. "You do not have to tell me any more, MaryAnn, not if it is too painful." Because he was fairly certain he knew the rest of the story. He wanted her to trust him enough to give him the details, but her distress level was rising, and with it, he noted with interest, the animals in the surrounding trees grew even more agitated.

MaryAnn had never told anyone, and she wanted to tell him. The constriction in her chest had grown; the feeling of being drawn inside was terrifying, almost as if the very essence of her was being sucked into a small, dark place, to be held in tight confines. She wanted to throw out her arms and kick her legs to prove to herself she was still in her own body and not tucked inside a box.

"I tried to tell my mother, and she told me it was a dream—a nightmare that perhaps I'd remembered as I ran. She didn't want me to go running anymore and neither did I. I never did it again. And I never went into a forest after that." It had taken all of her courage to come here to this place to help Solange and Jasmine, to find Manolito and try to get him out of wherever his mind had locked him. Her courage was waning, and she wanted the comfort of home.

"Because it triggered the memory?"

"The feeling of terror and being unable to breathe. The fear of being locked away and unable to get out." MaryAnn moistened her dry lips, her hand creeping up to his neck, fingers curling around his nape. She needed to feel the strength of his larger frame, the heat of his body and the steady beat of his heart.

Manolito remained silent, simply holding her while she stared up at the stars and ignored the animals surrounding them. Surprisingly, she felt no threat from them, only a kind of kinship, a rush of sympathy and concern toward her. She took a breath and let it out. She was going to tell him all of that memory because she was absolutely certain it had occurred, and it was the only real way she could face it.

"The woman clawed her way through the brush. We were being chased and she was sobbing. I knew she was hurt, but she clung to me, forcing herself to cover the miles until we came up to a house, a vacation home for a lady and her husband who had been friends with the woman carrying me. The lady came out. I remember her face, frightened, concerned, shocked when she saw blood everywhere. The woman handed me to her and told her they were trying to kill us, that they would kill me. She pleaded with the woman to save me."

She had to stop because her throat constricted again and there was that terrible tightness in her chest that came more and more often. She buried her face against him, a shudder going through her body.

"MaryAnn." He stroked a hand down her hair, rubbed circles of comfort along her back. "Did you recognize the lady? The neighbor? Was she familiar to you?"

She didn't know. How could she know? Her heart pounded wildly and her breath came in ragged gasps. The admission burst out of her without her consent, without her permission, the declaration shocking her. "She was my grandmother." She choked, gasped for breath, her fingernails biting deep into his skin. "The neighbor, who took me, was—*is*—my grandmother."

He wrapped his arms around her and held her close, protectively, one hand shaping the back of her head, fingers moving in her hair gently as he massaged her nape to soothe her. He hadn't expected the feelings—the *emotions*—that assailed him. He was shaken by the sheer intensity of sensation coursing not through his body, but through his heart and mind. He murmured softly to her in a mixture of Carpathian and Portuguese languages as she wept in his arms.

She felt small and lost to him, and far too vulnerable. MaryAnn was a woman of confidence, not this soft bundle so shattered curling in his arms, burrowing into him and not even aware she did so. Her distress was so great that waves of it burst over him and spread throughout the rain forest, disturbing all the creatures.

"How could they do that to me?"

He waited. She still kept that barrier firmly in place, not allowing him access to her mind—to her pain—or even to memories. And he suspected she had more.

"My parents should have told me. That woman . . . I know her. I feel her here," MaryAnn pressed a trembling hand to her heart. "I ache thinking of her. She sacrificed her life to save me, just as the man did."

"Most parents would willingly sacrifice their lives for their children, MaryAnn. There is no greater love." He kept his voice gentle, hypnotic, although he was careful to keep from pushing or adding a compulsion. He kept her wrapped in warmth and safety in the only way he could, outwardly, when his every inclination was to push forward, to soothe and make everything all right for her. It was difficult to suppress his instincts to take her over. She was not a woman to be taken over.

Manolito nuzzled the top of her head with his chin and then brushed dozens of small kisses into her hair. A mixture of emotions poured from her. Grief. Anger. Feelings of betrayal. Guilt for thinking even for a moment anyone else might have given birth to her.

"I love my parents. We're a normal family."

She opened her mind again to him, and images of her childhood leapt into his brain. She was attempting to prove to him, and to herself, that her memories of growing up within her family were true and real, and everything else was simply an illusion, or a bad nightmare. He could see her parents holding and kissing her, swinging her into the air, laughing and happy with her. She had been surrounded by happiness and love her entire life.

"They love me."

There was satisfaction in her voice, but she was clutching his hand and her nails bit deep into his flesh. He looked down at their joined fingers and could see the hard knots beneath her skin, the curve of her nails, thick and strong, one not covered in polish.

"It is obvious they love you," he agreed and brought her hand to the warmth of his mouth, pressing his lips to the knots, smoothing them, gently tugging with his teeth until the nail piercing his skin was lifted and she relaxed a little more.

"I don't know what I'm supposed to think," she said, sounding vulnerable and lost.

His heart reached for hers instinctively. "No matter what your past was, MaryAnn, you are still you. Your parents loved you and raised you surrounded in that love. If they are not your birth parents, it does not in any way change that fact."

"You know there's more to it than that." She jerked her hand out of his and sat up, facing away from him, toward the treetops. She could see the highway in the canopy, the branches touching, serving as a long strip from tree to tree where even the larger animals could travel quickly.

She swallowed the lump in her throat threatening to choke her. "My whole life has been built on a lie, Manolito. I don't have the history my parents have given me. I don't have the stability of all the structure I thought I had. I don't know who I am. Or what I am. Growing up, I sometimes had flashes of memories, and each time, my parents explained it away as inconsequential, when really, it was very important."

"Maybe they had reasons, *sivamet*. Do not judge them harshly when you do not yet have all the facts."

"It isn't happening to you. Your entire life isn't being ripped apart." She flashed him one smoldering look over her shoulder and turned away again. "And then you come along and add to it all by claiming me, by binding us together in a ritual I don't have a choice in. And now I'm becoming something else. How do you think you would feel if it was happening to you?"

"I don't know, but is becoming a Carpathian so terrible?" He swept a hand through his hair, wishing he had his entire memory back. "You will be able to do so many things that you cannot do now. You will see, in time, that there is no reason to worry." Her life as his lifemate would be perfect. He would make it perfect. "It seems unreasonable to be upset over something you cannot change."

His voice was so calm it set her teeth on edge. He spoke as if they were having a philosophical discussion, not contemplating irreversible and dramatic changes to her life. Fury burned through her. "Reasonable? I shouldn't worry about being forced out of my own body? You're taking me over, telling me what I have to do, and I should just go along with it because you say so. How nice for you to live in your comfortable skin and know who and what you are. Claiming me doesn't change your life at all, does it?"

"It changes everything." His voice was gentle with emotion— emotion he could feel because she'd given him that gift.

He didn't understand the enormity of what he had done by binding them together. He didn't seem to even understand how her life would be affected. She would have to watch her family die. She would no longer be the person she'd always been. Even the chemistry of her body would be different. Everything about her would change, and she had no choice in the matter. Manolito would remain the man he'd always been, only he would have color and emotion restored to him. He might think it would all come right in time, but the change wasn't happening to him.

Adrenaline pumped through her body and with it—fury. How could someone else arbitrarily decide her life for her without her consent? Without asking her? Manolito. Her parents. Even her beloved grandparents. How could they just decide what was best for her and not only leave her out of the decisions, but even withhold knowledge?

She leapt up before Manolito had an inkling she was going to move. There was no slight movement of her body to indicate a shift. She simply moved all at once, leaping to her feet and over the railing before he knew what she intended. Heart in his throat, he leapt after her. They were one hundred and fifty feet in the air. The fall would kill her.

MaryAnn! He called her name even as he pursued, sending air to keep her floating as he streaked downward, but she was already on the ground, crouched low in a fighter's stance.

He slowed his descent to study her. Her hair was thick, long and wavy, gleaming a blue black as it cascaded down her shoulders and back. Her hands curled into claws, and the amazing bone structure in her face stood out beneath her taut skin. She backed away from him as he settled in front of her.

"I want to go home."

He knew she was in good hands—his hands—yet her voice trembled and she looked so frightened he felt terrible.

"I know you do, MaryAnn. I will get you back to your home as soon as I can." And he realized it was true. For the first time, he realized she might need Seattle. She might need that cold, rainy city just as much as he needed the rain forest. "I promise, *csitri*, when I can fully leave the land of shadows, I will escort you home."

MaryAnn drew a deep, shuddering breath. "You promise?"

"Absolutely. I give you my word, and I have never broken it in all my centuries of existence." He held out his hand to her. "I am sorry I cannot understand what you are going through." If she opened her mind to his, he could feel her emotions, not just visibly see them, but she held tight to her resistance.

MaryAnn looked around her. "I don't know how I got here." She looked up at the top of the canopy. She couldn't even see the deck he had constructed. "How did I do that, Manolito?"

He kept his hand extended to her. The leaves were rustling around them. Shadows moved. He took a step closer to her. MaryAnn put her hand in his, and he pulled her into his arms and took to the air, taking them to the protection of the deck he'd woven. She stood on the platform, her arms around his neck, her face buried against his shoulder, trembling with the truth.

"The truth," he murmured softly.

MaryAnn jerked away from him. She knew it was the truth. She had been that infant someone had hunted through a forest and nearly killed. Her parents had hidden the truth from her for years. The foundation of her solid world was shaken, and she needed to find a way to quiet the growing thing inside of her so she could come to terms with what was happening, but she didn't want Manolito to throw the truth of her life in her face.

Manolito looked around at the various leaves. Some broad, some lacy, some small and others large, all a dull silver instead of gleaming as they should. The safeguards were in place, keeping out all enemies so he could spend time with her, trying to ease her into his world. He had intended to bring her fully over so she, too, was wholly *Karpatii*. Instead, he had forced her to bare her soul to his, to risk everything for him. Now he needed to give something back. Something of equal value. She had given him truth; he could do no less.

He paced restlessly across the small confines of space. "You gave me truth, MaryAnn, when it cost you. I have something to tell you. Something that shames me, and not just me, my entire family. What is inside you is noble and strong, and I doubt you need fear it. I have no such secret to share with you, although I wish it were so."

She blinked away tears and looked at him, somewhat shocked. He appeared nervous. It was the last thing she expected of a man as confident as Manolito. Her natural compassion rushed through her, and she put her hand on his arm, flooding him with warmth and encouragement.

"Do not aid me in this," he protested, shaking his head, but once again she had opened her mind to his, surrounding him with the brilliant colors and her soothing personality. "I do not deserve it."

He didn't deserve to be so smug about claiming her, but she pushed that sudden thought down and gave him a look of support. Manolito continued to pace, so she sank down onto the flowers, surprised that once again they released their fragrance, filling the air with soothing scent. Drawing up her knees, she wrapped her arms around them and rested her chin on top, waiting for him to continue.

Manolito took a slow, careful look around and wove more safeguards, this time enclosing them within a sound barrier to give them even more privacy. "Sometimes the forest has ears."

She nodded, not interrupting, but somewhere in the pit of her stomach she was beginning to believe that what he was going to tell her was of monumental importance to both of them.

Manolito rested his elbows on the railing and looked down at the forest floor beneath them. "My family was always a little different from most of the other warriors around us. For one thing, most families never have children within fifty to a hundred years of one another. Of course it happens, but rarely. My parents had all five of us with no more than fifteen years separating us, other than Zacarias. He's nearly a hundred years older, but we were raised together."

She could instantly see the problems that might go along with such closeness, particularly young boys feeling the first taste of power. "You had a gang mentality."

There was a small silence while he absorbed that. "I suppose that could be so. We were above average in intelligence and we all knew it; we heard it enough times from our father as well as the other men. We were fast and learned quickly, and we heard that, too, as well as it being drilled into us what our duty was to be."

MaryAnn frowned. She'd never thought about Manolito or his brothers being children, growing up in uncertain times. "Even then, were more males being born than females?"

He nodded. "The prince was concerned and we all knew it. So many children died. The women were beginning to have to go aboveground to give birth, and some children could not tolerate the ground in infancy; others could. Changes were happening, and the tension grew. We were trained as warriors but given as much schooling as possible in all the other arts. Resentment began to grow in us when others, not quite as intelligent, were given chances at higher learning while we had to hone our fighting skills on the battlefield."

"Do you believe, looking back, that you had reason for that resentment?" she asked.

He shrugged, his powerful shoulders rolling, the muscles in his back rippling. "Maybe. Yes. At the time we did. Now, as a warrior and seeing what has happened to our people, certainly the prince needed us to fight. The vampires were growing in numbers, and to protect our species as well as the others, our fighting skills were needed perhaps more than our brains."

He sighed as he looked down from the treetops. "When we first came here, you have to remember, there were few, almost no, people at all. We were alone, only occasionally pitting our skills against an enemy. Five of us with our emotions growing dim and the memory of our people and our homeland fading along with the colors around us. We thought that was bad. And then we began to face more and more old friends who had turned. Our lives as we had known them as Carpathians were long gone."

MaryAnn's teeth bit at her lower lip. "Did your prince give you a choice to leave the Carpathian Mountains? Or did he just send you?"

"We were given a choice. All warriors were told of what was to come and how we were needed. We could have stayed, but honor would never have allowed that. Our family was considered as having among the best fighting skills."

"But you could have," she said, persisting. "Your fighting skills must have been needed there as well."

"Considering what happened, yes," Manolito agreed.

For the first time he tasted bitterness on his tongue. They had agreed to go when the prince had put out the call to his oldest warriors, thinking, believing, the prince knew the future, knew what was best for his people. When the ranks thinned and their enemies moved in, the prince had aligned himself with humans. All had been lost when they had tried to protect their human allies.

Centuries later, now, when he could once again feel, he was still angry over that decision, still disagreeing and not understanding how Vlad could have made such a mistake. Had sentiment overruled reason? If so, no De La Cruz would ever make such a mistake.

"You're angry," she said, feeling the waves of his antagonism washing over her.

He turned around to lean his hip against the railing. "Yes. I had no idea I was angry with him, but yes, I am. After hundreds of years, I still blame the prince for going into a battle they couldn't win."

"You know that wasn't what decimated your people," she pointed out as gently as possible. "You said yourself, as young as you were, growing up, you noticed the lack of women, and babies weren't surviving then. The changes were already happening."

"No one wants to think their species is slated by nature, or by God, for extinction."

"Is that what you think?"

"I do not know what I think, only what I would have done. And I would not have taken our people into that battle."

"How would the outcome have been any different?"

"Vlad would still be alive," Manolito said. "He would not be among the fallen. We would not be left adrift—with so few women and children, the sheer odds make it impossible to keep our people alive. Add to that our enemies, and we are lost."

"If you believe that, why did you save Mikhail's life? I heard about it, of course. Everyone was talking about what you did for him in the caves when he was attacked. If you don't believe he's capable of leading the Carpathian people, why risk your life for his? Why die for him? Especially if you had already seen me and knew you had a lifemate. Why would you bother?"

He folded his arms across his chest and looked down at her from his superior height, a frown on his face. "It is my duty."

"Manolito, that is ridiculous. You aren't a man to blindly follow someone you don't believe in. You may have questioned your prince's decision, but you believed in him, and you must believe in his son or you would never have gone into battle with him, pledged your allegiance to him or given your life for his."

"I did much more than question my prince's decisions," he said.

She watched the shifting of shadows across his face, the flicker of torment in the depths of his eyes. Now they were getting somewhere. Now he was going to reveal his deepest guilt. She knew what he was going to say before he said it, because his mind was deeply merged with hers and she could see the guilt there, the fear that he had betrayed a prince he admired, deeply respected and even loved.

He didn't see it that way, and that fascinated her. He didn't realize how much he admired Vlad Dubrinsky and how upset he had been at the prince's ultimate defeat and death at the hands of their enemy. More importantly, he didn't realize that his anger was at himself, for going, for choosing to fight in a remote land for people who cared nothing for the Carpathians.

"I betrayed Vlad every time I sat down with my brothers and questioned his judgments and decisions. Riordan and I told you some of it earlier, but it was a very watered-down version of our talks. We made an art of it. Picking apart the prince's every command and examining it from every angle. We believed he should listen to us, that we knew more than he did."

"You were young, not yet grown and still able to feel emotion." She knew that much because his emotions then had been very strong. He had felt superior, both physically and intellectually, to many of the other fighters. His brothers had all been the same, and they enjoyed their debates on how best to serve their countrymen, how best to steer the Carpathian people through the perils of each new century. "Was it betrayal, Manolito, in your hearts and minds, when you debated, or was it merely trying to discuss ways to better the lives of your people?"

"It may have started that way." He pushed both hands through his hair. "I know we clearly saw the fate of our people when few others could see the future. We did not need to have precognition, only our brains, and it was irritating that others could not see what we saw."

"Did the prince listen? You must have gone to him."

"As head of our family, Zacarias did. Of course he listened. Vlad listened to everyone. He led us, but he always allowed the warriors to speak in counsel. We may have been young, but he respected us."

MaryAnn watched the raw emotions chase across his face. Manolito faced vampires and mages with poisoned knives stoically, his features stone, yet now he was upset, his past too close to the surface. She wanted him to understand that the boyhood memory wasn't one of betrayal. She sought the right words, the right feelings . . .

Do not! The command was sharp and pushed at the walls of her mind. "I do not deserve the warmth you send to me. Nor do I deserve the feelings you are trying to plant in my memories."

She blinked at him, shocked that he would think she would try to plant anything in anyone's mind.

"We came up with a plan, MaryAnn. In our arrogance and superiority, in our belief that we knew more than any other, we came up with a plan to not only destroy the Dubrinsky family, but all enemies of the Carpathian people. The Carpathians would rule all species. And the plan was not only brilliant and possible, but it is being used against our prince as we speak."

His voice broke on the last word, and he hung his head in shame.

14

MaryAnn took several breaths, unable to see into his mind. She didn't know if she had pulled away or if he had, but she could only stare at him in disbelief. Manolito De La Cruz was loyal to Mikhail Dubrinsky. She had seen his heroism. She could see the scar on his throat where he had nearly been killed. It took a great deal to kill a Carpathian, but someone had managed to do so while he had been protecting the prince. She would not believe even for one moment that he was involved in a plot to destroy the Dubrinsky family.

"I don't understand your thinking, Manolito. My friends and I talk politics all day and we often don't agree with our government, but that doesn't mean we are traitors to our country or people."

Enclosed as she was inside the bubble preventing sound from escaping, MaryAnn couldn't hear the birds or insects. The silence seemed deafening. His misery was overwhelming. It was strange that she couldn't read his mind, yet she could feel his emotions, so strong and deep. The shame. The anger. The guilt. Even a sense of betrayal.

"Tell me." She made it a command this time. If she was his lifemate as he claimed, then he needed to share this with her. It was eating him alive, and she began to realize, as she watched him stare down at his hands in a kind of wonder, that at that moment, he was more in the realm of the other world than with her.

She caught his hand and tugged until he sank beside her on the cushion of flowers. "Manolito. This is destroying you. You have to resolve it."

"How does one resolve betrayal?"

She tightened her fingers around his. "Did you set out to make a plan to overthrow your prince?"

"No!" His denial was instant and strong.

And the truth. She could hear the ring of honesty in his voice.

"Not my brothers and certainly not me. We were just talking, complaining perhaps, debating certainly. But that was all." He dropped his head into his hands and rubbed his temples as if they were aching. "I honestly do not know how we began to flesh out the details. I do not know how or why an actual plan to overthrow our prince began, but later, when we were angry, we spoke of it for real."

Ever since his brother Rafael had killed Kirja Malinov, he had tried to remember. All of his brothers had tried to remember. At first they sat quietly around a campfire debating the pros and cons of all decisions Vlad had made. "There was only one other family with children as close together as ours: the Malinovs. When our mother gave birth, so did theirs. We grew up together, my brothers and the Malinovs. We played together as children, fought together as men. The bond between our families was so close. We were different from other Carpathians. All of us. Maybe because we had been born close together. Most Carpathian children are born at least fifty years apart. Perhaps there is a reason for that."

"Different in what way?"

He shook his head. "Darker. Faster. Stronger. The ability to learn to kill came too fast, long before we were out of our normal childhood. We were rebellious." He sighed and leaned over to rub his chin in the wealth of her hair, needing the feeling of closeness. "The Malinov brothers were lucky. There was a beautiful female child born to their family about fifty years after Maxim—the youngest boy—was born. Unfortunately, their mother did not survive long after the birth and their father followed her into the next world. The ten of us became her parents."

She felt the sorrow in him, sorrow that hadn't dimmed through the centuries in spite of the intervening years when he could no longer feel emotion. It was still there, eating at him, tightening his chest, roiling in his gut, choking him until he could barely breathe with it. She saw a child, tall, gleaming black hair, straight and thick, flowing like water down to a small waist. Huge, bright eyes, emeralds shining from a sweet face. A mouth made for laughter, nobility in every line of her body.

"Ivory." Manolito whispered her name. "She was as much ours as theirs. She was bright and happy and caught on to everything so fast. She could fight like a warrior, yet use her brain. There wasn't a student that could outthink her."

"What happened to her?" Because that, after all, was what had led up to the bitterness she often sensed in Manolito's mixed emotions toward his prince.

"She wanted to go to the school of mages. She was certainly qualified. She was bright enough and could weave magic that few could break. But we, all of us, her brothers and my brothers, didn't allow her to go unescorted anywhere. She was a young woman and chafed under ten brothers telling her what to do. It didn't matter to us; we wanted to see her safe. We should have seen her safe. She was the beauty that we were fighting for, striving to protect. Her laughter was so contagious that even the hunters who'd long ago lost their emotions had to smile when she was around."

He pressed her hand to his heart so hard she could feel it pounding in her palm. "We forbade her to go to the school and study with the mages until we could go with her and see to her protection. Everyone knew our wishes and should never have interfered. But, while we were away at a battle, she took her plea to the prince."

A shudder went through his body. He actually rocked his frame just once for comfort, but MaryAnn felt it and knew that the bite of sorrow was deeper than most would have conceived. Time certainly hadn't healed the wound. She wondered if the loss of emotion all those years kept the pain fresh, so that when the males could feel again, even past emotions were enhanced and vividly alive to them.

"The prince had no right to usurp our authority, but he did. Even knowing we had forbidden it, he told her she could go." His voice trailed off to a whisper, and he pressed her hand harder against his chest, as if to ease the terrible ache there.

"Why would he do that?"

"We believed that his oldest son, one we do not name, was already showing signs of illness. The Dubrinsky line holds the capacity for vast power, but with that comes the need for a vaster power to control it. Madness reigns if discipline does not. Vlad's eldest son had been looking at Ivory, though he was not her lifemate. We would have slain him had he touched her.

The tension was becoming palpable every time he returned to our village. I myself pulled my blade on two occasions when he had cornered her near the market. It was strictly forbidden to touch a woman who was not your lifemate, yet there was no question it was in his mind to do so, given the opportunity."

"I thought Carpathian men didn't ever look at women other than their lifemates."

"When they are young, some do, and there is an illness in others, a need for power over the opposite sex, that taints them. It is a type of madness that often takes the very powerful. Our species is not without its anomalies, MaryAnn."

"Why wasn't he stopped?"

"I do not think many wanted to believe a son of the prince could have the sickness in his veins, but we knew it. Zacarias, my oldest brother, and Ruslan, the eldest Malinov, went to Vlad and told him of the danger to Ivory. The prince sent his son away, and there was peace for some time. Vlad's son was returning, and when Ivory asked for permission to attend the school, it was an easy way for Vlad to get rid of an immediate problem. He thought, without her there, his son would be okay."

He ran his hand through his hair. "In truth, he knew better. Vlad should have come to terms with his son's illness and given the order to kill him. Without Ivory there, he had more time to study the matter and perhaps find a different resolution."

"So he allowed her to go."

"Yes. He sent her away without one of us to protect her. He neglected to send word to us, either, because he knew we would return at once."

She shifted, circling her arms around him to hold him close. "What happened?"

For one moment he dropped his head onto her shoulder, nuzzling his face against the warmth of her skin. He was cold and couldn't seem to get warm. With a small sigh of resignation, he forced his head up, forced himself to look her in the eye. "You are my lifemate. Destiny decreed what is between us. I am many things, MaryAnn, and know myself well. I will not let you go. You will have to learn to live with my sins, and I owe it to you to tell you the worst of it."

She kept her gaze fixed on his, reading more sorrow than betrayal. His love for Ivory had been strong, as had, she suspected, the others' in both families. With so few women, such strong, protective males would have felt it was their duty and pleasure to protect and serve that one small child. To fail must have been intolerable.

"When word came that a vampire had attacked and killed her, we were all devastated. Worse, we were in a killing rage. Ruslan and Zacarias for the first time were not the cool heads they always had been. They wanted to slay the prince. We all did. We blamed him for countermanding our orders and ultimately causing Ivory's death." Manolito slowly shook his head. "We could not find her body to even try retrieval from the shadow world, although any and all of us would have gladly followed her to make the attempt."

MaryAnn's heart jumped. The shadow world, land of mists, the place where the Carpathians went after death. Where Manolito still partially dwelled. "How can you follow someone to such a place?"

His gaze flickered. "Rumor was, only the greatest warriors or healers attempt such a feat, or a loved one—a lifemate—but any of us would have gladly gone. And obviously it can be done. Gregori did it and then you."

She hadn't realized what she was doing when she'd stepped into that other world. At times she still didn't want to believe it was real. "I didn't know what I was doing."

"Apparently it is dangerous to one who is not yet dead."

She sent him a small, reluctant smile. "Maybe it was a good thing I didn't know that. But none of you could follow her path, because you didn't have her body."

"If the spirit leaves the body, the body must be guarded until the spirit returns and enters it; otherwise our enemies can trap us in the other world for all time." He shrugged his shoulders. "Suffice it to say, only the dead go there. The reason must be great for a living person to attempt it."

"That's what Gregori and your brothers did, then. They followed you into the land of mists and shadows and brought your spirit back," MaryAnn reiterated, wanting to understand. He was still partially there. If that was so, she had to find a way to bring him wholly into their world again. This was far beyond her realm of expertise.

"Yes, but we did not have that chance with Ivory. She was lost to us for all time, and we seriously began to question Vlad Dubrinsky's judgment. He had no right to interfere in family matters. It made no sense to us. If his son was mad and he did nothing, was it possible the madness was in him as well? The more we'd discussed what he'd done, the stronger our anger became. We began to think of ways to end his rule. One step led to the next. We realized the other species who were allied with us might fight with Dubrinsky to keep him as ruler, and the Carpathian people would be divided, so we figured out how to get rid of everyone else. The jaguar-men never stayed with their women. The women already were mating with humans and choosing to stay in that form. It wouldn't be difficult to turn the remaining women against their men and to capitalize on the brutality of the animal form."

"Which is what eventually happened."

He nodded. "Worse, MaryAnn, there is no hope of saving the jaguar race. Even if ten couples survived, it is too few to save them."

"Evolution may have played a larger part ·than you think. Because you spoke of a plan, one, by the way, you reasoned out intellectually by observing what was already happening, doesn't mean you had the responsibility of the destruction of the species. You aren't a god."

"No, but we did nothing to aid the jaguar in seeing their own destruction. We left them alone, and while we did, the Malinov brothers implemented the plan and helped to push the jaguars to their own extinction. If they have done that, what other parts of the plan have they begun?"

MaryAnn waited, watching the shadows chase across his face, watching him flex his fingers as though they were aching. There was a new note in his voice, the soft rumble of a growl, every bit as sexy as his hypnotic velvet voice, maybe more so. The notes played over her skin, making her feel edgy.

"The humans fear Carpathians because they fear vampires. The legends had to come from somewhere. Whispers and rumors of killings and the loathing and fear grew until the Carpathians were no longer allies of humans. We are now hunted and killed. And with the werewolf, the one ally that we knew had the power to stop us, it would be easy enough to do the same thing, to drive a wedge between the species, divide and conquer. The werewolves were elusive anyway, and driving them underground or secretly stamping them out by arranging killings would slowly dwindle their ranks as well. Eventually someone would have to step into the seat of power to clean up the mess."

MaryAnn drew back, her breath coming in a ragged gasp. "You didn't do those things, did you?" The masculine scent of him was in her lungs, surrounding her with every breath she drew. Maybe it was the sound barrier he'd erected, but she couldn't stop the thrill of drawing his essence into her body, or the way her muscles clenched and her blood sang just being near him.

She wanted to react with the objectivity of a counselor. It was second nature to her, but something else, something wild, was building so that she watched the rise and fall of his chest, the tiny shift in his expression, the crinkle of the lines around his eyes, the shape of his molded mouth and wanted—no, *needed*—to offer comfort without words.

"No, of course we didn't. We knew what we were doing was wrong. When the grief subsided and we could see reason, we knew it wasn't Vlad's fault any more than it was ours that she was dead. We stopped talking about it and threw ourselves into the hunt for the undead. We became fiends, so much so that all of us lost our emotions much faster than we should have. We made a pact to protect each other, to share what we could of our memories of affection and honor, and we have done so. When our prince put out the call to go to other lands, we answered. The Malinovs did the same. We were sent here, to South America, and they were sent to Asia."

She leaned in close to inhale more of him, all the while lending him soothing warmth and trying to suppress the rising tide of need. What was so different about him? His confession of wrongdoing? Had that made her more sympathetic to him? Or the fact that he still mourned that lost little "sister"?

She had been angry with him for thrusting her into his life without her consent, for removing her choices, and for not understanding the enormity of what he had done, but she couldn't help the strength of her emotion for him in trying to understand. For trusting her with his greatest shame. And she knew that was what he had gifted her with.

When he reached out to push a strand of hair from her face, his fingers brushing across her sensitive skin, she shivered.

"The Malinov brothers came to us before we left and wanted to talk." His voice roughened, and the sound scraped over raw nerve endings, a seduction she hadn't thought possible. He bent his head, pushing her hair from her shoulder, and his tongue touched her pulse. "They wanted us to renounce the prince."

Tiny flames danced along her neck and throat, edging down toward her breasts. Her nipples peaked beneath the thin top, and her body felt soft and pliable and so achy she burrowed closer to him. "But you didn't." She was positive. She knew he respected Vlad Dubrinsky in spite of the terrible tragedy.

"No, we did not. We could not." His voice held absolute conviction. "And at that time, neither did the Malinovs. They swore allegiance to him."

And she loved him for that. For knowing right from wrong. For having such strong loyalties even when he loved the Malinov brothers so much. They had been his family, yet he had known, all of his brothers had known, that to turn on the prince was to turn on their people.

"No, of course you wouldn't." She ran her hand up and down his arm, feeling the definition of his muscles beneath her palm. So hard. She closed her eyes, briefly wanting to feel him skin-to-skin. She wanted to seduce him, to take him into her body and fill the emptiness she felt inside of him.

His eyes came alive with such stormy turbulence that her heart jumped. The dark black irises glowed amber—almost gold, taking her breath away. That wildness in her, that place she never wanted to acknowledge, leapt forward in recognition, and she leaned close before she could think, before she could stop herself, brushing his mouth with hers, breathing for him, taking the adrenaline into her own body. Taking his need. Taking his desires. Taking him.

He kissed her back, his tongue sliding into the silken heat of her mouth. Every nerve ending leapt to life. Whatever anger he still held toward his prince, toward himself or even toward the Malinovs slid away, leaving his blood pounding for her.

His arms went around her, and he pulled her even closer, body to body, his mouth on hers, his pulse thundering in her ears. They were merged, mind to mind, and she felt the sudden shift in him, the way every cell recognized her, wanted her, *needed* her. His teeth tugged at her lip, nipped and teased and demanded. Heat flared, driving away the cold of his skin, pushing out the shadows and sorrow of old memories until there was only this—the ultimate feeling. Sheer bliss.

"I want to feel your skin against mine," he whispered. His hand was already sliding up her leg, along her calf, up her thigh, inside where she ached and craved and needed him. Where she offered him a refuge and haven. His knuckles moved in small circles against her damp core while his mouth ravaged hers.

Around him, the world dropped away. Both worlds. Shadows receded until there was only the bed of flowers and the fragrance and scent of man and woman calling to each other. He brought both hands up to hold her in his arms, hold her against him, one hand cupping the back of her head as he lowered her to the cradling vines. He wasn't wild this time, didn't want to be. He took great care, slow and easy, wanting to taste every inch of her, wanting to take them both on a silken journey of pure sensation.

She reached up to push back his fall of silky hair, so long and luxurious, thick, thicker even than she remembered. His hair had been beautiful, but now, maybe because every sensation seemed so much more to her, his hair seemed longer, a thick pelt she wanted to stroke and caress and bury her face in. More than anything, she wanted to comfort him, make him feel whole and alive and so much better.

Her hand shaped the nape of his neck and she lifted her mouth to his. His kiss matched the lazy, slow movement of his hands as they slid beneath her top to cup her breasts. His thumbs teased and flicked, with that same languorous pace, creating pinpoints of flame that radiated from her breasts to her belly to melt into a pool of molten liquid between her legs. Her body was instantly slick and hot and already eager for his.

She loved his mouth. The feel and shape of it. The way it was so hot and commanding. No matter how gentle he began, within moments his mouth took over hers, drugging her with kisses, sending flames spinning into a vortex of need. His hands slid over her skin, leaving her writhing for more, so gentle, so patient, that it shocked her when he suddenly tore her blouse open, sending buttons scattering everywhere, lowered his head and covered her breast with his hot, greedy mouth.

She arched into him, cradling his head, stroking his hair, whispering encouragement, asking for more.

Manolito lifted his head to look down at her. She was so beautiful, offering herself up to him to make the past all better. If anyone could do it, she could. He was aroused beyond anything he'd ever thought possible. Whether she knew it or not, she was in his mind, heightening his needs, showing him her eagerness to please him in any way he wanted—or needed. She was his own personal playground, but this time, his lust was wrapped in love. He knew it absolutely. There was no way not to love her when she gave him everything without reservation, when she had the courage to hand her body over to a man as dominant as he.

He dragged the skirt from her body, rid himself of his too-heavy clothes and knelt over her, staring down at her full, ripe breasts. Her nipples were hard and eager. Her legs were slightly spread, so he could see the slick, wet invitation of her body calling to his. With a small growl rumbling in the back of his throat, he lowered his head once again to hers. She opened her mouth to him, accepting the hard spearing of his tongue. His teeth tugged at her lower lip, bit at the soft bow as his tongue teased and thrust. Beneath him, her skin heated to a smooth, sensitized silk, so that every time he rubbed his body over hers, she shivered and trembled with eagerness.

Her hands dropped to his shoulders, nails digging into his flesh, trying to hold on, as he deepened the kisses, rough now, demanding, making each one hotter and more addicting than the last. She was drowning, with no way to surface, his hands hard and hot on her body, his tongue capturing hers over and over, drawing it into his own mouth, his lips taking control in the way his hands did.

His palms slid possessively over her breasts, fingers tugging at her nipples. Arrows of flames streaked down her belly and darted between her thighs. She moaned softly, the sound vibrating down his spine and around to his groin, to hum through his erection. He wedged his knee between her thighs, opening her further to him.

He blazed a trail of fire from her lips to her neck, to the pulse beating frantically there. His teeth nipped and his tongue swirled as he listened to the surge of blood pounding in her veins for him. It was music—sheer music, setting his own blood surging in answer. It was only MaryAnn who could do this for him—quiet every demon, set his soul soaring, bring poetry to his life in the midst of too much reality.

She began to ride his thigh with a helpless little cry, struggling to assuage the need growing in her. He could feel the gathering of inviting moisture against his bare skin where she rubbed restlessly, and it felt so sensuous he could barely hang on to his control.

He flicked her nipple with a quick, hard stroke, and she jumped beneath him, already so sensitized that when he covered her breast, drawing the creamy flesh into the fiery heat of his mouth, she arched her body more fully into him, her cries driving him further into a frenzy of desire.

Her heart was loud, pounding out a rhythm to match his. He made his way down her body, gliding over the silky surface until he could clamp his arms around her thighs and lift her to his greedy mouth. He had woken craving the taste of her, almost more than the hunger for blood. He covered her intriguing little slit with his mouth, tongue flicking and stroking her clit. Her first release was hard and fast, her muscles tightening until the sensitive nerve endings were on fire, but he didn't stop.

MaryAnn tried to push away from him, but his strength was too much. All she could do was thrash wildly beneath him in an effort to escape his wicked mouth, which only incited him more.

That's it, sivamet, *burn for me. Go up in flames. Scream. Become mine completely.*

His voice was a rough whisper in her mind. His mouth suckled as his tongue assaulted her. It was too much, too fast, her body too sensitive.

I can't. You're going to kill me. Maybe not kill, but certainly destroy everything she had been, remaking her into someone else, someone highly sexual, someone who would need his hands and mouth and body for eternity. It was frightening to be so out of control, to have her body taken over, to have endless sensations build and build relentlessly. The second climax rushed over her, and she screamed his name, a plea, either to stop or for more, she honestly didn't know.

No, ainaak enyem, *I am loving you the only way I know how. I am giving you everything I am and taking everything that you are.*

He heard the growls of pleasure rumbling in his throat, knew the sound vibrated through her sheath, just as it vibrated through him. Her womb spasmed. He tightened his hold and took more, demanded more. This time he thrust his tongue hard and fast, pressing against her ultrasensitive spot while he drew the sweet honey from her body, lust and love gripping him so strongly he shuddered with it. His marauding mouth flung her into a third orgasm. She let out a keening wail.

Manolito, please. Please, please do something. Anything.

He rose above her, his features harsh with lust, his eyes filled with love. The combination was almost her undoing. Her heart seemed to stop for a moment, then began to pound so hard her chest ached. He lifted her hips again, dragging her over the thick bed of flowers so he could rest her legs on his broad shoulders, the pulsing head of his cock lodged in her entrance.

She held her breath, everything inside her focused completely on that one burning spot. The knot of nerves throbbed in anticipation. He surged forward, the thick length of him driving through the tight, silken muscles already so inflamed and swollen that the friction threw her into an even harder climax that didn't seem to stop. He buried himself completely, feeling the velvet walls contract and squeeze, the rippling sensations so strong he groaned with the need for control.

There was none. There could be none. The scent and feel of her tight sheath surrounding him, milking him, drove him past all sanity, and he plunged into her over and over, pistoning long strokes into her, letting the fiery sensations take him completely.

Manolito. There was fear in her voice. In her mind. She clutched at his shoulders, nails biting deep, head thrashing back and forth as she lifted her hips to meet his sensual assault.

You are safe, sivamet. *I've got you safe. Relax for me. Let me take you riding the clouds with me.*

He clenched his teeth, trying to hold on when every part of him wanted to let go, to explode into another dimension altogether. There was no longer shame or pain or other worlds around him or in him. There was only MaryAnn, his other half, and the sanctuary of pleasure she provided.

Let go, päläfertiil. *Fly with me.*

MaryAnn felt him then, in her head, sharing his body's pleasure, sharing her pleasure, so that their minds heightened the experience even more. Every deep stroke sent shock waves coursing through her, through him. Every thrust sent the lightning streaks racing through them. Sweat glistened on their skin as they reached together, each one wanting the other's ultimate pleasure.

He drove his cock deep, hard, into her pulsing, silken sheath.

She was strangling him, her muscles tight and swollen from the multiple orgasms, sending fire streaking through his body. Impossibly, he felt his erection grow, locking down inside of her as his balls drew up and hot seed jetted into her depths. Pulse after pulse while her body shuddered with the power of the eruption, pleasure consuming him, shaking him.

Beneath him, she screamed, her release tearing through her, her eyes glazing over, her face stretched taut with shock, the orgasm almost too intense to bear. The leaves above her head glittered like silver stars, and the edges of her vision narrowed until she could only see him. His shoulders and chest blocked out the world around them as he began to lean forward with infinite slowness over the top of her.

Manolito allowed his incisors to lengthen. His body was still hard, still locked in her body. The movement of his body pressed the thick hard length of him against her most sensitive spot. She shook. He let her see it coming, wanted her to know what he was doing. "Be still," he whispered when he felt her tremble, when he saw her eyes widen in what might have been fear. "I would never harm you, MaryAnn."

His teeth sank deep right in the same place he had marked the swell of her breast. She cried out as the pain gave way to another erotic shift. Her body pulsed and wept around his, tightening with exquisite rhythm. She wrapped her arms around him as he took her blood, holding his head to her, giving him everything she was.

When he finally lapped his tongue across the spot, closing the wound, he kissed her gently. Strangely, he had the desire to bite her again, to sink his teeth in the hollow of her shoulder and lap at the sweet-tasting liquid of life. Resisting, he slowly withdrew from her, savoring the feel of her sheath reluctantly giving him up. He rolled over, pulling her on top of him so that she was lying stretched across him like a blanket.

He lay beneath her, feeling the imprint of her body over his, the soft mounds of her breasts, her nipples pressing into his chest. She was soft, wet flesh, silky smooth with her lush curves. He could feel her heart beating, feel the heat between her legs, hear the sound of her blood rushing hotly in her veins. Her fingers settled in his hair. She was perfect. The moment was perfect.

"I dreamt of you last night," she murmured, lifting her face to nuzzle his throat. Her tongue teased his pulse point, her teeth nipping at his skin. "I dreamt of your body in mine and screaming your name. It was such a beautiful dream for a while." She licked at his skin again, her tongue lingering on that small spot. "But then the wolves came . . ." She trailed off and kissed his throat, pressing her lips to that spot, wanting more, much more, hungry for the taste of him. Her jaw ached with the need, her teeth feeling longer and sharper as her tongue slid over the edges. She nuzzled his shoulder, nipped again.

Beneath her, Manolito went still. His hands settled around her arms like vises, and he jerked her up. His black eyes held such danger, such menace, she turned, searching the canopies of the trees for a reason. His stillness brought her attention back to him.

"What?"

Very slowly he put her from him and sat up, shoving his hands through the wealth of black hair. His gaze went back to her, cold and hard and utterly menacing. His mind was gone from hers, leaving her shivering, rubbing her hands up and down her arms.

"Manolito, what is it?"

"I dreamt of you last night," he said softly in a tone that raised goose bumps up and down her flesh. "I dreamt of my body buried deep in yours, of things I did to you and you crying out with pleasure. And then the wolves came . . ." Just as she had done, he trailed off.

She sat up as he had done, drew up her knees, wishing she could don clothes as easily as he was doing now. "Sharing a dream bothers you? Why? Don't you think it can happen, especially as we're so connected?"

"Carpathians do not dream." He pulled his hair back and secured it with a leather tie. "We sleep the sleep of the dead. Our hearts and lungs shut down to rejuvenate. Our brains do the same. We cannot dream."

She wasn't certain what he was telling her, but her mouth went dry and her heart picked up a harder, faster rhythm. "You probably dreamt it as you awakened, or went to sleep."

"How do you explain my tolerance to the sun? I have been unable to walk in the early morning light for centuries. Even with clouds and severe storms, the sun hurt my eyes, and my body grew leaden. Yet I stayed with you until almost noon. Explain that to me." His voice was low and harsh, whipping at her with some unspoken accusation. "I rose with the sun out, yet my skin did not burn or blister."

"How can I explain such a thing? I know little of Carpathians and lifemates. Perhaps once you have your lifemate, that too is restored to you." She dragged her blouse to her and slid it on. "You ruined the buttons."

Impatient, he waved his hand, and she found herself, not in her own clothes, but a cotton T-shirt and jeans. *Jeans.* Not the dress he'd asked her to wear for him, but the trousers he didn't like. She swallowed fear, trying not to cry as she began to braid the long, thick mane of hair, needing something to do to escape his cold gaze. They'd just shared something few, if any, would ever experience in a lifetime, and he was rejecting her, pushing her away. It felt like a slap in the face.

"You were going to bite me," he said. "I saw it in your mind."

She pushed back away from him until her back was against the railing. "Was I? I wanted to, yes. But then, I saw that you intended the same. You took my blood and wanted me to take yours. You wanted to bring me fully into your world, and you wouldn't have asked me. You were going to make the decision without my consent."

"You are my lifemate. I do not need your consent." There was dark emotion flickering in his eyes. Little amber lights began to glitter through the pure black obsidian.

Anger pulsed through her. "You know what? I don't need your consent to leave, and I'm going back to the house." She stood up, and her hands gripped the rail when he stood up, too. He towered over her, looking every inch a predator.

"Actually, you do need my permission. And you will stay here and hear what I have to say. I want to know the truth, MaryAnn."

She narrowed her gaze on him. "You wouldn't know the truth if it bit you in the butt."

"You did bite me. And I took your blood on several occasions."

She tilted her head at him. "Is that my fault? I didn't ask you to. In fact I didn't even know the first time you did it."

"What are you?"

"A very pissed-off woman."

He stepped closer to her, so close she could feel the heat of his anger. "You are werewolf. And you are infecting me with your blood."

15

MaryAnn stared at him for several long seconds, and then she began to laugh. "You are totally crazy."

Manolito didn't look in the least amused. If anything, his expression hardened even more. "I am not crazy. I smell the wolf in you, and if you are honest with yourself, you can smell it all over me."

She shook her head, but the laughter faded. "This is insane. I know Carpathians are shapeshifters. I'm not. I've lived my entire life as a human being. My parents aren't werewolves. I doubt such a thing exists."

"Why would you doubt it when you have seen jaguar-men and vampires? When you know the Carpathian people exist? Why should you have trouble believing in werewolves?"

Perspiration beaded on his forehead. Carpathians sweated blood, she noted. He brushed at his temples.

"Then where are they? And if they really exist, and I'm one of them, why didn't you recognize it sooner?" The sweating blood thing was eww, and she so wasn't becoming Carpathian. She'd much rather be a wolf!

"Because I have not seen or heard of the lycans for centuries."

She put her hands on her hips. "So let me get this straight. You were all in love with me and ready to turn me into a Carpathian when you thought I was human, but now it's different because I might be turning you into something else." She raised her chin another inch in challenge. "What you mean is, it's perfectly okay for me to give up who and what I am, but not so much for you."

He frowned at her. "I was born to be Carpathian. It is who and what I am."

She pressed a hand to her churning stomach. "You hypocritical male chauvinist, Neanderthal, asinine idiot. I must have been out of my mind to think I could live with someone like you."

He waved her opinion of him aside. "We are lifemates. Of course I will do whatever is necessary to complete the conversion and bring you to my side completely, but I have to study this problem from every angle. I have never heard of a werewolf and a Carpathian mating. The blood of the wolf is as powerful as the blood of the Carpathian."

"I don't shapeshift."

"The wolf lives within you, part of you. It is not the same way I take another form. The wolf is your guardian and will emerge when needed. You have felt him close to you. That is why you have flashes of memory. And it is why both of us can take the early morning sunlight. Only my eyes were affected by the sunlight, not my entire body. You have not burned in the sun in spite of the fact that my blood flows in your veins. The change should have already begun to take hold."

"And you think I've known all along and somehow have tricked you? If there is a wolf in me, now is the time for it to come leaping out. I just might go for your throat." Furious, she shoved at his chest to move him out of her way. "You should hear yourself. Do you really think I'd want to spend the rest of my life with a man who has no regard for my feelings?"

"I have every regard for your feelings."

"Right! Which is why you accused me of 'infecting,'" she spat the word in a fury, "you! Like what I am is some taint. Some disease. You know what, Manolito De La Cruz? You deserve to be stuck in hell. And I'm an idiot for even thinking a relationship with you could be anything more meaningful than hot sex."

She went to the edge of the deck and, gripping the rail, looked down. She'd jumped once, but now it seemed a very long way. The thing inside her, the *wolf*, he suspected, stirred, recognizing her anger. She swallowed the sudden fear in her throat and turned back to him, her heart pounding hard enough for him to hear it. Her own head was beginning to hurt, a buzzing sound, like thousands of insects driving her crazy, reverberated through her mind. Her skull felt too tight, and her brain began to pulse and throb in time to the surge of blood rushing in her veins.

"You know." He made it a statement. "You were fully aware

of my taking your blood. You wanted to take mine. You wanted the taste of me in your mouth. Hot and sweet and bursting with life. That is not human behavior."

"You made me want that." It came out in a whisper. She pressed her hand to her churning stomach. Between rage and fear she should have found some kind of balance, but all she felt was disoriented, swinging back and forth.

"I did not. I did not force your compliance. The call of the wolf was on you."

MaryAnn turned away from him, her heart pounding. Everything was making sense. It shouldn't be. She couldn't accept what he was saying. She didn't want a wolf inside of her. She didn't even know what that meant, or how it was possible. "Take me back." She didn't look at him, couldn't face him. She felt very alone. "I want to go back now." Feeling alone made her angry all over again. When he'd faced his worst moment, she had stood with him, but he rejected her. *Rejected her.*

"You have completely closed yourself off from me."

"You idiot!" She wanted to leap across the deck and smack his face. Was he really that obtuse? Taking a deep breath, she forced herself back under control. "Did you hear me? I asked you to take me back." Because she was going home. As fast as she could get back to Seattle, where life was normal and she didn't have wild cravings for idiot men from centuries gone past.

"MaryAnn, neither of us has a choice. We have to work this out."

Her chin came up, dark eyes glittering at him. "I have a choice. I refuse to have my life taken out of my hands. You *rejected* me when you thought I was changing you from being a precious Carpathian. As far as I'm concerned, you've forfeited every right to me as your lifemate. I asked you to take me home. And I was polite about it." She wasn't feeling so polite now. Her nails were digging into her palm. The buzzing in her head grew louder. Her mouth felt coated in copper.

"I did not reject you."

"Really? Well, as far as I'm concerned, you're a coward. You want me to take all the risks. You want me to become something unknown and frightening, and I have to accept it because fate somehow decreed we should be together. Well, I refuse to be with anyone who insists on me risking everything, but he won't risk anything at all. *Take me home now.*"

It was a command, a compulsion, and for the first time, she realized she had not just thought it—or said it. She had thrown the command into his mind, furious with his double standard. Furious with herself for letting him take her over. More frightened than she'd ever been in her life, because she suspected there was no turning back and that even if she made it home, whatever was inside of her would refuse to quiet.

She was psychic, just as they all had said. She had been using her ability all along, without being aware of it. She looked up at him, and her breath caught in her throat. He was looking down at her, black eyes glittering with menace. He was every bit as furious as she was, and much more frightening.

"I said no. You are not going anywhere."

She leapt at him, raking at his face with her long fingernails, missing him only by a scant breath as he grabbed her arms and gave her a hard shake. "Do you think to command me?" He shook her again. "Me? Your lifemate? You dare to try to influence my mind? To attack me?"

Who was she conspiring with to try to trap and kill him? She had deceived him. Even as the words slipped out, even as he entertained the idea that she would harm him, he rejected the thought.

What was he doing and thinking? Had he truly lost his mind? Was he the coward she called him? He had gone into battle with the vampire without flinching. No one had ever questioned his courage, yet he was bullying his lifemate when she needed love and reassurance. He was accusing her of things the innocence in her eyes, in her mind, belied.

Was this his true personality? Or was it some manifestation of the wolf mixing with his Carpathian blood? Both species were dominant. Both demanded instant obedience, the wolf perhaps more. Who knew what secrets that elusive society had kept? It was obvious they had gone underground and still existed, but he had no way to understand what was happening—the thick mane of hair, the increased sense of smell, acute hearing, the driving need to keep his mate beside him, his scent all over her.

He was angry with himself, not her. He should have recognized the wolf traits in her, been more prepared for the consequences of taking her blood. He had been consumed with her, so much so that when he woke he had needed to feel her body wrapped around his even more than he needed blood for sustenance. In all the centuries of his existence, that had never happened. She was in every thought he had, taking him over until he knew he couldn't survive without her. Worse, when her mind was withdrawn from his, the other world invaded and he was left in the gray shadows, wandering, trying to figure out a way to reconnect wholly his spirit and body.

He couldn't force her to accept him. He couldn't get into her mind and stay merged; nor could he persuade her of the consequences of keeping that mind merge from him. And as she had withdrawn from him, he could no longer sustain enough power to keep his spirit wholly in the land of the living. Around him, the colors faded until everything was dim and grayish, and when he looked at his hands, he could see through them. His brain felt as if it was bursting through his skull, his temples pounding with pain. Ordinarily he could shut off pain, but it was impossible. His tongue felt funny, thick and coated with copper.

MaryAnn struggled in his grip, opening her mouth with the intention of blasting him, so hurt she wanted to crawl in a hole and pull the earth over the top of her, so angry she thought she might take another swipe at his face with her too-sharp fingernails, but something about him caught her attention. She pushed down her own hurt feelings and forced her mind back to reason.

"Manolito, is your head hurting?"

He nodded, pressing against his temples hard. "I shouldn't experience pain like this. I do not understand." *Unless it is the wolf. Unless it is this woman, trying to pretend to be my lifemate when she is really a puppet of the vampire, bent on my destruction.*

She caught that and flinched, nearly backing out of his mind, afraid he would hurt her more with his insults, but then she caught a sound. A buzzing. Like a million insects, only much worse than what she was getting in her brain. Her breath caught in her throat. Instinct told her to pull back fast, but she forced calm. She was psychic. She had the ability to read minds. She'd been doing it for years; she just hadn't been aware she was doing it. There was nothing to be afraid of. She just had to figure out how she did it.

She let her breath out and reached for him, filling her thoughts with him, wanting him to feel better, wanting to take away his pain and see what—or who—was harming him. The buzzing grew stronger, louder, pushing at her brain, making her feel so sick she ran to the railing and leaned over it, but she held on, determined to push further. Voices. Soft. Insistent. Crawling up and down his mind. Slicing at his brain.

"Manolito." She caught his hand and held on tight. "We're under attack. *You're* under attack. I can hear them. They're trying to get you to kill me."

He didn't hesitate, his hand enveloping hers. "The undead. Maxim seeks to trap me from the other side." It all made sense now, and in a way it was a relief to know he wasn't crazy. He hadn't turned on his lifemate. It hadn't occurred to him that he would be vulnerable in the shadow land, but it should have. His body was alive, and part of his spirit had returned to that of the living, which meant the dead would be aware he didn't belong with them.

"How can he do that when he's dead?"

"Maxim's spirit still remains in the land of ghosts, and that is where my spirit is. He must be attacking me from within." He pulled her close to him. "I do not want your last memories of your lifemate to be those of rejection and anger. I cannot believe the way Maxim could reach an ancient as battle-savvy as I am supposed to be. I fell under his influence like an inexperienced fledgling." He brought her knuckles to his mouth. "Forgive me, MaryAnn. I would not have hurt you for the world. It is my privilege to protect you, yet at the first test, I have failed you."

"No you haven't," she said. "Just tell me how we're going to make him stop." Because whatever Maxim was doing, Manolito was suffering; she could see it in his eyes, feel it in his mind. "Tell me what to do."

"I have to enter wholly into that world, and my body will be vulnerable to attack. If they kill you, or they destroy my body, I am lost. They must have a plan."

She stuck her chin out. "I can go there with you. I'm pretty certain I know how."

He shook his head. "No. It is much too dangerous. I can travel in the shadow world, because my spirit was drawn there, but you are alive and you do not belong. They were aware of you the instant you entered. I think they can kill you there."

"I think he's killing you in that world right now."

"He will not kill me." He caught her chin in his hand. "Listen to me, MaryAnn. This is important. I was upset when I discovered that I was changing, becoming wolf, just as you are changing and becoming Carpathian, but not for the reasons you think. Not for the reasons I gave you. Whatever influence Maxim has on me, at this moment my thinking is clear. Other psychic women have successfully converted to Carpathian. It was a painful process, but they are healthy and happy and living lives they seem to embrace. I expected no less for you."

He bent down to brush a kiss on top of her head. "Discovering the wolf changes the equation. There is no precedent. We have no idea what could happen to you if I convert you. We have no idea the effect the wolf would have on me. I can tell I am more aggressive and dominant, and you indicated you already had a problem with me in that area. I do not want to take a chance with your life. Until we know more, we have to be careful. I could become dangerous. You could be killed. We just do not know."

MaryAnn leaned into him, needing to touch him, beginning to feel panic. There was something wrong with the way his eyes were focusing. "Stay with me," she whispered, clinging to his hand. "Stay with me, Manolito."

"I have to go back there. Whatever Maxim is doing is there in the meadow of mists and ghosts, *sivamet*. I cannot be in two places at one time and fight him."

"Then I'm going with you."

"You cannot. My body will still be here unprotected. I am sending a message to my brother to come at once to get you to safety. He will know what to do with my body." He cupped her face in his hands, thumbs sliding over her silky skin. "You are the most important person in my world, MaryAnn. I cannot risk you. Please do as I ask and wait here where you are protected for Riordan to come. I cannot worry about you and fight Maxim at the same time."

She stared up at his black, glittering eyes, realizing there was nothing she could do to stop him. He believed he had to protect her, and he would. He would die for her. He would kill for her. He would do anything for her. No matter the consequences to him, he would go where the vampire had all the advantages.

His smile was gentle, the pad of his thumb sliding over her lower lip. "What makes you think he has the advantage, *csitri*?"

"He's meaner than you, and much more cunning. And he's had time to plan."

His smile widened, until he looked wolfish. "I do not think you have to worry about who is meaner or more cunning. He has had time to plan, but he is counting on me trying to stay in this world. He will send others here. They will come, so do not leave until Riordan is here to escort you."

He was already fading, his spirit slipping back, away from her, away from the living world. MaryAnn tried to hold on to him, but there was no use. He was gone, and only his body remained, a shell, faded and drawn, no longer vital. There was enough spirit left for him to sink down, leaning his back against the railing, and then that, too, was gone and she heard his call.

Riordan. I have great need of you. MaryAnn is unprotected, and the vampire will send everyone he has to slay her. You must get to her.

The answering in his head sounded slurred and demonic. She could barely make out that he was speaking another language, one she didn't understand. Abruptly Manolito pulled away, confused. The voice was so distorted, he couldn't tell whether he was speaking with his brother or not.

MaryAnn took a deep breath and let it out. She could do this. She had successfully merged with Manolito when she had wanted to; she could do the same with Riordan. All she had to do was follow the original path Manolito had used.

Riordan. Her first attempt was hesitant, but she felt him stir and latch on to the path immediately.

MaryAnn. What is wrong with Manolito? Juliette and I are transporting Solange and Jasmine to the ranch. Neither is safe here. I can tell he is in trouble, but I cannot reach him.

She swallowed the surge of fear. *How long will it take you to get back here?* Her stomach did a hard roll, but she dug her fingernails into the railing and waited.

We are starting back now. If we take Jasmine and Solange home to the others, we cannot aid you in time. We're turning back, so hold on. Can you reach Manolito? Can you get to him and hold him to this world?

MaryAnn glanced at Manolito's body. If she went to find him in the shadow land, his body would be completely vulnerable. *I can go to him when you get here, and I know I can bring him back.* She put much more confidence in her voice than she actually felt. Accepting she was psychic and could talk telepathically wasn't easy. Her brain kept telling her she was crazy. *Hurry, Riordan. I don't think we have much time.*

The monkeys in the surrounding trees screamed a warning. Birds erupted into the sky, wings flapping hard, stirring the air so that she scented intruders. Jaguar. A human she believed to be mage. He had the taint she associated with vampire on him. And one other. Her heart thudded hard as her nose wrinkled. The wind carried the scent of decay. Vampire? She was not equipped to deal with a vampire.

MaryAnn rushed to the railing and peered down. Oh yeah. She was in deep, deep trouble. She could see the jaguar emerging from the forest of ferns along the embankment. His fur was dark with water, and as she looked down, he lifted his head and looked right at her. Their eyes met. He bared his teeth.

She ran her hand down her thigh. At least Manolito had provided her with a pair of designer jeans, one of her favorite. She could die looking good. She took a deep breath, considering her options. If she ran, they might follow her, but she doubted all three would, and that would leave Manolito's body vulnerable. They would certainly destroy it and with it—him.

You must leave, MaryAnn. The mage will unravel the safeguards, and you cannot face jaguar, mage and vampire. Go now.

Manolito's voice was far away and thin, his spirit in another realm.

I'm not leaving your body here for them. Riordan's coming.

You cannot wait too long. You cannot face a vampire alone.

She certainly didn't want to face one, alone or with an army.

I don't think you have to worry too much about me going anywhere near them.

He seemed so far away that she had to fight down panic.

How had he become so important to her so fast? She'd thought it was physical attraction and nothing else. He was so incredibly beautiful. No man had ever looked at her the way he had. She was intelligent enough to realize that the danger and macho inherent in his personality were also a huge moth-to-flame draw for women, but she was too logical to succumb to a man for that. Maybe all along she'd wanted the attraction to be those things because it kept her safe. Loving Manolito De La Cruz would be too much like jumping off a cliff.

MaryAnn exhaled. She had already taken the plunge, somewhere along the way without even realizing it. It didn't matter that he was Carpathian and she was—whatever she was. Manolito was her other half, and she was going to keep him alive. She was going to do whatever it took to bring him out of that other world, back to the land of the living, back to her.

She stood up in plain sight of the jaguar, wanting him to feel the challenge. Wanting him to see he had a fight on his hands—or claws. Because they weren't getting Manolito's body. She would find a way to use whatever she was, whatever power she really had, to keep him safe until Riordan got there to take over. And then she was marching into the land of mists and ghosts—or whatever he called it—and she was dragging him out.

Below, the jaguar snarled in answer, revealing viciously long teeth. It gave up any pretense of hiding its intent and sprang onto the trunk of a large tree. Using claws, it dragged itself to the lowest limb and began to run along the canopy highway built of thick overlapping branches. The cat raced toward her, eyes glowing with venom.

MaryAnn watched the jaguar come, her pulse racing in time to the beat of its paws as it hit each tree, breaking small twigs as it came closer and closer. Her chest felt tight. Too tight. Her head hurt as if her brain had swollen and no longer fit inside her skull. Her teeth and jaw ached. Muscles contracted. Skin rippled as if something lived beneath it. The ends of her fingers began to split apart as they curved down. She felt herself being drawn into a tight, tiny compartment, into a small space with no way out.

Panic turned the edges of her vision black. She could feel herself, the very essence of who she was, being drawn into a vortex, whirling, shrinking, until she grew smaller and smaller.

MaryAnn flung out her hands, catching the railing to anchor herself, and with a small, terrified cry, she pulled back. Nails dug into the wooden rail, leaving behind deep grooves, while she breathed away the feeling of being swallowed alive. The jaguar leapt straight at her, claws extended, and she jumped back, tripped over Manolito's legs and landed hard on her bottom.

The jaguar slammed into an invisible wall and fell straight

down, clawing desperately for a purchase on the trunk or branches as it crashed through, breaking boughs along the way.

MaryAnn stood up slowly and cautiously peered down. The jaguar hit a larger branch and managed to hang on where it lay, panting, sides heaving, trying to catch its breath. Beneath the cat, a man emerged from the heavier foliage and lifted his hands in the air. A mage. And one who seemed to know what he was doing. Unlike the other mage, who had been tentative as he worked, this man barely slowed down as he worked to unravel Manolito's safeguards. The invisible threads woven so tightly together began to unravel so fast she could almost feel them falling.

She pressed her lips together hard and forced her mind away from panic. The moment the mage took down the safeguards, the jaguar would attack. She might manage to kill the shape-shifter, but she knew nothing at all about fighting vampires, even fledglings. And the mage was dangerous as well. What had she done last time to kill the mage? She couldn't remember. She hadn't killed him on purpose. She'd wanted him to go away.

The monkeys shrieked at the jaguar and rained twigs down on him. The jaguar snarled and leapt at one of the smaller ones in the lower branches. At once the entire monkey population went wild. The sound was deafening. MaryAnn realized the mage had already unraveled the sound barrier Manolito had erected.

Riordan. Get here soon. She tried to send the impression of the mage, vampire and jaguar to him.

She felt his sudden tension. *Can you get out of there?*

I can't leave Manolito's body unprotected. I don't think I have very much time before the mage breaks through. He seems to know what he's doing.

Manolito will have woven in a few surprises, but he most likely was looking for privacy, not expecting an all-out attack against the two of you.

"Just hurry." She whispered the last aloud.

There had to be a way to distract the mage. She concentrated on him, focusing wholly on his face, his expression, the way his lips moved as he mouthed the reversal of the safeguards Manolito had set. How could she stop him? Slow him down? What she needed was a way to get the earth beneath his feet to open, a big wide crack that would follow his every step if he tried to escape it.

The tree shook. The ground below undulated, throwing the mage off his feet. He glared at her as he crab-walked backward hastily, trying to avoid the crack widening in the earth. Her breath caught in her lungs and she went still. Was she doing that? Was it possible? Could she really have broken a branch from above the first mage and dropped it on him? The thought both sickened her and gave her hope. But how was she doing it? What else had she done? What else was she capable of doing?

For the first time she felt a twinge of hope. The agitated movements of the monkeys caught her attention. They were throwing leaves and twigs not only at the jaguar, but at the mage, as if they were firmly aligned with her. She let her breath out slowly. Had the animals been following her? Had they obeyed her when she told them to go? And the jaguars, even the shifters, had stopped when she'd given the command. She hadn't held them for very long, but for one instant they had obeyed her as well.

She rubbed her pounding head. It was about to split open. Her chest felt too tight, as if everything inside her was expanding and she was contracting, getting smaller and smaller. Her body felt as if it didn't fit, and hard knots appeared beneath her skin on every muscle. It was distracting and just plain freaky. For a moment she was shaken, wanting to run, but then she glanced at Manolito, so still, so alive looking, his eyes vacant when his body seemed so strong and virile. He wasn't running from trying to protect her, and she wasn't about to leave him behind.

Her spine stiffened, and she looked up at the animals in the canopy. So many of them. The sheer numbers were reassuring. *We really don't like that bad man, do we? He's trying to hurt me. Throw things at him. Big things. Drive him away. Don't let him put his arms in the air like that.*

The monkeys went insane, jumping up and down and shaking the branches of the trees, running back and forth, showing teeth and beating on their chests as their agitation built. She was beginning to get a feel for the flow of energy. It was small at first—she could only guess at what she was doing—but as the animals responded and the energy swelled around her, she became very aware of it. She took a deep breath and tapped into the seething cauldron of power, directing it this time at the snarling jaguar.

That man doesn't belong in your realm. They have tried to

enslave you. They've taken everything from you and are driving your people to extinction. See them for what they are. The vampire has put his mark on you. You were once a proud man; now you do another's bidding. They don't belong here.

The jaguar shook its broad head continually, looking confused. It took a few steps toward the tree as if it might come after her again, but it stopped, trembling.

The mage snapped a command to it and waved one hand, gesturing toward her.

Why should this man tell you what to do? Is he your master? Does he own you? You are jaguar. You own the rain forest. Whoever walks in it should walk with your leave, not the other way around.

The jaguar gave a coughing grunt and swung its head toward the mage, eyes blazing with fury. It crouched low. The mage froze. He began to talk quietly, chanting something while his hands gestured in rapid patterns before him.

Look out! He's trying to use power against you. Look at him. He's trapping you with a spell. Attack before he finishes. She put alarm and urgency into her thoughts.

The jaguar snarled at the mage, showing its teeth as it took several slow steps toward the mage. The mage gave way, backing up, this time holding out one hand to stop the large, menacing cat.

The thick hedge of ferns withered and turned brown, lacy fronds rolling back as a third man stepped from the bushes. He was, by turns, beautiful and then grotesque. MaryAnn blinked several times, trying to bring his true form into focus. With a casual wave of his hands at the monkeys, they fell into an uneasy silence. He spoke a word to the jaguar, and the shapeshifter halted.

MaryAnn touched her tongue to her suddenly dry lips. She was looking at a vampire—the epitome of evil. He looked up at her and smiled. His jagged teeth were stained with blood, and his skin seemed stretched tight against his skull. The next moment he was a gorgeous man, with a wide, engaging smile.

"Come down and join us," he invited softly.

She felt the buzz in her head and knew he had embedded a compulsion in his voice. She forced a smile, then waited a few beats to gather massive amounts of energy to project into her voice and mind, so she could turn his own compulsion back on him. "I'm quite comfortable actually, so you can go ahead and leave."

The vampire blinked. Frowned. Shook his head as if he couldn't remember what he was doing.

"Yes, you want to go. Leave this place." She poured power into her voice.

He turned away from her, just for a moment obeying her command, swinging his body around toward the ferns.

Her breath caught in her throat and she struck. *Now! Now attack. All of you. Hurry. Take them before they destroy you.*

The jaguar leapt on the vampire's back, teeth sinking deep into the skull. At the same time, the monkeys dove at the mage, biting and hitting, swarming over him in large numbers. Birds took to the air, wings flapping as they buzzed around the combatants, raking with their talons.

The mage went down beneath the sheer numbers. MaryAnn wanted to turn away, the sight sickening her, as the jaguar bit down hard and blood gushed, running in streams down the vampire's head. He roared his rage and caught the jaguar in his hands, dragging the cat away from his body with his enormous strength and wrenching at the head. The crack was audible to her, even in the midst of the shrieks and cries of monkeys and birds.

The vampire glanced at the mage, buried under the mountain of bodies, and then he slowly turned back to face her. His head was punctured, the skull shattered under the jaguar's strong bite, but it didn't seem to faze the undead. The eyes were glowing with red-orange flames, the mouth opened wide in a grimace of hate.

He stood there for a moment simply staring at her. Then he flexed his fingers, allowing the nails to grow and curve into claws. Still holding her gaze, he flew through the air and landed on the trunk of the tree beside the one she was in and began to slither up the side. He looked frightening. An abomination. Just like one of the vampires in the movies, a dark, unnatural apparition of evil bent on killing her—on destroying Manolito.

For a moment terror gripped her. The safeguard wouldn't hold long. Manolito hadn't meant for it to be a protection so much as a sound barrier. Riordan wasn't there to save her. If she was going to live, if she was going to keep Manolito's body safe, she had to do something fast.

Already she could feel the power surging in her body. Once again her head pounded, this time even stronger, faster. As if her body already knew the way and was only seeking her permission. The idea of letting go of herself, of her own identity, was almost more terrifying than the vampire crawling up the tree trunk.

Her jaw ached, popping painfully. Tendons and ligaments pulled while the muscles in her body contorted, hardening into tight knots of pain she could visibly see beneath her skin. Her stomach lurched. She fought down panic. Even if she didn't do this for herself, she had to do it for Manolito.

Images strobed through her mind so quickly they nearly made her sick. They moved so fast she couldn't sort them out or focus on any one, but they were of wolves walking on two legs. A collective memory. Her skin stretched tight, too tight. Her vision clouded, edged red and black. Once again her fingers curved into claws, an involuntary action she couldn't stop. Pain exploded through her.

She tried to breathe, tried to force herself to let go, but her mind just wouldn't surrender. Her mind just wouldn't let her go. What if she was trapped?

The tree shook. The vampire shrieked, the sound skating down her spine and striking terror in her heart. He had leapt onto the edge of the platform, just outside the railing, and he was working fast at unraveling the safeguard. She had only moments to make a choice.

MaryAnn put her hand on Manolito's shoulder, touched his face. He was somewhere else, fighting for her. He was counting on his brother to come and protect her and protect his body, but she was all he had. She took a deep breath and let go.

At once she felt the very essence of who she was sucked down, spiraling and getting smaller, as if she were folding in upon herself. She was fully aware, but her dominion over her own body was diminishing rapidly. Everything in her screamed to resist, but she kept her gaze fixed on Manolito, and the sight of him gave her the courage to surrender.

As the essence that was MaryAnn retreated, the fury of the wolf sprang out, passing her as it went. She felt the inescapable power of it, the enormous strength of body and will. The sentinel. The guardian. It leapt to take her place, to fit into her body, stretching and molding muscle and bone to suit its steely frame.

She was aware of her skin bursting, but there was no pain. She couldn't feel the sensation of her bones and body re-forming, or her organs shifting; there was only the feeling of being protected and safe deep within.

At that moment the vampire tore through the barrier, and with a hiss of hatred, it sprang at Manolito's body. The wolf leapt to intercept, body changing fully in flight. They crashed together, the wolf growling, the vampire shrieking. All around them the rain forest erupted into screaming monkeys and birds, as animals reacted to the terrible sound of battle.

16

Manolito moved quickly through the barren shadow world, seeking the darker edges where the undead gathered in packs to wail while they waited to know their fate. He had the illusion of wearing his body, striding over the uneven ground, making his way through the tangle of huge roots, just as if he were still back in the rain forest, but he was too light, almost floating, and when he looked down, his hands and arms were transparent. He could see the rotting vegetation on the ground as he passed through on his way to the mountains of jagged boulders that marked the entrance to the meadow of mists.

A few spirits frowned at him as he strode by them, a couple lifted a hand as if they might recognize him, but for the most part, he was ignored. It was strange to him that as he glided through the forests and hills, he could clearly see that two types of people populated the land, where before he hadn't noticed.

The meadow seemed to separate those who had little or no remorse for the things they did in their former life from the ones who struggled to understand where they had gone wrong. Few had been around to greet him.

As he approached closer to the meadow, heat and steam rose to envelope him. Where before the mists were simply gray and dank, with no feeling of hope, now the air was even more oppressive and seemed thick with tension, as if uneasiness walked the land. In the distance he heard the sounds of mocking laughter, the whisper of voices calling his name. They waited for him, knew he approached.

Was it really possible for an army of the undead to find a way back to the land of the living? If so, he would have to find a way to stop them. He had to let go of his fears for MaryAnn and give this world his full attention. He couldn't be in two places at one time. He would have to trust that Riordan had arrived to protect MaryAnn from harm. He didn't dare touch MaryAnn's mind and accidentally pull her into the spirit world with him. He had to keep her from danger at all costs—even his life should that be necessary. He shut down all emotion and turned his attention wholly to the problem at hand.

If the vampires were acting to invade the land of the living, they had someone powerful helping them. Razvan or Xavier, the two most powerful mages in existence. Maybe both. No one else could wield that kind of power. And if Xavier and Maxim were allies working together to bring down the Carpathian people, Xavier certainly would have told Maxim if he was trying to find a way to tap into an army of the undead. Everyone knew Xavier called on shadow warriors, men of honor long gone from the world, their spirits imprisoned by the skilled mage to do his bidding. If Xavier could yoke the shadow warriors, he might find a way to harness the legions of undead waiting in the meadow of mists.

The way seemed longer, and more people tentatively greeted him, which surprised him. Before, the first time his spirit had arrived, most turned away with a quick gesture toward the meadow, yet now the inhabitants seemed to accept him. As he moved closer to his destination, he felt an easiness spreading and realized that when he had arrived the first time, his spirit had been dark, close to turning, so close that even within the land of the dead, he had been considered closer to vampire than to hunter. The atmosphere around the meadow hadn't bothered him and he had instinctively sought it out. Now his spirit must appear brighter, more normal. The growing stain across his soul had receded because of MaryAnn. He owed her more even than he had known.

He came to the meadow and halted, staring out over the expanse of sinkholes and shifting soil. It looked like a spongy marsh, and when he put his foot on it in experimentation, he sank to his ankle. His body had no real weight here, so the reaction made no sense. He hesitated, studying the barren land. Only a few scattered weeds and thistles grew in the center of the marsh. Dark reeds lined the edges, bent like old straws. Steam rose from vent holes, and minerals of all colors—dim, not bright—rimmed boiling mud ponds. The sludge quivered and popped, splattering large, dark spots of oozing mud and adding to the rising steam.

The mist lay heavy over the meadow, a gray-green vapor that reeked of sulfur. He stood for a time studying the rising plumes of hot gases and wondering why it had been so easy to cross it on his first visit.

"You look lost, Manolito." A voice greeted him from behind.

Manolito spun around and found himself face-to-face with Vlad Dubrinsky. Emotion welled up sharp and fast, a piercing shock that threatened to shake his confidence. Joy. Guilt. Shame. Amazement. Pride. Vlad Dubrinsky had been more than a prince to him. When their own father had chosen to follow his lifemate into death, Vlad had stepped in to fill the gulf left by the death of their parents. He'd guided Manolito and his brothers, mentored them, respected their counsel. Yet, in the end, they had repudiated him for trying to save his son when he knew there was no hope.

"My prince. I did not expect to find you in such a place."

Vlad stepped forward and gripped his forearms in the timeless greeting of respect between warriors. "It is good to see you, old friend."

"I do not understand how you can be in this place."

Vlad's eyebrow shot up. "You do not? This is where we wait between worlds, Manolito."

"Wait for what? I came here and found only condemnation. Accusations. Invitations to join the undead."

"You are not quite spirit, yet not quite one with your body."

"I was killed, yet my brothers held my spirit to earth. Gregori went down the tree of life to retrieve me, but I woke too soon. My spirit and body had not yet had time to meld together, so I walk in both lands."

Vlad gestured across the meadow. "You do not belong with the vampires. I can see by your spirit you have not succumbed to our darker nature."

"I was close. Too close."

"You do not want to go to their resting ground. They cannot kill you, but they have devised ways to torture and drive the spirit mad. They cannot leave this place without accepting their own guilt, yet they will not. They blame everyone around them.

I suspect many would like to get their teeth into you. Come with me to the campfire of warriors. We will once again talk."

"My body is vulnerable in the other world, Vlad, and there are conspiracies I have to uncover in order to keep our people safe. I believe Maxim is raising an army of the dead and hopes to find a portal from this land to the living."

Vlad stopped moving to frown at him, then shook his head. "I should have guessed he would be up to no good. Come. It is a small way and we might be of use to you. In any case, Sarantha will want to see you. Give us news and let us give you aid."

"I still do not understand how you can be here, waiting for judgment. You were never close to turning. You served our people with honor."

"Do you believe, after all this time, that I never made mistakes, Manolito? I made many. I tried to do my best, but like any man, I had my failings. You should know that better than most. I tried to save my eldest son at a cost to many others. Was that a wise decision? Or even a fair one?"

"You could not have known what would happen."

"Of course I knew. I did not want to believe it, but I had the gift of precognition. I knew, yet I set the course because I could not bear to destroy my own son. When I confessed to Sarantha, she begged me not to let him die, and fool that I was, I chose the path of destruction for all our people. I am responsible for many things that should never have come to pass. In the end, the job that should have been mine was shouldered by my son Mikhail."

Manolito could barely accept what he was hearing. All along he had felt guilt and shame for condemning Vlad's decision. He loved him and respected him, and yet he had felt a traitor for plotting to overthrow him.

"It was not in the best interest of our people." He choked on the words, on the lump growing in his throat. The Malinov brothers had lost their beloved sister, Ivory, and so had the De La Cruz brothers. She had been their light, the reason they all continued their hope and belief in their people. With her death, the darkness had descended on all of them, triggering a chain of events that could still very well lead to the destruction of their entire species.

"No," Vlad agreed, his tone very even. "It was not. I am

no deity. No Carpathian male is. We are all capable of great wrongs."

Manolito swallowed the tight ball of condemnation welling in his throat. What could he say to that? He had done things in his life, many things, he regretted. At the time they were done without emotion, but he could remember every single incident, and the worst crime had been against his own lifemate.

He hung his head. "What you say is true. I was close to turning when I heard the voice of my lifemate. She was under the protection of Mikhail and Gregori, along with several other Carpathians. I cared nothing for the laws and I took her blood without her consent or knowledge, binding her to me."

Vlad nodded his head. "It was a challenge to you."

"To get through their ranks and claim what belonged to me? Yes. Am I sorry for it? I do not know the answer to that. I am sorry I did not reveal myself to her and tell her my reasons for taking her life out of her hands without consent, but I do not think doing so was wrong, only the way I did it."

"Our people have lived long beside humans, and our rules are different for reasons, Manolito. We were given the ability to bind our lifemate because without that our people would have died out long ago. Few will ever be able to understand that, but if we do our best to love and respect our women, always putting them first once they are in our care, we have a better chance that other species will come to understand and accept us."

"The world has changed a great deal in your absence, Vlad, and with it, our people. I have found it difficult to accept the new ways."

Vlad clapped him on his shoulder, the touch so light Manolito barely felt it. Vlad's body was even less distinctive than his. "We all have flaws, Manolito, and we all have to work to overcome them. There is no shame in that. Come, greet Sarantha and give us all the news of our loved ones."

"I truly have little time. MaryAnn, my lifemate, is guarding my body and I believe she will be attacked. I have to stop Maxim before he figures out a way to leave this place with an army of the undead."

Vlad shook his head. "He cannot find a way out of this world."

"Do not be so certain. Maxim works in league with Xavier."

Vlad turned his head slowly, the smile fading from his face. "Xavier still lives?"

"We believe so. And his grandson, Razvan, works with him to destroy our people. We are almost certain that Maxim's brothers are all involved in a plot to destroy Mikhail, a plot I helped to devise." Manolito refused to look away from Vlad as he confessed. This was the man he respected above all others, with the exception of his brothers. This was the man he'd once thought of as his father. And this was the man whose downfall he'd helped to plan. He would not lie or shy away from the guilt and shame of his deed.

Vlad remained silent for a long moment. There was no flicker of disappointment or disgust on his face; he simply locked gazes with Manolito and stared him in the eye. "Do you think it comes as a surprise to me that you and your brothers entertained the idea of bringing down the reign of Dubrinsky? You were always intelligent and you saw my crime. You knew what I had done. In trying to save my son, I did betray our people. You had every right to question my judgment. It was not sound."

"We did not have the right to plot your downfall or the destruction of every other species we were allies with."

"To take me down, you would have had to take them down." Vlad nodded his head. "It makes sense, of course." He waved his hand toward a small grove of trees. "Please come for a few minutes. A few of us guard this area to keep newcomers from wandering into the land of the fallen ones."

Manolito matched his steps, although, as much as he wanted to talk to Vlad and even get advice on the elusive werewolf species, he was impatient to confront Maxim and get back to MaryAnn. A sense of urgency was growing inside of him.

He had been expecting Vlad to condemn him. Maybe it would have been easier to face what he'd done if his prince had been angry. "I am sorry," he said quietly. Sincerely. "I had no idea the plan would ever be implemented. I had no idea the Malinovs hated you so much. In the end we talked for hours, and Zacarias and Ruslan agreed that we all would remain loyal to you and serve you with honor. We took a blood oath."

"You and your brothers have served our people faithfully," Vlad said. "Even here we get news as warriors or vampires come." He pushed through a wall of ferns. "Ah, here is Sarantha. My darling, I have brought a guest."

Sarantha turned, her smile lighting her face, and her eyes brightening the dull colors around them. "Manolito. It is wonderful to see you, although I have heard rumors you walk in both worlds. How are my sons and their lifemates? How is my granddaughter? I understand she is quite lovely. You must tell me everything, all the news." She hugged him, her body light and insubstantial against his. "You must have a lifemate or your spirit would not be so bright. Tell me about her."

Vlad laughed. "Give him a chance to speak, my love. He is in a great hurry."

"Forgive me. I am just so excited to see you." She patted a spot by the campfire. "Do you have a few moments of your time to give to me?"

"Of course." He leaned over to kiss her cheek. "Mikhail is a wonderful leader. You would be proud of him. His lifemate is a good match for him and is helping to lead our people back into a more cohesive society. Jacques and Shea have had a son, a boy. I was gone before the naming ceremony, so I do not know what they have called him. I heard that Savannah, your granddaughter, is expecting twins."

Sarantha threw herself into Vlad's arms. "I wish we could see them."

"Someday," Vlad said, enfolding her close. "We will be united with our loved ones. We are moving from this life to the next very soon."

She nodded and turned her face up to his to brush a small kiss along his chin. "And your lifemate, Manolito? Tell us about her."

"She is courageous. And beautiful. And she makes me want to be better with every rising." Manolito frowned, wanting information without giving too much away. "Vlad, tell me what you know of the guardians. The werewolves."

Vlad sank cross-legged to the ground. "Little is known of their society, although legends abound. I think they started most of the myths to keep people frightened and away from them, but then that backfired and they were hunted by humans. They live in human form most of the time. They exist on all continents, or did in ancient times. Few can ever tell them from humans."

"How can they stay secret even from us?"

"They do not have brain function all that different from a human; they simply use more of the brain, as we do. Most of the time, the wolf stays silent within them, so they appear completely human."

"What would happen to a wolf if he became Carpathian?"

"Cross the species?" Vlad glanced at Sarantha. "I do not know. I have never heard of such a thing."

"Can it even be done?" Sarantha asked.

"I have no idea," Manolito said. "But humans have been successfully brought into Carpathian society. As werewolves are psychic, it is theoretically possible."

Vlad let his breath out. "I am glad it is not a decision I have to make. A wolf and a Carpathian. The combination might be lethal."

"Or exciting," Sarantha interjected. "Two species of equal power."

"What would it do to the person? To their body and mind? What would they become?"

Vlad opened his mouth and closed it abruptly. "I see your dilemma." And he did. Much more than Manolito might have wanted him to see. "I cannot help you. As far as I know, it has never been done. Both bloodlines are of equal power. I do not know which would emerge victorious, if either."

"And what do you know of Xavier?"

Vlad sighed and reached for Sarantha's hand. "In truth, it is long since I had to make decisions for my people. I am grateful that I can simply exist without my choices having impact on anyone other than my lifemate. Even speaking of Xavier is difficult. He was a good friend. One I believed in. One I loved as a brother. He betrayed us as no other could have done."

"Why?"

"Greed. Jealousy. He wanted to be immortal. I tried to tell him there was no real immortality—after all, we too can be killed—but he came to believe he was superior and should have the kind of longevity we have. Unfortunately, all of our safeguards were founded on mage spells—spells he provided. Over the years we added to them, but the weave of energy is the same, and that made us—and still makes us—vulnerable to him."

"When you were such good friends . . ."

"He wanted me to give him a Carpathian woman. I tried to explain about lifemates, but he refused to see reason. We had many arguments, and he became convinced that I was deliberately keeping him from being immortal because I feared his power. Eventually we began to separate our two societies, although he maintained the schools for our fledglings to learn. Rhiannon was one of his best students and he decided to keep her for himself. He had her lifemate murdered and he took her. He must have planned it for a long while, because she was Dragonseeker and few could have held her against her will, let alone got her pregnant. Yes. We have heard that he had children by her." His fingers tightened around Sarantha's. "There was nothing I could do to stop him, and now he is trying to destroy our people."

"He was evil then and he is now," Manolito said. "He has banded with the Malinovs and is implementing the plan we devised. Now that we know what he is doing, Zacarias will take word to Mikhail and we will send out emissaries to each of our allies and try to stop him before he goes any further. But first, I have to stop Maxim."

"Oh dear," Sarantha looked at her lifemate. "Maxim is such a troublemaker. He cannot accept his mistakes. He refuses all responsibility, and until he atones in some way, until he learns, he cannot move on."

Manolito pushed himself to his feet. "I cannot stay longer. I fear for MaryAnn's safety. It was an honor to see you both."

"I will come with you and see what I can do to help," Vlad volunteered.

Manolito shook his head. "You know you cannot. This is my problem to solve. I am trapped in two worlds and cannot live in both. This is my burden alone, sir, but I thank you for wanting to shoulder it with me." He gripped his prince's forearms in the time-honored manner and then leaned down to kiss Sarantha. "I will give your love to your family."

"Be well, Manolito," Sarantha said.

"Live large," Vlad added.

Manolito strode back through the trees, looking back once for a glimpse of the leader of his people. Sarantha and Vlad had their arms around each other, their bodies giving off a faint glow of light that seemed to grow stronger, more blinding in the midst of the gray, dank world. The sight of them, so in love, so bound to each other, made him long for the same thing with MaryAnn. He sighed and resolutely turned back to face the path to the meadow. A slight wind blew through the leaves in the small grove of trees but failed to reach him, even when he lifted his face to try to feel the breeze.

How could he uncover Maxim's plan? The vampire would never trust him, never believe he had come over to his side. What was left? Vlad had said that the undead had devised ways to torture and drive one mad. How did you drive a spirit mad? Or for that matter, torture one? He frowned as he mulled it over. A war of the wits then. There could be no other answer. For good or evil, he had to risk everything for his people—and for MaryAnn. If he was wrong . . .

He shrugged and proceeded to the belching, steaming meadow where the veil of mist hung low and the bubbling pools of mud spit out dark, ugly stains. Maxim and his army of undead waited on the other side. He could see shadows moving in the dull gray of the mist, eyes glowing red and voices rising on the steam.

He streaked across the space, avoiding the plumes of steam and sudden hissing geysers as they spouted into the air, throwing more of the dark mud in all directions. He burst through the veil of mist, straight into the center of the vampire circle.

Maxim hissed his surprise and stopped dead, arms still raised in the air. The chanting faltered, and the others forming the circle around Maxim stepped back, covering their faces.

Maxim forced a smile, showing the pegs of his stained teeth. "I see you have returned to us, old friend. Join us in our little ceremony."

"I certainly did not mean to interrupt you, Maxim. By all means, you and your friends continue with what you were doing."

"You do not mind, then?" Maxim asked, with a faint, deadly smirk.

"No, of course not." Manolito folded his arms across his chest.

Maxim raised his arms and began chanting once again. The vampires circling him moved their feet in a hypnotic pattern and began to lift their voices in a mesmerizing incantation.

Manolito deliberately walked around Maxim, studying him from every angle, watching the flow of his hands, committing each movement to memory.

Maxim sighed and dropped his arms. "What is it?"

"Carry on, Maxim. I am just contemplating where I have seen this particular spell used. I believe it is one of Xavier's earlier works, when he first was attempting to bind the shadow warriors to him. We studied him, remember? He was a brilliant man."

"He *is* a brilliant man."

"Not so much anymore," Manolito said in disagreement. The other undead had once again stopped their chanting and were watching. "He has grown senile. He lives off the blood of our people, but he was never meant for longevity and his mind is going." He stepped closer to Maxim and lowered his voice so only the master vampire could hear. "He no longer can produce new spells. He has to have others, lesser mages, do it for him."

"You lie!" Maxim hissed. "I know you lie."

"You know I do not," Manolito replied calmly, once more circling Maxim. "You have always been of superior intelligence. I do not flatter you when I remind you of that. You could reason things out. Xavier lacks the ability to think of anything new. He relies heavily on the things he knew before, and I doubt he remembers much of that." He stopped again on the vampire's other side and whispered in that ear. "Why do you think he seeks the book?" Xavier had compiled his spells into one book, now guarded by the prince of the Carpathians.

Maxim growled and swung his head back and forth, his eyes glowing with red-hot flames. "He is a powerful man."

Manolito nodded and once more began walking in a circle, moving his feet in a dance pattern as he went, watching the master of the undead try to follow the intricate, hypnotic steps. "Very powerful. In spite of the fact that he no longer makes up his own spells, he is still a powerful mage. But he cannot do what he promises you and your brothers. He cannot open the portal to allow your army of the undead to come forth. That's why he has given you the ancient spell of the shadow warriors."

Maxim continued to turn in a circle with him, following his every movement with suspicion. When Manolito stopped and leaned in close, he automatically did the same.

"He knows Vikirnoff's lifemate can send the warriors back to their own realm. He was using her spells, and now he no longer has control of her. He's left with nothing, but dares not let Ruslan and your brothers know the truth. Of what use would he be then to them?" Before Maxim could answer, Manolito once more took off circling.

The vampire gripped his own head in agitation and screamed, the sound rubbing across nerves like sandpaper. "It does not matter, Manolito. Xavier did not figure out what to do; Ruslan did, and he is always right. *Always.* Zacarias was a fool to follow Vlad instead of Ruslan. We had a code, a blood oath, and you broke it."

"Our blood oath was to one another and to the prince, Maxim. The De La Cruz family was always loyal to the Malinovs."

"We gave you the opportunity to join us. We talked all night of it. You insisted on following the prince and his murdering son." Maxim spat out the last words, his face contorted with hatred and rage. He stepped up toe-to-toe, staring Manolito in the eyes, so that the red flames burning in his sunken eye sockets were plainly visible. "Betrayer," he accused. "You deserve to die."

Manolito didn't flinch away from the foul stench of Maxim's breath or the savage hatred on his face. "I did die. How else would I be here?"

"You went back, and that means it is possible. Xavier will find a way to return me to the others or he will die a long, painful death. He knows not to betray us. Our memories are long, and you will suffer for your betrayal."

"Will I?"

Maxim's fury erupted so strong there was no containing it. He threw back his head and howled, reaching to seize Manolito's shoulders with his claws, the talons piercing deep and tearing through the flesh so that blood ran and the other vampires erupted into a frenzy, racing forward in an attempt to lick at the dark red streams.

For one moment, pain burst through him, bright and hot, twisting his gut and beating at his brain, but Manolito quelled his body's reaction and stayed perfectly still as the vampires swarmed around him. He shoved down his revulsion and smiled at Maxim, his gaze calm. "Do you think to trick me so easily? It is an illusion. Nothing more. You cannot kill what is already dead. I have no body in this place. These fools want to believe, but even they can only taste the dirt on the ground as they root around."

Contempt on his face, he touched one with his foot as the undead clawed at the barren ground. The noise was hideous as they all tried in vain to get to fresh blood. Growls and hisses, animals gone mad. "This is what you have been reduced to, Maxim? You were once a great man, and now you wallow like swine in a pen."

Screaming with rage, Maxim struck him repeatedly in the face, shredding flesh with his long yellow nails. It was difficult to stand still under the attack, to keep his mind from believing what was happening was real. Flesh appeared to fly in all directions. Blood splattered everywhere.

Manolito kept his arms loosely at his sides and forced the smile to remain, even when the other vampires went mad, trying to shove bits of his flesh into their mouths, going so far as to sink teeth into his shoulders and chest. It was one of the most difficult things he had ever done in his life, standing there while the undead gathered around him in a feeding frenzy, tearing the flesh from his bones and trying to eat him alive.

He kept his mind fixed on MaryAnn. He thought of her smile, her hair, the way her eyes lit up when she laughed. Ah, the sound of her laughter was warm and bright in his mind, drowning out the sound of the vampires tearing at him. He fixed his mind on every detail of her body and the way she wore her so-fashionable clothes. Her red heels and her soft boots. Even here, in this land that made no sense, she came to his rescue, keeping her courageous image between him and madness.

"Enough!" Maxim shouted and waved the vampires away from Manolito. The undead obeyed reluctantly, some crawling along the ground trying to scoop up flesh and blood and getting only handfuls of the alkaline dirt. Some caught Maxim's legs and fawned, begging for more, their faces smeared with mud. He kicked them away from him impatiently and glared at Manolito. "Get the sneer off your face."

"I am not sneering, Maxim. I feel only pity for the creature who used to be my friend and was once a great man. Now you are content to serve these worthless ones. You have become worm fodder by your own hand. And you have lost the one thing that mattered—your keen intelligence. How could a man with a brain as sharp as yours ever believe a word Xavier said? It makes no sense that you or Ruslan—or any of your brothers for that matter—would waste your time on him."

Manolito was careful to keep the flattery to a minimum as he brought the vampire's focus back to the mage. Maxim was cunning, and he would notice if Manolito went overboard. He kept his tone very cool and slightly filled with contempt, which he knew would grate on Maxim.

The master vampire sucked in his breath, the air whistling between the jagged pegs of his teeth. Manolito could see him struggling for control, for dignity. He stepped away, placing his hands behind his back and schooling his face into even lines.

"You are mistaken about Xavier, Manolito. He will bring my army through the portal and no one will be able to defeat us. You cannot fight the dead." He laughed without mirth as if he were very amusing.

Around them the other vampires began to pull themselves together, following Maxim's example, opening their mouths wide to let out sounds that were a terrible parody of laughter. The din was grating, a wild screeching that echoed through Manolito's head and set his teeth clenching. He forced a flash of his teeth, keeping his gaze fixed on Maxim's, trying to read whatever was behind that evil mask.

"Do you really believe that, Maxim? Do you think Xavier has the power to bring you back? He created the shadow-warrior spell when he was at his peak. Now he is an old worm, feeding on the blood of young children and claiming lesser mages' magic. Do you really believe he can bring you out of here?"

"*You. You* are going to bring us out," Maxim snapped, the truth spilling explosively. Spittle sprayed from his mouth and the flames in his eyes leapt even higher. "So smug like always, little man. That is what you really are. Your brothers knew the truth. You are a little man who whines to become someone of importance. You think to fight us, but you cannot. You never could. You dared to enter my world, and you had the opportunity once again to join us. Twice I have given you the chance."

"You wanted me to slay my lifemate."

"You would have joined our ranks and served me. With your brains, we could have gone far, but you never could see the bigger picture. You wanted to fawn on that fool Dubrinsky. And you never understood, not even Zacarias understood: Vlad Dubrinsky betrayed you for his son. He betrayed all of us for his son."

Manolito stiffened, his mind racing. The answer was right

in front of him if he could just fit the pieces of the puzzle together. Maxim wanted to tell him, wanted to show his superiority; Manolito just had to have patience and lead him in that direction. "Do you think your childish taunts are going to impress me the way they do your ridiculous dogs?" Deliberately his gesture took in the vampires desperate for Maxim's attention. "I am a hunter. I have been a hunter for a thousand years. You have become amusing, the greatness in you long gone. You turned yourself into a puppet for the likes of Xavier."

Maxim looked as if he might explode. His eyes spun in the deep sockets, glowing red orange and yellow. He spewed venom from between his teeth, the acid landing on Manolito's skin, where it sizzled and smoked.

Manolito remained stoic beneath the attack, never blinking, never changing expression, simply watching Maxim with that same small smile of contempt that continued to get under the vampire's skin.

"You know nothing. *Nothing.* You also thought your intellect superior to everyone's. You and your precious brothers. Zacarias ordering us to follow that murdering, sniveling prince. Dubrinsky could have a female killed, but not his own son, and the De La Cruz brothers follow like puppies."

Manolito rolled his shoulders in a casual shrug. "Like you are doing with Xavier. Believing in his lies. He does not want to be fodder for the undead. He will tell you whatever you want to hear."

"I *saw* the portal," Maxim snapped. "And she will return. You are the conduit. She will come for you when she hears you screaming."

Manolito felt his heart jump, but he kept his expression the same, careful to keep his gaze filled with contempt and not blink at the revelation. He had expected it, but hearing it brought fear for MaryAnn. He pushed emotion down somewhere deep and faced the master vampire. "It will be interesting to see you do that."

"At this very moment my puppets do my bidding, attacking her while your body lies vulnerable. We will burn it and there will be no hope for your return. She will hear you screaming and she will merge with you fully as she did before. Once she is here, we can use her living spirit to return."

Manolito tasted fear now, but he forced his heart to beat with an easy rhythm. "And just how do you intend to make me scream, Maxim? So far you have failed utterly."

Maxim smirked. "There is only one capable of following every path of communication." He waved his arms, satisfaction glowing in his eyes. "Meet Draven Dubrinsky, Mikhail's older brother."

Manolito turned, and Vlad's son stood behind him, glowing with the power of his family's legacy, his eyes bright with hatred, his handsome face twisted with malice.

"She will come for you," he agreed. He stood tall, his arms out from his side, and Manolito felt the power of his mind-merge the moment it hit him.

17

The vampire crashed through what remained of the barrier surrounding MaryAnn, shredding Manolito's safeguards. The creature's talons were extended in an effort to reach Manolito's body as it sat on the deck high in the canopy. The werewolf met the undead in midair, the two slamming together, the wolf driving the vampire backward with the force of her forward momentum. Like a child protecting a cub, she slashed relentlessly at the vampire as they fell together.

They dropped toward the forest floor, the wolf on top of the undead, the two writhing forms breaking branches as the vampire hit bough after bough with his back as they fell one hundred and fifty feet. All around them the jungle came alive with the noise of the battle, the shriek of hundreds of birds, the cries of the monkeys, the growls of the vampire and the crack of splintering wood as they plummeted the distance.

The vampire clamped his spikes of teeth into the wolf's shoulder and tore, savaging with talons, raking at the wolf's belly. MaryAnn felt the talons digging deep; she could even hear the sound of flesh and fur being torn from the wolf. Her stomach lurched, but the wolf knocked the head aside, tearing the teeth from her shoulder, ignoring the blossoming pain as flesh shredded and blood spattered across the leaves.

The vampire hit the ground, half-formed, trying to dissolve out from under the wolf, but MaryAnn's guardian was relentless, teeth driving for the throat, claws digging through the chest wall for the withered, blackened heart. It was instinctive, an age-old legacy passed in collective memory from one generation to the next. Deep inside where nothing could touch her, MaryAnn vowed never to go anywhere without her pepper spray. The wolf could have blinded the vampire with it and at least given herself a reprieve from those terrible teeth.

She landed on top of the vampire, and they rolled, the vampire hissing, its breath fetid. The creature reeked of decaying flesh, offending the wolf's acute sense of smell. The vampire grabbed the wolf and threw it, taking the opportunity to dissolve into vapor and stream upward toward the deck on the canopy.

MaryAnn's heart crashed against her chest. She heard herself screaming, tried to reach, tried to take over the body so she could get to Manolito, but the wolf was already in motion, leaping up the tree branches with incredible speed, springing for the vampire as he reformed beside Manolito's body. This time the wolf caught the vampire's head in her claws and wrenched. The vampire's neck snapped and the head flopped to one side. Growling, eyes glowing with hot rage, the creature lowered his shoulder and drove the wolf backward, once again taking them over the edge of the railing.

MaryAnn felt herself falling, felt the slam of branches against her back, but all the while the wolf was in control, muzzle burrowing toward the prize of the undead's heart. Blood coated the wolf's body, burning like acid, searing bone-deep, but the guardian refused to stop. In desperation, the vampire threw himself off the wolf, and both landed hard on the ground.

Riordan De La Cruz materialized out of the air, just as the vampire lurched to his feet. Riordan slammed his fist deep into the chest of the vampire and ripped out the heart. Tossing it to one side, he whirled to face the wolf. The guardian staggered as she managed to stand, shaking with the pain and trauma of her injuries.

Riordan lifted an eyebrow. "MaryAnn?"

The wolf nodded and reached behind her for support, leaning against a tree. She nodded toward the heart as it rolled toward the vampire's body.

"Yes, of course." Riordan reached toward the sky, covering his shock. At once storm clouds boiled and thunder rolled. Lightning veined the darker clouds and then slammed into the heart and incinerated it. Next he directed the white-hot energy toward the vampire's body.

To MaryAnn's astonishment, her wolf leaned into the crackling energy stream. Rather than incinerating her, the energy dissolved the acid-laced blood from her arms and body. Staggering back, the guardian once more leaned against the tangled roots of a tree, her sides heaving, breath coming in ragged gasps. Pain burned through her body, but she had kept Manolito alive. She couldn't wait another moment to check on him. To touch him. She needed him desperately.

Leaping to the lower branches of the tall tree, she climbed her way to the deck. Manolito was still sitting, his body a little slumped to one side, but he looked as if he were resting. She let out her breath and sank down beside him.

MaryAnn reached for her body, thanking the sentinel, grateful for the aid it had provided. She could never have defeated the vampire in her more fragile human body. It gave her a sense of gratitude to the other species who shared the world with her, thankful that they cared enough to keep everyone as safe as possible. The wolf made her feel safe.

You are the wolf, the feminine voice inside assured her.

MaryAnn closed her eyes and expanded, drawing the guardian deeper into her soul. This time the process was much faster, as the wolf leapt for its den and she emerged, with much more ease than she had let go. Her body reshaped with a minimum of distress, although the moment she was in her human form, the pain of her wounds escalated until tears burned and she bit down hard on her lip to keep from moaning.

"I have destroyed the jaguar and mage as well, and cleaned up the mess the vampire's blood caused in the soil and on the trees and foliage, so I am coming up."

MaryAnn didn't understand the warning in Riordan's voice for a moment, until she looked down at her body. She needed clothes. She had no clothes. Panic rose. Her clothes were her armor. Her courage. Her fashion sense got her through everything. She couldn't face him without clothes on. She actually began to hyperventilate.

"No! You can't come up here. I'm not dressed."

He muttered something in his impatient tone, and she found herself in a faded plaid shirt, loose-fitting jeans and very old sneakers. Then he was standing in front of her, frowning.

"I am going to have to heal your wound. I will need to take a look at it. Vampires have been leaving little parasites behind lately when they bite."

She barely heard him, too busy staring down at her clothes in dismay. "I know you don't think I'm going to be wearing these—these . . ." She trailed off, her fingertips holding the hem of the shirt out while she looked up at him, appalled.

His frown deepened to a scowl. "Those are called clothes."

"Oh, no they're not. Rags maybe." She patted her tight braid to make certain it was still intact. She might be fighting vampires and jaguars, but she was going to look good doing it. "These are not clothes." Moving her arm, when her shoulder was already on fire, had her wincing visibly. Of course he saw it. He was far more interested in the vampire bite than her fashion problem.

Riordan crouched down to examine his brother. "Juliette never worries about her clothes. She just wears whatever."

"I'm well aware that girl needs a serious makeover," Mary-Ann said. In more ways than one. Juliette also needed a few counseling sessions on dealing with overbearing men.

Riordan glanced up at her, and his smile made her breath catch in her lungs. For just one moment, in that sliver of moonlight, he had looked like his brother. The flash was there and then it was gone, and her desperation to be with Manolito grew.

Riordan straightened slowly, as the smile faded from Mary-Ann's face. "You did well. I owe you a tremendous debt. Our entire family does, MaryAnn. Thank you for saving my brother's life."

The sincerity in his voice was her undoing. If she'd been wearing her best clothes, she could have handled it all with dignity, but no, he had to put her in some horrible, wretched outfit and she just crumpled under the pressure. She heard herself blubber. He looked alarmed and even took a step back, holding up one hand.

"Don't cry. That was a compliment. Don't start crying. Your shoulder must be hurting. Let me take a look at it."

"It's the clothes." She hiccupped. "Change them fast."

"Give me a picture, then."

He sounded as desperate as she felt. She could not stand here sobbing like a baby when Manolito was facing that other world and whatever lay within it. She had to get to him. For some reason, just the thought of that spirit place gave her chills. She took a deep breath and pictured herself wearing her favorite Versace jeans, Dolce & Gabbana tobacco-colored, jersey halter top with gold leather straps and draped neckline that lay artfully over her breasts, and her favorite boots, the Michael Kors, simply because they were so stylish and comfortable and went with everything. Accessories were everything, so she went all the way and added the braided belt and chunky bracelet and necklace she'd always wanted but couldn't afford.

She took a deep breath and let it out as soon as the clothes settled onto her skin, fitting her like a glove, providing her with her suit of courage to face the next challenge. "Thanks, Riordan. This is perfect."

She expected him to give her his little sneer, but instead he studied her appearance with care. "You do look wonderful. I thought you looked fine in the other clothes, but these suit you somehow."

She smiled, feeling a little camaraderie with him for the first time. "Thanks for getting here so fast. I didn't know what to do with that thing. He just kept coming at me." She shook her head, frowning. "Well. Not me. My guardian."

"The wolf."

He said it with respect, and her heart lightened even more. MaryAnn realized what that meant. She was the wolf. It dwelled in her, silent and waiting, emerging when needed, content to stay quiet unless compelled to action. She was the sentinel, and the animals around her recognized the guardian in her for what it was. And they respected her. Riordan respected her. But more, they *accepted* her for who and what she was.

"You are Manolito's lifemate," Riordan said. "And you more than meet every expectation." He bowed low, a courtly gesture of respect. "He could not have found better. You keep many secrets, little sister."

She felt the grin spread across her face; she couldn't help it. "The wolf? She comes out upon occasion and kicks serious butt." She felt so proud saying it, so matter-of-factly. The wolf. *Her* wolf.

"I had no idea there were any lycans left in this world. Now I think they are far cleverer than any of us gave them credit for. Of course they still exist, and we should have known that. They were always content to stay in the background."

She leaned against the railing, swaying a little. "I was hoping when they got hurt they could just heal themselves the way you do. And I would have liked the ability to produce clothes with my imagination. There are a few lines I can't afford, but I sure can imagine myself wearing them."

He caught her arm to steady her, lowering her until she was sitting beside Manolito once again. "I have good news for you, MaryAnn. Manolito is quite wealthy, and you will be able to afford whatever line of clothing you prefer. It is good to keep the illusion of being entirely human at all times, but if you need, once fully Carpathian, you will be able to manufacture clothing at will."

Her heart jumped when he said that. Fully Carpathian. She still had to deal with that. And she wanted to be with Manolito De La Cruz forever. He was going to drive her insane with his arrogance, and he was going to have to learn what it was like living with a woman who was every bit as stubborn as he.

"Do you understand what that means?" Riordan asked.

"Not really. How could I?" Whatever he was doing to her shoulder was taking her breath away. It hurt like hell, and she was really glad she could stare down at her perfect boots and admire the square toe and really nice leather.

"You will be wholly Carpathian. Juliette was upset to lose her jaguar. She can call her cat, shifting into the shape and feel of it, but it is not the same. She doesn't feel a sense of loss, but I know it was difficult when she first thought of it as a loss."

"Really? I'm more concerned with losing my family. My grandparents and parents are very important to me. I don't much care for the idea of watching my friends and family die."

Riordan didn't know that her blood was infecting Manolito with the wolf, just as his blood was giving her the traits of Carpathians. Her fingers slid into the long, thick hair of her lifemate. She tasted the word and the depth of its meaning. He was hers. As much as she belonged to him, he belonged to her. Whatever was happening to her was also happening to him. What would Riordan have to say about that? How accepting would he be then?

She rubbed at her pounding temples. "Did you hear anything?" She looked around her, raised her face and sniffed the air. How often had she done that and never realized why? How often had she reached into people's minds without being aware she was doing so to extract the information she needed in order to help them? And the animals . . . She looked around her at the monkeys in the trees. They had all come to her aid when she needed them. Even the jaguar, under the enthrallment of the vampire, had fought to break the spell and do her bidding.

"The wolf is good," she said with satisfaction.

"Of course. What did you think?"

"Monster with teeth tearing apart the screaming teen with his claws and devouring the entire family while the littlest one looks on from the closet vowing to kill the hairy beast someday."

Riordan snorted, his brief smile of amusement fading as fast as it had appeared. "It can happen. There are a few who go rogue, but the wolf society, in the past, and I suspect now, always did a good job of policing their own kind. They live as humans, at least they used to prefer that, usually near the forest or jungle, or they took jobs with animals to help protect them. They rarely revealed themselves unless there was extreme danger to someone under their protection. Their numbers were dwindling even before ours. They were too spread out, the packs not close enough to interbreed, and we suspected they tried to breed with humans but weren't successful and eventually their species died out."

"Why would you think that their blood wouldn't convert a human?"

"We didn't think Carpathian blood could successfully convert a human. Juliette thinks that over the years, more humans than we realized had blood of the other species in them as well, maybe not much, but still, genetically they are probably linked."

"But you think the wolf blood isn't as strong as the Carpathian blood and that Manolito will convert me with no problem?"

She felt more than saw Riordan's hesitation. "I know he must convert you or he will not survive."

"That's not what I asked you." She pulled away from him so she could see his eyes. "What are you afraid of?"

"I do not know what will happen when he converts you," Riordan answered honestly as he reached one more time to examine the bite mark. The area was burned from the blood and saliva, as well as raw and torn. She was shaking, but didn't seem to realize it. Her fingers bunched in Manolito's hair as if he was her anchor, but she didn't seem aware of that either. "When I converted Juliette, the jaguar fought hard for life."

"Manolito converted Luiz."

"Luiz was dying. It was the only chance the jaguar had of
survival. A small part of him lives, just as a small part of Juliette's jaguar lives within her, but it isn't the same, and although
they can take the shape of a jaguar, they are not the jaguar. Does
that make sense?"

Her heart jumped. She liked her wolf. She was proud of it.
And somehow, although she'd only just found out about it, the
guardian had been there all along, shaping her life, helping her
without her knowledge. She didn't want to be anything else. She
thought of herself as human. Maybe Juliette was right and most
humans did have a genetic connection to some of the other species, but whatever the reason, she liked who she was, was comfortable in her own skin, and she didn't want to change, not if it
meant letting go of who she was. What she was. Not if she had
to let go of her newly found wolf.

But could she give up Manolito? Let him die? Let him turn
vampire? "He can't turn vampire when he knows he has a lifemate, can he? If I don't become what you are?" Her heart thudded in time to the pounding in her head. She wasn't certain
which hurt worse, her head or her shoulder. The vampire wound
burned clear to her bone.

She suddenly needed to touch Manolito's mind. To merge
with him. She fought the urge, knowing he didn't want her to
come into the shadow land with him, but it was difficult when
she needed his touch so much. She almost couldn't breathe, la-
boring to find a way to draw the air into her lungs. Was it her?
Or was it him? Was he in trouble?

"Of course he could go mad with need. It is worse to know
one's lifemate is there and one still cannot be saved. He will do
what is necessary, MaryAnn, and in the end, you will be glad
that he did."

She hurt everywhere now, her back and legs and arms, as if
someone had beaten her. "I need him." She admitted it and
should have been ashamed, but all she could think about was
getting to him.

Riordan frowned. Tiny pinpoints of blood dotted her forehead. It was unlike MaryAnn to let a statement like he had
made go without rebuttal, and she never would have admitted
her need of Manolito to him. Something was very wrong. He
had to make certain the tainted blood wasn't spreading through

her system like poison. "Just relax. I am going to heal you in the way of our people."

She took a breath and leaned closer to Manolito, needing the warmth of his touch, the feel of him close to her, but he felt cold, lifeless, his spirit a great distance from his physical body. "I have to go to him."

"Breathe. Let me do this. He would want me to." Riordan kept his voice as soothing as possible. MaryAnn had had too much to contend with in the last few days. She looked worn out, and by tomorrow night, when they next arose, in spite of what he would do here, she was going to feel the effects of crashing through branches to the ground.

He took a breath and released his body, allowing his physical self to drop away so he could become the necessary healing light of energy. He entered her body to survey the damage. The vampire had purposely infected her blood. He had not ripped and torn big chunks of flesh away; rather he had punctured deep with his razor-sharp teeth, using a sawing motion to inject thousands of tiny parasites into her bloodstream. Why? Why not try for a kill? The wolf was unexpected, but that should have pushed the vampire to defend himself with even more vigor.

The vampire had gone for the most damage he could inflict, rather than for a kill. The jugular was left intact. He had raked and torn at the wolf's belly, bit the shoulder, but not a single wound was a kill target. No vampire had that kind of control during a life-and-death battle—not unless he was programmed. And who could manipulate a vampire, even a lesser vampire, when his life was at stake? By nature, vampires were selfish and cunning. Riordan observed the parasites teaming in MaryAnn's bloodstream with dismay.

He entered his own body. "This may take a little while. Are you feeling sick?" He hadn't detected poison, so the vampire hadn't injected a lethal chemical into her.

"It can't take too long. We have to help Manolito."

He studied her face. Aside from looking so weary, she didn't appear to be alarmed, so she didn't know. He would bet his life the wolf did. "Rest," he advised, more for the wolf than for her. Because the wolf was going to be needed later; he was certain of that.

MaryAnn closed her eyes and leaned her head against

Manolito's shoulder. Riordan stood over her, shedding his body
so that he could fight the battle against the parasites the vampire had left behind.

~

Manolito stared in shock at Draven Dubrinsky. The man was
long dead. Why hadn't Vlad warned him that his son resided in
the meadow of mists and shadows? Draven, like his father and
Mikhail, was a vessel for the power of the Carpathian people.
He would know the exact tone, the exact path, mind-to-mind,
even of lifemates.

Manolito's heart jumped, his belly knotted, but he kept his
pulse steady and strong, his features expressionless. His first
thought was to warn MaryAnn. To do that, he would have to
merge with her. Would that pull her into the world enough that
Maxim would be able to grab her?

He let his breath out slowly, keeping his mind away from
MaryAnn, blocking her out so that if Draven touched his mind,
he wouldn't be able to find her, or even a hint of a path to her.
She wasn't Carpathian. Draven couldn't automatically search
her out as he might a full-blooded Carpathian female.

He refused to look at the son of Dubrinsky, choosing to keep
the battle between him and Maxim. He knew the Malinovs,
and he was more than willing to match wits if that was what it
took to keep the Carpathians safe. "You cannot drag her into
this world through me. Not with the likes of him."

"Do not be so sure of yourself, Manolito. That was always
your downfall. You and all your brothers." Bitter contempt
curled in Maxim's voice. "How do you think your woman will
fair against one of our most powerful?" His laughter was soft
and mocking. "I do not think so well."

Manolito frowned as the rain forest closed in around him. He
saw MaryAnn sitting beside his physical body, knees drawn up,
one hand twisted in his hair. There was blood on her shoulder
and down the front of her. Her shirt was torn. He couldn't see her
face, but she seemed to trust the man standing so close to her.
Riordan. His brother. Bending close to examine the wounds.

He should have looked protective, but there was a furtive,
cunning quality about him as he stood over her, like predator
over prey. He turned his head and smiled at Manolito. Riordan's
face blurred and became that of Kirja, one of Maxim's brothers.

Manolito's heart nearly stopped. He held himself still, afraid of moving, of triggering the attack on MaryAnn. Everything in him told him to reach for her, to warn her . . .

Maxim leaned close. "Humans are so easily fooled."

Manolito closed his eyes as relief swept through him. "I do not think so. And as I recall, my brother Rafael ripped Kirja's heart from his body and sent him to the deepest pits of whatever hell is waiting for the likes of him." A human might not sense the danger, but the wolf would. A guardian would have sprung forth instantly had a vampire been attacking MaryAnn.

"I hope you are certain."

With that, Kirja knocked MaryAnn aside and, in one quick motion, slit Manolito's throat where he sat so helplessly. Mary-Ann cried out and tried to crawl away, but the vampire dragged her back by her ankles, flipping her over and ripping the clothes from her body. He kicked her ribs viciously and then bent down to punch her relentlessly in the face. She rolled away, and he grabbed her by her hair and dragged her over to Manolito, holding her there while he forced her to watch him lapping at the blood pulsing from her lifemate's throat.

Manolito discovered there were far worse things than physical torture. He told himself it wasn't really MaryAnn, but his eyes and brain refused to believe him. He told himself Kirja was long dead and gone from the living world, but the blood and screams were all too real. He shuddered as Kirja continued to beat her. He felt his stomach rebel when the vampire committed further perversions on her, every atrocity Maxim could think of, and he could think of many.

Manolito had no way to stop the images, so he tried to shut down his emotions. There was no way. In this land, he was meant to feel emotions—they all were—and the emotions were amplified a thousand times. He knew now how the undead could drive a spirit mad. He couldn't compartmentalize; he had to feel every blow, every sick, disgusting thing MaryAnn had to endure. His lungs burned for air. His hands trembled. He curled his fingers into a fist to . . . what? They had no bodies. This was a mind game. They were waiting for him to break. The hope was that he would merge with MaryAnn to check on her, to ease his own suffering.

He shook his head. "I will never let you have her, Maxim, no matter what you do to me. No matter what you show to me."

Kirja plunged his fist into MaryAnn's chest and pulled out her heart, holding it high in the air while she screamed. Manolito's body jerked, but he stood impassive. If his fate was to endure the next centuries feeling her pain and watching her torture, he would do so. They could not have her. It may have been only minutes, or hours—time meant little in this place—but it seemed lifetimes, centuries, watching the other half of his soul being forced to endure whatever Kirja, Maxim or Draven conceived. The sound of MaryAnn's pleas and screams, the images of her torture were burned forever into his heart, his mind and even deeper into his soul.

"He cannot love her to stand there like that," Draven said. "Any man would break if he saw his true lifemate so brutally handled."

Manolito looked through him. Draven Dubrinsky would never know what love was. Manolito knew. He felt it in every blow of Kirja's hand, every kick of his feet, every touch on MaryAnn's body. An illusion. All illusion.

He forced a smile when he could feel blood running down his body in rivers of sweat. That, too, was an illusion. "A game, Maxim, that is all. You play games with me and you know I will never break. You know me. So keep it up if you must, but it seems childish, even for you."

Maxim snarled, showing his pegs for teeth, and waved the illusion away.

"Acknowledge me," Draven snarled, already furious that the Carpathian male wouldn't look at him.

"I have no wish to speak with you, see you or in any way render you real," he said, watching Maxim more than Draven. Vlad's son had power, but it was Maxim who had the cunning and the hatred enough to return to destroy the Carpathian people.

"I find it—*distasteful*—Maxim, that you would choose to spend time with one such as this. He caused the death of our beloved sister. You may have embraced him, but I do not wish to spend time with him. Do not think I fear one such as this reject from the Dubrinsky lineage. Long ago I would have welcomed the chance to take his life. It would have been nothing against the loss of one such as Ivory, but still, I would have welcomed it, as you should have, Maxim."

He kept his gaze fixed firmly on Maxim, his tone dripping with contempt.

Maxim growled, spittle running down his chin as he swung his head from side to side in a threatening manner. "Do not use that condescending attitude with me. Your disloyalty proved long ago whose side you were on."

For the first time, Manolito allowed a whip of anger to seep into his voice, and he lashed Maxim with it. "Do not dare use the term disloyal when your sister's murderer stands at your side. You have sunk lower than I thought possible, becoming the dog for this foul abomination. Crawl on your knees to him, Maxim, like those who seek your approval. Lick his boots if you must. I have no further business with you, not when this . . ." Deliberately he waved his hand toward Draven. "This . . . piece of garbage is your master."

"I am *royalty*," Draven snapped. "*You* should be on your knees to me."

Manolito didn't bother to spare him a glance. He kept his gaze locked with Maxim's as he conjured up a picture in his mind of Ivory. For him, she was as fresh and as pure as the last time he'd seen her, her memory such a part of him it would never fade. He sent it along the path of their blood bond. Ivory with her laughter and her bright soul shining. Ivory flinging her arms around Maxim and kissing his cheek. Ivory standing outside the Malinov home, sword in hand, blindfolded in the middle of the circle of her five brothers and the De La Cruz brothers as they taught her to fight.

Stop it! Maxim screamed, pressing his fingers to his eye sockets.

Manolito projected the loving memories as relentlessly as Maxim had tormented him with MaryAnn's torture. Ivory as a young child riding on Maxim's shoulders. Her first time in the air with her brothers surrounding her, keeping her safe, Ruslan always beneath her, Maxim and Kirja on either side, while Vadim and Sergey prowled the air in front and behind. Her laughter. The moon illuminating her brightness as she raced down the stairs to greet them when they returned from battle.

Stop it. I beg you. Stop it.

Because in the meadow of shadows and mists, the ghosts could feel every emotion. Hatred. Bitterness. Sorrow. Regret.

They were meant to feel it like the lash of the whip, driving home their destructive path. It was why Manolito so acutely felt the emotions pouring into him, even when he knew the scene of MaryAnn's torture was illusion. He was meant to feel what he had not all those long centuries.

Maxim had no choice but to feel the love for his sister. Emotions poured into his mind with every memory. He covered his face with his hands and fell to his knees.

"You stand with the man who would have done those very things to her that you wanted done to my lifemate. Should I show you what was in Draven's mind? The perversions he would have inflicted upon Ivory?"

Manolito would never have been able to do such a thing, but he knew Maxim would conjure them up in his own mind. He would know that he stood shoulder to shoulder with the one who had ultimately taken Ivory from them. He planned evil with the one who would have committed the ultimate betrayal of her.

"No. I cannot think of her."

There were so many memories. Manolito felt the tears in his own heart. Ivory. He had loved her as a sister. She had brightened all their lives with her generous spirit and compassionate nature.

"You have done what you intended, Manolito."

They all whirled around to face the couple who had come up so quietly behind them. Vlad and Sarantha stood hand in hand.

"You should not be here," Manolito said. He glanced at Draven, at the snicker on his face, and wanted to smash something. Vlad and his lifemate deserved so much more from a son. "This is my mess, and I will find a way to clean it up." He wanted to spare them the pain of facing the monster Draven had been. Somehow, he knew Ivory would have wanted that rather than revenge.

"You have destroyed their plans and managed to bring Maxim to the realization of what he has done. He will not aid his brothers," Vlad said. "Your time here is over. I have yet to do my duty and then ours will be, too."

Manolito looked down at his hands. They were no longer transparent. He closed his fingers into a tight fist and then opened his hand once again.

"We stand with you always," Manolito said, knowing Vlad would understand he meant every De La Cruz.

"You and your brothers have been loyal to our people," Vlad said. "I trust that you will aid the jaguars as best you can, and give that same loyalty I have always counted on to my sons."

Sarantha stepped close to him and touched the scars. "You saved Mikhail's life. And you saved our son, Jacques, by stepping in front of Shea and taking the poisoned knife. You also saved our unborn grandson. I thank you. It is not enough, but it is all I have to give."

Vlad gripped his forearms. "Go now. Leave this place. You do not belong here anymore. Let me take care of the business I should have centuries ago. Live large and well, old friend."

Manolito stepped away. He felt himself reaching for Mary-Ann. For his brothers. For life. He stopped for a moment to observe Vlad and Sarantha face their son.

"You have had many years here, Draven, and we have stood by you, but no longer. Even here, when you are given the chance to redeem yourself, you refuse. We accept your decision. Go now, from this place to the next."

"No! You cannot. I am your son." For the first time, the smirk was gone from Draven's face. He threw himself at his mother, wrapping his arms around her legs. "Do not let him condemn me. He cannot send me away."

"*We* condemn you, as we should have so many years ago, Draven," Sarantha said, conviction in her voice. "Go now. Perhaps in the next place you will learn far more than we could ever teach you."

Draven screamed as black smoke curled around him, pouring from his body to surround him. Shadows moved along the ground, skittered over the trees. The vines pushed up from the earth, long, tangled barbs on the seeking tentacles. The vampires stood mesmerized, some with smiles, others with nervous scowls, but all frozen as Draven tried to run.

The vines reared back, coiled like snakes, and then lashed out, circling Draven's ankles. They yanked hard, and he fell into a nest of greedy claws reaching out of the ground for him. One moment he was there, wrapped in the barbs, his mouth opened wide in a now-silent scream, the next he was gone, swallowed by a black hole.

There was silence. Sarantha dropped her head on Vlad's shoulder. He held her close, protectively, sheltering her against his larger body. Manolito could feel the pull of his own world drawing him, and he went, eager to get back to his own life-mate, to hold her in his arms and shelter her the way Vlad had Sarantha throughout their centuries together. When he glanced back, all he could see of them was blazing light, and then that, too, was gone and he was back in his own body.

MaryAnn gasped and threw her arms around him, fitting neatly, perfectly, into his frame. He smiled over her head at Riordan. "Thank you," he said simply. And meant it.

18

"Are you all right? Did they hurt you?" MaryAnn skimmed her hand anxiously down Manolito's chest. "I was so worried about you."

"No, *meu amor*, but you—I saw you with blood on your shoulder and belly." He touched her bare shoulder where the angry marks showed, then tugged up her shirt to examine the bare expanse of flesh.

Riordan cleared his throat. "I am still here."

Neither looked up or acknowledged his statement.

MaryAnn ran her hands under Manolito's shirt. "How did you get out of that place? I was right, wasn't I? Maxim was trying to kill you." She went up on her toes to press half a dozen kisses down Manolito's throat. "You are free of the shadow world for good, aren't you?"

Riordan scratched his head. "I just want to say one word here. Vampire. Are you listening, Manolito? She fought a vampire."

That got through. Manolito pulled her closer and this time did a long examination of the wounds.

"I removed all the parasites, if you're interested," Riordan said.

Manolito swept her once again against him, raining kisses along her shoulder, his heart leaping in his chest and then settling into a steady rhythm. He should have thought of their blood. If they had managed to pull her into their world with the infected blood in her system, the blood would have called to them. Xavier might have been able to find a way to resurrect his dead army after all.

"I have to check, MaryAnn," he said, framing her face in his hands. "I have to be certain nothing can harm you."

"*Hello!* That's such an insult, bro," Riordan said, but he couldn't help the grin spreading across his face. They had it bad, those two. Stubborn as mules, but still, they had eyes only for each other.

MaryAnn buried her face against Manolito's throat, circling her arms around his neck. "Take me somewhere safe where I can breathe." She wanted to touch him, inspect every inch of his body to make certain he hadn't been harmed.

"We actually have a few things of importance to discuss," Riordan tried again, knowing it was in vain, but figuring he could rack up a few teasing jabs he could pull out later on his brother. Big bad Manolito was putty in the hands of his life-mate. "You know, things like the wolf. Bad blood. What happened in the spirit world."

Manolito lifted MaryAnn into his arms, ignoring his youngest brother. "I know a place you will love."

Riordan rolled his eyes. "I guess I'll just leave you two alone." His grin widened when neither looked his way. "I can take care of Solange and Jasmine for the night, if you two—you know—want some alone time." They didn't even appear grateful for that. He shook his head and dissolved. There was no use trying to get anything of importance out of either of them tonight.

MaryAnn closed her eyes and laid her head against Manolito's chest, turning her face up to the night sky. She might never get used to flying through the air, but as long as he held her so close, she could enjoy being in his arms. The wind and mist were cool on her face, and she felt safe as he whisked her over the canopy toward his surprise destination.

It didn't take long to find the entrance to the underground cavern Manolito had discovered years earlier. The island had only two sections where the terrain rolled into what could be called hills, and they were covered in thick forest. A waterfall poured into a pool that fed the stream running down toward the river surrounding the island, picking up strength as it went, rushing and frothing over boulders and smaller rocks until it poured into the larger body of water.

MaryAnn looked around her as he set her on her feet. "It's breathtaking." Flowers wound up and down the trunks of the trees, blossoming in every vibrant color possible. The sound of the water added to the beauty and wildness of the place, yet it seemed a private cocoon where no one would disturb them.

Manolito waved his hands at the waterfall, and the heavy stream parted to reveal a ledge behind it. He caught her up and leapt, taking her through the spray to set her on the other side. "This was an incredible find."

"It certainly is beautiful," she agreed, trying to still the uneasiness in her as she looked around for bugs. Bugs and bats. "Aren't there like a zillion different kinds of bugs in caves?" Her voice came out in a little squeak.

Manolito laughed. "You just fought a vampire, MaryAnn."

"Yes, well, I don't think the wolf is going to come leaping out because I see a crawly thing—no matter how scared of it I might be."

He laughed. "Good point."

He flicked a hand toward what appeared to be a crack in the rocks, and at once light threw the narrow tunnel behind it into relief. Slipping inside, Manolito stepped back so MaryAnn could get a clear view of the walls of a tunnel leading deeper under the hill. Rows of torches cast dancing shadows along the way and illuminated the drawings covering the rock walls.

He gestured for her to go in front of him. When she hesitated, he caught her hand and tugged her to him, nuzzling her neck. "Your wolf will love this place."

She relaxed against his body, tilting her head to look up at him. "I'm sure she will, but I was thinking more along the lines of a five-star hotel. Is that really asking too much? I mean, come on, Manolito, a *cave*. Do I look like a woman who goes exploring dark places where bugs congregate?"

She hadn't even mentioned the bats, and maybe she was getting all girly on him, but really, didn't Carpathians believe in hotels? "I don't have enough bug spray for something like this."

"I will take care of the bugs for you. Give it a chance. You will love it."

She sighed. He had that smile and those eyes, and the sound of his laughter, even though the sound was in her mind, made her stomach bottom out. She was merged with him and read how "cute" he found her. She would never have described herself as cute, but what the heck, she'd take it when he was enjoying himself. He wasn't a man to laugh much, so fine, she'd walk into his cave.

"I understand where you get the whole Neanderthal mentality if you hang out here all the time," she mumbled, but she slid through the crack, careful not to touch either side of the rock.

She swallowed fear and forced herself to walk a little way inside, just enough for Manolito to get through as well. They stood close, his body heat warming her as she studied the numerous drawings of animals on the walls. It was like an art museum of work over centuries of time. Crude stick figures gave way to more elaborate and detailed work, all holding a unique beauty and giving off a sense of timelessness. The paintings depicted a society of jaguar people. Some were in human form, some in the middle of shifting and some fully in cat form.

"Do you think they lived together like this at one time?" MaryAnn asked, touching one of the drawn cat's ears with gentle fingers. "There's a campfire. Men have their arms around women, and children are playing. Was it ever like this?"

"I never saw them that way, and I have been around a long time, but the jaguar and lycan really were secretive about their societies. I fought beside them a couple of times, but never saw them in their own environments."

"You should show this to Luiz."

He shrugged his shoulders. "Perhaps someday. It is a favorite resting place of mine, and we rarely allow anyone to know where we sleep."

There was something in his voice, in his mind, she caught. A sadness. Wariness. She stilled, leaning back into him. "You're afraid Luiz won't make it."

He wrapped his arms around her. "I find that having emotions, particularly fear, can be disturbing. I am worried about the possibility. I like the man. I thought I had converted him solely because you asked me to, but now I am not so certain."

She turned in his arms, her hand sliding under his hair to curl around the nape of his neck. "If he doesn't, Manolito, it isn't your fault. You've given him every chance, more than he ever would have gotten. And thank you—whether you did it solely for me, for him, or because he is a friend—thank you."

He kissed the tip of her nose. "You are very welcome." He framed her face with his hands. "I have to check for myself that the vampire didn't leave anything behind that could harm you. I need a minute."

"Riordan did a good job healing me. I'm a little achy, but other than that, the shoulder and my stomach feel fine."

He didn't argue, merely let his physical body drop away and his spirit enter hers, taking his time to make certain not a single parasite had hidden from Riordan. When he came back to himself, she was tapping her foot.

"Are you satisfied?"

"Yes. For now. Later I intend to inspect every inch of your skin."

"Fine. I'm doing the same to you."

He grinned at her. "Come, let me show you this place." He waved casually toward the entrance, and the crack in the boulders groaned and creaked so that she gasped and nearly climbed up his shoulders.

"What the hell was that?" She literally crawled up his body. "I think this cave is coming down on top of us, Manolito."

He tried not to laugh. She clawed for a purchase on his shoulders, her head swiveling left and right, her eyes enormous. He couldn't help it—the laughter spilled out to become a full-blown roar. "I am closing the door."

"Oh no, you're not." She had her arms around his head, practically blinding him. "And stop laughing. This isn't funny. I'm not getting trapped in a cave, not even for you. Gorgeous can only take you so far."

The two sides of the boulder ground together with a horrendous jarring, eliciting a screech of fear from her. The torches flickered and danced as if they might go out. She buried both fists in his hair and yanked. "Get us out of here."

Manolito wrapped his arm around her and pulled her back down so her feet were once again on solid ground. "We do not want light shining through the falls. The idea is to be safe here. We have air. I'll take care of bugs. Trust me, MaryAnn, this is better than a five-star hotel."

She stared up into his face. A woman could drown in the absolute love in his eyes. She let out her breath and found calm. "Well I want room service then."

"I intend to give you anything you want."

The velvet caress in his voice sent a shiver running through her body. "I don't know how you managed to get around all my defenses, Manolito, but you have."

His slow smile made her heart nearly stop.

"I cheated. I will probably go to hell if there is such a place, because I fear I do not have the necessary remorse in me for my actions. I stole you, MaryAnn, right out from under the noses of our best hunters."

She laughed. "You sound like you're boasting."

He kissed the corner of her mouth. "Maybe just a little. After all, you have to know your caveman can bring home the dinosaur."

She looked around suspiciously. "You'd better be joking."

He tucked her hand in his back pocket to lead her down the long, winding tunnel. Torches lined the way, burning brightly and showing her he was keeping his promise—there wasn't a single bug in sight.

"I've been thinking a lot about this Carpathian-wolf thing we have going," she said, trying not to keep staring at his butt. He had a nice ass.

His laughter was soft. "I was just thinking the same thing about you."

"What?" She tried to sound innocent.

"Ass. Butt. However you want to describe that particular portion of your anatomy. Yours is quite nice. I was just thinking how you looked in those red heels. You take my breath away, woman." She did a whole lot more than that. His body hardened and thickened with every step he took. With her mind firmly merged with his, knowing she was thinking along the same lines as he was only heightened the ache.

He wanted to get her out of her clothes and inspect every single inch of her body to make certain she was all right. And he wasn't going to let her out of his sight again—at least not for a long, long time.

He swung around and pulled her to him, kissing her hard, his tongue sliding into her mouth to tangle and dance and reclaim her all over again.

MaryAnn recognized the hint of desperation wrapped in the hunger. She pulled back, smoothing his hair. "What is it?"

Her voice. The way she effortlessly slipped inside his head, surrounding him with warmth and comfort, enveloping him in love—he felt it now, where it hadn't been before. He didn't know what he'd done to earn it, but he was grateful.

He pressed his forehead to hers and closed his eyes briefly, inhaling her scent. "They could not kill my physical body in the spirit world, so they tried to kill my soul."

She felt the involuntary shudder that went through him. "How, Manolito? Tell me how."

He knew she didn't have a clue that her tone held a hidden compulsion. She wanted to take the pain of those memories away. Her fingers stroked and caressed his hair, slid down to his shoulders and arms, and then back up. Every touch was meant to share, to soothe. His MaryAnn. There was no one else like her. He caught her chin and bent his head to fasten his mouth to hers. She leaned into him, her soft body pliant, fitting him perfectly.

"Tell me," she whispered.

He took a breath, fighting the images in his head. He couldn't go there again, couldn't let himself see her being brutalized. She gasped and he knew she saw, too.

"It's all right, Manolito. It didn't happen. Maxim tried to trick you."

"He didn't know about the wolf," Manolito said. "Your wolf." He tugged at her curls. "Your wolf saved us all the way around."

She smiled up at him. "Of course it did. My wolf is totally cool."

"Your wolf is hot," he corrected and turned her around.

The room was oval shaped and deep, wide and spacious. Thousands of colored crystals covered the walls. The lights from the torches picked up the many colors, scattering rainbow prisms dancing all around the room. The bed was enormous, a big four-poster of carved exotic wood, with wrought iron embellishing it. She stepped close to it, running her hands over one of the posts. The moment she touched it, she knew he had made it.

"This is real."

He nodded. "I like working with my hands. My brothers call it my vice." He led her around to the head of the bed, where she could examine the board there. Two small tables stood on either side, but it was the headboard that intrigued her. There were symbols, hieroglyphics, carved into the wood and several small iron rings embedded across it.

"What does this say?"

"It is in an ancient language."

"And?" she prompted.

"To bring only pleasure to *ainaak sivamet jutta*."

"You'll have to translate that as well."

"Forever to my heart connected. My love. Wife. Lifemate. *You*."

"You made this bed for me?"

"It was made for the other half of my soul. Yes. For you. I poured everything I felt for you into this. Every dream. Every fantasy. I tried to think of every way I could pleasure you and make certain I was ready for that. I studied every century's new ideas on sensual pleasure, every culture's ideas, and learned as much as I could."

The idea was almost frightening. "I'm not exactly all that experienced, Manolito."

"A mind merge is a wonderful thing," he pointed out. "So are you happy with the accommodations? We have privacy, warmth, and I can assure you, the mattress is the top of the line."

She had no doubt about that. Manolito didn't do anything halfway. "Okay, it's five-star all right. But where's the service?" she teased.

He smiled, his sinfully sexy smirk that seemed to burn slow and mean through her entire body. "I have plans to provide service all night. Did I mention I love your shirt?" His hands went to the leather straps circling her neck. The golden leather fell so that the soft jersey drape dipped even lower. It had skimmed the swell of her breasts, but now her nipples peeked out at him. "Oh, yeah, I like this top," he reiterated and bent his head to flick each nipple with his tongue.

She shivered as his hair slid over her skin, a fall of midnight silk she couldn't help invading with her fingers. "Take your shirt off, Manolito."

He stepped back, bringing her hands to the buttons. "You take it off for me." His black eyes seemed to scorch her skin.

MaryAnn slid the buttons aside one at a time, and with each one, her lungs became a little more labored. She used her palms, fingers splayed wide on his chest, to push the shirt aside and up and over his broad shoulders. She tugged it off and let it fall. His skin glowed in the dancing firelight. God, he was beautiful. Built like a man should be built. If that made her shallow, then all right, she'd accept that. She ran her palms over the defined muscles of his chest and then down to his six-pack and narrow waist.

Above her head, his features were strong—his jaw, his nose,

the high cheekbones. He kept his chin up, looking over her head as she leaned in to press kisses along every delineated muscle.

"You will need to remove my shoes before you can my trousers," he pointed out.

Her heart jumped and she glanced up at him through her lashes, but he continued to study a spot above her head. She moistened her lips and crouched down to untie his shoes. She knew he could simply wish his clothes away, but she didn't want him to and maybe he was reading that in her mind. She wanted the sensual discovery of unwrapping his body, a gift, a treasure, just for her.

He lifted his foot and let her slip off his shoe and sock, her fingers lingering on his skin, stroking his ankle and up his calf, before going to the next shoe. She set them aside and knelt up to reach for the waistband of his trousers. Her jersey top slipped further down to pool around her waist, leaving her breasts exposed. The cool air tightened her nipples even more, but Mary-Ann found it erotic to be kneeling in front of him, half-clothed, her breasts spilling out while he stood waiting for her to undress him.

Manolito's breath caught in his lungs. She was so beautiful, looking up at him that way, so seductive she was lucky he had enough control to give her whatever she wanted, because right now, he wanted to just lift her up and bury himself in her. She wanted to play. He watched the tip of her tongue moisten her full lower lip, drawing his attention to her mouth. She was inches away from the thick bulge in his trousers. He was separated from paradise only by that thin layer of material, already stretched to the maximum.

He closed his eyes briefly as he felt her fingers dance around the opening and then slowly peel the material aside. His erection sprung out, large and pulsing with need. Her cheek brushed the ultrasensitive head as she drew down his trousers, urging him to step out of them. Her fingers brushed back up his leg, inside his thigh, and then she cupped his balls in her hands. His breath left his lungs in a long rush. His cock jerked as she blew warm air over him, her lips barely brushing the broad tip.

He caught a fistful of hair and tugged, drawing her head up. "Lie across the bed for me."

"But I wanted . . ."

"I'll give you what you want. Do this for me."

Slowly, his gaze holding hers, she sank down onto the mattress. He pulled her legs across the bed sideways and gently pressed on her shoulder until she slowly lay back, her head at the very edge of the bed, hair falling toward the floor. Very gently he removed her boots and set them beside his shoes. The feel of his strong hands moving down her calves sent little tingles of excitement racing through her bloodstream. He tugged at her jeans until she lifted her bottom and let him slide them off. She was left draped across the bed with her top pooled around her rib cage.

Manolito moved around to the side of the bed where her head was, caught her shoulders and tugged until her neck was off the bed and her head was tipped back. Her breasts thrust invitingly into the air, her nipples twin tight peaks begging for his attention.

MaryAnn's heart jumped. She felt a little vulnerable and exposed in this position. The rainbow lights played lovingly over her body, almost spotlighting her. She could feel the moisture gathering between her legs, and every single nerve ending was alive with anticipation.

He spread his legs, taking a wide stance as he towered over her. His cock was engorged, thick and long, his balls smooth and tight. "Reach back for me," he instructed, his eyes on her mouth.

Her body trembled with the sudden desire to please him. To have him. To make him burn for her. He made her feel so sexy and wanted, with just a look, a brush of his gaze. She reached both arms back to cup his balls, to draw her fingernails lightly over his tight sac to memorize the texture and shape. The air left her body in a hiss and she smiled, running her tongue along her teeth. He wanted to be in control, but the brush of her fingertips, the light squeeze of her hands, the small flick of her tongue as she brought him to her mouth told her she had far more power over his body than she'd first thought.

He murmured something graphic, stepping even closer, his hands finding her long, curly hair. "Slide down a little more now, *meu amor*. That's it. That's what I want. You can take so much more of me this way."

Her head was back, throat arched, breasts thrust upward, her body laid out like a feast. To stay in control, he circled the base of his shaft with one hand and pushed the head against her waiting mouth, teasing her lips. Her tongue flicked out, and she did a long, slow lick, curling it at the end, like she was scooping ice cream out of a cone.

She made him wait. A heartbeat. Two. The world stood still. Time faltered and his heart lurched. Her mouth engulfed him like a silken glove, slid over his cock, her tongue swirling under the head and up over it, teasing and darting around while she suckled.

His hips jerked. A sound escaped, something suspiciously close to a rough growl. Pleasure burst through him, rushing like a drug through his system. More than pleasure. Love. With his cock in her mouth, he doubted he should have been feeling anything but lust, but maybe love drove his lust for her, because he couldn't imagine another woman more beautiful, or sexier. He couldn't imagine feeling this desire, so intense it was a wild storm crashing through him, for anyone else. His breath exploded out of his lungs. His body shuddered as the fire raced up his spine.

She ran another long, slow lick up and down the shaft, watching him, watching his reaction. He felt her in his mind, sharing the fire, sharing each wave of sensation she created as she drew him back deeper, her mouth hot and tight.

His hands bunched in her hair. His hips thrust forward, using his own hand to keep each forward movement short as he filled her mouth. Her tongue was a velvet rasp as she licked the underside, and then she was suckling again, drawing him deeper. Her eyes remained locked on his, tearing at his heart, his soul, as he watched her swallow him, watched raw desire heat her gaze.

She took him into her mouth, a long, slow draw, keeping her mouth tight, her tongue flat while she applied pressure and then whipped her head up fast, meeting his thrust, taking him deeper, so that streaks of fire spread through his groin.

MaryAnn felt her body going up in flames. Her breasts were swollen and aching, begging for attention. The junction between her legs throbbed and was drenched with heat. He was making rough sounds of pleasure, each one vibrating through her, so that the walls of her sheath contracted and rippled and begged for mercy. He was tugging at her hair with each thrust as he began to lose his control, pulling her toward him as his thrusts deepened.

"Harder," he encouraged.

She felt him swelling and knew by his husky groan he was close. She couldn't move, locked beneath him, his hands controlling her head, the short, tight movements as her mouth moved up and down his shaft. He directed the arch of her neck, allowing her to take more of him.

"Relax your throat for me," he instructed, his breath coming in harsh, ragged gasps. "Yes. Like that. Like that. Squeeze down." The thrusts were faster now, short and hard, but he used the leverage to go deeper, the tugs on her hair sending pulses of pleasure shooting through her body.

"You have to stop, *sivamet*." His voice was hardly his own, so gravelly, on the edge of desperation. Because he couldn't. Because even though he locked her down in the traditional way of his kind, he couldn't leave that hot, moist cavern, so tight as she suckled at him. It was such a carnal pleasure to indulge in, to be indulged. "Stop before it's too late."

Traditional way of his kind. Where had that thought come from? Why did he have such a desire to hold her still while he plunged in and out of her incredible mouth?

MaryAnn wanted him, all of him, was desperate for him. She felt like a woman on the brink of sanity, starving for what he had to offer. His cock thickened. Jerked. Grew hot and full. There was something terribly erotic about lying all sprawled out, held tightly in place, knowing she was pushing him past all control, even as he was controlling her. She knew it was the wolf. She scented the musky call of the male wolf as Manolito thrust hard, his hands rough now, his cock jerking, the hot jets of semen exploding into her. It was the way of the wolf to dominate, and looking up at him, she could see the amber lights flickering in the black depths of his eyes.

He reached for her breasts, his fingers tugging at her nipples while her mouth pulled at him. Without warning, he simply bent over her, his long body covering hers, and buried his face between her thighs. She couldn't breathe. Couldn't think. Her body bucked and writhed as his tongue stabbed deep. She was forced to turn her head and release him, and all he did was crawl up her body and pull her hips up to his marauding mouth. Her vision blurred. Her body belonged to him. To his hands and mouth and the long, muscled length of him.

I want your heart and soul.

The whisper would have stolen her last defense if she'd had any. *You have them.*

You are safe in my keeping. And she was. As long as he lived and breathed, beyond that even, he would protect and cherish her.

His tongue found slick heat, warm honey, and he indulged himself, holding her there easily while he took what he wanted. Her hips bucked, her breath came in sobs, as he devoured her. Her body was primed for him, already shuddering with her first climax, and he was throwing her into the second one with the dancing of his fingers over and in her. She cried out his name, music to him, the soft, ragged, breathy sound, barely audible when she ground against him in an attempt to get relief. Her releases only added to the pressure building, forever building until she was chanting, *Please, please, please.*

Manolito raised his head and pulled her around to him, lifting her upright into his arms, pushing up with his body while he held her until he was standing. "Wrap your legs around my waist, MaryAnn." His voice was rough and mesmerizing.

"I don't have any strength." She didn't, her arms and legs heavy, her body still shaking from the series of orgasms. Even so, she locked her fingers on his shoulders while she circled his body with her legs.

"I have the strength for both of us. Just hold on, *sivamet.*"

She locked her ankles and closed her eyes as he lowered her over him. The broad head of his cock drove through her soft, tight folds, the friction on her already-sensitive nerve endings making her cry out and bury her face against him. "I don't know if I can do this," she whispered. "It's too much, every time, too much."

How could she survive when her body was already in meltdown? Her need seemed unrelenting, the pressure building and building as he withdrew and her muscles tried to grip and hold him to her.

Manolito caught her hair and pulled her head up so he could find her mouth with his. He needed to kiss her. To feel part of her, to be inside of her. He looked into her eyes and saw need there, hot and yet filled with such love. His heart jerked in his chest, and he kissed her again, using a gentle rhythm to entice her to ride him. His hands gripped her bottom, lifting her, showing her, feeling the silken heat flash through him when her muscles clamped down.

So hot. A searing fire streaking up his cock and spreading to every inch of his body. The primitive need to possess her was a dark lust that wouldn't—couldn't—be stopped. Heat, lust, love, passion and arousal all mingled together as the bite of her muscles clamped around him and silken walls tightened until he was strangling somewhere between pleasure and pain.

Manolito shifted again, tipping her back onto the bed so he was bent over her, watching them come together, watching her body stretch impossibly to accommodate his. The sight of her body accepting his was so erotic it shook him. Her tight sheath was velvet soft but scorching, so that he lost his ability to think, to control, until he was pumping into her, deeper and deeper, while the white-hot pleasure burst around him.

She rose to meet every drive of his hips, every thrust and surge, urging him to a harder, faster ride, until he felt her release ripping through her like a firestorm—catching him up in the vortex, sucking and milking while streaks of lightning raced over his cock and he exploded deep inside her, jet after jet pulsing while her body gripped him hard. He lay over her for a long while, gasping her name, stroking her back, fighting for control when his body no longer belonged to him.

Gently he lifted her all the way onto the bed and lay down beside her, his legs too weak to hold him up any longer. She burrowed close to him, her arms around his neck, her breasts pressed against him, body still shuddering with pleasure.

"I think I am alive," he said, faint humor in his voice.

"I'm not." She was tired. Exhausted, but every time he shifted, her body reacted.

He moved against her, his mouth trailing down her throat to the swell of her breast, and she held her breath as she felt his incisors prick her skin. Instinct was taking over and she wanted what he was offering. She arched closer, but he merely flicked her breast with his tongue, pulling back as he rolled over.

It was too late for him. He had taken her blood numerous times, so much so that he knew the infection raged in his body. His Carpathian blood prevented him from feeling too many of the effects, but still, the wolf was in him now. But MaryAnn, it wasn't too late for her. He just had to maintain control at all times. Making love to her was the most dangerous of times because the need, the craving for her blood was on him all the time.

She lay in silence for a long while, listening to the combined rhythm of their heartbeats. Finally she propped herself up onto her elbow, levering up onto her side so she could look at him. "Manolito, I'm in your mind and I can feel your need to convert me. You don't just want to do it; every instinct you have is demanding it."

His fingers curled around the nape of her neck. "That matters little to me. Your safety and happiness are more important than anything else."

"Riordan said you could still turn vampire."

"You misunderstood." His fingers began a slow massage to ease the tension out of her. "We are bound together. I cannot turn. I will choose a life with you, whether it is here or in your beloved city of Seattle." He flashed her a smile. "See? I am beginning to be able to read your mind at will, too."

"What does that mean? I don't understand."

"I will grow old and die as you do. The lycan have longevity as well, but not as Carpathians. When you give up life, so will I."

She was silent, studying his face, probing his mind. Delving deep, she found—the wolf. She had known all along it was emerging, but now she could feel its powerful presence. With that combined with his Carpathian characteristics, Manolito would be a difficult man to handle. It was fortunate she had her wolf to help guide her.

"I want to go back to Seattle to see my family often," she said.

"Of course."

"And you will be charming and not at all bossy."

His eyebrow shot up. "It is always said that I am a charming man."

"By whom? You and your brothers?" She gave a delicate sniff of disbelief. "When we go visit, you have to act civilized and not at all like a Carpathian or a wolf. I don't want my mother upset."

"Are you going to ask her questions?"

"I don't know. I haven't decided yet. But I do know if Solange and Jasmine stay in Brazil, wherever they are, they really need help. I think we should try to have a home near them as well as in the States."

"I agree, and that is a perfect solution. Jasmine wants to go to the ranch, but Solange, I think, will be a problem. And in truth, MaryAnn, I do not believe she should ever be near my eldest brother, Zacarias. He does not take no for an answer, and she would judge him very harshly, not understanding that his word had to be, and continues to have to be, law. He was what kept us all from turning vampire. The darkness is in him, and we all tread softly to try to keep from pushing him over the edge.

She could feel his sorrow and worry for his oldest brother. He obviously loved and respected Zacarias above all others. She brushed back Manolito's hair with gentle fingers and leaned forward to kiss him. The shadows in his eyes, the heaviness in his heart were almost more than she could bear.

"You think you will eventually lose him." She made it a statement.

Manolito lay back, locking his fingers behind his head, and stared up at the sparkling crystals covering the ceiling. He sighed. "Zacarias is a great man, *meu amor*, highly intelligent, and he wields much power. He has stood in front of my brothers, in front of me, shielding us from the kills to allow us more time. Each kill we make our souls grow darker."

"Can you, Riordan and Rafael try to . . ." She trailed off. What was she saying? Did she want Manolito to hunt the vampire?

He shook his head. "He would never allow us to do that for him. He believes he is responsible for us. I already see the darkness is strong in him. I was so close to turning myself, I should know. Even when I entered the other world, the other occupants knew. After a while the darkness runs together until you no longer know if you can resist the lure to just one time feel something. Anything."

"But three of you have found lifemates. That should give him hope."

"He cannot feel hope, not his own. He can only feel our hope for him. And even should he find his lifemate, I fear he would be too difficult for a woman of today's society to live with. Most of our lifemates are human or raised human. He is a throwback to a different era. You find me difficult. In comparison, I assure you, MaryAnn, I am a very modern man."

"I'm very glad to hear you say that, Manolito, because this modern woman has come to a decision, and it's my decision to make. *Mine*. You have to understand that I believe I do have rights. This is important to me."

"What decision would that be?" He sounded wary. He was wary. He wasn't about to free her from her obligations even if it was possible—which it wasn't.

"I want you to convert me. Now. Tonight. I want to share your life wholly with you." She ignored the storm clouds gathering in his eyes. "I didn't have a decision at any time along the way. So this is me, thinking it over, knowing what I'm doing and saying, yes, I love you and I want to be wholly yours."

19

Manolito bit down on his first response, forcing the sudden fear down. Emotions were much more difficult to deal with than he'd remembered. If he converted MaryAnn, and the wolf protested, it might kill her. No one, not even Vlad, remembered the pairing of a wolf and a Carpathian.

"Manolito?" Her fingers drifted over his face, tracing his cheekbones, gentle, filled with love.

He swallowed the lump in his throat and turned his face away from her so she wouldn't see him fight back the way she affected him. She shook him with her tenderness. With love. Being a lifemate seemed so simple, yet it was far more complex than he had ever considered. He wanted her conversion for himself. He had pride in what and who he was, but at the same time, he wouldn't—couldn't—risk her.

"Ask me for the moon, MaryAnn, and I will find a way to get it for you. But not this. Not when we do not know what will happen."

"You are changing. You said so yourself." She pressed kisses along his strong jaw and up to the corner of his mouth. "Whatever you are, I want to be. I've thought about this a lot. I had plenty of time while I was fighting off vampires and mages and jaguar-men. It's really rare to find someone you love, and even rarer to have them love you back."

"We will still have that," he said gently and reached up to pull her down on top of him. He couldn't look into her eyes and not give her whatever she wanted. "We will always have that." When had it started? When had she turned his world upside down? His stomach was jittery and his heart melted the moment he looked at her. His brothers would laugh if they knew. He rubbed his chin on top of her head, feeling her hair catch like tiny threads binding them together. With a thought, he removed her top, sending it sailing to the floor so he could smooth his hand down her soft back.

"Do you feel the wolf inside you?" She rolled over to pillow her head on his shoulder. "Because his scent is all over you—and all over me. He's there, I know he is, reaching for my wolf when we make love. That's probably why you're even more dominant than when I first laid eyes on you." He'd taken her breath away even then. "That's why you rub your body all over mine, to get your scent on me, and that's a wolf trait."

"It's a Carpathian trait."

She laughed, and he felt the sound moving through his body like small electrical currents. "Don't say that like it's a good thing. I'm not going into this relationship with rose-colored glasses. It has occurred to me you might be difficult to live with."

He bit her neck, his teeth gentle, scraping back and forth over her pulse while the breath caught and held in her lungs. "As long as you do everything I say, I think life will be easy."

The teasing note in his voice was almost as sexy as the way his hands came up to cover her breasts. He simply cupped the undersides in his palms, holding her close to him for a long moment before he slipped out from under her head, one arm wrapping around her waist and rolling her onto her side to face him. The way he did it, his hands so strong and sure, his movements decisive, sent a shiver of excitement up her spine.

She couldn't imagine never wanting him like this. The ache was so strong she thought she might die from the mixture of need, want and love. His body was firm and hot, hard and aching for her. She read it in his mind, felt it in the way his body was so thick and hard already, pressing against her thigh.

"You aren't going to distract me, Manolito," she whispered. "Don't you see how important it is that I make this decision for myself? It has to be my decision."

He nuzzled her throat, inhaled her warm, feminine scent, was pleased that his scent lingered over her skin. His tongue touched her pulse, swirled over the small, inviting dip before he pressed his lips to the temptation.

MaryAnn closed her eyes. Maybe he *was* going to distract her. Her heart beat in time to his. Her body should have been thoroughly sated, but, no, she was hungry for him all over again.

He touched her and she was lost. He looked at her and she was lost. She gave a little groan and reached up to wrap her arm around his head and hold him to her. "I'm so pathetic when it comes to you."

His lips brushed her shoulder when he smiled, sending little darts of fire streaking over her skin to the swell of her breasts. At once she felt achy and tight.

"No more than I am with you," he murmured and shifted closer so that his mouth could wander across the soft, firm mound.

His tongue touched the small spot where his mark had lingered for so long, and at once she felt it burn and throb. Her body answered between her legs with that same burning and throbbing sensation, only a thousand times more powerful, so that she shifted restlessly.

"Does it matter to you that I want this?" Was that her voice, so breathy with anticipation she could barely recognize herself?

"You and what you want always matters," he replied, lifting his head, his black eyes searching hers.

"I need this, Manolito. Like you need my body and heart. I need the same from you. You have to trust me enough to know my own mind."

"It isn't a matter of trust, MaryAnn." He rolled over, away from her, but not before she caught a flash of uneasiness in him. Of wariness. Of something pushing close to desperation.

She didn't understand his mixed feelings. It was simple enough. Riordan had brought Juliette into his life. Manolito had brought Luiz. Now that she knew what her wolf was, now that she understood the protection and strength that it gave her, she loved it, but she loved Manolito more. She wanted a full life with him. She'd caught glimpses in his mind of what the reality would be if she did not become Carpathian. She would not be able to go to ground with him, and he would often need to rejuvenate. She would be aboveground, suffering the effects. There would be no days for him, few nights for her.

"We can't live like that, not and be happy the way we were meant," she said.

He turned back to her, his palm cupping the back of her head. "I can make you happy, MaryAnn. Through it all, I can do that."

"But I couldn't make you happy. I want this for myself, not for you. Because for the first time I know what life can be like sharing it with someone else. I feel as if I've been handed a miracle."

A smile softened the hard edge of his mouth. "That is the way I feel, MaryAnn. You are that miracle, and to chance losing you . . ."

"Why would you lose me? Juliette made it through."

His fingers raked through his hair. "It is different."

"How? Explain to me how it is different."

Exasperated, he sighed. "I see what you meant when you told me you were stubborn." He sat up and ran both hands through his hair again, shoving the long hair behind his shoulders and then abruptly leaning over to kiss her. "This is something you are absolutely certain you want to do?"

She curled her fingers around his nape and drew his head down to hers for another kiss. His mouth was like a heated furnace, ready to catch fire at the least provocation. "I want to spend every moment I can with you in the best way possible."

He let his breath out. "Do not think you will get your way in all things, *sivamet*."

She rolled onto her back, her hair spread across the pillow, and smiled up at him. "Of course I will."

He leapt out of bed and was gone. He simply dissolved to vapor in front of her eyes, streaming down the narrow tunnel toward the entrance. MaryAnn's heart slammed hard against her chest.

What are you doing? She sprang up and dashed after him, running barefoot, forgetting all about bugs and anything else to do with caves, in her concern for Manolito. She merged her mind with his, even as she used the wolf's speed to try to catch him.

He was not risking her without knowing what would happen. His resolve was absolute. He didn't want to be with her in case it all went wrong fast.

Don't you dare! She shouted it in her mind, his mind, burying as much compulsion in as she was capable of using. Her breath came out in a ragged sob. *Manolito. No. You can't do this.*

She felt the brush of his fingers on her face and then he was gone from her, pushing her out of his mind to ensure her safety. She felt the ground shake and knew the entrance was opened.

Putting on a burst of speed, she pumped her arms, racing to get there before he could close it.

The rock walls slammed together with a grinding noise that reverberated through her mind. She threw back her head and howled, somewhere between fury and terror.

If I do not return, the door will open at sunset.

She slammed both palms over the boulders, a sob welling up in her throat. *If you do not return, there is no reason for the door to open. Please, Manolito, I've changed my mind. I don't want this. Come back.*

I will not risk you.

It's my risk to take, she pleaded.

She felt his sigh in her mind, and again his fingers seemed to brush over her skin.

You do not understand. You are more than my heart. You are my very soul. There is nothing—no one—on this earth more important to me. I do not want you to feel the fire of conversion. I do not want you to ever experience pain. And I will not risk your life or sanity until I have risked my own first to know that it can be done without harm to you.

She pressed her hand to her mouth hard to stifle the weeping. Crying wasn't going to stop him. Compulsion wasn't going to stop him. *If you really love me . . .*

His laughter was soft in her ear. *It is out of love that I do this. Go back and sit on the bed and wait for me. If I return, we will complete the conversion. If I do not, go to my brothers and allow them to care for you.*

There was seduction in his voice. The image of her sitting on the bed naked, waiting for him to return to her, was in his mind. She wanted to throw something. She leaned down to find a loose rock on the cavern floor, wrapped her fist around it and, in a storm of rage, flung it at the door, furious that he would expect her to meekly wait for him. To think that he would come back and they would have sex. Wild, uninhibited wolf sex. Oh, God, he was so right.

Manolito. She tried again. *You matter as much to me as I do to you. At least let us do this together. Let me out. Or stay merged with me.*

I will not risk you.

He broke the connection once more and she felt alone. So alone. MaryAnn walked back to the chamber, her heart so heavy she felt it might shatter into a million pieces. If something went wrong . . . If she lost him now . . . How could he have done it again? Taken the decision making out of her hands? Anger faded away as realization hit her. If he didn't come back, she had nothing at all. There would be no reason for anger. No reason at all. Just emptiness, just a terrible black hole that would eventually swallow her.

"What were you thinking?" she whispered aloud, not certain if she was asking him or herself the question. She sank onto the bed, ignoring the tears streaming down her face, just letting them fall.

~

Manolito inhaled the night air, dragging it deep into his lungs. He felt the wolf inside leap forward, processing data every bit as fast as a Carpathian could. MaryAnn had infected him with her wolf's blood, and as the wolf inside had grown stronger, he had expected his Carpathian traits to either overcome it, or succumb to it, but so far, neither had happened. The wolf simply had taken up residence and remained quiet and alert. They seemed to coexist, but what would happen to him or the wolf, if he called it forth?

He turned his face up to the night sky. He loved the night, the beauty and mystery of it. He loved all things Carpathian. Was this what it had felt like for MaryAnn, to know who she was, to be confident and happy in her own skin? He had ripped that out from under her. He had expected her to accept his gift of life, of love, without ever really weighing the cost to her. For him, being Carpathian was everything. She had loved her life, was comfortable and happy in it. He had taken that as well, all without thought.

Manolito? Zacarias touched his mind, the connection strong in spite of the distance. *What are you doing?*

He felt the uneasiness of his brothers and knew he had inadvertently touched them, as they always did with one another before a great battle. A touch to say good-bye just in case things didn't go the right way.

I am all right, Zacarias. I have made choices I regret. Given the chance, take care with your choices so you do not have regrets. I have learned that my way is right, yet so are other ways.

There was a small silence. Zacarias had always been able to see too much. *What you do is dangerous.*

Manolito gave a casual roll of the shoulders, shrugging off the comment even though his brother couldn't see him. *What we have done our entire existence has been dangerous. Please get the information to Mikhail that we face possible destruction from all sides. That is the least we can do when we aided the Malinovs in creating the plan to bring down the leader of our people.*

Nicolas has already begun the journey. I do not want you to continue on this path you have chosen. I cannot read anything but danger.

Live well, brother. Manolito sent his warmth and affection, but pulled away before Zacarias could get an inkling of what he planned.

"It is you and me, wolf," he said quietly. "And the night."

He felt the wolf stir and stretch. The creature was separate from him, two strong, dominant personalities sharing the same body. It wasn't an illusion. The wolf traits, the need to keep his female protected and close, those things were as strong or stronger in the wolf and doubled his own need to act on them. They shared feelings and sensations. They could—communicate.

Are you ready to do this?

As ready as you. She is my mate as much as yours. There was no hesitation on the part of the wolf. He didn't yet understand the Carpathian bond and what it would mean should Manolito die. MaryAnn would either follow him at once, or, if her wolf could keep her alive, it would be a slow, living death for her.

He shook his head, refusing the possibility. If he didn't convert her, she was right, they would have a difficult life, maybe the same slow, living death either way. Better to face the fire and burn quick and clean.

He called. The wolf answered. He reached. The wolf leapt. The change swept over him. Different. He forced himself to feel everything, to examine it all. The ripple of life beneath his skin. The itch of fur. The burst of teeth as his muzzle elongated to accommodate the sharp fangs. He was being drawn back, pulled inside, spiraling down and shrinking, the sensation claustrophobic. His guardian passed him, flooding him with assurance as the wolf sprang forward and took over his body.

Strength and power poured into him and through him, feeding the wolf. His mind expanded as the collective memories of generation after generation flooded his mind. Nothing like the werewolves in the movies. The full moon made them weak, unable to come out and protect their host body. Unable to answer the call of the wild when their charges were in danger. They headed up the organizations to save forests and animals. They worked tirelessly to combat the ignorance on wildlife, plants and the habitats, even the earth itself.

They were power and intelligence wrapped in sleek fur. Amber eyes and a dark pelt of black fur, the wolf looked into the glassy water to give Manolito a sense of who and what he was. There was no terrible movie monster, but a wolf worried as much for his mate as Manolito was for MaryAnn.

Packs were scattered across the world. Small. Tight. Hidden. They rarely came together unless the need was great, but they survived, buried deep in the community of humans, working, living and loving among them. Their greatest danger was the rogues, wolves who refused to be part of any pack, wolves who, like the Malinov brothers, felt they had a right to rule.

His wolf had searched the collective memories of all wolves and had never found an incidence of a Carpathian mating with a wolf, but neither blood had harmed the other. Manolito opened his memories to the wolf, allowing him to see what the conversion would do, sharing his fears for MaryAnn's safety. He was beginning to think of the wolf as another brother, a partner and friend. They knew each other, stood with each other, and his wolf would always, always protect MaryAnn, just as Manolito would always protect MaryAnn's wolf.

Manolito emerged into the night without a single loss. If anything, he had gained—in knowledge, confidence, and his ability to make a rational decision. It would eventually harm them to live without MaryAnn going through the conversion. She had known that instinctively, as well as reasoning it out. He had to accept the risk for both their sakes. If he didn't do it this night, he might not find the courage again.

He waved the door to the cavern open, knowing she would hear the rocks grinding together as he once more sealed them in. Striding down the narrow tunnel, he wasn't surprised when she came, tears running down her face, hurling herself at him, instead of waiting on the bed as he'd ordered. He kept the smile from his face, but his heart lightened at her reaction.

"What have you done? You're crazy, you know that?" Cream washed through the perfection of her coffee-colored skin as she flung herself at him. She was furious, yet still crying as she swung at him, letting the adrenaline rule her.

He caught her fists and jerked her against him, wrapping her up tight before she could hurt herself or him. "Easy, *csitri*. Do not hurt yourself."

She kicked back at him with her foot, angry all over again now that he was safe. "Hurt you, you mean. I can't believe you did that. What if you needed me and I couldn't get to you?"

"I had to make certain you were safe," he said, perfectly reasonable. His arm was around her waist, the other under her breasts, both pinning her arms to her sides to keep her from taking another swing at him. "My wolf is very interested in yours. He is worried that something will happen to her when you change, but I believe we are of equal strength. I think your little female is strong enough to go through conversion with you."

She wasn't quite ready to let go of being afraid and angry with him. He drew her up off her feet and moved backward, taking her with him, her body tight against his. His cock was already hot and engorged, pressed snugly between her buttocks.

"If you think I'm going to let you touch me . . ."

He bent his head to find the hollow of her neck. Warm. Soft. Inviting. His tongue found her pulse and teased with small flicks. His teeth scraped gently back and forth, flooding her channel with liquid heat. Her womb contracted, set up a throbbing ache. She flexed the muscles in her arm until he cautiously allowed one to escape. She wrapped it around his head and arched back into him, grateful he was alive and unhurt.

"You scared me."

"I'm sorry, *sivamet*. I had no wish to frighten you, only to keep you safe."

His hand came up to cup her breast very tenderly, his fingers tugging at her nipple, sending whispers of sensation floating through her body. There was something extremely sexy about being held like this, his arm locking her tightly to him, his body pressed into hers. He always made her feel sensual and beautiful and very wanted.

Voracious hunger glittered in his eyes as he bent his head to kiss her. His mouth ravaged hers, but his hands were gentle as they traveled down to the soft expanse of her belly. He rubbed small circles there, holding her chin, keeping access to her mouth. She shivered in anticipation.

"Lie down on the bed." His arms dropped away.

MaryAnn turned to face him, studying the stark arousal on his face, the thick erection standing against the hard muscles of his stomach. He nodded toward the bed, and she crawled onto it, deliberately sensuous, hearing his swift intake of breath as she moved her body with the grace of a wolf, slow and sexy, her breasts swaying and her bottom round and tight. She turned over and stretched out, not hurrying at all, letting him see every inch of her.

She knew he liked her skin, and with the flickering lights playing over it, the soft coffee color was shown off to an advantage. He couldn't take his eyes off her. He knelt over her on the bed, his hand sliding up the length of her leg to her thigh. His hands were warm and rough. Arousal tightened her womb, and she could feel ripples of need deep in her most intimate feminine channel. He was barely touching her, only with his dark gaze, so filled with lust, so aroused, she thought she might have an orgasm just from the light brush of his fingers and the look on his face.

Manolito covered her body with his own, kissing her over and over, taking his time, being as gentle and as patient as he could. His touch was tender as he aroused her body. He wanted her to know love. To feel love. To know that he would always stand with her and for her and he would worship her body with his. She would know, at the end of their time together, she would know she had been thoroughly loved.

He parted her thighs with his knee and lifted her to him, waited until her eyes met his, and then he joined them in one long surge that set lightning streaking through his body. Her muscles pulsed around him, tight and slick and oh so velvet soft.

He told her he loved her with his body, leaning down over and over to kiss her as he rode her, as he brought her to a gentle climax. His heart pounded at the enormity of what he was doing—of what they were doing. His own release sent another orgasm rippling through her. He kissed her again and sat up, pulling her into his lap.

"Are you certain?"

She nodded, her eyes trusting. His heart turned over. He drew

her into his arms, his mouth finding hers, kissing her again and
again, over and over as if he'd never get enough. She gasped as
his fingers flicked her nipples and sent an overload of sensation
to the junction of her legs, so that her body shuddered with
more pleasure. As if he had waited for that signal, he bent his
head lower, long hair sliding sensuously over her skin, pooling
in her lap as he found her breast. Teeth tugged, scraped; his
tongue laved and danced. He took his time, suckling for a moment, one hand sliding between her legs to catch her reaction,
the hot tightness, the gathering moisture.

He kissed his way back up to the swelling curve of her breast
and licked at the pulse point there. Once. Twice. His hand slid
over her cleft, rubbed, fingers pushing deep. He felt the ripple
of her silken walls closing around him, clamping down with
heated arousal. He sank his teeth deep. MaryAnn jerked in his
arms, threw her head back, her hips bucking against him, her
body riding his hand as he drank. The pleasure/pain of it rocked
her and, through her—him.

This was the Carpathian way. The need of a lifemate. Nothing
sated hunger, sexual or physical, as a lifemate could. Her taste
was unique to her and an aphrodisiac to him. It was the very essence of their life, a blood bond that could not be broken. He
reached for his wolf, sharing it with him, wanting him to understand, wanting MaryAnn's wolf to share that same bond.

He fed MaryAnn's arousal, wanted her to feel only pleasure, to heighten the experience of their ultimate merging.
Her life was tied to his for all time, and the blood binding
their union was as addicting as her body. He closed his eyes,
savoring the feel of her bare skin sliding against his. Every
nerve ending was enhanced, so that the smallest sensation
washed over him in waves of pleasure. He moved in her
mind, sharing how she felt—the soft satin, the hot silk, the
spicy taste.

He lifted his head, watched the two twin trickles make a
path down the sloping curve to the valley and below toward her
belly. He passed his tongue over the pinpricks, closing them,
and followed the twin trails over her breast, down the valley to
her stomach. His hair slid across her thighs as he circled her
waist, urging her to lie back as he licked every remnant of her
life's essence from her skin. He could feel the muscles bunch-

ing under his palm, tightening just the way her sheath tightened around his fingers.

He caught her to him and rolled, putting her on top of him. "Straddle me. Ride me." He was already bursting with need again.

"You can't possibly," she said softly, but she slithered down his body to find his pulsing erection with the heat of her mouth. "I guess you can."

His hands caught at her shoulders. He couldn't let her distract him, and her mouth—her magic mouth—just might do that. "Straddle me, MaryAnn." He gripped her thigh, tugged until she reluctantly gave him one delicious, very erotic swipe with her tongue and then obeyed him, crawling up his body until she straddled him.

She threw her hair back over her shoulder and rose above him, while his hand circled the base of his shaft so she could slowly seat herself. Her breasts swayed invitingly, lovingly, oh so temptingly, and he caught his breath, wondering at the sheer magic of her. And then she lowered herself, one exquisite inch at a time. It was torture, a painful pleasure as she took him into her sheath, so hot she was like a ring of white-hot fire, so soft she felt like living silk, so tight his breath strangled in his throat. He wasn't certain he would survive this night.

Manolito lifted his hands, and MaryAnn leaned forward to tangle her fingers with his. The movement put pressure on her most sensitive spot, and she nearly fragmented right there, but his hands dropped to her hips and locked her down tight on him, preventing movement. His gaze held hers. Hot. Aroused. Glittering. The intensity sent another wash of heat rolling through her. Commanding.

She knew what he wanted. The idea should have filled her with fear, or dread, or even disgust, but instead, it excited her, excited her wolf. She could feel her teeth, sharp now, pressing her for a taste of him. Manolito. The other half of her soul. He slid one palm under her hair until his fingers could curl around the nape of her neck and pull her down to his chest. Seated on him, her body throbbing with pleasure, she licked at the spot just above his heart.

The rush of his blood through his veins called to her. His male scent. The musky scent of the wolf and the heady fragrance of sex in the air—all combined to make her head spin. Her tongue darted out again, flicked over his skin. His cock gave an answering jerk. Her muscles tightened around him. She waited, listening to the steady beat so close to her ear. Rapid. Excited. Anticipating.

Her teeth sank deep, and the taste of him, the incredible gift of life, flowed into her. His harsh breathing deepened. His cock thickened, stretching, invading, sending fiery waves through her body. Her muscles spasmed, and he groaned, adding to her heightened pleasure. He tasted—like power. Hot and sweet and filled with sex. Who would have thought he could taste so good?

His body began to move in hers. Long, slow strokes, almost lazy. Steel encased in velvet riding between her legs, thick and long and driving her slowly insane. He was everywhere. In her. On her. Flooding her mouth, her body, enveloping her in a cocoon of love. His hands urged her hips up so that she concentrated on the fiery sensations as he nearly retreated completely. Then he forced her back down, holding her to the lazy pace so she could take enough for a true exchange.

The ride was the most sensual she'd ever had. His hands slid over her bottom, massaged, made small circles, stroked the long, velvety line between her buttocks, and then he'd urge her up again, in that slow, lazy rhythm. She moaned and swept her tongue across his chest to close the small wound. Her muscles were pulsing around his shaft and her breath came in gasping sobs. She looked down into his eyes.

He was staring back at her. Manolito De La Cruz. His eyes were the blackest of night in color, with streaks of amber, like small lightning bolts. And she could drown in the amount of love she found there. He didn't try to hide it, wasn't in the least shy about letting her see.

He held her hips and did a long, slow circle as he brought her down, so that the breath was driven from her body and the tight knot of nerves screamed at the intense sensation. Her stomach rippled with the fiery burst and her womb spasmed.

"Of course I love you. How could you not know?"

Her throat ached and tears burned behind her eyes. "I never thought I'd find you. I never thought I'd feel a love like this of my own."

"I will make certain you feel it with every breath you take," he said. Tightening his fingers on her hips, he drove his hips upward, filling her so full she cried out his name, her nails digging into his shoulders.

She thrust back against him, driving down, her body shuddering as mind-numbing pleasure exploded through her, as she felt his brutal release, the sudden swelling, the hot release so deep inside triggering wave after wave until she fell forward into his arms, exhausted, lying on him, locked to him, unable to move.

He held her to him, his lips in her hair, staring up at the crystal ceiling. "I have lived for centuries, MaryAnn, and never once did I believe it would happen to me. I don't think any of us really believe it will happen."

There wasn't enough air in her lungs to speak, so she pressed kisses to his throat, and then laid her head on his chest and closed her eyes, listening to the rhythm of his heart.

"I've looked into my heart and soul, and honestly, I think a man of our species is meant to claim his lifemate regardless of whether or not she is in love with him. I have destroyed so many vampires, and I think, given the choice of becoming wholly evil, murdering and preying on the innocent, or staking my claim and allowing my lifemate time to grow to love me—I believe it is the only recourse open to us."

She patted his chest. "Perhaps you might consider courting your lifemate first, getting her to fall in love with you and then claiming her." Her stomach suddenly cramped. With a small gasp she rolled off of him to lie on her back.

Manolito put his hand on her belly, feeling her muscles cramping. She cringed and pushed his arm away.

"You feel too heavy. And it's hot in here. Maybe you should open the door and let the night air in."

He rolled onto his side, careful to keep his body from hers. "The conversion is starting. You felt a part of what Luiz went through. I want you to stay merged with me at all times, Mary-Ann."

"There's no need for both of us to go through this. It was my decision." A blowtorch seemed to flash through her middle, so that she gasped and clutched her stomach. Beads of perspiration dotted her forehead.

"I'm not asking you. I won't survive just watching. I have to
be an active participant and so does my wolf." He leaned close,
took her hand in his. "Do you understand? Did you hear me?"

Her eyes were enormous, already glazed with pain, but she
nodded. "My wolf," she gasped. "She's trying to shield me. You
have to make her stop. We both need to . . ." She trailed off as a
convulsion picked up her body and slammed it back to the mattress. She curled into the fetal position, reaching for his hand.
"Make him talk to her. She can't fight this. It will destroy her, but
she doesn't want me to suffer."

Manolito didn't want to leave her, not even for a moment,
but she was panting, nodding, trying to hold on while the pain
wracked her body. She went to her knees, leaning over the side
of the bed, vomiting over and over.

It was happening fast, almost too fast. He reached for her, but
the convulsions started again. In her mind, he could feel her wolf
rising, trying to protect her. The wolf had no thought of saving
herself. She was a guardian and MaryAnn was suffering.

His wolf was a part of him. There had to be trust between
them, and neither wanted his mate to bear the pain. Manolito
kept his mind firmly merged with MaryAnn's, trying to shoulder the agony himself, but he let go of his physical body, allowing the wolf to take over.

MaryAnn thrashed, desperate to ease the pain, and her hand
collided with thick fur. She turned her head and the wolf lay beside her. His eyes stared into hers. Deep amber with thin black
lightning bolts through them. Beautiful eyes. Beautiful fur.

Let go. Let her come out. She heard the words echo through
her mind as she convulsed again, as the pain burned up through
every organ and into her very brain.

She might die.

*I will not allow it. If you do not, she will not survive. Can
you feel her fighting? She will never accept what is happening
to you without guidance.*

I don't know how to help her.

I do. Let her come out.

He was every bit as arrogant and protective as Manolito.
She didn't know if she could bear the pain in the small confines
of that space, but she didn't want to take the chance that her
wolf would die. She forced herself to let go, even though the
sensation was worse; she couldn't cling to anything, had no

anchor to hold on to. She heard her desperate scream, and then Manolito was there, in her mind, calming her, whispering to her. His wolf was there as well, murmuring reassurances.

The pain eased, became distant, although she could feel the convulsions wracking her body. She could hear the wolf panting and whining, crying out on occasion. She felt the soothing lap of a velvet tongue as her mate eased her through the conversion. More than that, she felt the two males shifting the pain to their own shoulders, working in conjunction with each other to take everything they could.

Hours, maybe days, went by. It seemed endless. Exhausted, certain she was going to succumb eventually to death, Manolito at last called to her to emerge.

She didn't have the strength. Her wolf didn't have much left either. They both lay panting, so worn out neither could move or respond. The alpha male nudged at the female, stroking his muzzle over her body, clearly trying to help her.

MaryAnn felt them in her mind again, Manolito calling to her. She had to go to ground. It was the only way to stop the pain for all of them—the only way to heal their bodies. She made a supreme effort and forced her way up, sending warmth and love to her wolf as it retreated.

Manolito gathered her into his arms, holding her close as he opened the earth and floated them both into it. Cradling her, he drew the rich, dark soil over them, commanding her to sleep the rejuvenating sleep of the Carpathian.

20

"Where are they?" Jasmine asked anxiously. She didn't like being without the Carpathian males in the house. She paced from window to window, staring out into the rain forest.

MaryAnn remained silent for a moment, touching Manolito's mind very lightly. "They are helping Luiz. He has risen as Carpathian, and he is very hungry."

Juliette smoothed back Solange's hair. "No one is out there, Jazz. I'd know. In any case, the men aren't that far away. I doubt anyone would try another attack."

"I just want to get out of here," Jasmine said, pressing a hand protectively to her stomach.

"We've sent for the plane," Juliette assured her. "We don't want you and Solange trying to make it through the forest to the ranch. It's too far and too dangerous. Now that we know the master vampire is using the jaguar-men to try to capture Solange, we can't take any chances."

"The ranch is on the edge of the rain forest," Jasmine pointed out. "It's still isolated from people. Maybe we aren't safe there, either."

Juliette exchanged a long look with MaryAnn, and both looked down at Solange.

She squeezed her cousin's hand. *It's all right. I know I won't be safe anywhere now. Don't tell Jasmine. I had hoped to stay at the ranch, but I don't want to put her in any more danger than she's already in. She's pregnant, Juliette, and she needs care.*

Juliette spoke aloud to reassure both her sister and her cousin. "There are several houses on the estate. One has been built just for the two of you, so you can have your privacy. Rafael and

Colby are Carpathian and they have their own home on the ranch. Colby's younger brother and sister live with them. Riordan and I have a home there as well. Nicolas and Zacarias share the main house. Manolito and MaryAnn will have their own home. Aside from that, the Chavez family resides and works on the ranch. They are well equipped with the knowledge and the weapons to fight the vampire or anyone else who happens to try to harm either of you. The ranch is the safest place you could possibly be right now, with eight Carpathians to guard you."

Solange sighed. "She's right, Jasmine. We'll probably be safer at the ranch than anywhere else. I need some time to recuperate anyway. And I've always loved horses."

Jasmine turned around, for the first time more interested in the conversation. "I didn't know that. You never told me."

Solange tried to look nonchalant. She rarely gave anything of herself away these days, not even to her family. "When I was younger I used to ride."

"I remember that," Juliette said. "You were such a daredevil even then. You always rode bareback and scared the heck out of Mom."

The light faded from Solange's eyes and she lay back again on the couch. Juliette and even Jasmine glanced helplessly at MaryAnn, as if asking what they should do.

MaryAnn waited until Jasmine was seated on the couch beside Solange before she brought out her nail polish. She held up the bottle. "Anyone want to use this?"

"I've never painted my nails in my life," Solange said, looking faintly shocked. "Can you imagine me with red nails?"

"Not red." MaryAnn gave a little shake of her head, frowning as if Solange had committed a huge fashion gaffe. "Passion pink."

"*Passion* pink," Juliette prodded her cousin. "That's hysterical. I've never seen you in pink anything, let alone passion pink."

"Why not red?" Jasmine asked.

"It would be wrong with her skin tone," MaryAnn said knowledgeably. "She has beautiful hands. You want people to notice them."

Solange put her hands behind her back. "I'm not interested in men noticing me."

MaryAnn laughed. "Silly woman. Do you really think

women dress up just for men? Some do, but the majority dress to give themselves courage in any situation. If you look good, you have more confidence. For instance, if you and Jasmine have to go to some dinner party, you're going to want to look your best so other women don't make you feel like a poor relation. Women are much harder on women than men are."

"You always look good," Juliette said. "What else do you do?"

MaryAnn looked left and right and then lowered her voice. "The secret weapon is cucumber."

Solange sat all the way up. "Jasmine, cover your ears."

MaryAnn, Juliette and Jasmine burst out laughing.

"Sheesh, Solange," Juliette said. "Get your mind out of the gutter."

"*My* mind is just fine, thank you. It's MaryAnn's I'm concerned about."

"You put them on your eyes," MaryAnn said, laughing even harder.

Solange's answering smile was slow in coming and very brief, but it lit her eyes. "I knew that."

It was the first time MaryAnn saw a flash of normalcy in Solange, as her guard slipped just for a second.

"I'll paint your toes and fingernails for you, Jasmine," MaryAnn offered. The key to Solange's cooperation, and maybe ultimately her healing, was her love for her young cousin. As long as MaryAnn kept every suggestion for Jasmine, Solange would push herself to get out of her comfort zone for the younger woman.

Jasmine glanced at Solange and then her sister. "I've never painted either one."

"Well it's time you did, then," Juliette said.

"And I think Juliette ought to try the cucumber," Solange suggested.

Juliette threw a pillow at her.

"On your eyes, your eyes," Solange said in defense.

"I'll paint my nails if you will," Jasmine said.

Solange shook her head. "No way."

Juliette nudged her again. "Solange is afraid we're going to think she's a girlie girl. A little fashionista."

"Hey!" MaryAnn managed to look affronted. "What's wrong with that? I still kicked vampire butt. I just looked good doing it." She didn't mention she'd been wearing fur at the time. She held out her nails. "And I only broke one."

"Your nails are long," Jasmine said in admiration. "I break mine all the time."

"But not polished. Come on, Jasmine. Solange will let me do her toenails. She can cover them up so no one knows. Kind of like wearing ultrasexy underwear and no one knows. It makes you feel beautiful, but you're the only one aware."

Juliette frowned. "Underwear? Who wears underwear?"

"Eew!" Solange threw the pillow back at her. "You're just wrong."

"Okay," Jasmine said, "I have to agree with Solange on that one. That's way too much information. I'll never be able to look at you again without picturing you . . ." She broke off, making a face.

Solange actually smiled. A genuine smile. It changed her entire face, lighting her eyes and making her look years younger. "Now you've got that image in my head, too."

She and Jasmine exchanged a look, making a face and simultaneously saying, "Ugh."

"Then my mission here is complete. I've managed to disturb you both." Juliette folded her arms, looking smug.

Jasmine laughed and held out her hands to MaryAnn. "If Solange is passion pink, what color am I?"

Everyone waited. MaryAnn glanced at Solange, who raised an eyebrow. "Hmm, I think you're more of a bubblegum." She extracted another small bottle from her bag.

"That's pink!" Solange pronounced, sitting back against the cushions.

"It is not," MaryAnn said indignantly. "There's a subtle difference."

"What else do you have in there?" Juliette wanted to know. She peered into the bag with the neat rows of polish shoved through loops. "I don't believe this. Check this out, Solange." She snatched up the bag and exposed the contents.

There was a small, awed silence.

"Just how many different bottles of nail polish do you have?" Solange asked.

MaryAnn took the bag back and opened the bottle of bubblegum polish. "I rarely leave home without at least ten. You never know what might happen, and a woman needs to feel good about herself no matter what." She heaved an exaggerated sigh. "I have no idea what the three of you did without me."

"Well," Solange said, sitting so far forward her nose was nearly in the nail polish as she watched MaryAnn apply it to Jasmine's fingernails, "we didn't wear passion pink or bubblegum, that's for sure."

"Here." Juliette grabbed the passion pink. "Stick your foot out, Solange."

"Wait!" There was panic in MaryAnn's voice. "You can't just do it that way. Here. She pulled out two small pieces of purple and orange foam. "You have to use these. They'll separate her toes."

Solange drew her foot up and tucked it under her. "Back off, cousin. You're not sticking anything that weird on my foot."

"Don't be such a baby." MaryAnn slipped the foam onto her feet and lifted them up into the air. "See. It doesn't hurt at all. I have another pair and they aren't purple."

Jasmine let out a cry of delight. "Look, Solange, they're pink."

Solange rolled her eyes but allowed Juliette to put them on her toes. "You'd better never tell anyone about this."

MaryAnn worked happily on Jasmine's nails, occasionally glancing over at Solange's toes. Juliette was making a mess, and making Jasmine laugh so hard she could barely keep her hands still. MaryAnn glanced several times at Solange. She seemed to be relaxing and allowing herself to have fun. It was a small step, but it was still progress.

MaryAnn found her favorite polish and began on her own toes while Jasmine blew on her nails and Juliette allowed Solange to work on her toes. Solange suddenly stiffened and glanced toward the door.

Manolito? MaryAnn felt his presence close. *Be careful with Solange. She really has suffered trauma; both she and Jasmine need help. Warn Riordan and Luiz as well, please.*

He flooded her with reassurance as he strode into the room. "Good evening, ladies. I trust you are well." He bent to brush a kiss on top of MaryAnn's head, pretending not to see Solange wince at his close proximity.

"How is Luiz?" Jasmine asked.

"He is fine. Riordan is with him right now. He has a few things to learn. Flying and shifting in the way of our people is not as easy as it looks." He winked at Jasmine. "Pretty nails. I like the color."

She smiled. "It's bubblegum."

Manolito casually took the nail polish from MaryAnn's hand and sat across from her, lifting her feet into his lap. "I patrolled the island, Solange, and saw jaguar tracks on the north side. I followed them to the river. It looked as if the cat went in." He spoke matter-of-factly, treating her as an equal, forcing her to do the same with him. He opened the bottle of polish and frowned at the smell.

MaryAnn flashed him a smile of gratitude for addressing Solange as if he didn't notice she could barely tolerate his presence in the room. It had probably been several years since Solange had been in the casual company of a man.

"I have a rather acute sense of smell," Manolito added, "and I couldn't detect a man within the cat, although the trail was several hours old. How do you tell the difference between a shifter and a genuine jaguar without being able to scan their brain? He wasn't close enough for me to pick up his brain patterns."

MaryAnn wanted to fling her arms around Manolito's neck and hug him.

I have learned a few things from being in your mind. His voice was a drawling caress. Her toes twitched, wanting to curl, and the brush, slick with polish, landed on her toe instead of the toenail.

Solange had been watching the process, fascinated by the sight of a large Carpathian male, essentially a predator, delicately polishing his lifemate's toenails. Her mouth twitched and she had to look away as Manolito glared at MaryAnn.

"Hold still."

"I am holding still. You did that thing."

"What thing?" Manolito asked.

You looked sexy and gorgeous and sounded like heat in the middle of a rainstorm. Behave yourself.

Solange cleared her throat. "When the jaguar-man travels, he usually carries a small pack around his neck." Her voice sounded low and husky, as if she rarely used it. She didn't look directly at Manolito, but she wasn't snarling. And she continued to work on Juliette's toes, as if it was the most normal thing in the world. "Often when he leaps for the tree, the bag rubs a small amount of moss off the trunk or branch. It's very small, but once you know what to look for, you can spot it."

"When we get back to the ranch, maybe you could take the time to show me," Manolito said. "That way when we go on our patrols, we'll know what we're looking for." His voice was every bit as casual as Solange's. He bent forward to blow on Mary-Ann's toes.

"Sure."

Silence fell, but it was companionable, not filled with tension. MaryAnn looked around the room at the women who had become her family. At the man who was her heart and soul, and she found herself smiling.

Manolito looked up, his black eyes meeting hers. Her heart jumped the way it always would when she looked at him, when she got lost in his gaze.

I love you, avio päläfertiil. "My lifemate. My wife."

I love you, too, avio päläfertiil, koje. "My lifemate. My husband."

It didn't get much better.

The cougar was going to turn. Tansy Meadows inhaled swiftly, biting at her full lower lip. Her heart was pounding; she could taste the familiar dryness in her mouth and feel the dampness on her palms. The rush of adrenaline began making it difficult to control her shaking hands when she needed desperately to be absolutely still.

Turn, baby. She whispered the encouragement in her mind, willing the animal to do so. *If you turn, I'll make you very, very, famous,* she promised.

The big cat stretched lazily, its sleek body rippling with muscle beneath the soft tawny fur. The end of its long tail twitched.

Tansy's heart nearly ceased to beat, then began to tap out double time. *Come on, little mama,* she coaxed, *turn for me.*

Her legs had long since lost feeling, so numb from inactivity that Tansy wasn't certain she would be able to leave the tiny ledge where she had set up her blind some months earlier. It didn't matter; nothing mattered except getting this picture.

The mountain lion was large, nearly eight feet long, very pregnant, and due to give birth any day now. The slate gray tip of its tail twitched again and again and Tansy remained utterly still, waiting her moment. Five long hours of waiting, anticipating. Five long hours of cramped, sore muscles, not to mention the months of preparation.

Come on, baby, a little more, you can do it. Get that beautiful face pointed this way.

The mountain lion arched her back leisurely, tantalizing Tansy with expectancy. The cat turned her sleek head, green-gold eyes glittering like sparkling jewels. Tansy exhaled slowly as she began snapping frame after frame with her camera. As if she knew she was the object of admiring eyes, the cat preened herself, lapping at her tawny coat with her long tongue. She grimaced, showing off her gleaming yellow fangs. She even managed something Tansy thought resembled a smile right before she let out a soft, whistling call.

Mountain lions hunted mainly at night. Tansy worked with both digital and film, capturing wildlife in their natural habitats. She had captured a beautiful photographic series of this particular cat bringing down an elk calf three weeks ago, but this was her first real break since. Cougars were elusive and difficult to photograph in their natural habitats. Whenever possible, they preferred a high vantage point, and their superior vision allowed them to spot humans long before humans spotted them. Tansy had been studying the female cougar, one of the most elusive animals in North America, for a long time in the hopes of capturing a cougar birth on film. She was lucky she had such an affinity with animals; even the wild ones didn't seem to mind her presence too much.

She continued taking as many pictures as she could, knowing every angle, every frame was going to yield gold. The background was everything she could have possibly asked for. The night sky, the moon and stars, the slight wind shifting the leaves just so and ruffling the silver-tipped fur. Her subject was quite cooperative, stretching, cleaning and displaying her long, sleek body from all angles.

Tansy particularly wanted a series of shots with various lights up close on the fur. The color was difficult to truly describe, especially with each individual hair tipped in that silvery gray, enabling the cat to disappear at twilight, to simply blend in to her surroundings and move without detection through most of her habitat during night hours. She wanted to get the sense of that camouflage in the pictures, of the stealth and power of the huntress, in contrast to the playful and motherly personality.

In the distance, overhead, the *thump, thump* of a helicopter, blades spinning fast as it made its way across the dawn sky, interrupted the silence of the night. The cougar froze, crouching low so the few bushes and blades of grass growing on the rock hid her. She bared her teeth in a silent snarl as she looked upward.

Tansy slowly lowered her camera and remained just as still as the cat, an inexplicable awareness of being hunted creeping down her spine. Her breath caught in her lungs, and for just one moment she was disoriented, a frightening feeling while on a narrow ledge with a wild cougar just a few scant feet from her.

She turned her face toward the sky as the helicopter flew directly over her. Just the sight and the sound of the aircraft was unsettling to her, and she bit down hard on her lower lip, peering at the craft in order to identify it, worried her parents had sent someone after her when she'd insisted she was exactly where she wanted to be. She had chosen this wilderness to get completely away from all human contact and the helicopter above her was definitely military, not forestry, and certainly not one belonging to her father.

The undercarriage of the helicopter glowed with green lights as it moved fast over her, a large bird of prey swooping low over the tall trees, and then just as suddenly dipping down below her line of vision, the noise fading quickly. She lay very still on the narrow ledge, her heart thundering in her ears. She forced air through her lungs as the lights disappeared. Her imagination was running wild—maybe she had been alone for too long, after all.

Movement snapped her attention back to the cougar as the cat gave one final, almost contemptuous lick along her muscled leg and leapt to the rock above her resting area in a single bound. Tansy knew her den was there. The cat had chosen a small cave to give birth to her kittens.

Tansy had been able to infiltrate two previously used caves to set up her equipment in the hopes she could somehow film the event. To her disappointment, the cave the mountain lion had chosen was totally inaccessible, which meant Tansy would have to spend another year or two studying the species and waiting for the next birth cycle after these kittens were raised. In the meantime, tonight's pictures were worth a fortune and would give her the money necessary to continue her work.

Tansy deserved a long soak in the natural pool and an even longer nap in the eventual midafternoon sun. Very carefully, she stretched her sore, tired muscles. Needles and pins rushed in where before there had been only numbness. The cramps would hit soon, grabbing at her calves and thighs, a protest against the long hours of being motionless. She had no real room to maneuver, the ledge was so narrow. She breathed through the needles, breathed through the cramps, flexing and stretching with care until she was certain she was able to climb the sheer rock face as she usually did.

There were tiny crevices where she could wedge her fingers and toes. Long ago she had rigged a rope for safety. It was often an effort to remember to use it; she was so accustomed to the climb. Now, however, she was grateful for its presence. She was far more tired than usual. The natural pool would be more than welcome and nothing was going to prevent her well-deserved rest.

Tansy stowed her precious camera and its load alongside the diary she kept of the cat's movements, in her strongest metal box at her camp. She locked the latches with not one but two heavy locks, and stored it well away from her food supplies, on the off chance a wandering bear became curious.

She was actually happy. Tansy stretched again. She couldn't wait to let her mother and father know. They'd been so worried about her after her breakdown, and they'd been so frightened when she started disappearing for months at a time into the wildest places she could find. Dropped by helicopter with her gear, she lived with just a daily radio call to assure them she was alive and well. And she was more than fine now. She had suffered through hell and come out on the other side. Happiness was a bright light spreading through her like a glow when she honestly couldn't remember feeling happy before.

She yawned, glanced at her watch, waiting for the arranged time for the call. Her mother had obviously been doing the same exact thing on her end, because when she gave her call sign her mother answered immediately. Sharon Meadows's bubbly voice was like a ray of sunshine and Tansy smiled just hearing her.

"You should see the pictures I got," Tansy greeted her. "I don't think anyone's ever managed to get so close to a cougar in the wild."

"You've always had an affinity for animals. They don't seem to mind you being around," Sharon agreed. "Even the meanest dog would turn into a love when you talked to them. But don't get too close, Tansy. You are carrying a weapon, aren't you?"

"Of course, Mom. How's Dad?"

"I'm right here, Tansy-girl. I wanted to hear your voice. Are you about to wrap it up?" Don Meadows asked.

"She's going to have her kittens any day. I thought I might be able to film the birth, but she tricked me and found the one place I couldn't get my camera into, but I should be able to photograph the kittens within a few hours after birth."

"Which means you aren't coming home." Her father made it a statement.

She laughed. "You two don't want me home. You're like a couple of honeymooners and I cramp your style."

"We want you with us, Tansy," Sharon said, and now worry crept into her voice.

"I love it up here," Tansy explained. "I know you don't understand, Mom . . ."

Don laughed and Tansy knew he was trying to cover for her mother. "She doesn't even like to camp in an RV, Tansy. There's no way she can understand how you want to live in the wild without all the amenities of a five-star hotel."

Her father had taken her camping all the time, but her mother had found excuse after excuse not to go with them. Tansy had been about ten years old before she realized her mother hadn't wanted to come along with them and that her excuses weren't real. Tansy, like her father, loved camping, and those summers had prepared her for her current work.

"I just don't like you being so alone all the time," Sharon said, forcing a brightness back into her voice.

"Mom," she assured, "this is good for me. I don't have all the craziness out here. I can't be around people, you know that—it's dangerous for me."

There was a small silence. She heard her mother choke and knew she was holding back tears. Tansy wasn't normal. She would never be normal, and her mother loved her and wanted desperately for her to be able to be like other women. To get married, have a family. It was all her mother had ever wanted for her. Sharon had never been able to give birth to biological children. She'd adopted Tansy and wanted for her all the things she couldn't have herself.

"Are you certain, Tansy?" Sharon asked. "I can't help you when you're so far away. I don't know that you're healthy and happy. Are you? Are you really, Tansy?"

This time the break in her voice was very apparent and

Tansy's heart clenched tightly. "It's all right, Mom. I'm all right," she said softly. "I'm happy here. I'm productive. I'm able to make a good living at this and I really love it. My mind feels clean and clear out here."

"I just don't want you to be alone all your life," Sharon said. "I want you to find someone, to be loved by him the way Don loves me."

Tansy pressed her fingers to her eyes. She was exhausted, and even over the distance, even with radio waves, she heard the pain and disappointment in her mother's voice—not at her—she knew that—but on her behalf.

"I love both of you," Don said firmly. "And for now, that's more than enough, isn't it, Tansy-girl."

Of course she wanted a husband and children, but she knew it was impossible. She'd accepted that and so had her father. Love for him, for his ability to understand how truly flawed she was and yet love her anyway, poured over her.

"Absolutely, Dad," she agreed, meaning it. "I'm really happy, Mom. And I'm not ill, even the headaches are gone."

"Completely?" Don asked, shock and hope in his voice.

Tansy smiled, happy to be able to tell the truth. "Absolutely, Dad." *And thank you for all the nights you sat up with me when I couldn't sleep,* she added silently.

"That's wonderful, dear," Sharon's voice was packed with relief.

"Do you need us to send more supplies? I'll get one of our pilots to make the drop."

"I'll make a list and give it to you tomorrow. I need sleep now. I've been up all night."

"Take care, Tansy," her mother said, her voice back to normal, once again upbeat and happy, as if by using her bubbliest tone she could bolster Tansy. "If you don't come back soon, your father and I will be on your doorstep."

Don snorted and Tansy burst out laughing. "Okay, Mom. Just another few weeks and I'll be home." She made kissing noises and signed off, feeling very lucky and grateful that Don and Sharon were her parents.

She had always felt loved by them, even though she was so different. She'd always been different. She detested touching objects. Even dinnerware and utensils were enough to set her off, crying and rocking, so distressed her parents would take turns comforting her, walking her up and down, singing to her. School had been a nightmare for her, and in the end they had hired private tutors—which had broken her mother's heart.

Tansy sighed. She had so wanted to be that girl her mother could share her life with. The proms, the late-night gossip sessions, the wonderful fairy tale wedding. Her mother would never have that, and Tansy wanted it for her, just as her mother wanted that life for Tansy.

Finally, after months in a hospital, she'd realized she couldn't be that girl—would never be that girl. She'd accepted herself for who she really was, flaws and all, and she'd managed to make a new life for herself. She was content, even happy, here in the wilderness.

Tansy powered off the radio and started down the trail leading to the natural pool. The hike to the basin was long and winding, but she was very familiar with it and could go fairly fast in spite of the roughness of the terrain. The rock formation was part of the reason she'd chosen this area as her base camp. The falls were beautiful, flowing down a series of smooth rocks to a natural pool below. The swimming hole was lined with rock so it stayed clean, and it was surrounded with flat granite so she had plenty of room to sun herself. The basin was the perfect place to spend a lazy afternoon after being up all night working.

Tansy liked to sleep in the morning, bathe in the pool and then catch a couple of hours of sun in the afternoon before returning to her camp and preparing for another evening's shoot. As a rule, mountain lions had a large territory—the females often covered fifty square miles—but the female was staying close to her small cave, and Tansy was absolutely certain that she was about to give birth any day now. She didn't want to miss her opportunity, or let the female get away from her. She'd heard of cougars changing dens at the last moment, and she needed to be watching the pregnant cat closely.

Tansy stretched out, trying to get comfortable on the smooth granite surface. Ordinarily, after a long night without sleep, she dropped right off in the warm sun. She tried to tell herself she was excited over her pictures, the months of work finally paying off. The truth was, since the moment that helicopter had flown overhead, she had a vague feeling of uneasiness, as if a storm were gathering off in the distance and heading her way.

The premonition persisted and was so strong, she lifted her head to search the sky for a sign of ominous, dark clouds.

A lazy hawk floated in the cloudless sky, catching a thermal and riding it just for fun. Tansy laid her head against her arm, and rubbed her cheek back and forth in a soothing gesture. It was crazy, but she felt as if she were being hunted. The area was secluded, restricted without a permit, well posted, impassable except on foot, or in winter, with snowshoes. The helicopter had shaken her more than she wanted to admit.

"Let it go," she whispered aloud.

She closed her eyes tiredly, searching for the inner contentment she always found after a great shoot. No one else could have gotten those pictures. Well, very few. She had a way with animals, as her mother had said. If she willed something in her head, oftentimes she could get the animal to cooperate, even the wildest. She had it all: the perfect job, the wild terrain and the peace the mountains always managed to give her. This was the life she chose, that she loved. More, this was the life she needed. No human contact whatsoever. At last she'd found a place she could be happy.

Tansy smiled in contentment. She was very tired and needed sleep. She only had a few hours of sunlight ahead. Nights on the mountain were always iffy. Let it all go and just sleep. When she woke, she could swim in the pool and then stretch out and dry off in the hot afternoon sun before making her way back to camp to prepare for this night's shoot.

~

"Are you going hunting, sir?"

Kadan Montague glanced up at the crew chief, sliding his .45 smoothly into the holster at his hip and locking it down. "Something like that." He shouldered his pack and slipped his knife securely into the scabbard before glancing at his coordinates. "This is it."

The crew chief, recognizing his VIP didn't want to talk, made certain the rope was secure and moved to the side to allow his passenger to step up to the open door. Kadan caught the rope with both gloved hands and waited for the pilot's okay. The craft steadied and he went down, fast-roping, settling to earth with a slight impact and stepping clear to give the away signal. His descent had taken seconds and the helicopter swung away, shifting toward the south, flying fast for base. It would set down at the ranger station and wait, no matter how long, for a radio signal to pick him up in the lower meadow as soon as he had the cargo ready.

Kadan took a long, deep breath of mountain air and looked slowly around him, feeling at home. Dawn was breaking over the mountain, spilling light along the ridges, turning shrubbery, leaves and granite to gold. Pine, fir and dogwood stretched as far as the eye could see, and huge towering cliffs of granite jutted up toward the sky. For the first time in a long while, he relaxed. No one was trying to kill him. He might be in for a long hike, but he could enjoy his surroundings.

He moved with complete confidence, with the steady gait of a man used to being out in the wilderness and covering a large territory fast. He was at home in any environment, having trained with the military Special Forces as well as with the GhostWalker teams. Arctic, desert, mountain and water training gave his body the fitness to hike the rigorous terrain. He enjoyed physical activity and, although he was tired from going through several time zones and being without sleep for several days, he was wholly focused on his mission.

He traveled in the direction he estimated would be the most likely to yield Tansy Meadows's campsite. The area had several possibilities, but she had specific needs for a long-term stay and that narrowed her options significantly. If she was anywhere in the zone he had targeted, he would run across her tracks. An hour into his hike, he found several trails leading upward into the higher, less dense forest and more toward the craggy granite, a good place for mountain lions. He worked his way steadily to the granite where there was more brush and fewer trees.

Kadan paused on the narrow, faint ribbon of a deer trail to take a long, slow drink of his water. He had the coordinates of the range she traveled in, taking amazing photographs for *National Geographic*, and he was certain the information he had was accurate. Tansy Meadows, psychic extraordinaire. The girl who could track serial killers with her mind. Some said she was difficult to work with, others said she was "freaky" but got the job done, and every single report he read on her said she was the real thing. Of course, now, the law enforcement agencies claimed she'd lost her talent in a climbing accident when she'd fallen and hit her head. He didn't believe it for a moment, but if he was wrong, he was wasting time he didn't have on a bad roll of the dice.

He had a few question marks in his mind about Meadows. There were no pictures of her, not a single one, and she worked for numerous law enforcement agencies, yet no photographs existed. He'd tried National Geographic, but they didn't have a picture either. Who had that kind of power? No civilian could manage to wipe out law enforcement records—unless there was never a photograph in the first place. There were plenty of articles in newspapers and her name was in numerous FBI and police reports across the country, and then there were her hospital records. No photograph existed there either, in which case that meant little Miss Tansy Meadows had to be red flagged, yet Kadan had high security clearance and the General even higher, and from what they could tell, no photograph of her existed. Period.

She'd been adopted at the age of five by Don and Sharon Meadows, a wealthy couple who made a name for themselves in the research, design and assembly of aircraft, specifically attack helicopters. Don and Sharon Meadows were major players in politics and frequently received government contracts for military research and design. The couple was well connected politically, but did that mean they had the clout to keep their daughter's photograph from appearing anywhere in the news? It was possible, but doubtful. It would take far more power and influence, and for what possible gain?

The first time Kadan had heard rumors of a teenager who could track serial killers was when he'd trained at Quantico. Controversy had raged over whether there was such a thing as psychic ability, and if one had it, whether it could really be channeled to track a killer. He had never entered into the discussions because he knew absolutely that psychic ability existed, but to harness it and be able to use it was a difficult thing. The police Tansy had worked with swore by her, but no one mentioned her training, which had been odd to him.

He continued upward, his gut telling him he was on the right path. There were no tracks yet, nothing to indicate the presence of another human being, but he was certain he was heading in the right direction. He was looking for a needle in a haystack, but he knew he would find her. Every instinct he had told him she was somewhere close. And he would bet his last dollar that she was lying her ass off claiming she'd lost her psychic abilities. If she had worked over and over with the police tracking serial killers successfully, he doubted if a climbing accident had suddenly snuffed out her talent as she had claimed when she came out of the hospital, refusing to even meet with police or FBI agents again.

His gaze scanned the ground as he moved at a steady pace along the narrow trail. The path was no more than a worn deer trail, zigzagging up and down the slope, but he spotted two places where the grass was crushed and a leaf bruised. Something moved through the brush recently. He stooped to examine the ground and saw a faint track. It was nearly four inches wide and the front two toes were not lined up, with one toe farther forward almost pointing and four toes all together. There were no claw marks, and the top part of the heel pad had two distinct curvatures while the bottom had three separate lobes. There was no question in his mind the track belonged to a cougar. He'd found the cat, now he just needed to find the woman.

The rangers had assured him the mountain lions were up here somewhere, and that meant that Tansy Meadows would be also. His mission was to find her and bring her back to aid him in clearing the GhostWalker name. She had the reputation with the FBI of being the real deal and the General needed Kadan to do damage control as soon as possible and to do that, Kadan needed Tansy Meadows. He had never failed in a mission yet and this one was too important.

He continued hiking using the winding ribbon of a trail. Occasionally he could see a partial track in the damper soil, and once he found a few tufts of fur in some brush where the cat had been rubbing. He decided she must be female—her tracks weren't deep enough to indicate much weight, and he hadn't come across any of the signs indicating a male's territory. This was one of the few times he had gone into the mountains without someone trying to kill him, and he found he enjoyed the peaceful solitude in spite of the urgency of his mission.

He took a couple of steps and then he saw it. His heart jumped in spite of his training, breath hitching in his lungs. The print of a small hiking boot was outlined in the dust of the trail, and superimposed right over the top of it was the print of the mountain lion. All along the cat had been stalking the woman—and he was certain it was a woman by the size of the shoe—probably walking parallel to her trail for some distance before dropping in behind her.

He swore under his breath as he cast around for more tracks.

There were older tracks indicating the woman used this trail often, and that the mountain lion often stalked her. He took a breath and let it out, forcing down a feeling of urgency. If the cougar often trailed her, that didn't mean this would be the day the cat attacked. He picked up his pace, following the pair back up the granite slope toward the cliffs.

The mountain lion continued her steady pacing, staying in the woman's track, but not moving faster as if to overtake her. If she was hunting, she wasn't in a hurry to catch her prey. As the sun grew hotter overhead, he continued his climb, taking another long, slow pull from his camel pack, allowing the cool water to trickle down his throat so he could savor it, feeling a little exposed in the open of the granite with giant boulders towering around him.

At night it was piercingly cold. By day it could be unexpectedly hot, or, without warning, a storm could move in with alarming force. He had no wish to be caught out in the open with lightning striking everywhere.

Kadan made it to the top of the rise and looked out over the spectacular view. In spite of the high altitude, he had no problem with breathing, his training standing him in good stead. He paused for a moment to take stock of his surroundings. The deep timber had given way to high ridges of granite and tall, castlelike formations. It was breathtakingly beautiful. Even he had to admit it, as much as he detested wasting precious time on such things.

Above him a long fall of frothy water spilled down, far below, into a pool of deep emerald green. The natural basin was made of granite, large boulders worn smooth from the constant assault of water. Something moved in the deepest end of the pool. He fixed his sight on the water's surface and the intriguing ripple came again. Without taking his eyes from the ever-widening circle, Kadan pulled his high-powered field glasses from the case at his belt and quickly adjusted them. Instantly the emerald green of the water shimmered within touching distance. He found himself waiting in anticipation.

Closer to the water's edge, to his left and near the lowest wall of granite, the water ringed, and something silvery gold appeared to break the surface for a moment. Kadan unconsciously held his breath. An otter? Were there otters up here? Were otters silver and gold?

She rose up out of the water, long wet hair streaming, gleaming and shimmering like skeins of wet silk. The droplets of water ran off the curves of her breasts, down her narrow rib cage, dipped in at her small waist to stream down her flat belly to the triangle of blond curls at the junction of her legs. She was naked, skin glowing in the sunlight, her tan so deep it emphasized the white-gold of her hair. She tilted her head to one side, brought her long hair over one shoulder in an unconsciously provocative gesture.

The wind shifted and carried her scent to him. Kadan's body tightened savagely in response. His body knew her instantly. She looked like some wild, pagan offering, untamed, seductive. *For him.* He went very still, his breath catching in his lungs. Instant awareness shook him. He certainly had his share of women, but he never reacted like this—a vicious, brutal response of his body and mind, everything in him reaching toward her.

"Whitney, you bastard," he whispered aloud. Not for one moment would he ever believe his reaction to be natural. It was too strong, too obsessive. Too unlike him.

He crouched down for a moment, feeling sucker punched. He'd joined the military, gone through Special Forces training, continued with water, arctic, desert and even urban training, and then he'd read the call for testing of psychic ability and he had gone immediately. He tested high, as he knew he would, and had been accepted into the military GhostWalker program. He'd agreed to be psychically enhanced. He hadn't agreed to be genetically altered, nor had he ever been told that they would match him chemically to a female.

As the extent of what had been done to the volunteers became apparent, Kadan had hoped he'd been one of the ones who escaped this particular hell. But he knew. His body knew. He tried to breathe away the monstrous hard-on that came out of nowhere. He pushed down the aggression as testosterone flooded his body with burning lust and a savage desire to possess. He'd never thought to ask any of the others what it was like, or even if all of their symptoms were the same, but he felt aggressive, dangerous, almost brutal, a primitive response preprogrammed into him.

Breathing deeply, he grabbed a handful of dirt, closing his fingers around it hard, as if squeezing the life from someone's neck. And where was the cat? He had to make certain the animal wasn't about to leap on her.

Once more he lifted the binoculars, breath catching in his lungs as she came back into focus. Even the way she wrung out her hair was sensuous, tipping her head to one side, the long golden strands rippling like silk as her hands squeezed the thick skein. Water beaded and ran from full breasts to belly and down to the vee at the junction of her legs. Her legs were slender, her butt firm as she waded toward the edge of the pool, the water lapping at her thighs. His tongue moistened his suddenly dry lips. He would give anything to lick the droplets of water from her skin.

Reluctantly he moved the binoculars from his fantasy vision to scan the surrounding forest and mountains. Nothing. He shifted his directions, quartering the area, looking high, branches, boulders. The mountain lion had to be there somewhere, invisible to his sight, maybe, but not to his gut.

There was no camp nearby that he could see, but it had to be close. He turned his attention back to the woman. This had to be Tansy Meadows. She looked almost as if this was a daily ritual, and if so, she wouldn't be hiking too far from her home ground.

There was no doubt in his mind that she owned his body and that meant she had to be one of the lost girls Whitney experimented on. The demented doctor had taken infants from orphanages all over the world and performed experiments on them. A few lucky ones had been adopted. He had her background information memorized. Her parents had adopted her when she was five years old. She had severe problems in school and other social settings. She'd worked with the police from the age of fourteen, tracking killers and kidnap victims with amazing accuracy. He should have known it was too accurate. He should have known her psychic abilities were enhanced.

Kadan took another long look around in an effort to spot the mountain lion. If it was there, the animal was well camouflaged. Every area he thought would be the perfect place to ambush her seemed serene and peaceful. He swung the glasses back to the natural basin.

She stepped from the shimmering emerald water, moving with grace and something else, something so seductive and innocent at the same time that his body screamed at him with urgent demand. His breath caught in his throat as she lifted her slender arms toward the sun, the action thrusting her breasts upward, the darker nipples erect from the cold. Kadan could feel the taste of her in his mouth. He took a slow, deep breath to calm the surging excitement, the exultation. His body, his mind, his very soul said she was the one. He was looking at his mate.

God help him, he didn't want to think that way—not now, not in the middle of such a huge crisis. He needed to be sane, to keep his mind and body under control. And he needed to use this woman, be ruthless if necessary. He swore softly under his breath and wiped his forehead with the back of his hand as he kept the glasses trained on her.

She stretched out, face down, on the flat surface of the rock, her body an offering in the afternoon sun. Her bottom was curved, well muscled, joining the long expanse of her shapely legs. It was impossible, even with the field glasses, to see her facial features; she was turned away from him, her face in the shadows. His imagination could not provide a face to go with her sensual body or the erotic way she moved. He watched her for a long while until her breathing became slow and even and he knew she slept.

She was sound asleep and a mountain lion had stalked her all the way down the trail to the basin. It was hidden somewhere above her, maybe watching. Again he scanned the surrounding area, appalled that she lay naked and exposed, where any hunter or wild animal might come across her. Fury burned in his belly, low and mean, and for a moment the ground around him trembled. He clamped down on his temper and forced air through his lungs as he sifted through every possible place the cougar could hide. He'd trained at the elite sniper school, taken the test of finding fifty objects hidden at multiple distances and he'd spotted every one, but the cat remained hidden.

He lowered the glasses. He'd been too long without sleep. He'd traveled to ten foreign countries in two weeks, working on forming a collective pool of multinational antiterrorist information for an elite assassination squad. The team would live in the shadows, travel to the kill zone, destroy all targets and fade away before anyone ever knew they were in the area. Each member would be totally anonymous so there could be no retaliation against families. Each member would be a Ghost-Walker, able to get in and out of a target zone like a shadow.

Kadan had been assigned the task and was pulling his team together when he was abruptly called home and given another mission—and this one was too important to mess up. He was known for his coolness under fire, his absolute calm in any crisis, his ability to lead his team and undertake any mission, to find a way to carry it out and get his team home again, no matter the odds. He sighed. He didn't feel cool or calm now; he felt edgy and mean. He was grateful his fellow GhostWalkers weren't around to witness his struggle.

Deliberately slowing his breathing, he took another drink from his camel pack. He was going to have climb down to the rocks below and find a way to convince her to join him, because in the end she didn't really have any more of a choice than he did. He had a feeling it wasn't going to be easy or pleasant, but completing the mission was necessary. And he had the feeling that if this woman had been given up for adoption years earlier by Whitney, she probably hadn't been chemically matched with him, which, quite frankly, was going to make things one hell of a mess. Whitney had kept her DNA and had programmed him, but not her.

He'd thought the task was going to be heartbreaking and difficult enough just convincing and perhaps forcing Tansy to partner with him in his investigation, but now, with the added threat of the physical pull between them, the mission had gone to daunting. She had suffered a breakdown, and by all accounts it had been real. He'd read the report carefully, as well as all medical records. She'd spent weeks in a hospital and months in seclusion with her parents. She'd been fractured, shattered, by her last case, her mind splintering and refusing to relinquish the evil voices of the killers she'd tracked, or the screams of their victims. He was going to have to ask her to let other, more powerful and vicious voices in. On top of that, he was going to have to somehow explain that he was paired with her.

Kadan found himself unable to tear his eyes from her. The longer he watched, the tighter and more urgently his body made demands. He had never experienced such sexual hunger. It seemed to fill every cell of his body, invade his brain, squeeze him body in a vise until jackhammers were ripping through him, driving out every civilized thought. He had to get some kind of handle on the link between them, or he would destroy any chance he had with her.

He sat down, folded his legs tailor fashion and closed his eyes, searching inwardly to center himself. He needed balance. The discomfort of the rocks, of his boots, of his body swarmed into his brain and he allowed it to wash over him, to form rings on the pool he focused on and disappear in the ripples of the water. He breathed long, deep breaths, searching inside himself for the truth of his strong emotions.

Fear for her safety. Both from animal predators and from human ones. This area was so isolated, it frightened him to think what would happen if she were found by some drunk hunter, or a man without scruples or principles. Any animal could stalk her while she lay defenseless in the sun: the cat already had. Anger. He examined the turbulent emotion from all angles. It was one he was not completely familiar with. Most of his life he had been cold and dispassionate in his dealings with people. That was what made him so good at his job. He had mastered his every emotion. Anger. It ripped through him. Boiled. Surged and pounded. Insisted on release like a heated volcano. Completely over-the-top, and he refused to let it to the surface. He had a mission and nothing—no one—got in the way of a mission.

He took another deep, calming breath, stayed in the pool of sanity while insane emotions swirled and clamored and finally abated, leaving him whole again. He opened his eyes and smiled. The smile of a predator. He came to his feet, unexpectedly fluid for such a large man. His eyes found her once again. The shadows were just beginning to reach for the soft curves of her body. He moved with sudden decision, finding the easiest way down the mountainside. It was steep and rocky and, as always in the mountains, deceptively longer than the distance seemed it should be. It took some hunting to find the steep, narrow staircase that actually led to the secluded basin. He made his way down as quietly as he was able. He wanted to study her while she slept, just take his time and let the image of her burn in his memory for all eternity. He wouldn't mind throwing one hell of a scare into her either.

MaryAnn frowned at Solange. "I'm not sure this was such a great idea. You may like being out in the open, but I feel very exposed here. I think staying in the house was a much better idea. I'm heading back."

She glanced down at her boots, covered with muck. No one was going to give her sympathy for ruining her favorite pair of boots, least of all jungle girl. She heaved a sigh. How in the world had she ended up in such a mess? Destiny. Her best friend. And where was she now? Probably snuggled up, safe and warm with her hunky man while MaryAnn slogged through a jungle filled with leeches, rabid leopards and the wild jungle chick.

"Out here I can smell them coming at us. We have more room to maneuver."

MaryAnn slapped at mosquitoes, drew out her bug spray and lavishly—and rather maliciously—depressed the button to empty half the bottle around and over her. "Okay, look. You stay and smell them coming. I'm going to curl up with a good book in the comfort of a cushy chair." She turned her back on Solange and started back along the muddy trail.

Why did everything in the rain forest have to be so wet? And the stupid rain fell *endlessly.* Bugs bit and snakes crawled and the wild jungle woman climbed trees and swung from the branches.

Jasmine fell into step beside her. "I think I'll join you."

"This is mutiny," Solange said, following them. "Jasmine, what has gotten into you?"

Jasmine pressed her hand tightly against her stomach. "I don't want to live in the forest anymore. I want to sleep in a bed and eat real food . . ."

MaryAnn swung around. "Real food? What does that mean? You don't eat grubs, do you?" She shuddered. "I've seen those survivor shows and let me just say, they're all nuts." Her gaze flicked to Solange. "Girl, it's got to be said. You've got a few issues that need to be addressed. Your clothes are a fashion emergency. And your hair . . ." She shook her head. "We're just not even going to go there."

"What's wrong with my hair?"

"Have you brushed it in the past two days?" MaryAnn countered.

"I haven't exactly had time."

"There you go. A woman always has time to brush her hair whether she's in the jungle or not." She looked rueful. "My hair grows in this kind of climate, but I haven't given up."

Solange opened her mouth and then closed it again, her tilted cat's eyes looking a little disdainful, a haughty expression on her face. "I'm trying to keep us alive and you're worried about clothes and hair?"

MaryAnn burst out laughing. "You're very good at intimidating people, aren't you? Is that how you keep everyone at a distance? I'm from the city, girlfriend, and I hang with some tough chicks. You're just not that scary, Solange."

Jasmine laughed. "Oh, she's scary, all right. She fights better than most men, and few people can go up against a male jaguar, even a female jaguar. But Solange can."

Solange bared her teeth at MaryAnn.

"My best friend kills vampires," MaryAnn pointed out. "She carries around weapons, goes through doors, turns into mist and generally is a major badass. Can I just say, not impressed?"

A faint grin flirted with Solange's mouth. "You really aren't afraid of me, are you?"

"Nope." MaryAnn flashed her an answering smile.

For the first time, Solange relaxed a little, pacing alongside her. "You're so . . . girly. But even when I know you dislike the rain forest, you still go out in it and do whatever needs doing. I can't quite figure you out."

MaryAnn waved her hand to encompass their surroundings. "This is your jungle, and there are all sorts of dangerous things in it, but you know your way around and you feel very comfortable in it. My jungle is the city. I grew up there and I'm comfortable with the danger I find there. I counsel battered women and victims of crimes. That means I have to go into places that most people avoid. I sometimes have no choice but to try to help them get out before they're killed. Isn't that what you do? Your world may seem a little more primitive than mine, but only because the men in your world have fur and claws. Mine have guns and fists."

"I never thought of it like that." Solange brushed back the strands of hair spilling around her face with the impatience of a woman who never paid attention to her looks. "I think of city women as being so prissy. They come to the edge of the rain forest and stand around in skimpy, inappropriate cloths so they can catch the eye of some idiot male. If I happen to be close by, they grab their men and look at me as if I'm trying to steal from them. I don't want a man."

MaryAnn glanced at her sharply. There was pain in her voice—even hurt—that some of the women would treat her with suspicion when she risked her life on a daily basis to save women's lives.

Jasmine moved closer to Solange, an unconscious sympathetic gesture. "I don't want a man either."

"All men are not like the ones you've run across," MaryAnn said. "The danger of doing the kind of work you or I do, or even something such as law enforcement, is that you see only the really bad things in life and none of the good. You two need to take a break for a while."

Solange held up her hand as they came to the edge of the forest just before reaching the house. She moved out on her own and MaryAnn couldn't help but admire her. She was obviously a capable fighter. She moved in silence, her body flowing with easy grace. She looked catlike, and—it had to be said—unbelievably sexy and beautiful. She barely made a stir going through the tall grasses. As MaryAnn watched, Solange went down on all fours, shifting, fur sliding over powerful ropes of muscle. She padded on four paws and disappeared completely into the tall grass.

MaryAnn let her breath out, unaware until that moment that she'd been holding it. "Now that," she said to Jasmine, "is intimidating."

MaryAnn sank down in the seat of the airplane, her heart so heavy she feared she would never be able to recover. Everyone slept. It mattered little that she knew they were Carpathian and during the day their bodies turned leaden. Somehow, their sleeping seemed all wrong when they should be mourning. They should be acting like Carpathians and trying to save Manolito De La Cruz. Hadn't she heard they could call back the dead? That Carpathians were immortal? How could they bring his body home and act so normal?

Everything was wrong. She glanced forward at the others lying so still. It was eerily quiet inside the plane. She could hear the engine, but there was no music or conversation, nothing at all. Just MaryAnn and the coffin. She tried not to think about it, tried not to turn her head and look back and see that plain wooden box Manolito was in. His family had brought him home, but then, when most of them had gotten off the plane at their main residence, Riordan, his youngest brother, and his lifemate, Juliette, told her they were going to their estate in the rain forest where Jasmine, Juliette's younger sister, was staying. They wanted to "bring Manolito home to the forest." Why wouldn't they want to bury him close?

MaryAnn passed a hand over her face. She was a women's counselor and she'd come for a specific reason—to help Jasmine—but all she could think about was the man in the coffin. Truthfully, she hadn't known him. She'd seen him once or twice and he'd nodded at her. Once, their eyes met. She'd felt that look all the way to her soul.

"Which is just plain stupid," she whispered aloud. "I don't know you."

But she felt she knew him. The moment his gaze locked with hers, she felt different. Beautiful. Excited. Hunted. Scared. Exhilarated. *She felt as if she belonged.* So many different emotions swirling inside of her. She hadn't gone to the Carpathian Mountains looking for a man. It was the last thing on her mind, and in truth, if Manolito had approached her, she would have turned him down.

Her gaze was drawn to that wooden box again. Grief flowed through her like a river. There was no combating the emotion, not when it made no sense. With a little sigh, she pushed herself up and slowly made her way back to the coffin, seating herself beside it, one hand sliding over the grainy wood. The gesture was more loving than she would have liked, much more intimate than she intended, but she couldn't stop trying to touch him.

Why are you haunting me? Why can't I just forget about you? You're a stranger to me, yet I feel as if a part of me is in that coffin with you.

But did she know him? Was she confused? She'd had a dream of him, an erotic dream of him pulling her into strong arms and holding her close, but instead of a beautiful setting—a dance floor, or even a bedroom—she was surrounded by a tiled bathroom. How stupid was that? She couldn't even fantasize the way other women did.

How he ended up in the bathroom with her, she didn't know. She went into the bathroom to get towels, she'd even taken them off the towel rack and pressed them to her face because they smelled of the fresh outdoors. Manolito was suddenly just there, materializing out of nowhere and robbing her of breath and sanity. He smelled so male. Looked so handsome. And maybe that had been the fantasy all along.

Men like Manolito De La Cruz didn't look at women like MaryAnn Delaney. He had too much money, too much power and moved in completely different circles. She was well educated, but, essentially, she knew the streets. He was elite. He was arrogant and impossible and everything she'd ever despised in a man, but when she looked at him, she could barely think or breathe.

It was no wonder she woke up with her heart pounding, certain he had wrapped his arms around her, pulling her against his hard, heavily muscled body. He whispered in her arms, she couldn't remember the words, only the intimate sound of his voice, so mesmerizing, almost hypnotic. His fingers trailed down her face, and his eyes—those gorgeous eyes—had drifted over her skin with possession, his expression stamped with such intense desire that her stomach muscles had bunched tight and she grew damp and hot between her legs.

Her hand went to the neckline of her shirt. He slid his fingers there, and she let him, let him touch her skin, the feel of his touch unlike anything she'd ever dreamt of. He traced her collarbone with the pads of his fingers and then slid the buttons open on her blouse. Her breath hitched in her throat, stilled in her lungs. She didn't move, didn't want to move or stop him. Her breasts felt swollen and achy and her nipples hardened to tight buds.

He bent his head slowly toward hers, all that black hair

tumbling around his head like a waterfall of silk. She'd never liked long hair on men, but his was so different. She longed to tunnel her fingers through it, but she couldn't seem to move. His face, as it came closer, was all angles and planes, his mouth sensual, his lashes long.

Her heart leapt as he kissed the corner of her mouth, nibbled along her chin and blazed a trail of kisses down her throat. His tongue swirled over her pulse there, but he moved on, kissing along the swell of her breast. She never once tried to stop him, or to move away. And when he cradled her close, she felt protected, not afraid.

His tongue teased and swirled, and her womb clenched. She wanted to give herself to this man. She'd never even been formally introduced, yet she was totally enthralled with him. She felt the scrape of his teeth and found it totally erotic. Arousal spread from her breasts to her belly and centered in her most feminine core. He bit down and the pain gave way to instant pleasure, a flood of sensation spreading through her like wildfire.

She felt his erection, hot and hard, pressed tightly against her, and then his tongue swiped over her breast and he buttoned her shirt, leaning down to kiss each eyelid. When she opened her eyes, his shirt was open and he traced a line across his heart with a sharp fingernail. His palm cupped the back of her head and he pressed her to him.

MaryAnn tried to wake up from her dream, a little shocked that she found taking his blood so erotic, but she knew Carpathians exchanged blood all the time, and somehow, in her fantasy, it didn't seem such a terrible thing to do.

She ran her hand along the coffin, the mark on her breast burning with the same intensity as the tears in her eyes. "You left me," she whispered. "You left me and I'm completely alone."

"MaryAnn, what are you doing? Wolves don't climb trees." Manolito stood on the forest floor, hands on his hips, looking up at the rain forest canopy.

A wolf padded the branch highway, picking her way delicately through leaves and twigs, placing every paw with care. Birds shrieked, rising into the air, until they nearly blotted out the moon, furious that the unknown creature had disturbed their roosting place. Monkeys screamed foul things and threw sticks and leaves at the birds as they followed the wolf through the trees.

The ground is wet. MaryAnn sniffed. *Up here the canopy protects my coat and my paws don't have to get muddy. There's also less chance of some crawly thing getting into my fur.*

Manolito tried not to laugh. Whether she was in human or wolf form, his woman was going to be a fashion statement. "You've got the entire forest in an uproar. The rain forest is home to thousands of birds and I think you've got them all upset."

The female wolf sniffed indignantly and raised her muzzle toward the sky, baring her teeth at the flapping, agitated birds. *They're so noisy anyway.*

There were a good twenty species screeching, the noise so loud that somewhere a jaguar coughed increasing the frantic cries. Beneath the network of roots, in the flowing river, a lazy crocodile floated closer to shore.

"If you don't come back down here, I'll have to come up there after you."

The wolf turned her head, eyes gleaming. *Is that supposed to be a threat?* She flicked her fluffy tail at him, and with one paw she brushed twigs and leaves off a branch. The leaves fell in a shower around his head.

Muscles bunched in his stomach. She was teasing him. He almost didn't know what to do. He ran across the forest floor, leaping over several rotting trunks and ferns, angling his point of attack to intercept her as she ran along the canopy highway. He jumped high, caught a branch and swung up, going hand over hand, deliberately showing off his strength.

He heard her soft laughter brushing against his mind. Monkeys screeched and a heavy boar crashed in the brush. The wolf in the trees raced ahead, using the thicker branches above his head to try to outrun him.

Neither noticed nor scented the jaguar, absolutely motionless, crouched in the tree limbs far above, watching the wolf with bright, hate-filled eyes. Around the thick, muscular neck was a belt with a small pack. One paw contorted, claws elongating into fingers so that he could undo his pack and put it carefully into the crook of the branches. His movements were patient and slow, careful, behind the heavy screen of leaves, not to draw attention with motion.

The screaming monkeys and crying birds along with the

fragrance of flowers drowned out everything worth hearing and smelling anyway. The silly monkeys continued to follow the wolf and the jaguar resisted the urge to leap on them and shred them. His head hurt, the strange buzzing refusing to go away. He even had tried tearing at his head with his own claws to rid himself of the noise, but now he had a better target.

Manolito had eyes only for MaryAnn. He raced through the trees, hand over hand, swinging from one branch to the next, a good hundred feet beneath her, using branches and vines to propel himself through the canopy maze. MaryAnn's soft laughter teased his senses.

As the wolf passed beneath it, the large cat sprang, the heavy body smashing down, claws ripping and teeth clamping on the wolf's scrawny head, biting down, going for a kill with a powerful skull bite.

Mist! Manolito ruthlessly took over MaryAnn's mind, pouring the image into her brain, holding it even as he began the shifting process for her.

The wolf dissolved beneath the jaguar, so that the cat fell heavily through the branches, slamming hard against several limbs before it was able to get a purchase with its claws.

Fury at himself burst through him, even as he shifted, leaping up the branches of the trees to get to the intruder. Manolito was shocked that the cat had escaped his observation. He realized just how emotions and the presence of a lifemate could be distracting enough to get them both killed.

The jaguar whirled around, teeth bared. The two heavy bodies met with a tremendous crash. Limbs cracked and splintered, raining down on the forest floor. Monkeys went crazy, hurling everything they could get their hands on at the two rolling cats. Sounds of the battle mixed with the cacophony of birds and wildlife protesting the interruption of the night.

MaryAnn found herself on the forest floor, looking up at the raking, snarling cats, shocked that their peaceful play had been shattered so brutally and so fast. In this forest, violence was an accepted way of life. Life really was about kill or be killed. Manolito and his brothers had lived their entire life with that creed.

A part of her screamed this wasn't her way of life and never would be. She wanted to go home. She let out her breath, stood up, and prepared to do whatever was necessary for Manolito's survival, because no matter where they were, *he* was her way of life.

A MUCH-ABRIDGED CARPATHIAN DICTIONARY

This very-much-abridged Carpathian dictionary contains most of the Carpathian words used in these Dark books. Of course, a full Carpathian dictionary would be as large as the usual dictionary for an entire language.

Note: The Carpathian nouns and verbs below are word **stems**. They generally do not appear in their isolated "stem" form, as below. Instead, they usually appear with suffixes (e.g., "*andam*"—"I give," rather than just the root, "*and*").

aina—body
ainaak—forever
akarat—mind; will
ál—bless; attach to
alatt—through
alə—to lift; to raise
and—to give
avaa—to open
avio—wedded
avio päläfertiil—lifemate
belso—within; inside
ćaδa—to flee; to run; to escape
ćoro—to flow; to run like rain
csitri—little one (female)
eći—to fall
ek—suffix added after a noun ending in a consonant to make it plural
ekä—brother
elä—to live
elävä—alive

elävä ainak majaknak—land of the living
elid—life
én—I
en—great, many, big
En Puwe—The Great Tree. Related to the legends of Ygddra-
    sil, the axis mundi, Mount Meru, heaven and hell, etc.
engem—me
és—and
että—that
fáz—to feel cold or chilly
fertiil—fertile one
fesztelen—airy
fü—herbs; grass
gond—care; worry (noun)
hän—he; she; it
hany—clod; lump of earth
irgalom—compassion; pity; mercy
jälleen—again
jama—to be sick, wounded, or dying; to be near death (verb)
jelä—sunlight; day, sun; light
joma—to be under way; to go
jörem—to forget; to lose one's way; to make a mistake
juta—to go; to wander
jüti—night; evening
jutta—connected; fixed (adj.). To connect; to fix; to bind (verb)
k—suffix added after a noun ending in a vowel to make it plu-
    ral
kaca—male lover
kaik—all (noun)
kaŋa—to call; to invite; to request; to beg
kaŋk—windpipe; Adam's apple; throat
Karpatii—Carpathian
käsi—hand
kepä—lesser; small; easy; few
kinn—out; outdoors; outside; without
kinta—fog; mist; smoke
koje—man; husband; drone
kola—to die
koma—empty hand; bare hand; palm of the hand; hollow of
    the hand
kont—warrior

kule—hear

kuly—intestinal worm; tapeworm; demon who possesses and devours souls

kulke—to go or to travel (on land or water)

kuńa—to lie as if asleep; to close or cover the eyes in a game of hide-and-seek; to die

kunta—band, clan, tribe, family

kuulua—to belong; to hold

lamti—lowland; meadow

lamti ból jüti, kinta, ja szelem—the nether world (literally: "the meadow of night, mists, and ghosts")

lejkka—crack, fissure, split (noun). To cut; hit; to strike forcefully (verb).

lewl—spirit

lewl ma—the other world (literally: "spirit land"). *Lewl ma* includes *lamti ból jüti, kinta, ja szelem*: the nether world, but also includes the worlds higher up En Puwe, the Great Tree.

löyly—breath; steam (related to *lewl*: "spirit")

ma—land; forest

mäne—rescue; save

me—we

meke—deed; work (noun). To do; to make; to work (verb).

minan—mine

minden—every, all (adj.)

möért?—what for? (exclamation)

molanâ—to crumble; to fall apart

molo—to crush; to break into bits

mozdul—to begin to move, to enter into movement

nä—for

ŋamaŋ—this; this one here

nélkül—without

nenä—anger

nó—like; in the same way as; as

numa—god; sky; top; upper part; highest (related to the English word: "numinous")

nyál—saliva; spit (noun) (related to *nyelv*: "tongue")

nyelv—tongue

o—the (used before a noun beginning with a consonant)

odam—dream; sleep (verb)

oma—old; ancient

omboće—other; second (adj.)

ot—the (used before a noun beginning with a vowel)

otti—to look; to see; to find

owe—door

pajna—to press

pälä—half; side

päläfertiil—mate or wife

pél—to be afraid; to be scared of

pesä—nest (literal); protection (figurative)

pide—above

pirä—circle; ring (noun). To surround; to enclose (verb).

pitä—keep; hold

piwtä—to follow; to follow the track of game

pukta—to drive away; to persecute; to put to flight

pus—healthy; healing

pusm—to be restored to health

puwe—tree; wood

reka—ecstasy; trance

rituaali—ritual

saγe—to arrive; to come; to reach

salama—lightning; lightning bolt

sarna—words; speech; magic incantation (noun). To chant; to sing; to celebrate (verb).

śaro—frozen snow

siel—soul

sisar—sister

sív—heart

sívdobbanás—heartbeat

soŋe—to enter; to penetrate; to compensate; to replace

susu—home; birthplace (noun); at home (adv.)

szabadon—freely

szelem—ghost

tappa—to dance; to stamp with the feet (verb)

te—you

ted—yours

toja—to bend; to bow; to break

toro—to fight; to quarrel

tule—to meet; to come

türe—full; satiated; accomplished

tyvi—stem; base; trunk

uskol—faithful

uskolfertiil—allegiance
veri—blood
vigyáz—to care for; to take care of
vii—last; at last; finally
wäke—power
wara—bird; crow
weńća—complete; whole
wete—water